UNDER
THE RADAR
HIGH STAKES

DEE J. ADAMS

UNDER THE RADAR
Copyright © 2018 by Dee J. Adams
ISBN: 978-0-9967990-4-1

Edited by Melissa Johnson
Cover Art by Croco Designs
Digital Formatting by Author E.M.S.

DEDICATION

This is for the next generation…for three people I'm very proud of…
Katelyn, Matthew and Sydney.

Follow your dreams and find what makes you happy and stick with it.

Mostly, just be happy.

Dear Reader,

I'm so happy to bring you the last book in the High Stakes Series! You might be wondering how this can be the final story, since two St. John brothers remain, but those men are not only brothers and best friends, they tend to do things at the same time...and that includes falling in love.

The road to love isn't always easy, but tack on a forced get-away and being hunted by gunmen and that makes it doubly hard. From the moment Eric and Zoe and Danny and Victoria laid eyes on each other in *Out of the Blue*, life wasn't quite the same for any of them. I hope you enjoy their adventure in *Under the Radar*.

Thank you for taking the time to read any of the books in this series. There are a lot of books out there and I'm thrilled you chose one of mine.

I love to hear from readers, so feel free to email me at deej.adams1@gmail.com.

Best,

Dee J. Adams

ACKNOWLEDGMENTS

As the High Stakes series comes to a close, there are some extra special thank yous that need to be said. First and foremost, thank you to my awesome pal, Lynne Marshall. I couldn't have gotten through this book and this series without you. You always kicked my ass when it needed kicking and I appreciate you so much for that.

As always, a massively giant thank you to Melissa Johnson—editor extraordinaire—for your patience and brains (not necessarily in that order) and your general knowledge of...well everything!

Many thanks to Suzanne Nussbaum Goldman and Vivianne Fernquist for answering so many realtor questions. I appreciate you both taking time from your busy days for me.

Thank you to Sara Marton-Young for all the help when it came to public relations. What a fun, fascinating world!

Thank you to Alex Vidal for your EMT expertise and setting me straight when I was sure I knew the right answer to something and in reality, I totally didn't!

Thank you to Jason Fitzpatrick for all your camping and hiking information and for your patience with all my emails!

To my old neighbor and amazing attorney, Tom Brown. Thank you so much for all your help in the law department. You saved me from making a potentially critical error! In short...you da' man!

Any mistakes are my own.

As always, thank you, Sean, for everything you do. There would be no books without you.

CHAPTER 1

HAZY CLOUDS THAT COVERED an almost full moon in the California sky mirrored Eric St. John's current foul mood, as he jerked his gray RAV4 to a stop in front of the grocery store. He spotted Zoe Turner pulling her white BMW into a spot three cars away and tamped down the conflicting emotions that always upped his pulse around Zoe. Why did such a beautiful package have to house such a pain in the ass? Renewed annoyance blazed fresh at her request for help. Check that, her *order* to help. He had enough on his plate without the curly-headed pipsqueak barking instructions at him. Ninety hour work weeks were kicking his ass for over a month and he felt as if he were drowning in corporate quicksand.

"She's on time," his brother Danny said from the passenger seat.

"Wonders never cease," Eric groused. He couldn't figure out how Zoe claimed she was always on time for appointments, yet usually kept them waiting when it came to anything involving this whole engagement party. They got out and he locked his ride with a double chirp. He'd debated taking a few minutes to change out of his suit after another long day at the office, but his conscience wouldn't let him be late.

Danny laughed. "You're just mad because she's bossing you around again."

More like mad he wasn't in comfortable jeans and boots like his little brother.

The lawyer in him wanted to argue his point, except Danny was right. It would've been nice to have a little respite from his future semi-sister-in-law who'd taken on the wedding of her sister, Casey, as if it were her own. *Do this, do that,* she'd been ordering him around for what seemed like weeks now and his brother hadn't even set a date yet. This was only for the engagement party. Hell, he wasn't even the best man! Why wasn't Blake doing all this shit?

Danny's eyes lit up when the other maid-of-honor exited the car.

"Might wanna put your tongue back in your mouth," Eric quipped as they walked toward the ladies. Danny had been sporting a woody for Victoria Lopez since the day they'd met her almost six months ago. Their little brother had landed on a reality show with Casey, Zoe's little sister and Vic's best friend. Since those two had fallen in love, Eric could tell that Danny hoped to use his little brother and their sister/friend connection to score with Vic. So far to no avail. Not to say that Danny was too upset about it. He had a list a mile long of women ready to jump when he called. But…who was Eric to judge? Just because he wanted more from a relationship didn't mean his brothers had to. Maybe it came with being the oldest and setting an example. He envied his parents' relationship and didn't think he'd find anything like it if he followed his dick to every willing woman's bed.

Danny elbowed him. "Hey, snap out of it. Don't want Cyclone Zoe to catch you day dreaming about her." He laughed and dodged the half-hearted punch Eric threw in his direction. Eric never should've confided that nickname to Danny. Five yards later they met Zoe and Vic at the front of the market.

"Here's your list," Zoe said, still dressed in her own beige suit as if she'd come straight from work as well. Damn, she filled out that suit nicely. Curves like Zoe's demanded attention. Unfortunately, his dick always noticed when she was around. Her fancy pumps added three inches to her five-three frame. Of course, no *hello* or *hi, how are you.* Just straight to business. His hackles shot up again. She handed him a thin sheet of paper with her name and picture at the top. *Zoe Turner. Realtor. Turning dreams into reality.*

Yeah right. Maybe if you had five, ten or fifteen million dollars to spend on a house. Zoe dealt with high-end real estate and made a fortune. It only made Eric more uncomfortable around her. She always seemed on top of the world whereas he felt trapped in a box of his own making.

He'd followed in his father's footsteps and gone to law school. His goal to land in the prosecutor's office got sidetracked when one of his dad's friends offered him an internship in contract law. That move turned into a solid position and a great paycheck. He loved that his bosses appreciated his work ethic and attention to detail. Loved how they occasionally fought over which project he'd tackle next. Problem was he hated the actual work and itched for something more.

"Eric, did you hear me?" Zoe said, looking up at him with beautiful blue-gray eyes. He glanced away, not ready to admit what it meant that he couldn't face her head-on. Tonight, she'd pulled her dark hair back into a thick bun, and a few runaway strands curled around her face. Unlike her sister's stick straight locks, Zoe's hair usually curled into soft ringlets that practically bounced when she walked.

Eric lifted the list in his hand. He hadn't heard her, but he was a lawyer for God's sake so he pretty much had it figured out. "Everything on the list is my responsibility. Got it."

"And remember, it's—"

"Teal. I know. Everything is teal."

Which he had to admit was better than pink. Thank God her sister wasn't one of those girly-girls who had to have pink everything.

"Hey, Vic," Danny said, giving Vic one of his calendar-model smiles.

Vic lifted a sculpted eyebrow. "Danny." Her coy smile was the same tease she'd been giving him for months now. She was the bane of Danny's existence. No woman had ever kept him at a distance for so long and Eric knew it drove Danny crazy.

Eric grinned for the first time in hours. Thinking about Danny's love life was usually good for a chuckle.

"All right, boys, let's get in and out. I'd wanted to do this hours ago."

The smile vanished. He really hated when she called them *boys*. "I told you we could've gotten everything without you." Eric let

3

Zoe and Vic walk into the market first and caught Danny ogling Vic's very fine ass in her yoga pants. Though he would've been surprised if she'd actually been working out since not a hair was out of place and her makeup was perfect. Her long strawberry blond hair caught the bright store light and lit the red streaks like fire. No doubt, she turned heads wherever she went and she knew it. She was the five-seven female version of Danny. They were practically made for each other.

"C'mon." Eric slapped Danny's arm and motioned him to follow in the opposite direction of the *girls*.

"One day," Danny muttered, finally taking his gaze off Vic. "One day, it's going to happen and she's going to be sorry she wasted all this time."

"Yeah, yeah. She'll kneel down at your feet like all the women before her." Eric doubted it. "I wouldn't hold my breath for that one, bro. She saw through you in two seconds."

Danny stopped and spread his arms wide. "What's that supposed to mean?"

Eric laughed at his brother's wide-eyed innocence. "Are you seriously going to play dumb?" He grabbed two hand baskets and shoved one into Danny's arms. "A woman that beautiful has been hit on most of her life, and she's smart enough to see your end goal. She knows your type from a mile away. She's not about to be a notch on your belt."

"Hey, there's nothing wrong with a little mutual gratification. It's not like the women I date are unhappy."

"They are when you quit calling, and that happens about a month or so after they start sleeping with you." Eric walked up the closest aisle.

"Not everyone is looking to get married the second after they have sex." Danny lifted a hand in the air. "I like variety. It's not a crime."

Shaking his head, Eric dropped the subject. "Here." He threw four packages of teal napkins into Danny's basket.

"What else is on there?" Danny asked. "We can split up and go twice as fast."

Eric ripped the list in half and handed the lower part to his brother. "There. I'll race you. Loser buys the next six-pack."

"Deal." Danny didn't even look up. He kept his eyes on the list and started toward the back.

The only good thing about shopping this late was the near empty market. It beat fighting the crowds and dodging squirrely kids. Looking up at the aisle markers as he walked along the back of the store, he caught Vic reaching for salsa in one lane as he passed. He headed to the fruit section to pick up the limes Zoe ordered. Then it was back to the other side and the pharmacy section for pain relievers. Really? They needed to buy pain relievers for an engagement party? Maybe Zoe was sneaking in a few things for herself and he got stuck with them on his half. As he looked for the bottle she wanted, he spotted three men entering the market…just as they pulled ski masks over their heads.

Eric's heart pounded against his ribs as they lifted huge guns and stalked toward the registers. He ducked back behind the shelves and set his basket down. Jesus, he thought his heart might vault out of his chest.

Danny. Zoe. Vic. He had to get them out. Or at least make sure they stayed down until trouble disappeared. But he'd have to cross the main aisle of the store to do that. He pulled his phone out, nearly sent off a text, but Danny never put his phone on vibrate and the sound would ping, potentially giving away his location. He didn't know about the ladies and he wasn't taking the chance.

Eric moved silently, checking the aisles he could see from his little pharmacy section before finding cover behind some toothpaste shelves. His palms sweated like a bitch. Reaching the end of the aisle, he peeked around the corner and spotted Vic at the very end just as she turned right and up another lane. Sweat popped out of his pores.

All the men were busy making the two female cashiers empty their registers as they nervously looked around the store. Unbelievably, they missed seeing Vic.

What were the chances he'd find and warn all three of them before the robbers got their money and walked out?

Not frickin' great.

He was about to turn and double back when something caught his eye. Zoe came around the corner, too preoccupied with juggling her full basket to realize there was trouble. A vase slid

5

out of her arms and she yelped, trying to save it. A slow-motion catastrophe played before Eric's eyes, yet it all happened before he blinked. The vase crashed to the ground, one of the gunman looked and fired. A double shot. Zoe's head snapped up a split second before she went flying backward. Eric's stomach rolled and bile choked the back of his throat.

"Go, go!" One of the gunman ordered. The guy that fired ran toward Zoe who'd fallen back into the aisle she'd walked out of.

Another man sprinted into the building. "What the hell happened?" All of the men started talking at once, voices panicked and loud, guns waving precariously.

Eric saw Danny silently run down the short lane, the commotion giving him precious extra seconds. He scooped Zoe into his arms as the gunman got closer. Eric picked up a candle in a glass holder from the end display. It was heavy, substantial enough to do damage. He got into position, closest to the end of the lane. Adrenaline ran like hot lava in his veins. He had one chance to get this right. When the gunman got in his line of sight, he rose from his crouch, wound up and fired that candle at the guy's head.

Ten years of little league and varsity baseball paid off as he hit his target with one strike. The guy hit the deck with a clatter. The noise bought him more trouble, but at least Danny got Zoe clear.

"Go!" A man's voice ordered. "Kill the son of a bitch."

Shit.

VIC TURNED UP INTO a new aisle, basket and list in one hand, phone in the other and her mind still on Danny's perfect ass. What she wouldn't give to run her fingers through his thick auburn hair with one hand while holding that ass in the other. Maybe one of these days she should break down and give the guy a sign, but common sense told her to hold steady. On the other hand...if she gave in—

Glass breaking followed by two shots exploding in the front of the store made Vic jolt midstep. "What the...?" she muttered. *Gunshots? No, couldn't be. That stuff happened to other people.* Her heart pumped so hard she thought anyone in range could hear it.

Her brain went straight into PR mode: How would she spin the story? What would she advise when it came to interviews? She shook off the unnecessary questions.

On the off chance she was wrong…

She quietly ran to the back of the store, glad to be in her cross-trainers instead of her normal three-inch heels, since she planned to hit the gym after this errand. She passed an aisle with brooms and took a second to grab one before continuing on. It wasn't much, but it beat nothing at all.

Seeing Danny turn the corner a couple aisles ahead with an unconscious Zoe in his arms had her frozen in her tracks. He ran to the back through a door marked employees only. Every bit of spit dried up in her mouth and Vic pulled out her cell phone and punched 9-1-1, her hands shaking seizure hard.

Real. It's real. The words rolled in her head like a non-stop wheel.

"911. What is your emergency?"

"Go!" a man's voice ordered. "Kill the son of a bitch."

Kill the son of a bitch? Vic's hands shook harder.

"Hello. What is your emergency?" the dispatcher repeated.

She was afraid to talk, afraid to make any noise. "Need help," she whispered. Couldn't they pinpoint the location by her phone? She peeked around the next aisle and saw Eric at the other end of the store crouched low, hiding behind the pharmacy shelves. A man with a gun came into view and turned to Eric, his back to Vic. Without time to think about it, she set her basket and phone on the floor and rushed down the lane, wishing she had a pan instead of just a broom and glad this little store had short aisles.

"You're going to pay for that, fucker." The man raised his weapon and Vic saw the end in Eric's clear blue eyes as he looked up the barrel of a gun.

"Excuse me," Vic said as she wound up and stepped into the open.

The man spun as Vic let loose with a home run before he'd fully turned. She slammed the hard plastic broom handle into the side of the guy's head, connecting with his temple and knocking him flat to the ground. His gun skidded on the floor. She would've gone after it, but gunfire erupted and she bolted back up the aisle she'd

7

come from. With a quick glance over her shoulder, she was happy to see that Eric had disappeared, hopefully to someplace safe.

DANNY SNAPPED HIS HEAD up at the second round of gunfire, his pulse beating double time. He thought he'd hit his quota of blood and guts during his lifetime. Apparently not.

"Run," Zoe whispered. "Get out of here. Get help." She hadn't been unconscious long if at all. She had a deep slice across her side and another on her upper arm. She was bleeding pretty good if the growing red spots on her beige suit were any indicators, but she hadn't shed a single tear. Tough as steel, this chick. "I'm serious, Danny."

He pulled his cell phone from his back pocket and punched 9-1-1. His brother was going to be pissed, but fuck it. Big brother didn't get to make everyone else's decisions. "Here. Talk to the police. Keep pressure on your side with the other hand. I need to get Eric and Vic."

She nodded and for the first time her eyes filled with tears. "Be careful."

Danny found a couple of aprons and wrapped them around her injuries to stem the blood flow, then he took off.

Crouching low, he inched his head out just in time to see Vic running toward the produce section. Why would she do that? She had to know there'd be an exit out the back. Unless she knew they were here and was trying to lead the gunman away from them.

Bullets sprayed the back of the store and Danny covered his head. He saw a man lying still at the very end of the aisle Vic had come from. Two down including the man Eric nailed. But how many more were there?

"Dammit! Get them," a male voice said. Two more rounds blistered the air. Jesus! Had those shots hit someone? There'd been two cashiers up front when they'd walked in.

Danny took the knife out of his boot. A knife he truly never expected to use. It had been there for several years now. Most of the time he forgot about it. Had to be reminded to remove it before he got on an airplane. And now...now he was thrilled he'd copied his younger twin brothers in their quest to protect themselves.

A man came around the corner three lanes away and Danny ducked down. With his gun drawn, he followed Vic's path. "Come out, come out wherever you are," the man taunted.

Danny rose as sirens wailed louder in the distance. Sweat prickled the back of his neck as he crept closer. He drew his arm back, knife ready to fly. Vic's life depended on this one strike.

"I see you," the man said, his voice silky soft and scary as shit.

Danny saw her too. Vic must have thought she could fool him, have him walk past her, but her shoe was visible behind the freezer in front of the meat section against the wall. Getting as close as he dared, adrenaline soaring, Danny whipped the knife and it landed right in the middle of the guy's shoulder blades. He spun and fired, but Danny was already moving, diving out of the way. The whiz of bullets rushed by his ear, as loud as the pounding of his heart, then he was rolling. He came up on his feet and sprinted to the end of the aisle, realizing that there was no sound anywhere.

Nothing.

He peeked out from the lane and checked both directions. Footsteps pattered at a run two aisles away.

"Danny?" a voice whispered.

He knew that voice. "Vic?"

She stuck her head out from behind a vegetable display, her pretty brown eyes wide and very freaked out. The urge to protect her reared up fast and hard. "Are there more of them?"

He shook his head. "Don't know. Where's Eric?"

"Psst." Eric waved from behind one of the check-out counters and slowly stood up. "I saw three come initially, then a fourth. Two are definitely down, the fourth guy bolted. Not sure where the other one is."

"I hit him in the head with a pan. Danny's knife made him stumble after he spun and I took advantage." Vic scooted from her spot and Danny opened his arms as she ran for him, connecting with a hard thwap. A wave of relief hit him gut deep.

Sirens blared closer and a car peeled out from the curb, catching their attention.

Danny felt every single tremor racing through Vic's body. This was *not* how he imagined holding her for the first time. Not at all. And shit...

9

"Zoe!" The three of them said it at the same time and bolted for the back just before police stormed the front.

CHAPTER 2

ZOE NEVER EXPECTED TO be—and despised being—in the spotlight. Again. The first time should've been enough. Not that anyone would connect her to the little girl who made national news after getting lost in the woods so many years ago, but it wasn't something she wanted to remember. She'd rationalized her part in her sister's reality show because people weren't tuning in for *her*. Making the front page of the local Los Angeles paper was even worse. Sure, she'd been mentioned in the real estate section, but that came with the territory of her job. The incident had even made television news since there'd been talk about it being an act of terrorism. Not the case. Nope...turned out it was just four idiots hoping to score easy cash by holding up a grocery store. Zoe couldn't wait to press charges against the assholes.

Now she was just another statistic in the war against guns and gun violence. Would it have done her any good if she herself owned a gun? Everything had dropped out of her arms after falling backward and she wouldn't have carried a gun to the grocery store anyway.

"Hey, sis." Casey strode into the room, her long, highlighted hair flowing behind her. "How are you feeling?"

Glad for the distraction, Zoe tried to sit up. She loved the new confidence her sister had found after dumping her ex and winning America's new favorite reality show, *Write Your Ticket*. Casey finding true love had been an unexpected perk in the process. "Fine." Mostly. She was still sore as hell, but no vital organs had been hurt with either bullet and with her doctor's blessing, she hoped to be released today. In another six or eight days, she could have the stitches removed from her upper arm and left side and be done with doctors altogether. "Did you bring my clothes?" Luckily the wound on her side didn't interfere with jeans or anything around her waist.

"I did." Usually Zoe did the *taking care of* so this turn of events didn't really sit well with her. Casey's smile was one Zoe had learned to be leery of. "I also brought something else," her little sis added.

"Dammit, Casey. I hate surprises. No surprises."

Her smile broadened. "Too late."

Before words escaped her mouth, Eric, Danny and Vic walked into the room. Eric held a bouquet of spectacular multicolored lilies, Danny had a box of chocolates and Vic presented a stuffed bear. She really couldn't be angry, but seeing them only made her feel embarrassed all over again. Yes, it was illogical that she should feel embarrassed for getting shot, but apparently she had no control over guilt. Pet peeve number one: *Not* being in control.

The three of them had been as heroic as any purple-heart recipient and all she'd done was take a bullet. Twice. She'd been so preoccupied with getting everything for Casey's engagement party that the rest of the world had faded away until it was too late.

But, okay, she had to be honest...who didn't like flowers, candy and stuffed bears?

"Hey, beautiful," Danny said, setting the chocolates at her bedside. "How're you feeling?" His playboy smile lifted her spirits. The guy was damn good looking and he knew it. Dark auburn hair, crazy gorgeous blue eyes like the rest of his brothers and a body built like a god. Not that he intimidated her in any way. Danny was miles from her type so it was easy to talk to him.

"Better. Thanks to you." He had saved her life by carrying her to safety. But the man she really owed everything to stood behind him and barely looked at her as he found a place for the flowers. "And thanks to you," she said in Eric's direction.

Eric glanced up and gave her a rare smile. Mr. Serious all the time. Did he ever have fun? It was odd to see brothers so close in age and looks and yet so very different in personality. Whereas Danny didn't ring any of her bells, something about Eric struck a chord. Eric didn't have the same playboy good looks of his younger brother, but all those hard lines and angles made him drop dead gorgeous just the same. Even his immaculate haircut appealed to her. Football player shoulders that tapered to a lean waist and drool-worthy ass on top of muscular thighs…there just wasn't any part of the guy that didn't warrant a second glance. Danny might be movie star perfect, but Eric…even in the sharp navy suit he wore now, everything about him screamed rugged sex appeal and her heart thumped a little faster whenever he was around.

"Vic told us they're supposed to spring you today," Eric said, stuffing his hands in his pockets. The red highlights in his auburn hair glistened in the sun streaming through her hospital window.

"Yeah, we wanted to make your departure as difficult as possible with as much shit as we could carry in," Danny added with a wink. Yep, adorable times ten. Sometimes she wished Vic would pull her head out of her butt and *do* the guy already.

"Nicely done," Zoe murmured, looking at all the gifts. "It'll be good to go home. I need to get back to work." She had a new listing and she was way behind. Her stomach pitched. If she didn't sell this house, she was in real danger of losing her job.

Danny's face perked up. "Oh, yeah? You selling Beyoncé's house?"

Zoe chuckled and immediately regretted it since it hurt her side to laugh. "No. I didn't know she had a house for sale. This is a place in Holmby Hills. Some CEO is moving to Europe and put it on the market."

"How much is this one worth?" Danny asked.

Eric shoved his arm. "Cut it out. It's none of your business."

In the short time she'd come to know the two oldest St. John brothers, she'd learned that Danny had less of a filter than his big brother. Much less. Maybe that was the difference. She just couldn't take Danny too seriously. Eric on the other hand…

"It can't be a secret," Danny continued. "Or it wouldn't be for sale."

Zoe shook her head at that deduction. "It's on the market for eighteen million." Honestly, she was hoping to get fifteen, but it all depended on the buyers. She watched Danny's eyes widen as he probably tried to figure her commission, which would be all of zero if she didn't get released and get back to work.

"Are you sure you're ready to bail out of here?" Vic asked as Casey pulled the clothes out of her bag and hung them in the small closet near the door. As usual, Vic had barely spared a glance in Danny's direction, and he was working overtime to be as attentive as possible. Probably hoping to show Vic exactly what she was missing. So far, it didn't seem to be working.

"Yes," Zoe said. "The bullets grazed me, they didn't go through me. Smashing my finger in the parallel bars during gymnastics did more damage than this."

"Ew. I remember that," Casey said, her face in a distasteful pucker. "That was gross." She glanced at Vic. "She had like twenty stitches in her little finger."

"It was eleven," Zoe clarified. The same amount that she had from both gunshot wounds now.

Eric's phone rang and he pulled it out of his back pocket and checked the screen. "Sorry," he said, glancing up. "I should take this." He walked into the hall as he answered.

"Did you guys reschedule the engagement party?" Zoe asked. That was just one more reason to feel bad. The fact that Casey and Brendan had cancelled their engagement party because she'd been hospitalized. Zoe had begged them to do it without her, but Casey refused to have a party when her maid-of-honor couldn't be there to celebrate.

"Not yet," Casey said. "Bren and I haven't had a chance to figure out new dates. He won't be back in town until next week."

"But I thought *you* were out of town next week," Zoe said, shifting to relieve the pull of stitches.

"I am, but it's only a couple of days. We should both be here the weekend after and we'll figure it out then."

Eric came back into the room, his face even more serious than usual.

"What?" Zoe asked. "Bad news?" She'd never been one to chit chat.

Eric's look to Danny spoke volumes and Danny's smile vanished.

"That was Dad," Eric said to his brother. Then he looked at the rest of them. "One of the guys that robbed—attempted to rob—the grocery store was just released on bond."

"What?" Fury pounded through Zoe. She launched upright and

regretted it in a nano-second when a zing of pain shot across her side.

Eric flinched, reached a hand out. "Easy," he urged softly... almost as if he felt her pain. He blinked before glancing around the room at all the surprised faces staring at him. "Someone put up the hundred thousand premium for the bail," he said, running a hand across his jaw and getting back on topic.

"How is that possible? Where does a gang member get a hundred thousand dollars?" Vic asked.

"Apparently someone has deep pockets," Eric muttered.

Danny swore quietly to the floor then looked up. "Do we know which one was released?"

"The driver. The one without a record."

Glancing between them all, Vic said what Zoe was thinking. "I guess that's not as bad as one of the other ones. I wouldn't want a third strike suspect on the street with a trial looming."

"It's still bullshit," Casey seethed from the foot of the bed next to Vic.

"Huge bullshit," Danny agreed. "They killed a cashier. That should've kept them all behind bars."

ERIC EXHALED, JUST AS angry and dismayed as everyone else in the room. "Hey, I'm not arguing. If I thought for one second one of them would've made bail I'd have asked the district attorney for a higher bond." He shook his head and ran a hand over his face. A boatload of frustration swirled in his chest.

"Well, this is pretty screwed up." Zoe hit the bedside button and the mechanism whirred as she propped herself up to get comfortable. It killed him that she didn't have the usual color in her complexion.

Eric forced himself to focus his gaze out the window. Looking outside made it easier to think because when he looked at Zoe, all those old feelings of helplessness reared up and smacked him in the face. Though she was in much better shape than Brendan had been after his family's ordeal, it still killed him to step foot in a hospital. He hated the smell, the sounds and the idea that people might be here as a direct result of an intentional act from another human being.

People sucked.

At the moment, life kind of sucked.

"Hey, big guy. Eric!"

He shifted his gaze to the spitball of a woman calling his name. "Yes, Zoe." Now what did she want? He couldn't really be short with her when she was laid up like this.

"Is there anything your dad can do to get this guy back behind bars?"

Didn't they all wish. Eric shook his head. "Not unless there's some new law I don't know about. As long as he made the ten percent bond, he's free to go. Nothing we can do but wait for the court date."

Zoe closed her eyes and growled. Despite the seriousness of events, Eric tamped down a grin. Every now and then, she was too cute for her own good. Every so often she showed a side of herself that he liked, and it was harder to keep his distance. Besides, they were going to be in-laws. There had to be some kind of taboo against dating a sister-in-law. Not that he even wanted to date her.

Jesus, where did that come from?

"So why *are* you all here?" Zoe asked after exhaling a hard breath. "Obviously it wasn't to tell me the latest news, since you just got that now. And as soon as the doctor signs off on my release and I get my home care instructions, I'm out of here."

"Exactly," Casey said.

Vic tossed her long hair over her shoulder. "We were all here when you came in and wanted to be here when you got out. In light of the release of one of the men who put you here, I think it's even more apropos to give you a giant escort home."

"That's sweet. If not excessive," Zoe added softly.

Though Vic may have been right, Eric had felt a bigger need to see Zoe home. He should've warned her the second she came around that corner. Should've stood up and distracted the gunman. He should've done something. Taken the bullet. She might've never been shot if he'd been fast enough.

The doctor came in and tossed them out as he talked to Zoe one last time. Then a nurse came in and gave her home care instructions. By the time she got dressed and Casey wheeled her out of the room more than an hour later, Eric was beyond stir crazy.

Together, the five of them left the hospital and Eric's anxiety morphed into a wall of protectiveness. He might not be Zoe's biggest fan, but he'd be damned if she got hurt again when he was around.

Eric walked to his SUV while everyone else waited with Zoe at the curb of the loading zone. Sun glared from a clear Los Angeles sky and the hair on the back of his neck stood on end as he walked through the parking lot. Without looking obvious, Eric glanced around at the mass of cars parked in the big lot. He didn't see anything out of the ordinary, but he sure as hell felt it. Made him wish he'd come down earlier to be ready for Zoe as soon as she made it out of the hospital. The mistake pissed him off and he hurried his pace.

At least most of the guys were still behind bars. But for how long? What if those deep pockets got deeper? Eric dismissed the idea, figuring the only reason the one guy made bond was because it was his first offense.

It was shit like this that had gotten him interested in law in the first place, but what had he done? He'd taken a position dealing in contract law and discovered he'd sold his soul for a decent paycheck. He didn't want to think about it. Instead of dwelling on his career, Eric hit the remote and listened to the double chirp of his SUV. After jumping in, he cranked the engine and headed up the ramp to pick up the gang.

The same nervous tension tickled the back of his neck as he pulled next to the curb.

The group climbed into his SUV and Eric headed out, keeping his eyes on the rearview mirror and the traffic all around him. He'd learned long ago to trust his instincts and he wasn't about to ignore them now.

DANNY DIDN'T KNOW WHY Eric suddenly had a bug up his ass, but contrary to what most of his family thought, he did have a brain in his head and clearly something was bothering Eric. "What's got—" His phone pinged and he glanced from his brother's granite features to see the message. Shitballs. From Nikki. He needed to figure out how to shake her. None of his usual excuses worked with her and she hadn't gotten the message. They'd had a good time, and for a few hours he'd thought maybe he'd found someone special, or at least someone to take his mind off Vic. He'd never obsessed over someone the way he had Victoria Lopez. Somehow, she'd crawled under his skin without him even realizing it. She'd never called him and hardly spoke to him, and yet he couldn't get her out of his head.

He'd definitely tried with Nikki, but ultimately he didn't click with her. Most girls took the hint when he didn't ask them out again. They understood when he turned down their invitations that maybe, *just maybe*, they weren't going to become exclusive. He read the message.

> *Realized I accidentally grabbed ur sunglasses when at ur apt. If u want them back, u'd better come to my place before it's cleaned out. Sorry I didn't get ur hints, but one of ur old girlfriends set me straight. The door is open. Sorry about what u find.*

What the hell? Nothing like a cryptic message to make him roll his eyes. It was going to take a couple hours for them to drop off Zoe and get her settled. Then he'd have to get his car at the apartment. His glasses had been gone this long…a little longer wasn't going to change anything. He had to give Nikki props for the drama factor. She was all drama all the time. Hadn't taken long to figure that out. Part of the reason he didn't want to continue things with her.

Vic and Zoe started talking about cream for reducing scar lines, and Danny added his two cents. He'd had his own scars to deal with after the beating he and his family had taken a few years ago when they'd been held hostage by a psycho trying to use them and his sister as leverage against her boss. To this day, he worked hard to forget that nightmare.

His questions for Eric could wait until tonight. His brother's constant glances in the rearview mirror had Danny thinking they were being followed, but conversation with the women in the back seat made it easy to see if they were being tailed, and they were not. Sometimes Eric was too serious for his own good. Yeah, Danny understood how the kidnapping had changed all of them and clearly not the same way. He chose to live life hard. Maybe too hard sometimes, but it suited him.

Eric took the other approach with more diligence than anyone had a right to. On the rare occasion someone got a smile out of him, it warranted a fireworks celebration. He took being the oldest brother way too seriously. On the other hand, seeing all of one's baby brothers getting the shit beat out of them could tend to wipe a smile off a big brother's face.

Three hours later, Danny pulled up to Nikki's place. He'd only been here once before, when he'd dropped her home after their first—and only—hook-up. She lived in the bottom half of a two level, Spanish style duplex with red adobe clay. It was a nice place she'd happened into by accident with very affordable rent for the area thanks to the old grandmotherly type lady who owned the building and took pity on her.

Nikki had that effect on people. The beautiful, but poor girl who just needed a break for her luck to change. So far, waiting tables hadn't put her in the sites of the Hollywood playmakers who could change her life.

It hadn't taken long to realize two things. One, they had nothing in common and two, she had an *unstable* vibe that radiated like a neon light. Danny had distanced himself. Or at least tried to, but Nikki had the game down. First, she left a makeup bag at his place. Now, these sunglasses she "accidentally" took.

Initially, Danny had planned to hand over the small bag at the door and say, "Hey, here you go. Sorry I can't invite you in, but I've got an appointment and have to run." Instead it had gone something like, "Hey…" and his mind shorted out seeing her in a tiny black mini skirt and a skintight white top that showcased her spectacular rack. The black fuck-me pumps on her slender feet accentuated her tone calves and lean thighs. He'd forgotten about everything he planned to say when a breeze lifted her long blond hair away from her face and she smiled at him, her green eyes offering everything.

Nikki had pushed him back, sauntered in, swinging her hips, licking her lips.

"Look, I don't think—"

She closed the door behind her and flattened him against the entryway wall. "Good. Don't think," she said. "I have some time on my hands." She kissed his neck, right in the sensitive spot beneath his ear and blood rushed below his belt. "I thought maybe if you weren't doing anything, we could..." She whispered something about needing to remove a new lace thong because it was itching her in the most obscene places. Then she'd placed a hand on the growing erection in his jeans, and he didn't hear anything except the roaring in his head as she kissed the holy hell out of his mouth.

It took twenty seconds for his brain—his big brain—to kick into gear and ease her away from him. There was a desperation to Nikki that he hadn't seen at the club, but it came through in her constant voicemails and texts. Danny had been honest about not looking for something serious and she'd been right on board, or so she'd said.

"Look, Nikki, this isn't what I had in mind." Her eyes looked a little wide and panicked, and Danny rushed on. "You said yourself you were only looking for a little fun the other night. I don't want you to get the wrong idea about us."

"What's wrong with a little *more* fun," she said, trying to get at him again, but Danny pulled back.

There came that vibe again, the little something spiking the hairs on Danny's neck.

She asked about seeing each other again, and he shrugged and was honest. *"Not sure. My schedule is packed."* He didn't lie, didn't tell her they'd see each other again when he didn't plan on it. Her face fell, but she walked out the door, probably trying to figure out the next seduction, knowing her.

Days of phone calls and texts followed. Initially, Danny had replied. He'd been as honest and friendly as he could be, but when it became clear that Nikki had no plans to let it go, he'd stopped responding. But with this last text about his sunglasses, his patience pretty much snapped. He'd been looking for his shades for days. He always set them at the front entry table. The table where Nikki had her bag and wrap. She'd scooped it all up when she'd left, probably taking his sunglasses on purpose.

Danny should've let it go; they were only sunglasses. Except they were his favorite and they cost a chunk of change. Besides, picking them up in person, he could talk to her face to face and tell her why things wouldn't work out between them. He simply wasn't ready for an exclusive relationship. He'd take the blame. He was an asshole. He got it. Wasn't it just another reason for her to let him go?

Still, the cryptic message seemed like a shit-ton of bad mojo. It had been a lot of years since he felt that kind of anxiety. He was not a fan of the feeling.

Danny walked up to the duplex, and the bubbling fountain in front of Nikki's place didn't soothe his nerves. He knocked on the door and got no answer before remembering her text. *The door is open.*

He turned the knob. It opened. He tried to quash the apprehension making his skin crawl. "Nikki? Hello?" Dammit, he wouldn't be here if he'd just called Vic like he'd thought about doing dozens of different times. Why hadn't *she* called *him*? Didn't modern day women like being in control? He took a few more steps in, the quiet of the apartment only weirded him out more. "Yo, Nikki. I'm here. Where you at?" He peeked into the dining room on the left where tons of knickknacks and clutter littered every surface. Stacks of magazines and bins of all sizes covered the floor and the old leather sofa. He moved into the kitchen that circled around to the hallway. "Nikki. Enough of the hide-and-seek. Where are you?"

His heart thumped faster as he walked slowly through her place, his mouth went spit dry. He listened harder in the hallway, heard a faint drip in her bathroom. The door was cracked the tiniest bit and Danny waited on the outside. "Nikki?" He knocked softly with a knuckle. After no response, Danny pushed the door open wider. Blood red water in the old claw foot tub sent his stomach into his throat. Nikki lay in the tub, her head at an odd angle, her face as bone white as the porcelain she lay against, and her eyes open and sightless.

"What the fuck," he breathed out, barely containing the urge to vomit. Woodenly, Danny got to her side and felt for a pulse. "No, no, no…" Her skin was icy. "C'mon, c'mon." He searched for her carotid and pressed down. Maybe… "Shit," he breathed. Nothing.

He stood on shaky legs and backed up, saw the note on the counter addressed to him. Didn't want to open it or know what it said. His conscience argued that he must do both. With fingers trembling, he opened the flap.

> *Danny,*
>
> *Your glasses are on my dresser. I'm sorry I was such a burden. I never meant to drag you down, but apparently I was really good at it. Now you don't have to worry about me coming around anymore. I wish you'd taken the time to see what we could've had. I hope you're happy. Have a nice life.*
> *Nikki*

It was just like being ambushed again. On that horrible day when he'd walked through his house, turned a corner and received a baseball bat to his gut. The surprise, the pain had sent him to his knees gasping for air. Then someone had followed up the attack with a hard punch to his face. He'd ended up on his side, clutching his stomach when a booted foot kicked him in the kidneys. The pain had exploded in his torso like an inferno.

Danny blinked the memory away. His legs almost didn't hold him up as he staggered out of the room. He fumbled for his phone. His hand shook as he punched 9-1-1. After explaining the situation, he disconnected even though the dispatcher was still talking to him. He called the first person he could think of.

"Yo. S'up," Eric said. "I only have a minute."

Danny swallowed the bile in his throat. He opened his mouth, but nothing came out. He tried again. "I need you. Like now."

There was the tiniest of pauses. "Okay. You have my full attention. What's going on?"

His fault. The whole thing was his fault. Nikki killed herself, but he may as well have done it himself. She'd thought she was a burden to him then took her own life. Pressure built in his head, and his heart thundered out of control.

"Danny! Talk to me! What's happening?"

A bathtub of blood was happening. His mouth watered like he might lose his guts and he swallowed again. "I just got to Nikki's place."

"Dude, what did I tell you about—"

"She's dead. She sent me a text, she left a note. I found her." His voice broke and everything inside of him crumbled. It was the mental equivalent of that day at home so long ago. "I can't..." He couldn't talk, couldn't think. And still, the pressure built, like a bubbling volcano ready to explode.

"Dano, where are you? I'm on my way. Where are you?"

"Uh... I don't... Highland. South of 3rd." His brain spun and the hallway circled in front of him. The smell of blood permeated his senses. "I have to go. I can't..."

"Danny, hang on, bro. I'm on my way."

Danny heard Eric talking, his voice far away as he gave someone orders, then he was back on the line talking to him, but Danny didn't hear a word he said.

The din of sirens blared in the distance and Danny slid down the wall in the hallway, his gut in his throat and his conscience in tatters all around him.

CHAPTER 3

Nine months later

VIC TURNED THE KEY and cut the power on her black, convertible Mercedes. The stillness of the underground parking garage made her as itchy as the morning downtown traffic she battled to get here. Her stomach twisted in knots as she checked her watch. Eight minutes early. Eight minutes until setting eyes on Danny for the first time since Casey and Brendan's New Year's Eve party over six months ago. A party where he hadn't had a drink, hadn't smiled and only talked with his brothers for a few minutes before bailing hours before the ball dropped. Never in the history of any New Year's party had Vic heard of a single man leaving before the possibility of a midnight kiss. Never. To say that he had changed was like saying the Las Vegas strip had a few lights.

Walking toward the elevator, Vic adjusted her black dress. An odd sensation tingled along her nerves and she glanced around the garage, the hairs on her neck standing up straight. Not a sound and no one around. Clearly, she'd been watching too many horror flicks lately. She'd be beyond ecstatic to get this *horror show* of a trial even started. The four of them had suffered through more continuances than Vic could keep track of and this morning they'd been summoned to the District Attorney's downtown office.

Riding the elevator and thinking back on that night, months ago, while waiting for Zoe in the emergency room, Vic remembered Danny's comforting arm around her shoulder. The way she felt safe with his rock-solid frame right next to her. Since the second she'd run into his arms in the market, it had seemed as if she belonged there. For those few hours, she'd let herself go. She'd moved the barriers aside and let him hold her. Deep down, she knew it wouldn't last, mainly because she'd never let it. With his gorgeous blue eyes, muscles to salivate over and smile to kill for, Danny was trouble. The kind of trouble she put behind her with her second and last cheating boyfriend.

Attraction to Danny aside, Vic felt a bond with the St. John brothers that comforted her. They all owed their lives to each other in a round-robin of saves, and Vic didn't intend to forget it. She'd liked these two men when they met last summer during the reality show that brought them all together, but now a new layer of respect took up residence in her heart. The St. Johns had as much bravery and smarts as they had good looks.

The elevator doors opened and Vic spotted Zoe already there. "Been waiting long?"

"No." Wearing a white wrap-around top over black business slacks and three inch black pumps, Zoe looked lean, mean and ready for business. "Only beat you by a minute."

Vic glanced around the empty hallway. "So, before the guys get here, has Casey said anything about Danny? Is he any better?" Vic didn't know much other than someone in Danny's world had committed suicide and it was the catalyst for his big personality change. Just because Vic never intended to be with the guy didn't mean she wished him ill.

"Better?" Zoe thought about the word. "I wouldn't say better. He's just a new version. A different version." She lifted a dark eyebrow. "I don't believe for a minute that you haven't grilled Casey about him. Why ask me?"

Scowling, Vic took a step back. "I've hardly talked to her. Apparently, she not only doesn't have time to plan a wedding, but she doesn't have time to talk to me either."

Zoe chuckled. "Yeah, being famous is a bitch."

"Look, I know she's busy and she's under a lot of pressure. The last thing I want to do is hound her about Danny."

"But you'll hound *me* about Danny." Zoe said it as a statement. "Look, I swear, if I hear anything, you'll be the first to know, but I imagine you're about to find out for yourself any minute now."

The elevator dinged and the doors opened. Eric came out first, dressed in a sharp black suit, with Danny right behind him. Vic's unease quickly turned to shock at Danny's new super-short haircut. All that glorious auburn hair, gone. What had he been thinking? Vic had to admit, the haircut brought out the spectacular blue of his eyes and defined all the angles in his face.

Danny barely glanced at either of them when he mumbled a *hey*.

"Did you check in yet?" Eric asked, glancing between her and Zoe.

Zoe popped a breath mint and shook her head, intent on rearranging the contents of her purse. Funny, the way she avoided Eric whenever they all got together, which admittedly wasn't often.

"Not yet," Vic said, squaring her shoulders and trying not to stare at Danny. "We just got here too."

"I'll do it." Danny didn't wait for a response he just strode to the receptionist at the end of the hall, his respect for the whole process clear in his wardrobe choice for the day…a green polo shirt that defined all the delicious muscles in his arms and faded jeans and boots. Not that it mattered what he wore. He looked good enough to eat in anything…and nothing too, no doubt. Mm-mm… There was just something about his perfect ass in a pair of jeans that turned Vic into a cat on the prowl.

"Do we know what this is about?" Zoe asked. They'd been staggering court appearances since learning early on that the defense wanted more time to construct a case. Vic nearly laughed at that since they had *no* case. But the justice system didn't seem to care about victims' rights in certain circumstances and this was one of them. Usually at least two of the four of them were present at every hearing to witness every damn continuance the defense requested. The whole process had caused nothing but A's. Aggravation, annoyance and a hell of a lot of anger, especially for Zoe who wanted to put it all behind her.

Eric shook his head and shrugged in response to Zoe's question. "No clue. It's got to be something significant to get us all down here first thing in the morning."

True that. Vic checked her watch. She had to be at her office in Hollywood for a staff meeting at nine-thirty. One of her biggest clients—Seger Hughes and his wife Ashley—had a baby on the way and the company wanted to optimize the news with the release of his new music. She'd have to haul ass if she got out of here later than nine.

Danny strode toward them, his jaw clenched and his brows pulled together in the unmistakable sign of surly. The man had done a one-eighty on her. To make matters worse, all Vic had done was think about him ever since. She compared every smile to the ones Danny used to give her, every cheesy pick-up line to the smooth way Danny handled a first meeting. She even compared biceps. It wouldn't have been hard to hold her ground with the old Danny, mainly because she'd already been successful at it. She was done being any man's conquest. She had yet to meet a man—other than her father—who had been true to one woman. Her heart had been broken one too many times to risk it again any time soon.

Vic blinked out of her haze as Danny closed their small circle and folded his arms. Averting her eyes from all those muscles crossed over his chest, she caught the sour expression on his face.

"There is no meeting," he told them flatly. "This was a waste of time."

"You mean the meeting was cancelled," Zoe said. "Because we all clearly got a call from Craig's office to be here this morning." She spread her arms indicating the four of them.

"I mean, I was just told that 'Assistant District Attorney Craig Simon is in court this morning and never called for a meeting.'" He made air quotes with his fingers.

"What the hell is that about?" Zoe groused. "Who screwed up?"

Vic understood Zoe's frustration. She felt it too. Thinking about that night still made her palms sweat and her heart pound harder. She'd never been so scared in her life. Seeing Zoe on the floor with blood all over her clothes and hands. It had been a defining moment for her. She could control the little things in her life, but the big things…the crazies that didn't play by the rules, those were out of her control. Everything could end in a heartbeat. With one bullet.

"Maybe it was just a communication error," Eric finally said. He tipped his chin toward his brother. "Did you ask the receptionist?"

Danny nodded. "Yeah. She doesn't know anything about a meeting and there's nothing in Simon's book. She didn't call us and she doesn't know who might've. Until we talk to Simon himself, we're at a dead end." He leaned toward the wall, almost grazing her arm in the process, and pushed for the elevator. "On that note, we can take off."

He smelled like clean soap and woodsy aftershave and every feminine part of her cried at the injustice of it all. All the St. John brothers were cute, but something about Danny just flipped her switch. Yep, Danny St. John was a tough man to resist, and he was the exact thing she loved most. A man who knew how to rock the sheets. Any woman who looked at him knew it. So did every man. Women ogled him and men envied him.

Vic had no problem going after a man she wanted, but something about Danny warned her off early on. It didn't matter that his smile woke up every X chromosome in her body. It didn't matter that she *wanted* to take him to bed, because she had a feeling he'd wipe the floor with her. He'd show her the time of her life and walk out the door.

She was done being a doormat. Done being cheated on and done with trusting a man with her heart. *How are you going to find a man if you never trust one?* Leave it to her conscious to ask the obvious questions. It was easier to ignore that obnoxious voice.

"You okay," Eric asked Zoe. The guy had intuition like Eminem with verses. Vic liked how he saw through Zoe's tough exterior. Though she'd never admit it, the whole process had made a huge impact on Zoe's life, and Vic wasn't sure she could help her.

Sex. That's what Zoe needed. Vic just didn't know how to get her friend to cut loose or where to find a guy for her to cut loose with.

"We only have a week until the preliminary hearing," Eric said. "It'll be good to finally get that over with."

"Can't happen soon enough," Zoe mumbled. She checked her watch. "I need to go. I have an appointment in a little while."

Eric watched Zoe as if trying to see inside her. Maybe because she sounded so pissed, but they all understood why. The usual friction snapped between them like an electric shock. It was apparent to anyone who cared to notice.

Hmm. Zoe and Eric? Was he what Zoe needed? Zoe had never mentioned him as a possibility, but maybe that was because her sister was going to marry his brother.

Following Zoe was Vic's best chance to get out of the building and away from Danny so Vic jumped on the bail train. "I have to go too. Busy day at work." PR was a never-ending job and the firm she worked for represented over two dozen heavy hitters between show business and sports. That didn't include the two dozen up and comers who expected her to pave *their* road to stardom.

The foursome took the elevators down and Vic gave a wiggly-finger goodbye to the St. John brothers when they exited at the lobby. Apparently, Danny had a friend working security and he wanted to stop and say hi. Vic breathed a sigh of relief when the elevator doors closed.

The elevator continued to the parking garage. "I've never seen you like that with a guy," Zoe stated, staring straight ahead.

Vic jerked her head. "What? What are you talking about?"

Zoe lifted a dark eyebrow. "Why don't you just do it and get it over with. Afraid you won't get to the door before he does?"

"Zoe Turner, that is the meanest thing you've ever said to me. I'm telling Casey." Vic faced the elevator doors, horrified that Zoe knew her so well. Sure, they were friends, but Vic's *best* friend was supposed to be Casey, not Casey's big sister, Zoe. Ever since that reality show when Casey had paired her sister and Vic together as her two outside-the-house sources, a new friendship had grown. Now that Casey spent most every waking minute with her fiancé, Brendan, Vic and Zoe had bonded even more. And bond they had; over lunches, coffees, and now a shooting and subsequent trial.

Zoe snorted at the threat. "Go ahead. Tell her. Casey will agree with me."

Vic rolled her eyes...mainly because Zoe was right.

"He's exactly your type," Zoe went on. "Although it seems like he's trying a new tactic. The old cold shoulder."

Ah ha! So, Vic wasn't the only one who'd noticed that. At least her instincts still worked.

"I don't know why you're keeping him at a distance...unless..." Zoe finally faced Vic as the elevator hit Vic's floor, a questioning smile on her lips. "You're really into him?" Her narrowed eyes widened. "That's it, isn't it? You actually do like him. Ha." She faced front as the doors opened. "I knew it. I told Casey, but she blew me off."

Vic strode past her, turning at the last second. "I am categorically *not* into him." But the door closed on a smiling Zoe before she finished her sentence. "Fine," Vic murmured, walking to her convertible. "Maybe I *am* into him. And maybe the sky will fall this afternoon too." She cocked her head at the abnormal tilt of her car as she got closer. Dread worked its way up from her middle to her chest. Both tires on the driver's side were flat as pancakes. "Dammit!" She spotted a note under her windshield wiper and looked around the garage as a tingling sensation lifted the hair on her nape. With her heart hammering way too fast, she pried the note away from the window and opened it. The typewritten words glared up in large print.

Call your lawyer now and cancel your testimony at the preliminary hearing next Monday or face immediate consequences.

Heat rushed through her veins. Anger. Rage. And fear. Definitely fear. She looked around the garage again. A car engine grew louder in the distance as Vic fished for her phone and pepper spray in her bag. A familiar white BMW came around the corner and relief whistled through her veins. She flagged down Zoe who stopped behind her disabled car.

"*Two* tires?" Zoe said, after rolling down her window. "You couldn't have one flat, you had to have two?"

Glad to have reinforcement, Vic opened the note toward Zoe. "I've got way more than two flat tires. Read this." Vic took a closer look at the back tire, and fresh anger burned her blood. "The whole side wall is slashed! I can't believe they did this."

"Punks," Zoe stated. "You're not going to bail on testifying, are you?"

"Hell *no*," she barked, looking around the big garage. "I need to call the police and the auto club so they can come change the tires."

"You only have one spare in the trunk. One tire change isn't going to do you much good with two flats."

"Shit." She hadn't thought of that. "Okay, so I need a tow. That's still auto club." She checked her watch. "I don't have time for this crap today." One of her clients had a huge birthday bash coming up and she was in charge of the details.

Zoe pulled her car into a spot across the aisle, got out and scanned the area.

"What are you doing?" Vic asked. "Don't you have a meeting to get to? What are you looking for?"

Craning her head, looking at the roof and all the angles, Zoe walked toward her. "There have to be security cameras down here." She pointed near the exit doors. "There. I'll bet security has it on film."

"That would be shocking. And doubtful," Vic murmured. "But worth a shot, I guess."

A familiar gray SUV rounded the corner and Vic recognized the St. John brothers inside. Eric slowed to a stop and Danny rolled his window down. "Everything okay?" he asked.

"Only if you think threats and flat tires are okay," Zoe said. "Otherwise, not so much."

Vic held out the note as Danny got out and strode closer. He scanned it then bent and surveyed the damage. He turned to Eric who was leaning toward the passenger side of his SUV. "Deliberate," he called to his brother. "Park it."

Eric parked in the only open spot at the end of the row and stalked back, shaking his head when he got up close and personal with both tires and looked at the note Vic held out. "Damn."

Took the words right out of Vic's mouth.

"You okay?" Danny asked.

"I'm pissed, I'll tell you that. Those little shit-turds are *not* going to scare me from testifying."

Danny stepped toward the elevators and pointed at Eric and Zoe. "Why don't you guys wait here. Make sure who ever did it doesn't come back for more. Vic and I will go talk to security. If Ethan can't help us, he'll know who can." Ethan must have been his friend.

In the lobby, Vic pulled out her phone to call the office. She was going to be late no matter what happened at this point.

Danny knew exactly where to go and Vic let him take the lead as he explained the tire damage and she called the police. It took fifteen minutes for the man in charge to access the footage. The aggravation compounded when they discovered the person who slashed the tires and left the note had crept between the rows of cars and kept hidden from the cameras. It would take a serious amount of time watching the garage footage to find the person or potential car he'd driven in with, and Vic didn't have the time to wait. Nor did she plan to wait for the two hours she'd been quoted for the police to arrive.

They headed back down to the garage. Vic broke the uneasy silence in the elevator, acutely aware of the *new* Danny. "Thanks for expediting that process. I don't think I'd have had the same success on my own."

Danny's gaze roamed from her ankles all the way up to her eyes, sending a wave of heat swirling low in her belly. "I can safely say you wouldn't have run into any problems." The air sizzled between them and Vic's heart thumped faster. "But you're welcome. Just sorry about your car." He glanced away. "On the bright side, tires are easy to replace and you're safe."

The elevator doors opened and Danny stepped out, scanning the area before Vic—still caught up in the visual compliment—fully processed his words.

"Anything?" Eric asked as they got closer to Vic's car.

Vic shook her head. "No, they're going to need a considerable amount of time to scroll through all the footage. They'll get back to me if they find anything. Danny suggested I leave the note with his friend Ethan to give to the police when they get here. They said it'll be at least two hours."

"Which really means four hours," Zoe tossed in. "Call the auto club and have them pick up your car when the police finish. I can drop you where you need to go now, and you can grab a ride to whatever tire store they take your car. It's doable. The police aren't going to find anything with your tires. They'll be more interested in the note, but I'll snap a few pictures just in case."

Glancing between the guys, Vic crinkled her nose. "Thanks for sticking around and helping me out."

"It's all good," Eric said. Danny just nodded his agreement, keeping his gaze focused on everything but her.

"C'mon," Zoe said, motioning to her car. "Hop in. You probably need to get out of this garage to get reception, so let's get out of here."

Vic slid in the passenger seat and leaned her head against the headrest. "If I ever get my hands on the guy that did this, I'm going to…" What would hurt the worst?

"Rip his balls off?" Zoe asked.

Vic tipped her head to the side. "That works."

Zoe drove up the remaining levels to the street as Vic searched for the auto club number among the cards in her wallet. One day she'd have to organize this sucker. Once outside of the structure, she had enough bars to make the call.

Zoe slowed at a red light, which quickly turned green and she continued through the intersection.

"What were they thinking?" Vic glanced at her as she waited for someone to pick up on the end of the phone. "Even if I don't testify that still leaves—ZO—" The words turned into a scream as a massive black grill slammed broadside into the car. Adrenaline exploded as airbags burst from the dashboard and door and felt like bricks against her arm and face. Impact sent them careening across the street. The world whizzed by as the acrid smell of burning rubber stung her nostrils. Everything went topsy-turvy and the sound of metal scrapping against road blocked out everything.

The scariest—and maybe last—ride of her life.

CHAPTER 4

"JESUS!"

"Fuck!"

The words came out simultaneously from Eric and Danny as they watched the accident unfolding before their eyes. A monster truck—black with a huge grill—T-boned Zoe's white BMW on the driver's side. Impact sounded like a bomb. Her car flipped and skid, landing on the side and practically wrapping around a streetlight. The truck fishtailed and burned rubber out of the intersection. No plates. Cars swerved and jerked to a stop, and shaken pedestrians got out of their cars.

Danny kept his eyes on the mangled car as Eric swerved to the right and parked. Together, they took off running at full throttle. Danny's pulse pounded as hard as his boots on the pavement. Judging by the damage to the car, he didn't see how anyone could've survived the accident. The car rested passenger side down. Black smoke drifted from the engine. The whir of the motor died as they reached the car.

"Zoe! Vic!" Eric called.

Shit, trying to get to them was going to be a bitch. Incredibly, the windshield hadn't busted although the driver's side window had a gaping hole in the corner where something had penetrated it.

Fire erupted from the engine as the guys circled the car and peered through the windshield. Front and side airbags had activated. Danny couldn't see past the white chalky residue mixed with black smoke in the interior.

"We have to get them out! Can't wait for the fire department!" Danny shouted to Eric.

His brother nodded. "We have to get Zoe's door open," Eric said over the commotion, stripping off his suit jacket. Sirens blared in the distance, but they sounded too far away.

"Give me a leg up," Danny ordered as they stood near the trunk.

Eric didn't argue. They didn't have time. Besides, Danny beat him the last time they benched pressed. Eric cupped his hands and heaved Danny onto the side of the car. The whole thing had been demolished from the truck. Danny braced himself on the wrecked frame and tugged the door. It didn't budge. Panic and adrenaline fought a battle and he took another stab at it, roaring as he yanked with everything he had. The door cracked an inch and with help from Eric, they pulled it open.

Black smoke mixed with white airbag powder made his eyes water.

"Zoe! Vic!" Danny shouted. The air cleared enough to show Zoe slumped over, the seat belt holding her against the seat. Danny adjusted to slide in when her head lolled to the side and she opened her eyes.

Zoe looked up, her cheek and chin raw, probably from the airbag. Both women were moving around—albeit slowly—working at their seatbelts.

"You guys okay?" Danny asked, trying to figure out the best and fastest way to heave Zoe out. They didn't look to be injured aside from road rash from the airbags, but anything was possible.

"Been better," Vic murmured. The smoke got thicker and blacker as each second passed.

"We need to get you two out of there. ASAP. Zoe, grab onto me and unbuckle—in that order." Gravity would drop her on top of Vic otherwise. "I'll pull you out." She did as he said just as a pop and hiss sounded. Flames licked out from the foot well along with more nasty black smoke. Danny heaved her out, handed her off to Eric and went back. He hoped those were sirens in the distance and not his ears ringing from the crackling fire in the engine.

Vic was preoccupied with something and Danny lowered himself in the car, bracing one foot on the console and one on the steering wheel. "C'mon, c'mon," she mumbled, the panic clear in her voice.

35

"What are you doing?" Was she trying to get her purse? Crazy female. "Victoria!" Her full name came out of his mouth for the first time in an effort to get her attention. "Leave it!" he said, reaching for her. The car's interior heated up by the second and his eyes burned from the smoke. Panic squeezed his chest. He had to get her out.

"The strap is stuck over the belt release!" she yelled at him, her brown eyes both frustrated and scared. Her chin and cheekbone had similar scraps as Zoe's. Thank God the airbags had worked. "I can't release the seat belt and I'm locked in too tight to budge." She coughed, the smoke choking them both.

Danny reached for the knife in his boot. The second time this thing had come in handy in less than a year. "Are you hurt?"

"I think I'm okay."

"I'm going to cut the belt so be ready," he said. She braced herself against the side window and he sliced through the belt. Flames grew from the engine and made their way toward the dashboard. Sirens blared closer.

"Danny!" Eric's voice seemed to come from far away.

"Almost there," he shouted over his shoulder. "Can you stand up, Vic? Put your hands on my shoulders. I'll lift you out. Eric will help you on the other side. Let's move it." They didn't have much time before the whole car lit up. He kicked in a new foothold through the air vent, sending a fresh burst of black smoke into the car, but he didn't trust his balance on the steering wheel with Vic's weight.

She didn't hesitate and Danny wrapped his hands around her hips and lifted her. It seemed as if miles of toned legs passed in front of his eyes as she reached for the window. He knew Eric had her when her weight disappeared. Flames arced higher in the interior and scorched Danny's foot and side. He grabbed the car frame and heaved himself up and out, the frame burning his palms.

Eric caught him as he unceremoniously fell backward. A second later, flames fully engulfed the car. "Cutting that a little close, don't ya think?" his brother chided.

"Just how I roll," Danny said, getting to his feet. He found Vic next to Zoe at the curb and away from the burning car. Dozens of bystanders watched and other cars had stopped. Glass and car parts littered the intersection. Other cars had fender benders as a result of the commotion.

"Where's the dickhead that ran into us?" Vic asked. Her voice shook as much as her body. Her black dress was smudged and ripped beyond repair.

Eric signaled with a thumb down the street. "He took off after he hit you."

Zoe stared at the burning wreck. "My poor car."

"My two flats are looking like the beginning of something," Vic muttered.

Something bad. But Danny kept the words internal as he locked eyes with his brother. Neither one of them believed in coincidences. The note. The two flat tires that put Vic and Zoe in one car and made it easier to take them both out. "You're thinking what I'm thinking?" he asked Eric.

"That the warning on Vic's car wasn't an idle threat," Zoe said, her attention snapping between them. "It was meant for all of us and intended to get us into the same car."

Eric met her gaze. "And the phone call getting us all to meet here was for this purpose."

Danny nodded. "Because the preliminary hearing is only a week away. With no witnesses…" He let the sentence trail off. It would've been easy to set the plan in motion, especially if someone had been watching them. He looked around the chaotic scene as the hairs on his nape stood at attention. "We're being watched right now."

Vic scanned the crowd as well. "Oh my God. I feel it too." She wrapped her arms around her middle and winced.

"What? What's wrong?" Danny scanned her from head to beautiful toe. The road rash from the airbag did nothing to weaken his never-ending attraction to this woman. He shut down the thought the second it made an appearance. No attraction to anyone. Not for a long time and maybe not ever. He didn't deserve it.

Vic bent her elbow and they discovered a nasty burn on her arm. "I didn't even realize it until just now."

Danny motioned to the paramedics who'd finally made the scene. "Let's get that looked at."

Vic crinkled her nose, but relented. "Fine. My boss is going to hate this."

"Don't even bring up bosses." Zoe shook her head in a move that conveyed serious trouble of her own at work.

"The good news is that taking a ride in an ambulance means no waiting in the ER. I call that a win." The old Danny might've hit them with a wink, something to persuade them into doing what he wanted, but that guy was long gone. Vic had never seemed interested in him anyway, so he needed to get over it. Just as well at this point, because all his focus was on the new business. If he didn't look at a beautiful woman, then he didn't have to think about his chances of getting her into bed. So far his new mantra had been working. Nine months and counting.

Eric and he followed two ambulances to spend another aggravating chunk of hours in the ER.

"**WHAT DO YOU MEAN,** 'you don't know if all the witnesses are still going to testify'? I thought I made myself *more* than clear when we talked about this." Liam Collier snapped the mechanical pencil in his hands and took a deep breath. Pushing away from his large mahogany desk, he stood in front of the wall of windows that overlooked mid-city Los Angeles. At six-one, he was still a formidable opponent. His salt and pepper hair used to be the only thing that hinted at his sixty-five years. "You promised me this would be off the table by tonight."

Trevor crushed the urge to squirm. Being summoned to his father's office meant trouble...mainly for him. The huge opulent space made him feel small, just as his father intended. Gray walls closed in on him and he shuffled a step to his right to avoid the sun's glare, glad the cream carpet masked the sound. "I know, Dad. I really thought everything was going to be taken care of by the end of today. The cashier is definitely off the table." She'd received the picture of her young son along with a very clear directive. *Testify and he dies.* "I said I'd handle it and I will."

"You'd better." Tipping his head back and forth, Liam's silence unnerved Trevor the way it usually did. He held his hand in front of him as he often did the past few months, and Trevor saw the tremor in his hand and arm in the window's reflection. Liam fisted his hand before shoving it into his pocket. The diagnosis of

Parkinson's disease had cut his dad's already short temper in half. Long seconds ticked by before he said anything else. "I still don't understand what you were doing with those misfits in the first place." He gritted the words out between clenched teeth.

The misfits in question were his friends—guys who'd had his back for more years than his dad ever had—and Trevor had been driving the getaway car. He should've taken off the second he heard the first shots, but instead he'd run in. By the time he'd actually peeled out, the cashiers had run from the market, and Alex had opened fire on them, killing one. The other had seen enough to identify him and his car, but he knew better than to bring that up now.

It had been his idea to rob the place. A dare to the guys because they were so amped for action. He walked a fine line when it came to living his life and pleasing his father. He wasn't dumb enough to outright piss off the old man. He'd seen him at his worst and had zero desire to conjure up that kind of crazy. Not that he worried the old man would give him a double tap to the head. Being an only child gave him a little breathing room in that area. But if Liam Collier had a heart, it was cold, black and shriveled beyond repair. Any of his ex-wives would testify to that. So could the dead men in his wake...if dead men could talk.

"Tell me again, why it took so long for you to deal with this situation."

Trevor cringed at the ice-cold tone of his dad's voice. Sometimes he wished the man had kept his secrets to himself. But when Trev had turned twenty-one, his father had taken him out for his first *legal* drink. The camaraderie—they'd never before shared because his dad hadn't been in his life until he turned eighteen—grew exponentially with each passing whiskey on the rocks until Liam had admitted his true line of work. Dear old Dad was a hit man. An honest to God, shoot-them-between-the-eyes hit man. And he'd sunk the fortune he'd made killing people into a tech business that offered all sorts of gadgets and electronics to the highest bidder.

Liam turned and Trevor rushed to answer his question.

"I was told Alex's family was taking care of things. I was misled," he added, because it was true. Alex's brother, Mondo, had assured him all the witnesses would be handled. That had suited Trevor fine since he didn't particularly want to go to jail for murder.

"Misled or stupid?" His dad's question boomed through his thoughts.

Trevor clenched his jaw and bit back the urge to tell his old man to fuck off. Who'd been stupid not to get a doctor's opinion on his shaking hand for so long? Who waited to find out he had Parkinson's until his whole arm shook with tremors?

"How many times have I said that you can only count on yourself?"

Enough that Trevor wanted to shove those words down his father's throat. He could have too since he matched him in height and weight. "I have it handled. I've got guys watching them right now." He'd even gone a step farther by using one of the company's prototype bugs to make sure he kept a bead on the four remaining witnesses. Of course his dad would pitch a fit if he knew, so Trevor kept the information to himself. Once the job was done, he'd snatch the bugs right back and no one would be any wiser. He considered those little devices his get-out-of-jail-free cards, because if one of his buddies did fuck up, at least he had a way to find those four and make sure they never testified.

"You'd better have it handled," his dad finally said after staring him down for the better part of a minute. "Because I'm not leaving all of this to you if you don't." He gestured to the plush office and building his dad owned.

Fury raged in Trevor's gut that the old man would do this to him. "I'm your only son." *You'd leave me out in the cold?* Trevor kept the question to himself, because yeah, the bastard would, and his mom told him as much years ago, before she died. He'd left him as a child, no reason to think he wouldn't do the same now.

"Exactly," Liam stated. "And my only son needs to be deserving of the legacy I leave him. I didn't work my ass off for years just to hand everything over to a boy who has yet to become a man."

Trevor grinded his teeth so hard he thought he might crack his molars. He was twenty-five fucking years old. At what point would Dear Dad see him as a man?

Stress. Parkinson's had the old man completely jacked up. No one deserved it more. Especially when his dad refused to take any medication for fear of side effects. The shaking just got worse every day.

His dad snapped his fingers in front of his face. A nasty habit that drove Trevor crazy. "You know what you have to do, and you have to do it before the preliminary hearing. Your future depends on it." Liam blinked his cold, dark eyes once. Slowly. "Now go. I don't care how you do it, as long as you make sure those people don't testify. And don't get caught. The sooner the better. Trevor…"

Turning to go, Trevor stopped when his dad called his name.

"Cover your tracks."

Trevor strode out of the office and headed to the hospital. Maybe he could fix this problem right now. After all, who'd expect a hit at a hospital?

CHAPTER 5

ERIC—WITH DANNY SITTING shotgun—followed the ambulance carrying Zoe and Vic to the ER. Zoe had a goose egg on her head from something, and though the doctor wasn't set on admitting her, he did want to keep her for observation for a little while. And Vic's burn required more attention than the paramedics on scene could provide.

Three hours into the wait—after Vic had her arm cleaned up and bandaged—Eric ushered her into a different treatment room where Danny sat with Zoe. The fact that Danny hadn't wanted to hang with Vic while she got patched up told Eric his brother was trying to avoid her. A year ago, Danny would've been all over staying by Vic's bedside.

Eric didn't mind keeping Vic company when he knew sitting next to Zoe would test his restraint. He'd want to help her and she'd argue. He wasn't sure why she disliked him so much, but he didn't want to upset her when she was hurt.

While Vic took the spot Danny vacated, Eric motioned his brother out to the hallway. "How's she doing?" he murmured.

"Seems fine," Danny replied. "She won't call her parents. Said having them hover when she was shot nine months ago was more than enough to last her a lifetime." He lifted a dark eyebrow. "Not that I blame her. Her folks are definitely special."

Eric snorted. He'd only spoken with Zoe and Casey's parents a couple of times, but they seemed to be two of the most uptight and repressed people he'd ever met. "Did she at least let Casey know?"

Danny shook his head. "Nope. Casey's in the middle of a tour and Zoe refuses to bother her when she'll be out of the hospital by the end of the day."

"She hopes," Eric added. His phone rang and he checked the screen. "Finally. It's our lawyer." He took the call. "Hey, Craig. I think I already know the answer to this, but you never called a meeting this morning with me, Danny, Zoe and Vic, did you?"

"No, I didn't." Craig sounded concerned. "But I do have some news you need to know. I got a phone call a couple of days ago from Elda Martinez, the cashier from the market. She told me she won't be able to testify at the preliminary hearing."

Eric's stomach turned. "Did she say why?"

"The only thing she said was that she had a family and it was her job to protect them. She mentioned that there are other witnesses and we wouldn't need her testimony anyway. My guess is she's being threatened and she's too scared to admit it."

"She's not the only one being threatened," Eric said, gesturing to Danny for them to go back into the room. Zoe and Vic deserved to hear this too. Eric put the call on speakerphone and explained everything that happened with Vic's car, the note and the ensuing accident. Eric wiped a hand across his jaw, hating the silence on the other end of the line.

"So, this accident with the monster truck was probably no accident at all," Danny said, jumpstarting the conversation. "Since our testimony could put four men in jail for twenty-five years to life, it looks like someone's warnings are escalating. Would this be probable cause to arrest the guy that's out on bail and put him into custody?"

"Only if the police find evidence that links him to the threats or the tire slashing or the accident, and that's going to take time no matter what."

"And you're sure none of the store's video cameras caught anything?" Vic asked. She sounded like she was ready to bail from testifying too.

"Positive. That's why the robbery took place that night. One of the suspect's little brothers worked in the back and knew the system was down." There was a short pause on the line. "What you need to know is Collier's dad has been under investigation for years. Money laundering, possible murder and trafficking…the list goes on. I don't need to tell you your testimonies are very valuable. My concern is that Liam Collier will do anything to keep his son out of jail. Maybe he's worried that his own reputation puts his kid at risk behind bars, maybe he just doesn't want a prison record for his kid, or—and this is the most interesting— maybe he thinks his son might flip on him for a lesser sentence. Hey, I could be way off base here, I don't know. Anything is possible. Either way, in light of what's happened, I think it's worth a call to the police to see about getting you all protection."

Eric shot a glance to Danny. They'd been down this road once with one of their little brothers. "Our experience is that the police department doesn't have the funds to protect witnesses."

"I didn't say it was going to be easy. Let me make a few calls. I'll get back to you. In the meantime, you all watch your backs and stay safe."

Eric ended the call and glanced around the room. Vic rubbed the side of her nose, Zoe sucked on the corner of her bottom lip and Danny stared out the window. "Vic, I understand if you don't want to testify."

"Stop right there, Eric. I'm not letting these punk-ass jerks scare me into keeping my mouth shut. It would've been nice to hear that one of those damn cameras had been working, but whatever."

"Zoe?" Eric asked.

"Don't even," she said, narrowing her smoky blue eyes. "What Vic just said goes double for me. I'm not letting them get away with this. Not for one damn minute."

A few hours later, as they still waited for Zoe to get the all clear, Danny paced the small treatment room. His inability to sit still grated on Eric's nerves. Just as Eric opened his mouth to tell him to sit down or take his 5K into the hallway, Danny stopped and faced them all.

"Let's disappear on our own," he said.

"What does that mean?" Vic asked from the bedside chair.

"It means, let's not wait for the police to decide whether or not we qualify for protection." Clearly little brother had been thinking the same thoughts as Eric. "There's got to be a place we can go." He looked between the three of them. "Someone here has to know somebody who's either out of town or has an empty space available for a week, or even a few days. Wouldn't hurt if we moved around. The point is to lay low."

No one said anything and Danny pegged Zoe with wide eyes. "Dude! You're a realtor! You've got to have tons of empty houses for us to camp in."

Zoe's jawed dropped to her chest. "I can't move us into an empty house in Beverly Hills! Are you kidding? You think I *want* to get fired? And don't *dude* me! *And*, what makes you think I can just up and walk away from my job for who-knows-how-long?"

Vic tipped her head from side to side. "Fired vs. dead. I'd go with fired. Just sayin'..."

"Figures," Zoe sniped. "It's not your job! It's mine! My bosses aren't nearly as cool as yours."

Vic crinkled her nose in response.

Eric sympathized with Zoe's dilemma. He had the same one. A week away from work could cost him his job. The only thing he had going for him was the massive amount of vacation time he'd accrued the past few years so maybe he could get away with it. *Work. Holy shit.* An idea tussled in Eric's head. Danny did have a point. And Eric potentially had the answer. "Dean's out of town for a month," he said, softly, mostly to himself.

Three pairs of eyes locked on him. Damn. Maybe that wasn't as much to himself as he thought.

"Dean? Who's Dean?" Danny sounded hopeful.

"One of the partners at the firm. Dean White."

"And no one's watching the house?" Vic asked.

He sighed. Came clean. "Well, kind of. It would be me. I know he stopped the mail. He doesn't have any pets to feed. He told me he was even turning the water off so he wouldn't come home to a busted pipe somewhere. I'm just the backup in case a neighbor calls with some sort of problem. Last time he got a house sitter, they had some big party and trashed his house. He said never again."

"Great! We're set." Danny started pacing again. "You must have the key then, right?"

Nodding, Eric regretted bringing it up. "He told me where he hides it. And I have the security code to his alarm system."

"This is perfect!" Danny said incredulously.

Eric stood, ran a hand across his jaw. *Shit!* Could he do this? Could he really waltz into a boss's home with three other people and keep his job? Was he insane?

"Bro, it's not like we're going to trash his house," Danny insisted. "We just need a place to lay low."

"How many bedrooms," Zoe asked.

"Do you need the square footage too?" Danny asked. "You're not selling it, Zoe. We just need a place to crash."

"Because, *dude*, if it's a one-bedroom condo, we're not going to fit. Oh my God, I can't believe I'm even talking like I can do this. I really can't."

"Again," Vic murmured, "sleep on the floor/miss work vs. die. Kind of a no-brainer, Zoe."

Zoe rolled her eyes and Eric empathized with her. His little brothers gave him the same attitude plenty of times. "Eric, answer the question. How big is the place?"

"Two bedroom. He had a little get together there when I first started with the firm. I might've taken a small self-tour to scope out the place. It's not so much a family home as an entertainer's home. Big kitchen, den and living room. Huge backyard with a pool and tennis court."

"Sounds like a winner. Let's do it. Where's it at?"

"Danny..." The warning in Eric's voice was one Danny was very used to.

"Bro, this is exactly what we need. We're not going to trash the place. You won't get fired. Hell, I will personally clean every inch before we leave."

"That I'd like to see," Vic muttered.

Danny ignored her and kept his gaze on Eric. "Where's the house?" When Eric hesitated again, Danny continued, "We're talking about our lives here. You know it's the right thing to do."

Eric shook his head. "Not the right thing." He exhaled a long breath. "But maybe the best thing. They aren't exactly the same."

Danny strode over and clapped him on the back. "Good man!"

"So, where's the key?" Zoe asked.

Seeing the struggle in her eyes softened Eric's mood. "There's a fake sprinkler head in the front planter box and the key is inside that."

"Awesome! Now all we have to do is figure out logistics. Piece of cake."

Eric glanced at the ceiling at his brother's enthusiasm.

Hours later, when Zoe was finally released, the four of them piled into Eric's car and headed to the guys' apartment first. After Danny and Eric packed a bag, they decided to split up.

"I'll take Vic to her apartment. You can take Zoe," Danny said. "Text me the address and we'll meet you at your boss's place as soon as we can. I'll call one of the detectives to let them know we've found our own safe house. Sound good?"

Eric ignored the quick double tap of his heart at the thought of being alone with Zoe. But after everything she'd been through, he just wanted to keep her safe. "That's fine." He noticed the almost surprised look in Vic's eyes before it disappeared. For a guy who'd been doing his best to avoid a woman, Danny seemed to have a change of heart when it came to Vic.

By the time they met at the home in the valley, the sun was setting. The ranch style house, situated in a quiet cul-de-sac, made the perfect place to hide.

"You'd think this guy would have a gate around his house," Zoe said, meeting up with Vic and Danny on the sidewalk.

"None of the others do," Vic noted. "Maybe no one's been burglarized over here."

"Hard to believe," Zoe muttered.

Eric scanned the long Cape Cod blue ranch house. Closed, thick shutters barred curious eyes from peeking inside. The zero-scape yard contrasted with the Japanese boxwoods lined around the structure. The house looked like any other suburban home, but the inside had been designed for a bachelor with money. The surrounding homes seemed just as boring on the outside. Eric couldn't explain the nerves chasing down his spine, but chalked it up to essentially breaking in to his boss's house.

Dean had shown him the security panel over a year ago and after gaining entry, Eric plugged in the code to disarm the system. Everything seemed fine until he got to the pound sign. Damn button wouldn't work. "Shit," he hissed. The clock continued to tick. If he didn't get the alarm disarmed in sixty seconds the house alarm would start blaring.

"What's wrong?" Danny asked.

"The pound key won't register. All the other numbers took, but this one is stuck."

"Let me try." Danny shoved Eric over and hit the button. Nothing happened.

"Twenty seconds," Eric murmured.

"Shut up." Danny tried again, this time with his thumb and nothing happened. The red light and beep, beep, beep of the ticking clock had Eric's palms sweating.

"Ten seconds."

"Son of a bitch," Danny seethed, pushing the button repeatedly as hard as he could.

Eric pushed him aside and tried again. "C'mon, you piece of crap." He tried one more time angling the push and the red light turned green and stopped beeping.

Danny dropped his chin to his chest. "Tell Dean to get his fucking key pad fixed."

"No shit," Eric groused.

With the alarm dilemma behind them, the guys headed down the hallway. Vic stuck her head out of a bedroom door, a smile on her face. "We call the master." She winked and smiled.

It was the first bit of levity they'd had today and Eric needed it. Although once he glanced into the second bedroom, he bit back a groan. Two twin beds. They'd never fit on those mattresses.

The day had only added to the scramble his life had become. Danny didn't like to see how much Eric hated his career and had taken to pressuring Eric to leave his job. The only reason Danny hadn't pushed him about joining his adventure business today was because of the accident and subsequent information. Eric didn't see how he could legitimately leave his very lucrative job at the law firm. Not that he didn't want to. If he thought he had something solid, he'd jump ship in a minute, but responsibility had been ingrained in him since birth apparently.

Late that night, lying on top of one of the twin beds his hands stacked behind his head, Eric watched the almost full moon through the slats of the shutters over the window.

"You could at least take off your shoes." Danny snorted. "It's not like we're going anywhere anytime soon." He'd put on sweats earlier and stretched out in a similar position on the next bed.

"I'm too wired," Eric said softly, listening to the quiet of the room. He hadn't changed out of his clothes. From the first minute they'd walked into this house, he'd had a bad feeling, and that feeling was growing worse.

"I know what you mean," Danny muttered. "Hey, have you given any more thought to what—"

"Shh." Eric put his hand out when he heard something outside the window. He sat up and listened harder.

Danny tilted his head and listened too.

Silence in the room stretched out and just as Eric was about to say never mind, he heard the softest whisper of sound outside the window.

Danny eased off the bed and dug his feet into nearby cross-trainers at the same time he reached for his knife sheathed in the pair of boots by his jeans.

Eric reached for his own knife and motioned for Danny to go out to the hall, but all hell broke loose when the window imploded. Glass rained over everything and a man landed like a thunderclap into the room.

CHAPTER 6

ZOE DEBATED TAKING MORE ibuprofen, but she wasn't nearly as sore as she expected to be after the accident and even her headache had disappeared. She should've knocked out the second her head hit the pillow of the giant California king bed, but her brain wouldn't shut down long enough to let sleep come. Even in the opulence of the completely redone house, she couldn't relax.

She'd talked to her bosses, who'd been more understanding about missing work than she thought they'd be. Of course, she'd used the accident as the excuse, but it was true so she didn't feel too bad. Vic had made her point very clearly in the hospital. Zoe's job didn't matter if she was dead. Zoe would've taken the opportunity to talk to Vic, but her friend's even breathing next to her indicated she was sleeping.

Damn she was angry. Angry that they were being threatened to this extent and angry about the car accident today that was not an accident at all. The extreme lengths that these men were going to scared her and pissed her off at the same time. How was she supposed to sell her own condo if she wasn't there to show it? How was she supposed to keep her job if she wasn't there to do it?

Something moved in the bushes just outside the window in the corner of the room. Zoe's pulse leapt as she sat up in bed.

"Did you hear that?" Vic whispered almost soundlessly.

"I thought you were sleeping." Zoe's voice wasn't much louder.

"Tried. Not successful."

They heard the tiniest scrap on the glass and both of them bolted out of bed. "Stuff the pillow under the blankets," Zoe ordered softly. "Shoes," she said next as she grabbed her flats.

Before they could leave the room, an explosion of sound came from the front of the house and Zoe swung Vic into the closet, followed her in, and shut the door as the window in their room blasted apart. Seconds later, heavy footsteps crunched over broken glass.

Fear and nausea erupted in Zoe's gut like a geyser. Grunts and thuds coming from the hallway marked the sounds of a fight and she held her breath, waiting for someone to pull open the door. She'd pulled Vic into a death trap by jamming them into this closet.

Bullets erupted outside the door and Zoe slapped a hand over her mouth to hold back a scream. The noise stopped and long tense seconds passed as Zoe and Vic stared at each other, the whites of Vic's eyes clear in the dark. Before Zoe knew what happened, Vic slammed the door open and pounced on the man in front them, putting him in a chokehold while hanging onto his back. It was the same thing Casey had done when she'd fought off her ex last year. The gun bounced on the floor and Zoe scrambled to reach it, her hands shaking and breath billowing in and out of her lungs.

The gun was old. A separate chamber for each bullet, but he must have reloaded all the chambers because it was full. No wonder the shooting had stopped. Zoe used her palm and pushed the barrel into position as she stood.

Scuffling continued outside the bedroom, the sound a hellish backdrop to the struggle happening in front of her eyes.

Tired of Vic hanging onto his back and choking off his air, the man fell backward, hard, landing directly on top of Vic and dislodging her hold. He flipped and had his hands around her neck in a second. A ski mask covered his face. Vic struggled beneath him as Zoe got into position, the gun pointed right at the guy's chest.

"Stop!" she screamed, but he didn't even look up. "Stop, I said!" Nothing, and Vic's struggles lost their impact as the breath was literally squeezed from her lungs.

With her heart pounding, her palms soaked with sweat, Zoe fired a shot, close range. A hole broke open on the man's shoulder and he fell back. Vic's audible gasp of air barely registered with Zoe. Dazed, the man staggered to his feet. The gun shook in Zoe's grip as the man slowly backed up toward the window and climbed out. Sucking in much needed air, Zoe took a few seconds to steady her trembling hands. Didn't happen.

Chaos still exploded in the house as she rushed to Vic's side, stashing the picture of the man's dark eyes and bloody shoulder in a deep corner of her brain and concentrating on her friend.

"Thanks," Vic whispered, her voice raw. "I thought that was it for a minute." She pushed herself up and coughed into her elbow. "Wow."

The door burst open and Zoe spun, lifted the gun at the same time she fell back on her ass.

Eric lifted both hands. "It's me! It's me!" A trail of blood ran from his lip to his chin and a nasty scratch marred his cheek. The urge to make it better, to take away his pain blossomed in her stomach and caught her completely off guard. "Are you two okay?" He looked between them.

Zoe exhaled a shaky breath and lowered the gun as he took in the destruction, the bullet holes covering the lumps in the bed and the two of them on the ground. "Yeah. Mostly. A guy busted in through the window and I got his gun when Vic pounced on him. I shot him, and then he left. Must've decided he wasn't going to win without his gun."

"C'mon. We need to get out of here," he said. Vic took one outstretched hand and Zoe took the other and he practically lifted them both off the floor. "You want me to take that?" he asked, glancing at the gun in her trembling hand.

Zoe nodded and gave it to him. Chills raced up her spine at the fact that she'd shot a man.

"Don't give him a second thought, Zoe." Eric tugged her closer and looked her straight in the eyes. "He doesn't deserve any compassion from you. Not an ounce of regret or second guesses. Got it?"

Zoe swallowed hard and met his gaze. His blue eyes drilled into hers and he looked so damn sure. For a second, she wanted to be tucked close against him, feel his arms around her until she could breathe steady again. Instead, she let some of his determination embolden her. Anything to help shake off the terror.

They followed Eric into the hallway. Blood marked up the walls and several windows had been busted apart.

"Oh my God," Vic whispered, her voice still raw. "What happened?"

Danny came from the other side of the house. "They're gone." Blood streaked across his cheek and a bruise formed along his jaw. "I don't think they expected a fight like the one they got."

Zoe swallowed the urge to be sick. "How did they find us? How is this happening?"

"Good questions." Eric looked at Danny. "No one knew we were here."

"We must have been followed," Danny said. "I'm not taking any more chances. Here's what we're doing. I'm calling the detective. Giving him this address and telling him what happened and what to expect. The four of us are walking out the door, going straight to my storage unit, grabbing the gear we need and we're going off the grid. What do you say?" His gaze passed over all of them.

"We can't just leave the man's house like this," Vic replied.

"She's right," Eric said. "While you call the detective, I'll call Blake and put him in charge of clean-up after the police are done. He owes me for drop off and pick up the last time he flew out of LAX." He looked at all the damage. "This might almost make us even."

AFTER BLAKE ARRIVED AT the house, Danny—with Vic riding shotgun—followed Eric to their apartment for the sixty seconds it took to drop off his SUV. Eric and Zoe piled into his Jeep and he continued to his storage unit.

"When did you start renting a unit?" Eric asked from the backseat. "I thought you just kept everything in Mom and Dad's garage."

Danny glanced at the cuts and bruises on Eric's face, figured his own face probably looked as bad. "Close. I rented Mrs. Ford's garage a couple of months ago." The eighty-five-year-old neighbor down the block had watched the boys grow up since they were born. The woman had lost her husband in a car accident ten years ago and lived by herself, all marbles intact. "All my equipment's there. We can load up and hit the road tonight. She's got a bathroom attached to it, too, so we can clean up. Before I forget, now is probably a good time to shut down all our phones. I wouldn't be surprised if the police tried to track us. Let's not make it easy for *anyone* to find us."

No one replied, but they all produced phones and shut them down.

"It's not like we'll have cell service in the mountains anyway, so we're just shutting down a little early," Danny added.

"Makes sense," Zoe said. Danny glanced at her in the rearview mirror. She looked extra pale. He didn't blame her. It'd been a hell of a night so far.

"What if she wakes up while we're in there?" Vic asked. Her voice sounded like razor blades, and Danny shoved back the anger welling up inside over someone trying to strangle her to death. Just because he'd wanted to keep his distance didn't mean he didn't feel protective of her. "She might call the police if she thinks she's being robbed."

Danny shook his head. "That's the beauty of renting from her. I have access twenty-four seven. At nine o'clock every night she takes out her hearing aids and goes to sleep. She can't hear a damn thing when they're out. Trust me. I had this conversation with her when we made our agreement."

"Poor lady," Eric muttered from the back.

"Are you kidding?" Danny said, taking offense at the insinuation. "She loves me. I pay on time and I bring her souvenirs from most of my outings." Beach glass was her favorite and she had a nice collection at this point. Danny cleared his throat and watched the road, suddenly self-conscious about his outburst. Mrs. Ford didn't know anything about the reason his life had changed so much, she'd just been happy to help him when it came to accommodating his business needs. He'd outgrown the space in his parents' garage and was on the verge of spending serious dough for a public storage unit when he'd run into Mrs. Ford during one of her walks.

"What about her car?" Eric asked. "Doesn't she need the garage?"

"You're so out of the loop." Danny shook his head. "She gave up her license and her car a couple of years ago. It's just a big empty space waiting for something. Her words. I had to convince her to take money. She didn't want to charge me anything."

"Aw," Zoe said from the back. "She sounds lonely. I'll bet she loves talking to you when you're loading and unloading everything."

Danny nodded. He figured renting the space helped both of them. He got the square footage he needed and Mrs. Ford got a little companionship.

"Hey, wait a minute," Eric said. "Is that why you've got a gut now? She's been feeding you her cookies and cakes, hasn't she?" Mrs. Ford's baking skills were legendary in the neighborhood.

"Fuck you. I don't have a gut!" Yeah, maybe he'd gained a couple of pounds, but mostly he worked it off during his outings. Although if he kept taking her up on all the sweets she constantly baked and fed him, then work out or not, he was going to weigh three hundred pounds by this winter. "Shh, we're here," Danny said, glad for the excuse to drop the subject.

He pulled into the long driveway and cut the engine near the garage. Like the house they grew up in down the block, the garage sat in the back of the property, away from prying eyes. Danny hit the clicker Mrs. Ford insisted he have, and the door slid up smoothly with barely a sound. He purposely kept that sucker oiled and quiet.

"Bathroom's in the back," he said softly. "I gotta get out of these clothes before I start packing." No reason to state the obvious. He and Eric had too much blood on their clothes to pretend nothing major had just happened.

They all bailed out of the car and the guys unloaded their luggage. Danny grabbed his pack with clean clothes and headed to the bathroom where he stripped and wiped down with a damp washcloth. Exhaling a hard breath, he caught his reflection in the bathroom mirror. Blood streaked across his cheek and a bruise blossomed along his jaw. Facing down the men who'd broken into the house had been reminiscent of the fight his family had endured years ago in their own home. The only difference was that this time, Eric and he had been somewhat prepared.

Had Eric not acted as quickly as he did, had he not put his skill to immediate use as soon as the man busted through their window, they might not be alive right now. His quick knife to the man's side had sent him back through the window almost as quickly as he'd jumped in. The gunshots coming from Vic and Zoe's room had happened after the guys had run to the commotion in the main part of the house.

Danny had been lucky to be in the right spot when one man had crept into the kitchen with his gun out. He'd slammed his straight arms up and knocked the gun loose from the guy's hand after which a fight ensued. Danny had the sore ribs to prove the man packed a punch, but it didn't compare to the last time his ribs hurt. Adrenaline and rage made great partners in battle. Between Danny and Eric, they'd fought off three men, all of whom ran as soon as the opportunity presented itself.

He still couldn't believe that the other three had gone along with his idea, especially Vic and Zoe. But they had, and now he was hell bent on putting his plan to action. After splashing water on his face, he dressed in clean jeans and T-shirt and got out of the bathroom.

He saw that Vic was rifling through her bag with her gorgeous ass in the air. He tore his gaze away and realized Zoe was watching him with a raised eyebrow. Zoe then grabbed Eric's hand. "You're next. Come with me. We need to get you cleaned up." Danny caught the surprised look on Eric's face, but let it go. Big brother deserved a little TLC.

Over the past nine months Danny had accumulated a ton of extra gear. He'd discovered that not all his clients came prepared so with some bargain shopping—and raiding the attic since his mom had kept tons of stuff they'd grown out of over the years—he'd loaded up on different essentials for multiple sports. This trip required his extra backpacks, flashlights, knit hats, scarves plus a bunch of other gently used, but clean items just waiting for action. Methodically, he grabbed what they needed and set it aside.

"Can I help?" Vic asked in a scratchy whisper.

God it killed him to hear her. If Zoe hadn't shot the man who'd choked her, he would have. His gut tightened that he hadn't been there to help Vic. He'd been dealing with his own fight at the time.

"Sure," he said to stay focused on the task. "You can grab what you need out of your suitcase and fit the essentials into this." He handed her a purple backpack. "I've got warm weather gear in that box if you want to rummage through and find coats, boots and gloves for you and Zoe." He handed her another pack, this one black. "She can use this."

This was either the best idea he'd ever had or the absolute worst. He couldn't imagine either Vic or Zoe camping out or roughing it anywhere, but that's exactly what they were going to do. Neither of them balked as they'd surveyed the blood and destruction they'd passed on the way out of the house. The fact that they'd all survived was nothing short of a miracle.

Eric and Zoe emerged from the bathroom and everyone got into packing mode.

Danny had been slowly building the business to accommodate mountain hikes, but he hadn't done anything more than local day treks and quick weekenders. He'd planned on snagging a brother or a friend to test out a trail he mapped in the Sequoias. In fact, he'd just downloaded a fire and parking permit a week ago in hopes of going right after the preliminary hearing, but he never dreamed he'd be putting it to use this way. This party was bigger than he anticipated, but he had enough resources to cover the five night trip in their immediate future.

He'd actually researched a new trail the park had just opened up to hikers. The grand unveiling of the new visitor center wasn't set for another couple of weeks, so it seemed like the perfect place to disappear for a few days.

Climate change had kept the temperature higher than normal and although it was bound to get cold in the mountains, it shouldn't be miserable. At least he hoped not.

Tents, freeze-dried food, bear canisters and other gear lay scattered on the floor waiting to be packed.

"How rough is this terrain, Danny?" Vic asked.

"Not honestly sure." He kept his focus on stuffing the food pouches into a pack. He'd planned to taste test all of them and weed out the good from the bad, but at this point he was just glad he had enough food to survive this spur of the moment trek. "It's a new trail that just opened up."

Vic's response was just short of a growl. Yeah, this was not a trip full of happy campers.

Danny stopped packing. Didn't move a muscle. This was a dumb idea, partly fueled by his business plans, and not everyone's welfare. They could just as easily hit the road and use cash for motels until the hearing, but that required a stop at an ATM and a way for police to find them. The detectives weren't especially happy with their immediate departure. Not that Danny blamed them, but sticking around to discover the cops weren't going to find anything of value didn't make much sense. The guys who'd invaded the house all wore ski masks, so they had very little to go by in terms of descriptions.

"What's wrong?" Zoe asked.

He looked up to find two sets of eyes watching him. "Nothing. Just thinking."

Vic and Zoe exchanged looks before their gazes landed on him again.

"Honestly, I'm gauging this plan against anything else and this seems the most viable, the best way to disappear."

"Look, it seems extreme," Vic said. Every uttered word reminded them all how closely they'd come to losing her tonight. "But, personally, I'm okay with disappearing if it keeps us safe. Let's let the forest hide us for a while. We can survive a camping trip. Right, Zoe?"

Zoe hesitated a fraction of a second before nodding. "Sure. It's not like I have a job where I need to be present." She clamped her mouth shut, swallowed hard and avoided eye contact. "Forget it. Let's just do this. We're wasting time."

VIC LET THE RHYTHMIC drone of the road soothe her senses. Not that she could get comfortable in the back seat of Danny's Jeep, but it beat an early grave. No matter how much she tried to deny it, her whole body ached from the car accident and her throat still felt raw and swollen. She'd seen the bruises on her neck when she'd cleaned up in the small bathroom. She glanced to her right, glad to see that Zoe had fallen asleep. Danny had thought to bring pillows and blankets for the car ride, along with a bottle of ibuprofen. Damn considerate of the man. He had a little bit of everything stored in that garage. What kind of man thought that far ahead?

Just when she thought she was done thinking about him, he

went and did something nice. Hearing more stories about their neighbor Mrs. Ford made it hard to quit crushing on him.

She could go months without seeing him and be fine, but the second they were in each other's company, all her girl parts waited in breathless anticipation for an errant touch or a sizzling look. Neither of those had happened today, with the exception of him pulling her from the car earlier and that didn't really count considering the circumstances. But it had been the most heroic thing any man had done for her, so it wasn't easy to set aside or forget. She'd probably never forget the feel of his hands on her hips as he lifted her over his head and into his brother's arms. A line of tingles chased down her spine remembering how effortless he made it seem.

Now she had to wrap her brain around roughing it for the next five or six nights. Six nights until the preliminary hearing when they could finally get this process to the part that mattered. Their testimony.

She'd just avoid looking at Danny's rock-hard body and shocking blue eyes. She wouldn't let the low rumble of his voice melt her underwear or stare at the hands that she wanted touching every part of her. All she had to do was survive Danny.

And the weather. She shivered thinking about the cold. Though she loved scenic views and serenity in all its forms, she didn't consider herself an especially outdoorsy person. Not that she had doubts she could handle it.

One of her favorite things was surprising people. She enjoyed when someone thought one thing of her, and she turned around and did something completely out of character. Of course, surprising her best friends rarely happened these days.

It would've been nice to surprise Danny by being outdoorsy, but now he barely looked at her. She'd been shocked when he volunteered to take her home to pack earlier in the day, especially since he'd avoided her at the hospital. Even if he hadn't said much, she'd felt safer having him there. And Eric...he flat out wasn't her type. Sure she appreciated the package. All the St. John brothers had looks and bodies for days, but Eric lacked the free spirit she craved in a man.

Danny, on the other hand, he had enough free spirit to fill a small town. Maybe that's why he scared her so much. He was the kind of guy she went for…but more. Only problem was she could see herself falling hard for a man like him. Zoe had pegged her right in the elevator.

Glancing in the rearview mirror, she caught Danny's gaze before he looked back to the road.

"You should try and catch some sleep while you can," he said, his low voice soft in the quiet car.

Eric looked over his shoulder. "Glad Zoe passed out. Just wish she'd get more sleep than this drive is going to give her." Without their cell phones and GPS, he had a map folded neatly in his hands.

"It's better—" she cleared her rough throat, "—better than nothing." She cringed at the sound of her voice, nothing attractive about sounding like a baritone. Vic adjusted the warm blanket on her lap and leaned against the pillow next to her. "Besides, Zoe is way tougher than you guys think."

Eric snorted, shook his head and lifted skeptical brows before closing his eyes and leaning against the head rest. Yeah, Zoe was beat up, but she'd never cop to it. Vic wouldn't either for that matter. Not in this lifetime.

"How are *you* doing?" Danny asked, his gaze catching hers again in the mirror.

No lying to herself. She liked that he cared. "I'm better than I sound. Don't worry."

He nodded "I meant to ask you earlier… Your boss okay with the situation and the unexpected time off this requires?"

"Mostly. It's going to require some shuffling of projects, but—" She coughed and cleared her throat again. "I should be covered. It just means I won't have any vacation time for the next five years or so."

Danny's gaze jerked to hers in the review mirror. "Seriously?"

She shook her head and grinned. Sometimes she loved how gullible he was. It was a very cute trait for such a smart man. "Okay, I'm exaggerating. Maybe two years is more like it. My boss is pretty cool and I'm good at my job, so I'm not going to stress about it." She had a feeling Zoe couldn't say the same about her bosses, but she was so close-mouthed about her job, it was hard to tell.

"I'm sorry about today," Danny said.

She glanced at Eric and his closed eyes. He probably wasn't paying attention to their conversation. "Which part?" There was so much to choose from.

"All of it. The car accident. Tonight at the house."

"It's weird. Somehow it feels like days ago instead of hours ago."

He nodded. "I was thinking the same thing while I was packing the bags. It's like a weird dream. More like a nightmare, I guess." It was quiet for a moment, with only the sound of the wheels eating up the road. "Every time I see those bruises on your neck, I…"

Vic couldn't control the sudden quick beat of her pulse. "You…what?"

Shaking his head, he glanced at her again in the mirror. "I want to hurt that man."

"Trust me, you're not the only one, but at least Zoe nailed him good in the shoulder." She'd never forget the fear of having the air squeezed out of her. She'd completely frozen and concentrated on defense instead of offense. She wouldn't make that mistake again. Nor would she forget the look of shock on that man's face when a bullet blasted into his shoulder, knocking him back. She shuddered at the memory. If she learned nothing else from the experience, she had to remember to attack because she was no match for a big man's strength.

"I know," Danny said. "It just pisses me off that he got his hands on you like that. That he nearly…"

Vic heard the tension in his voice—like he might be strangling the man even as he said the words—so she didn't press him this time. She understood. "Thanks." Her barely-there voice cracked and the word squeaked out, but Danny heard her. He nodded and set his attention back on the road.

A foreign sense of camaraderie sunk into her heart. She liked knowing that Danny wanted revenge on her behalf. It was another side to him she hadn't seen and though she wished the circumstances were different, she appreciated seeing more parts that made up the man.

"Get some sleep," Danny said. "The less you use your voice, the faster it'll come back."

Vic gave him a thumbs-up, which he saw in the mirror. She didn't want to know what time it was. The day was going to be endless, just like the one before. She leaned against the pillow and let the sound of the spinning tires lull her to sleep.

CHAPTER 7

DANNY DROVE TOWARD SEQUOIA National Forest with Eric in the passenger seat navigating. On the bright side, driving in the middle of the night ensured less traffic, which made the almost four hour trip northeast that much faster. He'd debated a farther destination and ultimately decided that they needed to be close enough to ensure returning in time for the court date.

He didn't know what to expect, but quiet hadn't been it. Everyone had fallen asleep during the drive. It gave Danny way more thinking time than he wanted.

For nine months, he'd tried to get that blood red bath and Nikki off his mind. It didn't matter how many jobs he did or how hard he worked trying to get his business off the ground, the vision always came back to him when he least expected it. All the violence and blood tonight had triggered memories of that day in gruesome detail. With those images came gut churning nausea loaded with a thousand-pound heaping of guilt. He should've seen how unstable Nikki was after the first damn drink. Should've seen the signs, like the way she'd attached herself to his side like a damn barnacle on a whale. Not to mention all the others. *Signs she'd covered up*, his conscience reminded him. Still, he'd missed something huge and he couldn't afford to let that happen again. Never again.

It didn't matter what his family said, he felt responsible for Nikki's death. He never should've slept with her. He should've taken the time to talk to her instead of rush her out of his apartment that last time. It almost felt as if part of the guilt bled over to tonight and not being there to help Vic. Yes, Zoe had saved her and she was okay, but—

"Sun's going to come up soon. How about we stop up ahead for breakfast," Eric said, breaking him out of his thoughts.

Danny welcomed the distraction. "Sure. Sounds good." He pulled up to the small diner just outside the park entrance. Only fair to give Vic and Zoe one last shot at a sit-down meal before roughing it. Eric too, for that matter. He hadn't done this since they were teenagers. Five nights for three novice campers was bound to be a challenge.

Danny tried to look forward to the adventure as another step in growing his business. The water sports had taken off during the summer. His kayaking, surfing and diving expeditions had all gone off so well that he had more business than he could almost accommodate. Time to expand, and this trip was the perfect way to explore and keep everyone safe at the same time. He only hoped the lessons and excursions he'd cancelled for the next five days wouldn't bite him in the ass, but he offered half price deals in his short messages and hoped that eased the sting of his last minute bail out.

Breakfast turned out to be almost as quiet as the drive up. They sat in a corner booth so everyone had a clear view of the front door and saw anyone who entered. Local pictures of the nearby park dotted the wood paneled walls, and fans circulated slowly overhead.

Tension between the four of them crackled with the few exchanged sentences. Danny got it. Last night had been scary as fuck. Not something easily forgotten or swept under the rug.

A fresh shot of guilt arrowed through his chest, a feeling he'd—unfortunately—become accustomed to. Leaving the scene last night weighed heavily on all of them. God, he'd knifed a man... Stuck a blade into his side and watched the shock of pain in his eyes. The man had acted on Danny's split second of surprise and leveled him with a hard right before cutting his losses with his bleeding friends.

"Dude deserved whatever he got." Eric's words echoed in his head. *"They made a choice, Dano. It was us or them. This was self-defense and you have every right to protect yourself and the people around you. I know you know this."*

True. Their whole family knew this lesson. Still, the violence...

Maybe it was leaving it all behind that had him so off kilter. On the other hand, how was sticking around going to change anything? As Eric had stoically informed him, *"Surviving's only going to make us a bigger target. It's only going to bring in more hired guns."*

They'd even talked about hiding out at their parents' house, but neither of them wanted to put their mom and dad at risk. Not after everything they'd been through during the kidnapping four years ago.

This trip was under duress. Zoe and Eric had serious boss issues, and Vic was finally looking at him with heat in her eyes when he didn't want her to. Funny how life worked in mysterious ways. He hadn't touched a woman in months. Didn't want to. He avoided the blatant stares and batted eyelashes from the single women in his tours. Business was business and he had no time for pleasure.

He glanced up and caught Vic's warm brown-eyed gaze.

"You've been pretty quiet," she said, tilting her head…almost as if she could see through him. "You doing okay?" Sun splashed in from the window two tables away and glinted off fiery red strands in her strawberry blond hair.

"Yeah, sure." That was a first. Vic had never asked how he was in the past. He glanced at the other two at the table but they seemed immersed in their menus. Danny cleared his throat and opened his menu. He wasn't that hungry and his stomach still churned picturing all that blood last night. But he pretended to be into the menu to get Vic's gaze off him and onto something else.

"How cold is it supposed to get tonight?" Vic asked.

"Mid-forties," Danny said.

She shivered across from him. "Chilly."

"You'll be fine. The sleeping bags are designed for twenty-degree weather. You might be too hot." His gaze flashed to hers. He hadn't meant that to sound sexual, but that's just how she took it. Her checks turned a pretty pink—even the scraped up one—and they both looked away. Shit. He did not want to lead her on and completely regretted how hard he'd come on to her when they'd first met. "The tents help too. Keeps the heat in. You'll be fine."

Luckily a server came by, took their order, picked up their menus and headed off.

Danny would've felt like a class-A fool if they'd been on this trip for any other reason than their safety. It couldn't have been more awkward.

"How big are the tents?" Zoe asked.

"Two person tents," Danny said.

"They have a little mud room at the entrance," Eric added. "They're fun." He grinned, obviously remembering one of their many camping trips. "You can stash your packs, shoes, whatever in the front and have room to spread out the sleeping bags in the big part."

Danny remembered when they used to take turns making the twins decide who was going to sleep in the small section. It gave them more room when their parents had all four of them sleeping in the same tent. It always cracked them up watching Blake and Brendan argue or come up with some competition to decide who slept with the big boys. Big was relative since there was only a year between each of them. Eventually, their dad caved and bought another tent. It was nice only having to share the space with one brother instead of three.

"And you seriously...enjoy sleeping on the ground?" Vic's question made Danny smile despite his mood.

"Yep. Seriously." He'd wait and give them their surprise tonight when they set up camp.

"How many times did you say we were moving again?" Vic asked.

"Five," Eric said. "We'll hike in and get to the first stop early afternoon and set up. Then we'll break down tomorrow morning and trek to the next." He glanced between Vic and Zoe. "And so on."

"But if we go that far in, we won't make it back in time for the hearing Monday morning," Zoe said.

"The plan is to curve around the visitor center so we're hiking in more of a semi-circle," Danny explained. "The midpoint will be as high as we get."

Zoe gave a huff. "Well, glad we can be your guinea pigs." Except he wasn't sure she meant it. She hadn't seemed completely on board with this idea from the beginning. Danny wasn't even sure what convinced her to finally cave, but he was glad she did. They were better off sticking together if someone wanted to hurt them. Strength in numbers. Besides, he didn't see how anyone could've followed them. Blake might be the private investigator, but Danny would've noticed steady lights behind him the whole trip and there had been absolutely none that had kept up with his speed. He'd passed too many semi-trucks with an eye out behind him and they'd been in the clear.

"Just think of this as a vacation," Danny said.

Zoe looked incredulous at that. "Vacation?" She opened her mouth then promptly clamped it shut. She shook her head and pushed away from the table. "I need to run to the lady's room."

They all watched her go. "She okay?" Eric asked, looking at Vic.

"She will be. She's tough. Knowing Zoe, she's thinking about last night. It could mean a whole new investigation which is going to cut into our lives just like the robbery did. Besides, *I'd* be wigged out if I shot someone. She just needs to work through it and realize she didn't have any other choice. She's probably freaked out about her job too. Once we get going, she'll come around."

ERIC LOOKED AROUND THE area as Danny parked in back at the tourist center. Not one other car sat in the lot. Not a big surprise since it was just after dawn on a workday and the building hadn't opened yet. He got out of the Jeep and sucked in the fresh air like it might save his soul. Huge sequoias surrounded the area and flanked the building in a giant semi-circle. Maybe Mother Nature could erase last night's violence from his mind. The memory kept hitting him. Pouncing on the guy who'd busted into the room and being very aware of Danny fighting with another man in the hallway. Praying he could help his brother in time before it was too late. The noise, the chaos, the gunshots. It all kept replaying in his head like a nightmare.

For the first time, Eric felt a kinship with Zoe. Understood exactly what she might be going through since last night. Zoe just hadn't wrapped her brain around the fact that she'd saved Vic's life yet. That was the only difference between them. Eric had never stabbed anyone before, but now he knew how it felt to plunge his knife into skin and bone. Seeing those men ganging up on Danny in the front hallway had released a tidal wave of rage. He'd experienced enough horror to know that if someone put him in a life and death situation, he was going to do what it took to survive and he'd used his knife accordingly. All that blood. Not to mention all the damage to his boss's gorgeous house. He trusted Blake to fix the place up, but still didn't see much chance of keeping his job after that. Too bad they hadn't been able to hold one of them down before they all ran off. He squeezed his eyes shut then blinked them open. There was going to be plenty of time in the future to rehash last night and deal with the consequences and right now he had other priorities.

He took in another breath of air. Damn it smelled good. This was what he needed, time away from his stuffy downtown office and real air. He didn't mind ditching the tie that nearly strangled him every day when he put it on, either. He loved L.A. and couldn't imagine living anywhere else, but getting out of town and into the clear skies and gorgeous territory had to be good for something besides running.

He'd been putting Danny off every time his brother tried to convince him to go in on the business with him. He'd gone to school to be a lawyer, not some adventure guide. His folks would have a heart attack if he threw over everything he'd worked so hard for.

Danny was already making decent money with his ocean tours. Kayaking, paddle boarding, surfing. He had clients up the yin yang. This past winter he'd segued into winter sports with skiing and snowboarding at Big Bear. As far as Eric could figure, Danny's popularity came from word of mouth. He was patient and attentive when teaching any sport. Surprisingly, his clientele consisted evenly of men and women. Eric would've bet the female count beat the male, but Danny's appeal stretched across the board.

So yeah, business was good, but Eric wasn't sure it could support both of them, no matter how much Danny tried to convince him otherwise.

Loading up the backpacks and getting Zoe and Vic set with their gear took a little more time than Eric expected. Not that they were in a rush, but Danny had stressed that the sooner they hit the trail the farther in they could get before setting up camp.

Though Zoe was the least excited of them all, she at least kept her complaints to herself. He attributed her lack of enthusiasm to the circumstances and he couldn't blame her. Besides, not every sport or activity was for everyone. Maybe once she got out in the wilderness and experienced the beauty of Mother Nature's land, she'd change her mind.

Danny helped him with his pack—sucker had to weigh nearly forty-five pounds—then heaved his own over his back. All the gear stacked high and cleared their heads by a foot. Miraculously, he'd managed to include the bear canisters to store the food. With one last check in his Jeep and the locked storage container fitted to his roof rack, Danny hit the alarm. Checking the map in his hands, he headed toward the giant sequoia trees in front of them.

Eric rubbed his hand across the thick stubble on his jaw. His brother had busted his butt to make this trip as comfortable as possible for them. Along with keeping them alive, he knew Danny looked forward to converting them into nature-holics just to see if he could. The ultimate challenge so to speak. If he could convert the amateur, then he had a chance to build this part of the business with return customers and good word of mouth.

"Water bottles handy?" he asked as they set out.

"Aye, Cap'n." Vic saluted.

"Perfect." Eric sighed and swallowed his doubts. No turning back now.

A half hour into the hike, he bent to tie a bootlace and let Vic and Zoe pass him. Zoe was straggling behind, and Eric didn't want to lose her. He made a production of adjusting his pack as they went by. Zoe lost her footing on uneven terrain and Eric caught her before she fell. Chest to chest, they looked into each other's eyes.

"Thanks," she said, her voice soft. Her pulse beat fast in her neck.

Eric fought the urge to lean in closer, to smell the vanilla scent of her shampoo. "You're welcome." He steadied her, set her back on even ground, then followed behind her.

"Making sure I don't drop off a cliff?" Zoe gave him a behind the shoulder glance, her brows lifted with the question. If there had been a moment between them, it was now long gone.

"Too soon for cliffs," Eric said. "Danny said we'd hit those tomorrow if we make good time." He should've known she'd see through him in a second. Not much got by her. Not even his crazy overprotective compulsions. But both of the women had to be sore as hell from the accident, so his concern was legit.

Damn it. Eric realized the problem of walking behind Zoe. Keeping his eyes off her ass—in black lycra—might very well prove to be impossible. Those curvy globes swayed in front him like a carrot in front of a donkey. He was definitely an ass. He looked away, focused on the terrain instead.

Danny had done a great job of mapping out the hike and choosing the camping spot. Eric was certain his brother was going a lot slower than his normal pace, too, trying to ease the ladies into the trek. He'd never seen his brother so immersed in anything. Sure, Danny had changed in the last nine months. Who wouldn't, after going through what he had with Nikki. Anger flooded Eric's system. Maybe his feelings would be different if she hadn't left that goddamn note implying Danny caused her suicide. But she'd killed Danny's spirit probably faster than she'd bled out. Danny rarely smiled anymore and when he did, it was forced. He barely looked at women much less touch them. Of all the women Danny had dated and slept with over the years, all the women that tried to lock him down or corner him into a commitment, Nikki was the first to succeed and she'd done it from the grave.

Eric just wanted his brother back.

They stopped twice for water breaks before lunch, then continued another couple of hours before reaching the spot Danny had marked as their overnight stop. Not a moment too soon either, because Zoe looked ready to drop. Eric had quit asking her if she was okay because of the surly answers she shot him.

Tall, gorgeous sequoias surrounded the campsite and Eric had never been happier when all those pounds of gear dropped off his back. Jesus, that was a hell of a load. His shoulders were already screaming. Tomorrow was going to be twice the bitch.

Danny started unpacking essentials around the fire pit while Eric got working on their tent.

"Where's the port-a-potty?" Vic asked, indicating the area.

Danny looked around then mimicked her finger-twirl. "You're looking at it," he said. "You won't have far to travel." He flashed a smile, almost a tell of his former self, but he went back to work and the moment vanished.

Eric chuckled at the horrified look on Vic's poor battered face, but the exchange got him wondering. Could Vic pull Danny from his self-imposed emotional exile? God, he hoped so, because he sure as hell hadn't been able to.

Danny unfurled the first bright red tent, showing Vic and Zoe how to assemble it. "This is the only time I'm doing this," he said. "From here on out, your tent is your responsibility."

"Why is that?" Vic asked.

"Because it feels good to do something for yourself. To survive in the wilderness. No sense in doing this if you don't learn from it. Also, it's good to go out of your comfort zone every once in a while." Danny never stopped working as he talked, sliding supports through their holes in the tent lining and teaching all of them the fastest way to set it up. Dude had been practicing.

Eric was slower than Danny at setting up their tent—also red—but it had been years since he'd camped so he cut himself some slack.

Danny wiped the sweat off his forehead with the bottom of his T-shirt. "I have a surprise for you two," he said, glancing at Vic and Zoe.

Zoe canted her head. "If you tell me you've come up with a better idea than camping out for the next week, I'll love you forever."

"As much as I wish that were so," Danny said, "I think you'll like this too."

Eric envied his brother's patience. He hoped Zoe and Vic realized how hard Danny was working to make this plan as comfortable as possible for all of them. If they didn't appreciate his gesture then he'd definitely talk to them. Not that he'd have a clue what to say, especially when it came to Zoe. Whenever he looked into her eyes, some part of his wigged-out mind took a dive and caved to every instinct he had when it came to her.

WITH THE SUN ON its way down, Trevor checked the signal on his phone and followed the mountain road to the new visitors center. A jolt of panic pumped his heart faster and he took a deep breath for some equilibrium. So far he'd avoided listening to his father's voicemails. The old man probably ripped him another new one because the job hadn't been done yet. *Take responsibility. Be a man. Do the job.* The same old words on a brand new day.

Honestly, he couldn't really fucking believe it had come to this. Trevor shook his head, still in disbelief that his buddies couldn't get the job done last night. How could four tough gang-bangers take a beating and run at the hands of a couple of chicks, a jock and a yuppie. Didn't seem possible.

His dad's words rang in his head again. *If you want the job done right, do it yourself.*

In the parking lot near the back of the building sat St. John's white Jeep. Just as he'd been assured, the little tracking device worked even at this elevation out here in nowheresville. He hadn't expected the chase to be this extreme, but now that he realized their intention, he'd have to adjust. Maybe he could wait them out and strike as they left the area. He couldn't go in after them, not with the head start they had. The tracking device attached to the car, not them. No matter what he decided, he'd need gear and extra hands, but he could have a viable plan ready to go by tomorrow. They definitely had to stay close to the Jeep, which meant camping out. He'd give them just enough time to think everything was fine. Then bam. End of story.

Grinning, he looked in the passenger seat at his buddy. Kaleb had slept most of the drive, probably because he'd partied hard the night before. Just as well, because they had a lot to do to get ready for the next phase. Trevor didn't think too many of his friends were into camping, but they *were* into watching each other's backs, so they'd have to do one thing to accomplish the other. Seemed like a no-brainer to him. The four they were hunting had done him a favor by picking a remote location. Easier to dispose of the bodies. Sure, one day, they'd be discovered, but hopefully it would be long after he and his guys had split. Worst case scenario had him hijacking the safe full of cash his dad kept in his home office. Liam didn't think Trevor knew about it, but the old man was wrong about a lot of things.

He wouldn't go to prison. His dad had threatened that if he ended up behind bars, he'd disown him. No inheritance, no nothing. The SOB. Trevor wasn't about to give up his birthright for these pussies. Prison was not—and never would be—an option.

Trevor looked around the near empty lot and jogged to the Jeep. He pulled out his switchblade and slashed the sidewalls of two tires, same as he'd done to the convertible in downtown L.A. That plan had gone over perfectly until the fucking St. Johns had pulled the bitches out of the car. But he couldn't control everything, although he had the upper hand in this situation. Those four had no clue they'd been found. And when Trevor pounced, he planned to hit hard and with no mercy.

He got back to the car and punched Kaleb's shoulder, waking the asshole with a start. "Call the guys," Trevor said. "We need back up."

"What? What are you taking about?" Kaleb rubbed the sting out of his shoulder.

"We're going camping."

"You fucking lost your mind? I ain't camping."

Trevor ignored him. "We passed a sports store about twenty minutes back. We'll get what we need while the guys are on the way. After that, we can hit up the nearest bar. I have a feeling you're going to need a drink to get psyched for my plan. Stay here. I'm going to scope out the inside. See what we're dealing with." Trevor grabbed a cap from the backseat and pulled it low over his eyes then strode toward the visitors center. Once inside, he spotted two different cameras in adjacent corners of the open building. Two rangers working behind the desk, looked to be closing up for the night. He'd bet the money in his pocket, these were the men he was going to face tomorrow. Poor assholes had no clue what was coming.

CHAPTER 8

ZOE FELT LIKE SHIT for the attitude. It took her time to process things, accept things, and she had so much to go through that she couldn't keep up. And *until* she processed, she tended to react with snark. It was a personal flaw she was well aware of and one she hadn't figured out how to adjust. Yet.

She couldn't get rid of the images from last night. The violence, the blood. It all circled in her head like a nonstop merry-go-round. Everything was happening too fast. First Vic's tires and the note, then the accident, and finally the attack at the house.

And currently, *this*. She looked around at the red tents, huge trees, fire pit and so much dirt, still in shock that she was actually here. She'd sworn to herself at age nine that she'd never ever, *ever* again go camping. Not with Girl Scouts, not with family and not with friends. *Never.* She certainly didn't plan to bring up why either. It was one of those tidbits best left in the past. *But where else are we all going to hide?* A fair enough question. Until they had more answers, this decision did seem the most logical way to disappear and most importantly, she'd agreed to it.

She sure as hell didn't know where they were. That should count for something.

It wasn't Danny's fault she hated camping. It wasn't his fault that someone wanted them dead. All he'd tried to do was make the best of a crappy situation. He and Eric had hauled in God only knew how much weight on their backs, and that was *after* saving their lives last night, so she needed to cut the attitude and be thankful Danny had at least shown them how to set up the tent. It wasn't as if it was hard, but it would've taken her and Vic way longer to figure out which poles slid through which holes.

"Zoe can't help the snark," Vic said, beating her to the apology on her tongue. "It's her middle name."

"No it's not," Zoe said, exhaling a frustrated sigh. "Sorry, Danny. I'm upset at this whole thing, but I shouldn't take it out on you."

"Not a problem." He didn't smile and it made Zoe feel worse. "Anyway…" He untied a thick package below his backpack and headed to their tent. "I brought along an air mattress for you two. It's self-inflating. Easy to set up, easy to take down."

Vic's eyes rounded as if Danny had pulled out a frozen yogurt machine. "No way! Danny, this is so cool! Thank you!" She moved toward him like she might hug him, but Danny shifted to the tent opening and dropped to his knees, avoiding any contact with Vic like she might carry a disease.

"No big deal. You're welcome," he said, and got to work unrolling the mattress in their tent.

Zoe hadn't spent much time with Danny and didn't profess to know him very well, but the change in him since he'd found that lady in her bathtub was sad. The man was a born flirt, yet she rarely saw him smile anymore. She only knew the basics, what Casey had told her, but still it made her feel for the guy that he couldn't get past that incident. This camping trip—hell his whole business—was partially about him forgetting. It didn't take a psychologist to see that.

The funny thing…or maybe not so funny thing…was that Danny's about face had completely attracted Vic. The same woman who'd kept him at a very healthy distance, now sent him meaningful glances and opened doors to all sorts of possibilities, but Danny shut down every invitation. The tension between them sparked almost as much as the tension between her and Eric.

Eric hated her. It was no big secret. She caught his bored stares and terse replies. He didn't like when she asked him to do things. He was an independent man who followed his own rules.

But she still owed him her life. Yes, Danny had lifted her to safety after she'd been shot, but Eric had distracted the gunman from pulling the trigger a third time at point blank range. Though initially she'd been hazy after falling back into the aisle, she'd been cognizant enough to realize when a gun was pointed at her. Awake enough to see that whatever Eric had thrown at the guy's head had been the only thing keeping her alive. Yesterday, he'd caught her after Danny had hauled her from the car and last night he'd come to their rescue in the bedroom, even if he had been a few seconds too late. His words came back to her. *Don't give him a second thought, Zoe. He doesn't deserve any compassion from you. Not an ounce of regret. Got it?* His eyes had been so serious, so intense. She knew deep down he was right, she just had to come to terms with it.

So, yeah, she owed him her life, but that didn't change the way he looked at her. Like she might bite his head off at any given moment and feed it to her fish. Not that she had fish, or any animals for that matter, because pets of any kind required money, which she was running out of at a precariously fast rate. Heat blossomed in her stomach and burst up her chest and neck as she thought about it. If she didn't sell a house soon, she'd be in neck deep shit. Just another reason this camping excursion was killing her.

If Casey or anyone else found out her issues, she'd be mortified beyond belief. Everyone thought she was the successful realtor with money to burn, when the truth of it was not as glamorous. Selling expensive homes was lucrative in a good market. In a not so good market with fierce competition, the tables turned. Add to that a bad investment in the stock market along with condo and car payments, and her bank account had disappeared in the worst magic trick known to man.

Ugh, one more thing she didn't want to think about now.

She also didn't want to think about the last time she'd gone camping twenty years ago. A shiver trekked down her spine and she shook it off. What had started this train of thought anyway? Oh, right. Eric. So, yeah, he didn't like her and if their siblings were going to be married one day—provided they stopped touring long enough to actually tie the knot—she should probably rectify that.

So what if one look from him jacked up her pulse rate? So what if his touch seared her skin? She wouldn't let her hormones rule every move she made. She could totally handle this.

"Anything I can do to help?" she asked.

Eric looked at her from across the fire pit, his blue eyes blazing with disbelief. "You're offering?"

ERIC NEVER EXPECTED ZOE to lift a single manicured finger during this trip so her willingness to help surprised him.

"Sure." She cocked her head to the side. "I'm capable. You disagree?"

"No." He shook his head and tossed a sleeping bag into his tent before standing, wildly glad that she'd seemed to turn a corner with her attitude. "I think you're highly capable."

"So, what's the problem? Gimme a job."

"Okay…" He glanced around the campsite and landed on the bare fire pit. "You can haul in some wood for later."

Zoe's eyes widened and color drained from her face. "Oh…okay. I-I can do that. Sure."

She didn't sound so sure. Probably afraid to break a nail. "If you'd rather not, I—"

"No. No, that's fine." She swallowed and looked around the campsite. Sun glinted through the tall sequoias and the air slowly cooled with the setting orange ball. "I'll just…just go now." She headed toward the path that led them to this little spot and as Eric watched her go, a burgeoning respect grew in his consciousness. It didn't hurt that she had a sweet ass either, but he looked away, because he had no plans to entertain those kinds of ideas. He snorted at the errant thought of even *noticing* the fine curves of her butt. Again. *Shit.*

He checked his work. The tent looked good. It wasn't like the old days when they fit four boys into a small tent. Danny and he were barely going to fit in this thing tonight. But at least their body heat would keep them warm.

Next, he pulled out an ultra-light cook set and dinner for the night. He flipped the plastic pouch in his hand. "Rice with chicken," he murmured. "Just add a cup-and-a-half boiling water. Delicious." He snorted. "I'll believe it when I taste it."

He looked around at the gorgeous trees surrounding the camp. Listened to the scurrying of wildlife and the breeze through the trees. He took a deep breath of the fresh air and something clicked in his brain.

Maybe this is what he needed. Maybe a huge life change would ease the weight in his chest. "Or make it worse," he said under his breath. Jesus, he just didn't know. Pausing or ending his profession as a lawyer to be an adventure guide seemed like a pretty big stretch.

"What's got you daydreaming?" Danny said, tossing a navy blue sleeping bag at him.

Eric barely caught the nylon bag one handed before it knocked into his head. "Just thinking."

"Do me a favor. Leave the lawyer behind." Danny spread his arms wide. "Enjoy this while you can. In a few days we'll be back to the traffic and smog…and cooped up courtrooms."

Danny rarely made good points, but Eric had to agree with all of that.

"Here," Eric said, tossing the pouch with their dinner. "You're on cooking detail."

Danny scowled. "Why me? You're the picky one. You do it." He lobbed the package back.

Like a hot potato, Eric let it fly as soon as it hit his hand. "But you're so good at teaching us the ropes. You—"

Vic came out from her tent, interrupting them with a slow clap. "My God, you two are adorable. Really, you need your own show. Until then—" she raised her hands, "—give it here." Danny tossed the pouch and she snatched it out of the air. She looked at the package and raised her eyebrows. "Seriously? Dinner from a pouch?"

Something rustled in the bushes and all three of them spun toward the sound. A giant squirrel scampered out of a bush and raced up the nearest tree. Eric exhaled a slow breath and glanced at Vic and Danny.

"We're clearly in need of some R&R when a squirrel has the ability to make us jump out of our skin." Vic flipped the pouch in her hands and focused on the label. "I'm off to the stream."

Hopefully this trip would take the edge off all their apprehension.

VIC FOLLOWED THE BARELY there path toward the sound of rushing water, trying to ignore her screaming muscles and the ache from her burned arm. The car accident had been bad enough, but add the near choking along with the hike up here and she was surprised she was still upright. She had no idea how Zoe was managing it all.

Zoe was seriously one of the toughest chicks Vic knew, but last night had freaked her friend out beyond measure. Vic was just glad Eric had given that forceful advice immediately afterward. Zoe did what she had to do and Vic sure as hell owed her because of it.

Vic had always been envious of Casey having a big sister. Growing up without any siblings and having parents who worked all the time led to a lonely childhood. After last night, Vic almost felt as protected as Casey used to describe...as if she'd all of a sudden found a big sister she could call her own. Someone to watch her back and be a shoulder to lean on. Her chest tightened and her eyes stung. Stupid thoughts. Blinking the moisture away, she focused on the now.

Now they had to get through this camping hurdle. After last night, it should be a cakewalk. At least Danny had stopped earlier than she expected. Now everyone had a job, including her. Apparently, all dinner required—Cajun Style Rice and Chicken— was *add hot water*. She saw the smile Eric had tried to hide. Both guys assumed she and Zoe were too frail or chicken or girly or *something* to handle this trip. Not that she could really blame them, since they didn't know each other well at all. She couldn't wait to prove them wrong. Sure, she was used to the finer things in life. Sure, she liked her dresses and heels and mani/pedis. What was wrong with looking good? Looking good made her feel good.

But she wasn't an idiot either, and five nights in the wilderness meant suspension from her usual routine. She could do it. So could Zoe.

This trip, she planned to show the St. Johns exactly what she was made of. Actually, she was looking forward to sitting around a campfire and gazing at the stars. Or gazing at Danny. Either or both worked fine for her. She'd been set on ignoring him and all had gone as scripted until *he* started ignoring *her*.

During the reality show when they'd both been support for

their respective contestants, Danny had been all about making sure she knew he was interested. He'd even given her his number. Of course, she hadn't called. No way. But she hadn't thrown the number away either. Stupid. She should have tossed that piece of paper the second she got home, but she liked to look at his handwriting. The way he'd scrawled his name and number all messy and masculine.

Too bad the man she met during the show had disappeared. It made no sense that she missed his playboy smile and not-so-subtle innuendo. She'd avoided him because of those traits. Of course, if he hadn't changed she wouldn't be paying more attention now.

The rushing water got louder and Vic caught sight of the beautiful stream just outside the tree line. Tall sequoias reached for the sky and moss coated river rocks on the bank of the riverbed. She took in a huge breath of clean air and exhaled slowly. She hadn't been camping since her two summers during junior high. She'd had fun until the last summer when a massive storm had brought torrential rain and subsequently all the snakes out from their hidey-holes. And the wild boar incident… It was funny now, but back then…not so much.

Vic edged closer to the stream and filled the gallon container with cool, fresh water. She took an extra ten minutes to stretch sore muscles then headed back to camp. The chilly air made a nice reprieve from the heat of the day.

Zoe and Danny had returned with armfuls of wood, and Eric had arranged a grill over the fire pit so they could boil the water. It had been a year since she'd had a girls' night out and over a dozen years since she'd had a sleepover with a pal—not including pals of the male persuasion. Although it had been too long since she'd had that particular itch scratched. Maybe that's why she couldn't seem to take her eyes off Danny.

She looked forward to the night ahead with girlish anticipation. She smiled at the idea of Zoe and she tucked into their little tent, whispering and giggling into the night. That is if they stayed awake long enough. Starting tomorrow, the hikes got more intense until they circled the mountain and made their way around to the other side of their starting point. A hell of a way to kill five days and keep themselves safe at the same time.

The four of them worked together and had a decent dinner considering the freeze-dried meal came out of a metallic-looking bag. Hunger probably played a part since she scarfed her food so fast. The best part included s'mores around the small campfire afterward.

"Enjoy it while you can," Danny said, after chugging some water. "After this we'll be too high in altitude to have a campfire."

"How will we toast the marshmallows without fire?" Vic asked, happy her voice sounded less raspy.

"We won't." Danny's eyes barely looked her way. "You'll either eat them with uncooked marshmallows or skip them completely. Up to you. No campfires over ten thousand feet. It's too dry to risk it."

Well, shit. It made sense, but no one had told her that before. Despite the rain they'd had earlier in the year, summer had still been brutal. Wild fires had destroyed thousands of acres of land all over the country and California continued to dehydrate like a giant prune. Still, she'd figured with all the energy she was expending every day, this would be the one chance she had to indulge in dessert.

Zoe tossed a small twig at her. "You can still eat chocolate every night." That girl knew her too well. Almost as well as Casey did. She'd gone from one best friend to two and it didn't suck. Growing up an only child had been lonely and though she had friends from high school, she hadn't stayed as close as she had with her college roommate.

Vic ignored Zoe and kept her gaze on Danny. "Cold marshmallows it is." She held a poker face until Danny finally looked at her, then she gave him a smile, letting him see the invitation in her eyes.

DANNY PUNCHED HIS TINY camp pillow and tried to settle in. Fat fucking chance. He couldn't get Vic out of his goddamn head. He knew this excursion was going to test him, but he hadn't realized the extent. For months he'd managed to forget his attraction to her. Hell, he'd done a decent job of forgetting everything but building the business. But now, having her so close… She totally freaked with his mojo and he refused to be bated. Danny flipped to his other side.

"Would you stay still already," Eric muttered in the dark.

"I can't get comfortable." He'd been tossing and turning for over an hour and if he didn't knock out soon, tomorrow's hike was going to kick his ass all over the mountain. He'd grabbed a quick nap earlier after being up for almost forty-eight hours. He should be out cold now. "Sorry. Can't sleep."

Eric rolled to his back. "What's up? Wait. Let me guess. Vic."

Duh. She'd been making it abundantly clear that she was on board for any extra-curricular activities that this hike might lead to. She'd been eyeing him, smiling at him, tossing her hair, batting her lashes. For a woman who wouldn't give him the time of day when he wanted it last summer, her about-face surprised him as much as her attitude toward the camping situation.

Next to him, Eric sighed. "You know, a few months ago, you would've been all over that." He could've said nine months, because they both knew when Danny's sudden celibacy started. "There's no law against you taking her up on the invitation. She's a big girl. I think she knows what she's getting into with you. And I mean that in a good way."

Meaning Danny wasn't a long-term guy. No one thought of him that way and really, there was no reason anyone would. He liked women and made no secret of that fact. But ever since Nikki… He didn't dare touch another woman. The weight of her death hung on his shoulders like a two-ton elephant and it trumpeted in his head that had he been sharp enough, he could've stopped it. Had he picked up on her behavior a little quicker, he might've handled his texts or phone calls differently. Instead, he'd been too short, too eager to get rid of her.

Another ton of guilt heaped onto his shoulders.

"Dano…" The sympathy in Eric's voice grated on Danny's nerves like a bad pen on paper. "You didn't kill her," he said softly. "You can't put that on yourself. How many times do we need to tell you that? Everyone is responsible for one person in this world. Themselves. Cut yourself a break already. Don't you think you've punished yourself long enough?"

"What is long enough? How do I gauge a lifetime—Nikki's

lifetime—against—" his feelings? Danny scrubbed his hands through his hair. "Put yourself in my place, Eric. Hell, you're the one who takes responsibility for everyone in the family with *maybe* the exception of Mom and Dad, and that's a *maybe*. It's like you have some kind of gene that put you in charge of all of us." He sat up. "You know, it'd be great if you could tell me how to live with this. What's your advice when I close my eyes and see her in that blood bath? How am I supposed to get past it? Because I have no fucking clue?" He needed air. He kicked his legs out of the sleeping bag.

"What are you doing? Where are you going?" Eric asked, watching as Danny jammed his feet into his boots and grabbed his down vest.

"Out. For a walk." His brother took a breath and Danny waited for the words, but Eric surprised him and said nothing. Danny unzipped the tent and crawled out into the cool night. He just needed twenty minutes of alone time. To breathe, to shake off the mood that haunted him so often when the stars came out. He flipped on his flashlight and headed toward the stream, moving panther silent through camp so he wouldn't wake Vic and Zoe as he passed their tent.

The path seemed narrower in the dark and branches reached out and snagged his sweats as he padded toward the stream.

Okay, no big deal. Dodging Vic for so many months hadn't lessened his attraction. He'd just deal with it like a fucking man. He'd stay busy. He'd ignore her to the best of his ability and still make the trip bearable.

His hand caught the sticky mass of a spider web and he shook it off.

"Bearable," he muttered. "Yeah right." He was only fooling himself. Maybe he'd take Zoe aside and have her talk to Vic. "Or maybe you should talk to her yourself and tell her straight out to cut the shit," he murmured aloud. Knowing Vic, she'd play dumb. Or not. She was the most unpredictable female he'd ever met. All girly and feminine, but always on board for a raunchy joke. Her smiles lit a room like a skylight at midday.

Just thinking about her fucking smile had all his blood rushing south, making him harder than a two-by-four. "Cut it out." Yeah, as if talking to himself was going to help.

How the hell was he supposed to survive the next five days in her company, watching those long legs, that tight ass, hearing the sound of her voice and listening to her distinctive laugh?

"Suck it up, St. John," he told himself. He didn't know when he'd be ready to think about diving in again, but it wasn't now. Maybe not ever.

CHAPTER 9

"**DID YOU HEAR THAT?**" Zoe whispered, bolting upright. Sore muscles protested the move. "Something's out there." This went beyond the crickets and rustling leaves that had kept her up. Her heart thumped harder as she listened to the new noise. She should've been out cold and instead she couldn't relax enough to crash. "What if it's like the house last night? What if they know where we are?"

Vic flipped onto her stomach and peeked from the bottom flap of the side panel. "It's only Danny," she said quietly, her voice still rough. "And quit worrying. No one followed us and they have no way of knowing where we are. No one but us knows where we are." She whistled softly. "That man knows how to fill out a pair of sweats. Mmm, mmm. Probably answering nature's call." She slid back into her sleeping bag.

Her logic made Zoe feel better, but brought up another point. "Speaking of nature's call, did you know we'd have to carry around our used toilet paper with us in a Ziploc bag? That was news to me! I don't remember doing that when I was little." She adjusted her tiny pillow and lay down, wincing as her muscles cried out a second time.

"You were probably at a campsite with a port-a-potty or latrine back then."

"Very possible. I have no idea. The whole thing is a blur." Well, everything but getting lost in the forest for twenty-four hours. That had been a hell of an introduction to camping. It was weird how some of that trip was a complete blank and other parts were as vivid as if they'd just happened. To this day, thinking about it could bring on an anxiety attack that stole her breath and *those* embarrassed her. A grown woman had no business having anxiety attacks over something that happened so long ago, so it was easier never to talk about it.

Vic leaned up on her elbow. "So, if I ran something by you, would you consider it a minute before shutting me down?"

Zoe didn't have to see the puppy-dog eyes that won Vic everything from free coffee to concert tickets, because she recognized the tone in her voice. "I think you should stop talking so your voice gets better. Who knows, maybe by tomorrow you'll be good as new."

"C'mon, Zoe. Here me out."

"Ugh. I hate when you start off like that. What do you want? Just spit it out." Not usually a problem for Vic.

"You know how Danny told us about the hot springs farther up the mountain." That was midway into the trip. "After we set up camp and have dinner, I was going to try and convince him to take me down the path for a late night soak."

Zoe clicked on the small LED light next to her bedroll and saw Vic's hopeful strawberry blond brows lifted in question. "We'll certainly all be a little ripe by then. Let me guess, a little skinny dipping in your future?"

Vic's face lit up like the Macy's window at Christmas time. "I hadn't even thought about skinny dipping." Her face fell as she reconsidered. "On the other hand, that might be a little too obvious. I think I'll stick with something a little more traditional. Anyway, my point is, if things go as planned, would you mind swapping tents that night?"

Bam. There was the bomb she should've expected. Shaking her head, Zoe let her jaw drop open. "Are you seriously asking me to shack up with Eric so you can bang Danny?"

Vic had the audacity to look offended. "You know you sound a lot like your mom when you talk like that…well minus the words 'shack up' and 'bang.'"

Zoe clamped her mouth shut and sat up, all buttons pushed. She was absolutely *nothing* like her mom and Vic knew it. Her mother was so conservative, she made every other conservative look *liberal*.

Vic put a hand out and faced her. "Wait! Sorry. I didn't mean it. Look, it's not like I'm asking you to sleep with Eric. Just share his tent for the night…or however many nights it might turn out to be."

"Vic!" Zoe hissed, damn glad they were whispering. How could she ask this?

"Shh! C'mon Zoe. In exchange, I'll let you use my bath wipes to wash up. Honestly, I don't even know if Danny will go for it. He's changed so much. He's a totally different guy than when we first met him."

"True." Zoe huffed her indignation. Like bath wipes would even the deal. Vic's request shouldn't surprise her, but it did. Zoe thought Danny had been tossed into Vic's *never tapping that* pile. "What makes you think he'll bite?"

"Nothing actually. All I want to do is make the guy smile for a minute. It's like he's lost the ability. I mean, I never met that Nikki chick, but I'm sorry, what she did to him was uncalled for. Just because he was a player doesn't mean he deserved to get shit on like that." She gave Zoe her best pout face. "So, what do you say? If you won't do it for me, do it for Danny. The guy deserves a little relief."

"A little relief named Vic?" Ugh, Vic really intended to press this.

Her smile brightened up their little dim tent. "Ooh…I like the way that sounds."

Sure, it was all happy-happy-fun except for one little detail. "What about Eric?" Zoe asked. "Don't you think he'll have something to say on the matter? The guy can barely look at me, much less share a tent with me."

"That's a load of bullshit. Besides, maybe you should take a few minutes to talk to him instead of order him around. You might actually make a new friend."

"I do not order him around…" A definite silence met that statement, "…all the time," she added. "Just when he needs guidance, which happens to be more often than not."

Vic laughed. "You are so full of shit. You never gave him a chance. You went straight into *make everything perfect for Casey* mode without thinking about anyone else's feelings."

"If this is your way of buttering me up, I should tell you it's not working." Zoe might've been used to Vic's straight talk, but that didn't mean she liked it when it concerned her. She shut the light off and lay back down.

"C'mon, Zoe. What could you possibly have against Eric? He's nice, he has a good job and he's as gorgeous as his brothers. You're telling me you've never noticed?"

"Sounds like you're as interested in Eric as you are in Danny," Zoe said.

"Hardly and you know it. I'm just trying to figure out why *you're* not interested in Eric. Seriously Zoe, you need to date more. Get out, have some fun."

"I have plenty of fun." How had this conversation taken such a hard right turn?

"Yeah, because writing property listings and showing houses is so much fun. Give me a break. When was your last date?"

The fact that she had to think about it didn't bode well. "I don't know. I do remember that it was a total waste of my time. All he did was talk about himself for ninety minutes."

"You're never going to find a guy unless you go out and meet people."

"Gee. Thanks. Mom."

Vic sighed long and loud. "Why can't you at least give Eric a shot? He's one of the good guys and he's available."

"And his brother is marrying my sister."

"So? What does that have to do with anything? Just get to know him. Let him get to know you."

"Vic, let it go. Eric hates me. Haven't you seen the way he can barely look at me?"

"That's ridiculous. Eric doesn't hate you. He just doesn't know you the way Casey and I do. I'm sure if you guys just have a few minutes to talk without any interruptions, you might find you have some things in common."

Zoe snorted. "What could I possibly have in common with Eric?"

"Easy. For starters, you're both obsessed with making sure your siblings are happy."

She couldn't really argue with that. She shifted in the sleeping bag, searching for a comfortable position for her sore muscles. "What else?"

"You both want to be in charge. You both have high power careers."

That crappy reminder hit Zoe in the solar plexus. She didn't want to think about her career…the one hanging by a thread. If she lost the sale of the only listing she had, she'd lose her job. She was on probation already, because she'd lost four listings in the last two years. Then she had the matter of selling her condo. The place couldn't show itself. But only an idiot would stay in town knowing someone was trying to kill them. If she didn't have a life, the job didn't matter and selling the condo became her sister's job. Nothing like the thought of dying to wreck a night. Time to get back on topic.

"Who's asking Eric about the swap?" She lifted a finger in the air. "Wait. Let me rephrase that. When are *you* mentioning this swap to Eric, because I sure as hell am not doing it."

Vic's enthusiasm came out in her little gasp of victory. "I'll do it. I just have to find some alone time with him. So, if you see that an opportunity arises, scram."

Zoe didn't see Eric going along with this idea for a minute, but she of all people knew not to discount Vic when the lady wanted something. "Fine. Another question for you." She turned on her side and adjusted her pillow again. "What are you going to do if Danny avoids your call of the wild?"

Vic shrugged and settled deeper into her sleeping bag. "I'll deal with it." Her smile flashed in the darkness. "But he won't."

SPEAKERS PIPED IN COUNTRY music into the half full bar. Dim lights, scuffed flooring and faded red booths said this place had existed almost as long as the mountains around them. Trevor eyed the fifty-something bartender who set down their beers on the long slab of nicked oak. He slid a twenty toward the guy. "Keep the change." They'd found seats in the middle of the bar and Trevor hoped the brew would kick-start a fresh solution to his problem. There wasn't much he wouldn't try and he'd always gotten away with everything. His dad had often said he had an innocent man's face.

Twenty-five minutes ticked by and Kaleb hadn't offered any suggestions worth a shit. Trevor swiveled on the barstool, taking in the crowd; a couple of drunk empty-nesters, a foursome on a road trip, and three different sets of disgruntled neighbors out for a little pick-me-up. So far, no great ideas in sight.

The door opened and two men strode in, laughing as if they'd already consumed a six-pack before coming to the bar. They took two seats a barstool away from him.

"The usual?" the bartender asked.

"Sounds good. How's it going, Rusty?"

"Can't complain." The bartender—Rusty—pulled a couple of beers from the beneath the bar, popped the tops and placed them in front of the guys as he spoke. "Well, I could, but then I'd be an asshole." The men laughed. "You guys must've just got back," the bartender continued.

"Day before yesterday. Had a great trip."

"Yeah? Bring home anything?"

"Rus, that's the dumbest question you've ever asked. What you needed to say was, 'How big was the buck you bagged?'"

All three guys laughed and Rusty opened his mouth to answer when something caught his attention and he put a finger up. "Hold that thought. I'll be back." He headed to the other end of the bar to another customer.

"Here's to another hunting season. May the next be as successful," the second guy said, lifting his brew.

"Provided I'm still in town," the first guy replied. He clucked and shook his head before drinking to their toast.

"Aw, don't go and get all morose on me," the second guy said. "Something'll come along. You've been unemployed before."

"Not for this long, I haven't. If I don't get some money soon, the bank's gonna move in and take my place."

Trevor's ears perked up and his mind started spinning. He had two hunters and one of them needed money. What if, instead of waiting for his prey to come out of the forest, he followed them instead? The guy next to him needed work and Trevor had the perfect job. He listened to them talk about their rifles and reliving the hunt. Both guys were single and only got together a few times a year. The more they talked, the more Trevor liked what he heard.

"Congrats on your catch," Trevor said, abandoning his chair and moving closer. He gestured to Kaleb to follow him. "You guys been living in this area a long time?"

"Probably longer than you've been alive," the first guy said, taking a hit of his beer. The giant scar on the guy's cheek bisected his face and cut into a dimple. Man-made or animal-made? Gray peppered what was left of his sandy brown hair.

The bartender returned. "You guys want to start a tab."

Trevor reached for his wallet. "I've got it." He tossed another twenty, and the two strangers looked more interested. "I'm Trevor." He put his hand out and gestured over his shoulder. "This is Kaleb."

The first guy shook it. "I'm Henry. This is my friend Will. Thanks for the round. What's the occasion?"

A man who got straight to the point. Trevor liked him already. "I couldn't help but overhear that you two are hunters. Wondering if I can enlist your help to track..." How did he phrase this? "...some game?"

"What kind of game?" Henry asked.

Will laughed behind him. A ratty baseball cap covered his head and dark thick brows nearly met in the middle of his face. "Be serious, man, you couldn't give a shit about what kind of game if the price is right."

"I guess that's fucking true." They both laughed and chugged more beer. Henry glanced at Trevor. "I figured these beers didn't come for free."

Will shoved his shoulder. "Don't be such a cynic. Just listen to the boy. Go ahead, Trev. Let 'er rip."

"Okay, here's the deal. My house was robbed a few weeks ago and we actually have a hit on the guys that did it. Problem is they ran up here to hide. I want to catch them. Show them a little justice, if you know what I mean." He wasn't sure he had their cooperation and added another layer. Trevor swallowed hard and nodded his head. "They left my dad in a coma. I'm not feeling extremely forgiving, I'll be honest."

Henry set his beer on the bar and shook his head. "Don't know what the fuck this world is coming to. Sorry you had to go through that. Hope your dad comes through it okay."

Trevor nodded again. "I'm not asking you to do anything for free," he said. "I've got money." He pulled out the wad of cash in his jacket pocket. "I've got five grand here. I'll split it between you both. All you have to do is find the guys. Track 'em, you know? You could do that right? Track them?"

Henry snorted. "In my sleep." He chugged more beer.

"Does that mean you're in?" Trevor asked. "I've got another buddy headed up to help. Should be here first thing tomorrow." Only one of his friends decided to make the trip. The others were going to hear from him when he got home. "The guys we're following have a decent head start. I'm pretty sure they got here this morning."

Will waved off the concern. "That's not a problem. We can track anything."

Trevor let a half smile curve his lips. "Great. That's great. Does that mean you're in? I can count on you?"

"Two and half grand buys me five more months," Henry said to his buddy. "Maybe I don't have to move after all." He turned back to Trevor with a smile. "Cheers."

Trevor talked to both men and got the info he needed about the newly opened visitors center, still only partially staffed. He also got a list of what they'd need for the hike in case he'd missed something earlier. Fortunately, the college kid working the store had known exactly what they'd need and supplied it all.

At eight the next morning, with two of his crew backing him up, Trevor entered the visitor center as a ranger unlocked the doors. His pulse picked up as he fingered the gun in his jacket pocket. He'd left their new tracking buddies outside. The less they knew the better. "Good morning," he said, strolling toward the counter separating a few desks from the main lobby. "Wondering if you could answer a couple of questions."

Smiling, a middle-aged ranger behind the counter nodded. "That's what we're here for."

"Do just the two of you work up here? Seems really quiet."

"At the moment, yes, but we're looking to bring on a few more staff for next season." His co-worker joined him behind the counter, eager to help with any information. "Why, you looking for a job?" His affable smile faded when Trevor drew his gun.

"Not really interested in a job at the moment. But I will be needing your assistance for a little excursion I have planned."

The first ranger put his hand out. "Why don't you go ahead and put your weapons away. I'm sure whatever you have on your mind can be figured out without the need for violence."

Trevor laughed out loud, then shook his head. "Your guns on the counter. Now." He waited for them to comply before pointing toward the parking lot where a couple of cars had pulled up and people were getting out. "Just in time. Let me make this real clear. You control the next few minutes, make no mistake. Unless you want to die, unless you want those people to die, you're going to do everything I say. First, go tell all those people out there that this new area isn't ready for hikers yet. And if you want to make sure that no one gets killed, you're going to see them off to another visitors center." When the ranger made no move to come forward, Trevor leveled his gun right between his eyes. "Look, I've got enough guns to take out both of you and everyone in the parking lot. Your call." He lifted an eyebrow.

"I've got it," the other ranger said, moving to the far end to get around the long counter.

"Kaleb, why don't you go along with this ranger and make sure he tells those people how they can come back next week, but right now there's some government red tape keeping hikers from the area. Or whatever you have to say to clear out those people. Understand? Because otherwise, your friend here eats a bullet."

"I got it," the ranger said.

"Just what I like to hear." He glanced behind him. "Next on the agenda is pylons. We're going to close off the road that leads here." He canted his head. "Pylons, barrels, I don't care what you have, but point them out so we can block the road."

The ranger gestured to a door at the back end of the main lobby. "In there."

"Perfect. See how easy this is?" He gestured with his chin. "Open it up. Let's get what we need." He spotted two different cameras in opposite corners. He tipped his chin toward Bruce. "Go take out those cameras, brah. Destroy it all." Bruce nodded and pocketed his gun to do the job. "You're good with staying behind with our Smokey's right? To make sure they stay on board if the phone rings or anyone decides to drive around our little blockade."

"Always wanted to be a ranger," he replied.

Trevor laughed again. Bruce could handle these two in his sleep. He lowered his voice. "Don't kill them until the very end. Never know if you'll need them to get rid of any other people or rangers who come asking questions."

"Got it." Bruce's grin was as evil as the Lucifer tattoo that covered his neck.

Too easy.

CHAPTER 10

WEDNESDAY NIGHT AFTER A long hike, all four of them sat around a fire pit with no fire. Zoe looked up the rugged mountain where Danny pointed and saw over the tree line the very top of the A-frame wood structure he was talking about.

"It's the ranger station for this section of the park," he said, consulting his map. "It's probably another few miles up, but we'll be cutting around to circle to the other side of the visitor center by late tomorrow morning. If we had the time, I'd have liked to check it out. From the looks of it, it's significantly closer than the trek back to the visitors center with the exception of the rough terrain. Looks like a great place to scope out the whole park and take some pictures."

"So, rangers stay up there? For long periods of time?" Seemed crazy to Zoe. She couldn't imagine living out here full-time.

Danny shook his head. "They're in and out during the summer. There's a fifty-fifty chance someone's there. It could be locked up tight, although from the picture in this pamphlet you can still get to the upper look-out deck. Stairs are on the outside."

Zoe dragged a stick through the dirt, weighed the circumstances necessary for a fire at this altitude and decided she'd rather forgo the snow or rain for the dry pit. The sore muscles from last night had nothing on tonight's pain. Fairly certain that Danny had taken it easy on them today, Zoe stretched, happy to be off her feet without a thirty-pound pack weighing her down. They'd agreed to an early dinner and she'd scarfed down the freeze-dried Pad Thai so fast she wasn't even sure it tasted good. Although it must have, since she'd licked her bowl clean just like the other three. With her belly full and her ass planted firmly on the ground, she had no desire to get up for anything.

"Oh, oh, oh! I've got one," Vic said, clapping her hands. She'd practically disappeared under the big green coat Danny had loaned her, hiding the curves she'd been taunting him with all day in her leggings and long sleeve T-shirt. Her voice sounded much better too. Probably due to so little talking during the hike. They'd needed all their energy for walking.

"One what?" Zoe dared to ask. She had no clue what her friend was talking about.

"A ghost story."

"Are we telling ghost stories?" Eric asked, adjusting against the big log propping him up.

"We are now." Vic leaned forward, her dark eyes sparkling and Zoe caught the hint of a smile on Danny's face as he monitored boiling water with a nifty little item called a Jetboil. "Okay," Vic said, rubbing her hands together. "This happened when I was in my first rental after graduation. I was—"

"What was your major?" Eric asked.

"Communications. Zoe's was business." Vic shot her a quick glance, obviously going forward with her *let-him-get-to-know-you* plan. Zoe just shook her head because sometimes there was no stopping her friend. "So, I was in the laundry room—"

Zoe sat against the boulder at her back, watching Vic do what she did best, reel people in. Zoe knew this story. Wasn't sure if she believed it either, but Vic had a way of telling it.

"...swear to God, all the cabinets were open when I came back in. Just like in *The Sixth Sense.* It happened three times that day."

"And none of your roommates were home to see it and it never happened to one of them?" Danny asked, his eyes narrowed skeptically.

"The cabinet thing, no. But the toilet did flush on its own a couple of times when Savannah was in the bathroom. And then there was knocking on the ceiling every night. That was freaky. I was happy when that lease was up and I got out of there."

"How many of you in the house?" Eric asked.

"Three of us renting a three bedroom house. It wouldn't have been bad if the place wasn't haunted. What about you guys? Any good ghost stories?" She looked around their little dark fire pit lit with a lantern near Eric's feet. "No one? Seriously?"

"I got nothing," Eric said, shaking his head with a grin.

Vic frowned before her face lit up. "I know! Let's play a game."

"What kind of game?" Eric sounded less than enthused, but he'd never participated in one of Vic's games. As juvenile as they could sometimes be, they were usually good for a laugh.

Zoe grinned at the way they'd congregated around the pit, girls on one side, boys on the other. As if some invisible battle of the sexes was playing out. A light breeze whispered through the massive green trees and she had to admit the absolute serenity felt good to her soul.

"Truth or dare," Vic said, eyeing them all with a challenging stare. "Spin the bottle style."

The men groaned, which just made Zoe smile wider. They really didn't know Vic very well. She was a walking contradiction. A woman who changed her attitude as quickly as a chameleon shifted from pink to green. It wasn't a bad thing...once you got used to it.

"What does 'spin the bottle style' mean?" Eric asked. With a black thermal top beneath his brown sleeveless vest, he looked as devastating as he did in a suit. Zoe's heart beat a little faster every time she looked at him, so she bit her bottom lip and avoided glancing in his direction.

"It means..." Vic reached behind her and grabbed a half full bottle of water and placed it next to the fire pit. "That whoever the bottle points to first is the *askee* and whoever it points to second is the *asker*."

"And why are we doing this?" Danny asked around a blade of grass in his mouth. Wearing a blue-and-gray flannel shirt over a long sleeved gray T-shirt, he looked completely country. It suited him. Of course, she'd also seen pictures of him in a wet suit with a surfboard under his arm and he looked exactly like a California surfer dude should. He was a man who fit into his surroundings without missing a beat. In that respect, Danny and Vic had a lot in common. They both adapted to their surroundings without a hint of trepidation.

"Because. It's fun," Vic said. "And we've got time to kill

tonight." She spun the bottle. "So, first up to answer a question is…" The bottle stopped in Eric's direction. "Eric! Truth or dare? What's your poison?"

He shook his head. Didn't look as if he planned to play the game. "Truth," he finally said.

Vic looked at him and set her manicured fingernails on the bottle again and spun. "You will be answering a question from…" The bottle stopped and pointed at… "Zoe. What's your question?"

If only she knew.

"C'mon, we don't have four months. Now, please."

"Vic, take a chill pill. I have to think of something. You just sprang this on us thirty seconds ago." What could she ask him? Something universal. "Okay. Here's one. What are you most afraid of?"

Eric squinted his eyes and considered the question. "Most afraid of," he repeated. "Would have to be a zombie apocalypse. Yeah. I'll stick with that." His grin would've melted her if the cold hadn't been seeping into her bones. The black down coat she'd borrowed from Danny's stash wasn't doing a great job of keeping her feet warm.

"You guys suck," Vic announced. "This is supposed to be real." She spun the bottle and it landed on Eric again.

"Nope. I already answered. "Spin again," the man said.

She did and it went to no one so she spun a third time and got Zoe.

"Truth or dare?" Vic asked.

"Truth," Zoe said.

Vic spun again and the bottle pointed at her. She already knew most of Zoe's secrets, but the guys certainly didn't. "What was the scariest moment of your life?"

That was a no-brainer, but she wasn't about to admit it to the people around her now. She took a breath to share the second most obvious.

"Not the grocery store or the car accident," Vic said, before Zoe got a word out. "Something we don't know about."

Fine. Still not hard to come up with a runner-up. "Scariest moment had to be walking into Casey's apartment when the police finished their investigation after the shooting. I couldn't believe she and Brendan survived after seeing the damage."

Vic scrunched her nose. "What? That can't be…" she stopped at the lethal glare Zoe gave her. "Oh, whatever. Next." She spun the bottle and it landed on Danny. She looked up with the devil in her eyes. "Truth or dare?"

He blinked once, never taking his eyes off Vic's. "Dare."

Vic grinned and spun. The bottle landed on her. "Oh, goodie. Me."

Zoe inwardly cringed and glanced down. Poor guy. This could get uncomfortable.

Vic's smile matched the look in her eyes. "Okay." She scanned the campsite. "I dare you to run from here to that big forked tree and back."

Danny scoffed and stood up. "Piece of cake."

"Naked," Vic said.

"What?!" Danny put his hands out. "It's like forty-five degrees out."

"I know. And you're not even wearing a jacket, so this will be easy for you."

Zoe felt obliged to speak up. "Vic, that's not fair."

"Thank you, Zoe," Danny said with a nod of his head.

"At least let him keep on his boxers." She held back a grin.

Eric, who'd been obscenely quiet, suddenly barked out a laugh, but quickly covered it with a cough.

"I don't wear boxers," Danny muttered. "Boxer briefs."

"I'm okay with that," Vic said. She flourished a hand at him. "Go ahead. Strip to the B's then run like the wind."

Danny looked as if he wanted to *strip* the smile off Vic's face, but he whipped off both layers of shirts and *my-oh-my* the man was all sorts of built. So many ridges on his abs that his chest could've been a human slalom course. She remembered the conversation the guys had about Danny having a gut from eating the neighbor's cookies. If that was a gut, then she was six feet tall. He pulled off his boots then turned before dropping his jeans. His snug black boxer briefs displayed one of the finest asses Zoe had ever been privileged to see. He turned his head as he yanked his boots back on. "I'm not running around here in my bare feet. Not when we've got three more days of hiking."

Vic waved her hand. "Completely all right. Commence." She

99

lifted her perfectly arched brows and Zoe watched her fight to keep a straight face.

Huge props to Danny because he actually ran to the forked tree and back, not even attempting to hide the package in his ass snug boxer briefs—and wasn't that nice of him. He scampered into his clothes as if the air were on fire.

Vic finally lost her control and laughed her butt off.

"Okay, who's next?" She reached for the bottle, but Danny snagged it first.

"Oh no. You're done spinning this bottle. My turn." He spun the bottle and it landed on him. "Shit. Dare," he said without anyone prompting him and Eric lifted an eyebrow in a *have you* not *learned your lesson yet* way.

Then he spun again. Eric. "Dude, you're up. Don't make me hurt you after we're done..." He looked up and his eyes narrowed.

Eric just laughed. "Fine." He looked around the camp. "I dare you to...kiss Vic."

Vic snapped to attention. "What? That's not fair. I'm not part of his dare."

"You are now," Eric said.

Danny looked a little pissed the way his eyebrows slanted over his eyes. "Fine." He stalked over to Vic, yanked her up by the outstretched hand warding him off and bussed her on the lips. If he meant to pull away fast, he clearly changed his mind. Although no sooner had that thought crossed Zoe's mind than Danny pulled away, his gaze hot on Vic's wide eyes. A heavy silence descended for all of three seconds before Danny stepped back. "Next." He crouched low and spun the bottle again. It landed on Vic. "Truth or dare?" he asked her.

Still looking a little dazed and confused from the kiss, Vic looked him right in the eye as she sat back on her log. "Dare."

He spun it a second time and it landed on him. He looked up, with a barely contained smile on his face. "See that forked tree over there?" Danny asked.

Zoe bit her lip to keep her jaw from dropping to the forest floor. He wouldn't dare, would he?

Danny crossed his arms over his chest. "Run to it. With just your underwear on."

He did!

Vic snorted. "You can't do a dare that's already been done," she said.

"Really?" Danny seemed very amused by all this. "Okay. In that case, you can run to the tall skinny tree just past it."

"Danny!" Vic said. "That's total—"

"Karma?" he asked. "Yes, it is total karma." He motioned the same way she motioned to him. "Strip. Make it snappy. It's getting chilly out here." He watched her with hawk eyes.

Zoe clapped a hand over her mouth. Vic didn't often get what she deserved, but this was pretty hilarious on the karma scale of one to ten.

Like Danny, Vic gave everyone her back as she stripped off her clothes. Her pale white skin set off the hot pink bra and matching bikini underwear. Aside from her last name and eye color, Vic showed no sign of her father's Mexican heritage. Her complexion was as Irish as her mother's. She practically glowed in the dimming forest. Also, like Danny, she put her hiking boots back on before running fifteen yards to the designated tree and back. Zoe appreciated the lady's style. But really, with a body like hers, it wasn't a big embarrassment to run in skivvies' in a little harmless fun. She showed off the exact same thing in her bikini. Zoe had always envied her sister's long-legged height, and Vic had a similar build with more boobs and hips.

Watching her friend just made Zoe glad she'd picked *truth*. She glanced at Eric, expecting to see him drooling over Vic like most men, but caught him watching her instead. Zoe felt her cheeks heat as they shared a secret smile. Obviously, the tension between Vic and Danny was no big secret, and Eric seemed to be equally amused by their little pissing contest. Zoe looked away from Eric's intense gaze, hoping dusk covered her blush.

Vic dressed almost as quickly as Danny had, and the two of them squared off. Zoe couldn't help but chuckle at their competitiveness.

"Okay…" One of them had to put a stop to this. No telling what these two would end up doing given another dare. Zoe stretched her arms over her head. "We've worn out spin the bottle. Now what?" It seemed too early to go to sleep. There had to be something they could do.

CHAPTER 11

ERIC TOOK A DEEP breath of cool mountain air and followed Zoe's lead, stretching sore muscles. As amusing as watching Danny and Vic out-daring each other had been, he was glad they were done with the games and counted himself lucky that no one had called him out on his zombie apocalypse *fear*. The real answer would've made them all laugh. What was he afraid of? That was too easy. Failure. He was afraid of letting down his parents and his siblings...and himself. He'd worked so hard in law school, studying his ass off for years and passing the bar only to grab the first job offered and be miserable ever since.

No, zombie apocalypse wasn't his biggest fear, but dying a little each day sure as hell was.

A million stars twinkled in the clear night. What a difference being out of the city made. It wouldn't be bad to commune with nature more often. The fresh air felt good in his lungs.

"What are you thinking about over there?" Zoe asked from across the rock pit. She looked cute as hell with a dark knit cap over her crazy curls, a black down coat, black leggings and white running shoes. Should've known she had her eyes on him. She rarely missed anything.

"Not much," he said. "Just enjoying the outdoors. It's a nice change of pace from that brown shit we breathe in every day."

She looked up and nodded. "That's true."

Long seconds of comfortable silence passed before Eric's curiosity got the better of him. "You think those two are going to prank each other to death?" A grin slid across his face. It was pretty funny watching Danny and Vic sprint in their underwear in this cold. The four of them had drawn straws to see who had water detail and Vic and Danny had lost. They'd gone to the stream to refill and purify the water bottles.

Zoe laughed again, a contagious sound that had him chuckling as well. She shook her head. "No. I think they'll be fine. Have to admit, though…I don't want to be around for the next game of Truth or Dare." She stood and stretched.

"Or spin the bottle," Eric added.

"Or that," she agreed. Her smile faded as she caught his gaze. "Tell me, *is* there anything you're afraid of?"

Leave it to Zoe to bring up the subject he despised. She pushed his buttons without even knowing it. Or maybe she did. "You mean my zombie apocalypse isn't enough?" Eric stood too and dusted the dirt off his ass.

She shrugged. "I understand if you don't want to share. Just asking. I'm scared of a ton of stuff, so, I'm sure I have enough to cover the both of us."

He snorted. "You? Scared? When? You weren't even scared when you got shot."

"Hello?" Her eyes bugged out wide. "Bullshit to that. I was scared you and Danny were going to get shot trying to save me." She looked out to the trees. "I was scared that Vic and Danny were going to burn in my car when it was wrapped around a telephone pole."

He waited until she met his gaze. "Are you ever scared for you?" he asked quietly.

Holding steady, she finally nodded. "Sure. Everybody's scared of something. Even if it's only a zombie apocalypse." Her smile brightened her pretty blue eyes and Eric felt that ever-present attraction that came with looking at Zoe. She put one leg forward, bent at the knee and stretched the other behind her. "Okay, I've got a question. Oh c'mon, don't look so sick. It's a fun one." Her grin widened as she looked around for the others. "What's the worst thing you ever did growing up to one of your siblings? There has to be something. Little siblings can be so obnoxious." She switched legs.

He sighed. "All siblings. I do have a big sister." He rifled through his memories trying to come up with something good. "Well, my mom kept a pretty strict policy, so there's probably not as much dirt as you might hope for or expect." He stacked the now clean plates they'd used for dinner and chuckled as something came to mind. "I do remember one time my sister ate the last cookie when my mom had promised it to me. Jess totally knew that cookie had my name on it and she ate it anyway."

"Ooh. I see retribution in your eyes. What happened?"

"I filled up my water gun and soaked all of her *Seventeen* magazines. Then as I was running out of her room, she slammed the door on my hand. I screamed bloody murder just as my mom came running down the hall. Jess got totally busted since I was five years younger and she 'was supposed to know better.'"

Zoe's smile transformed her features. Her eyes sparkled with mischief. "How old were you?"

"I don't know. Nine maybe? I was completely terrified she was going to get me back one day."

"I can see how that might put you on edge," she agreed, nodding and still smiling.

"Other than that, it was just the regular battles over toys and whatever, until sports came along. Then we were hell-bent on destroying each other on the field." He would've stacked the cups, but they'd be using them tomorrow morning for coffee.

"Fun. Casey and I bonded over—" She stopped herself and Eric waited.

"Over what?" he asked.

She gnawed on the corner of her lip, a habit he'd never noticed until spending so much time with her. "Well, you met my parents. They have a pretty archaic view of the world. Casey and I had to stick together. We watched each other's backs."

Eric got the feeling she was leaving something out. "You guys are only a couple of years apart, right? I think the bigger the age difference the harder the relationship. My brothers and I are all so close together I don't remember a time when they weren't there. Now if you ask my sister, she'll give you a whole other story. She swears she raised us even though she's only five years older than me. To hear her talk, we were born when she was fifteen."

Zoe laughed and caught her bottom lip between her teeth. A zing of something sexual cut straight to Eric's groin and surprised the shit out of him. He zipped his vest half way.

"I'm looking forward to meeting her. Hopefully at the wedding," she said.

"You'll definitely meet her there. Nothing's going to keep her from the wedding. I think she's still shocked that the youngest is the next to get married."

Zoe continued stretching, alternately pulling an arm over her head and bending sideways then repeating the motion on the other side. The bulky coat covered her top, but Eric imagined those two gorgeous legs in tight spandex wrapped around his waist. *Shit.* He focused on her words. "I saw an interview with her and her husband after her movie won a Golden Globe. They seem really happy."

Eric nodded, thinking about all his sister had gone through before finding her happiness. "They're the real deal." Most everyone close to the family knew their story and Eric figured Casey had told Zoe. "Not the way I'd like to meet my significant other, but it worked for them."

"Yeah, so that was for real? He really shot her?"

Eric nodded again. "He really did. Trust me, we all fought over who was going to kill him first. But, lucky for him, he grew on us." Eric could say with certainty that watching his family be brutalized by a psycho was the scariest thing he'd ever lived through. Without his brother-in-law, Tanner, they'd all be dead. "I think our feelings changed after he saved us."

She snorted. "That would probably tip the scales for me too. Certain death is a bitch, but it's a good thing he turned out to be a good man. Take Casey's ex... You met him. There's a guy you wanna kill. Oh wait, someone did." Pausing, she sighed. "Damn. Sorry. I try to catch myself with comments like that, but sometimes they just slip out." She glanced at him. "What? Why are you smiling at me like that?"

"I've never seen you so...I don't know...jovial. You're always on the move, someplace to be, people to meet. You actually have a sense of humor."

"As morose as it is. Shocked you, did I?" She scratched her nose and tipped her head to the side. "I'm good at that. I do my best to keep people off balance and when they least expect it—wham! I play Truth or Dare and make them run in their skivvies. Vic learned it from me."

"Ha. I doubt it. I have a feeling Vic could teach us both a few things."

"Well, I certainly wouldn't argue with that. She is a bit of a wildcard. But she means well. Sometimes she's just a little...I don't know...needy."

Eric didn't like the sound of that. Maybe pushing Danny toward Vic was a bad idea after all. The last thing he wanted to do was set his brother up with someone who might hurt him.

"Don't get that look on your face. She's not needy in a Nikki sense."

Apparently, Zoe knew exactly what he'd been thinking.

"She's needy in a spotlight sense. She goes through men probably like your brother goes through women. Although, it's obvious Danny's changed. We all feel terrible about what happened, but it's not like he should blame himself for it."

"Yeah, try telling him that. I'm not sure what's going to pull him out of this funk." Eric saw Vic approaching from the stream. "Speak of the devil. Well, one of them, at least." They waited as Vic cut the distance between them.

"Consider us watered up and purified," Vic said. She looked between them and lifted an eyebrow at Zoe.

Zoe looked over her shoulder. "I'm going to...ah...take a little walk. I'll be back shortly." She wandered off and Vic set a couple of bottles near Eric's boots.

"Hey, as long as we're alone, I wanted to ask you something."

He kept a poker face because their being *alone* was clearly pre-planned. "I thought we finished playing Truth or Dare."

"Yeah." She chuckled but shook her head. "Not that kind of question. Look, I'm just going to be straight with you. I was hoping to...cheer up Danny."

Eric thought about that for a few seconds. "Cheer him up?" He might've been bent out of shape from the game, but he wasn't in a bad mood. "I didn't realize he needed cheering up."

"Oh, he does. He definitely does."

"And why does this cheering up require my—" He looked at her expectant face, both brows raised and her bottom lip between her teeth. *Oh.* Because she was talking about sex. "Ah. Cheering *up.* Got it." Eric maneuvered a twig through his fingers as he thought about it. "Just so you're aware, Vic, I don't think Danny's the same guy that hit on you last summer."

"Oh, he's not. I realize that."

"And you're hoping to change that?" Eric flicked the twig and stuck his hands in his vest pockets. "Let me get this right. He hit on you last summer and you took a pass. Now, knowing he's changed, you want to jump on the offer so that if he decides he's into you, you can take another pass? Do I have that right?"

"You do *not*," she said with a definitive nod. "I took a pass because I didn't want to be another in a long line of Danny's flings. The fact that he's changed has just made me realize that the light he used to have has kind of…I don't know…dimmed. I want him to shine again. Doesn't mean anything. It's not like I have any illusions of anything even remotely permanent and I'm pretty sure that's what he's always worked to avoid so we're on the same page."

"And you're telling me all of this, why?"

She sighed as if he were the densest human she'd ever encountered. "Because, I need a tent." When Eric looked back at the tent he shared with Danny, Vic thumbed behind her. "Not yours. Mine. But that means Zoe needs a place to crash."

Eric actually laughed at that. "Does Zoe know you're asking—" Dumb question number two. Of course, she did, that's why she'd split so fast after getting the stink eye from Vic. "And she's okay with it?" Shocker.

Vic nodded. "She's okay with it if you are. Basically, she's doing it for Danny."

"For Danny or for you?" he asked.

"It's no secret that Danny's changed. We all see it. Maybe he needs a night to remember what it's like to have fun, to let go and enjoy life. He hasn't done that in a long time. I'd think, as his big brother, you'd be on board for something that might help him move on."

He couldn't argue with that logic. He just wasn't sure if her plan was the best plan. "You know there are other ways to cheer a guy up."

She cocked her head to the side and her strawberry blond ponytail wiggled behind her. "Well, I can't bake him a cake." She spread her arms wide. "But I can make him feel good."

Eric put his hands up. "Okay. TMI. I don't need to hear more. I wouldn't be too sure that Danny's going to jump just because you snap your fingers." He kind of hoped his brother did, but wouldn't count on it. Hell, hadn't he been trying to administer his own type of medicine by daring him to kiss Vic in the first place? "Look, that girl wrecked him." He kept his voice low. So low that Vic stepped closer to hear him. "I never believed that anything could crush his spirit, but she did." Maybe it was wrong to be angry at a dead woman, but Eric was. He didn't know when he'd get over it either. Danny hadn't gone out of his way to seduce her. He'd made no promises or lied to her. But she'd basically chopped off his balls the day she'd written that note and killed herself. No one had been able to say or do one damn thing to bring Danny out of his funk and that ripped Eric up like a shredder at high speed. "I'm not going to stop you from trying, but I do have one thing to say." This time he stepped close and stared into her dark brown eyes. "If you hurt him? If you somehow make things worse for him...you will be hearing from me. And I guarantee you will not be happy about it."

Instead of getting defensive, which he half expected, Vic just gave him a lopsided grin, her eyebrows slanted in a little pucker. "That's very sweet." She nodded. "I totally get the protective thing. It would've been nice to have someone stick up for me like that when I was growing up." She glanced back toward a sound and they spotted Danny breaking through the trees. "Cool, we're good here. No worries. You get to stay in your tent with a new bunkmate and I get to try and rehabilitate your bro. All good." She stepped back as Danny approached.

"What?" he said when they both turned to him. He set two water jugs near the fire pit.

"Nothing," they both said at the same time. Eric refrained from an eye roll as Danny looked between them. Danny finally shook his head and went about prep for the morning.

ANOTHER DAY OF HIKING put them at their middle mark and brought them to the wondrous healing powers of the hot springs. Tomorrow they'd cut down and follow the trail back to the other side of the visitor center. Zoe regretted the end mainly because of the investigation awaiting their return. She dreaded reliving that night at Eric's boss's house. Then, of course, her job security—or lack thereof—still weighed on her mind and if she didn't get home soon, she was bound to find herself out of work and out of luck. They could've picked a hundred other options to lay low that would have given her access to the internet to do at least *some* work, but no...

After dropping their gear at the camp, Danny followed the path and led them to a rushing river. Off to the side, in an embankment, a small pond steamed with natural hot water. Manmade stone sectioned off the water from the nearby river and three separate hot tubs had been built off to the side. Paradise.

"This is going to be heaven on my aching calves," Vic said, bending to feel the water. "Oh wow. It's a bathtub." She stood with a smile on her face and Zoe knew exactly what she had on her little dirty mind. Which tub did Vic plan to use for her seduction?

They headed back to the clearing and set up camp. They'd fallen into a little routine on this third night and Zoe appreciated the way they all worked together to make the place comfortable. Of course, tonight, if everything went according to Vic's plan, Zoe would be sleeping next to Eric.

A foreign shiver trekked down her spine and she shook it off. Stupid. She had no reason to shiver. It wasn't like she even had a shot with Eric. Or *wanted* a shot with him for that matter. Sure, she'd been attracted to him the first time he'd held the door open for her. Yes, he was gorgeous with amazing blue eyes and superhero shoulders, but he'd never shown the least bit of interest in her and she wasn't one to linger where she wasn't wanted. Besides, he made it a little too easy for her to boss him around. She liked a guy who matched her and held his own. So far, Eric had been a little *too* accommodating.

"Up there," Danny said, pointing toward a natural lip in the mountain, "is a lookout spot. Might be a perfect place to watch the sunrise if you guys are game. Or we can just detour a bit and stop when we head out tomorrow. Supposed to be a great view of everything below us."

"How big a detour?" Eric asked, saving Zoe from the same question.

Danny shrugged. "Hard to tell. Fifteen, twenty minutes to get up, probably quicker to get down so we can hit the trail and start back. Not too bad. We can play it by ear in the morning and see how everyone feels."

The lookout rose about fifty or sixty feet above and off to the side of their camp with tall trees almost obscuring it from their vantage point. Getting there meant climbing up the back way, because there was no way to go straight up from where they camped now unless they wanted to climb a tree. Zoe didn't doubt it made for a pretty picture, and it probably would be a good selling spot for Danny if he decided to do this hike for his clients. It was the least Zoe could do and the way everyone looked at her as if she might be the reason they wouldn't make the hike, it kind of pissed her off.

"Let's do it. Sunrise at the lookout. Last person up is a rotten egg." Her still sore muscles wept silently.

After dinner when they'd cleared up the mess, Danny headed out for his usual solo walk in the forest. He'd been taking them every night, explaining the need to familiarize himself with the terrain, so no one was surprised when he headed out toward the hot springs when the sun went down.

Vic—with absolutely no stealth whatsoever—brought Zoe her pack with her sweats, toiletries and everything she'd need for the night. "Here you go. Thanks again." She didn't bat an eyelash as she turned.

Sitting at their little rock pit, Zoe had one thing to say. "Hey. Vic." Her friend turned and Zoe stared her down. "Do not make noise tonight."

Vic rolled her eyes. "Whatever." Then she disappeared into the tent. She emerged twenty minutes later holding a towel and looking much the same in her khakis, boots, shirt and big jacket. The telltale sign of her string bikini showed around her neck. And damn if she hadn't applied a little makeup. Zoe didn't realize she'd even brought any.

"Have fun," Zoe called after her. "Just not too much fun," she said more softly.

110

Eric came out of his tent. She should've been used to the jeans, boots and flannel shirts, but somehow this more casual look still caught her off guard. It was the direct opposite of how he usually dressed and though she often went for guys in suits, this side of Eric appealed to her in a rugged mountain man way. "Tonight's the big night, huh?"

Zoe cleared her suddenly dry throat. "I find it hard to believe that you didn't say a word to Danny." Zoe sipped from a mug of hot tea.

"Not me. I didn't want the repercussions. I'm going to be just as surprised as he is. Because I'm not telling him I knew about Vic's plan. In fact, I didn't know about any of this until you just now told me and asked to bunk with me tonight. My hands are clean." He brushed them together for emphasis. He was kind of adorable as he tried to clear his conscience.

"Do you think he'll turn her down?"

"I don't know. I have no idea how Vic is going to come at him so…" He shook his head, hands spread wide.

Good point. If Vic came on too strong she might lose him and if she played it too cool, she might not reel him in. "Yeah, I guess it's all in the approach." And dammit, if they stayed out there all night she'd miss the big attraction.

"What's the frown for?" he asked, taking a seat on the log next to her.

"No one asked us if we wanted to, maybe, have a minute in the hot springs. I mean we came all this way and I can't even enjoy the best part of the trip."

Eric nodded. "Good point." He picked up a gray river stone and ran his thumb over the smooth top. Zoe wondered how that same thumb would feel brushing over her nipple. Heat rose to her cheeks at the random thought. "I'd say Vic owes you big time for this."

"So big time," Zoe agreed, clearing her dry throat. "What about you? You didn't want to go jump into the water?"

"Don't get me wrong, I have nothing against hot springs. I'm just not a fan of the temperature change when I come out. A couple of years ago I visited a pal in Colorado and we went to one of those outside Jacuzzis. It was nice until we got out and into the seventeen degree weather and realized neither one of us had the room key. Nearly froze our balls off. Literally."

She laughed at the mental picture. "Sounds painful."

"Trust me. It was." His rogue smile caused a flutter in her stomach. She ignored it.

"I'm not sure if we should stay out of sight when they come back or just pretend like we don't know what's going on."

"Don't overthink it," Eric advised. "Danny's either going to follow Vic into your tent or he's going to be pissed as hell and I'll get to deal with him the rest of the night in ours. Until then..." He pulled a deck of cards from his jacket pocket. "Poker?"

Zoe crinkled her nose. She sucked at poker. Mostly she hated when everyone made fun of her for being so bad at it.

"I'll take that as a no." Eric sighed and stuck the cards back in his pocket.

CHAPTER 12

TREVOR CHECKED HIS WATCH then took a swig of water too heavy with iodine and grimaced at the foul taste. This purification shit sucked. Crickets chirped all around him and unidentified critters rustled in nearby bushes. Every one of his muscles ached like a bitch, but he kept it to himself. The longer they'd hiked, the angrier he'd gotten. Sitting on a fallen log, he swiped at a bug on his forehead.

"How much longer are you waiting," Henry said as he paced nearby. "Will told you they set up camp for the night. Doesn't get easier than this. Just do what you're gonna do and let's get out."

Trevor blinked and looked away from the man's disfigured face. "I will when I'm ready and not before." They'd all kept a healthy distance from the foursome, but the hunters Trevor hired for this gig were driving him bat-shit crazy. Will had started out ahead of them and backtracked with an update. Tonight was the night. Trevor figured three nights equaled plenty of distance between freedom and someone finding the bodies, especially if Bruce held his position at the visitor center.

Trevor had explained how his dad's home camera caught the women knocking on the door. They used a stalled car and dead cell phones as an excuse to get in the house. From there, their boyfriends had blown in and robbed his father of thousands of dollars then beaten him into a coma. Trevor arrived in time to see them and get a license plate number.

His new friends at the bar understood his need to handle this on his own and leave the police out of it. Justice needed to be done. The fools with the guns agreed with him. Add them to Trevor's crew of two, and they had plenty of manpower. Four of them on the trail and one back at the visitors center in case something went wrong and someone got away. With the Jeep disabled, one of those idiots would go inside looking for help. They just wouldn't be getting the kind of help they were hoping for. But Trevor wouldn't need that back-up plan, because he intended to be successful in the wilderness.

Cupping his hands, Trevor blew hot breath into his palms to warm up. "Just waiting until I'm sure they're out for the night. I want to do this as quickly as possible. No hassle. Just go in quiet and get it done. They don't have to know it was me that hit 'em. I just want them gone." So did his asshole of a father.

According to Dad, Trevor never did anything right. For once in his goddamn life, Trevor wanted to prove to his dad that he could handle anything. It was the only way Liam was going to let Trevor lead his own life.

Henry's rifle might be fine for hunting, but Trevor liked his AR-15 for this excursion. This mountain was going to see a lot of action tonight. Trevor looked forward to providing the show. The hike back was going to be a hell of a lot easier with this off his shoulders. He checked his watch again. He'd give it a little bit longer to make sure they were tucked away for the night.

VIC SPOTTED DANNY ON the giant boulder that looked out to the hot springs. In front of him, steam rose up from the water in a decadent invitation. Large pale stones circled several different pools of various sizes. Sitting so still, Danny looked like a Greek god, one leg bent on the rock, his arm rested on his knee. The serene picture didn't fool her. Danny might seem calm on the exterior, but inside he hurt.

Moonlight flooded the open area and the giant silver circle reflected in the gently rippling water.

She took a tentative step and snapped a twig. Spinning around, Danny jumped off the rock and faced her. For a second, standing in a fighting stance with so much scruff covering his jaw, he looked like an outlaw. "Sorry. Just me," she said, moving toward him. "Didn't mean to scare you."

Relaxing, he shook his head. "I thought you were calling it an early night." He resumed his seat on the boulder that overlooked the hot springs.

"Nope." She hung her towel on a nearby branch then stripped off her jacket and long sleeve top, very aware of Danny's double take.

"What…what are you…? I mean, I didn't know you brought a swim suit." She felt his eyes on her. "You took the bandage off your arm. Is that a smart idea?"

"The water is supposed to be healing right?" Vic did her best striptease without looking too obvious or taking too much time. It was flippin' cold! Her black bikini top made her white skin practically gleam in the moonlight. She should probably invest in visits to a tanning salon, but she didn't have the time or inclination to get her sun from a machine. She kicked off her on-loan boots and socks, stripped off her khaki pants and revealed her matching black bikini bottoms. Two tiny scraps of material that barely covered the important parts. Perfect. "This didn't take up much room, so…" She grinned and picked her way over the dirt path toward the pool of warm water, hoping he couldn't see the massive amount of chill bumps on every inch of her skin. "If we really are doing sunrise at the lookout then I want to enjoy this before I lose the chance." She dipped her foot into the middle pool. Deliciously warm. "Oh my God, this is heaven." Her feet sank into the soft bottom as she waded in and let the warmth ease her sore muscles. Saying goodbye to her straight locks the rest of the trip—because not one of these trees had an electrical outlet for her straightener—she dunked beneath the water and came up, her hair slicked back. She caught Danny's quick glance away from her. "You have to come in here. It's amazing."

He narrowed one eye. "Don't think so."

So much for her first attempt. "What's wrong? Afraid to get your hair wet?" Totally juvenile, but she didn't care. She cocked her head and lifted her eyebrows. Danny never backed away from a challenge.

"Just not in the mood."

The lame answer made her sad. The old Danny was probably always *in the mood*. "What *are* you in the mood for?" Somewhat of a loaded question, but why not. It was only the two of them.

"Privacy?"

That stung, but she hid the hurt. "Oh, ouch. Burn." She flipped to her back and floated in the warm water, hoping to divert his attention to her...assets. Keeping him in her peripheral vision, she felt his eyes scan her from top to bottom. Any second now he was going to strip and join her.

He scrubbed a hand through his short hair, jumped off the rock and turned to go.

"Danny, wait." Dammit. She didn't want it like this. Stroking toward the edge, she walked out into the very chilly night. Cold air attacked her wet skin and made for an icy blanket. The goose bumps returned. "You were here first. I'll go." She reached for her towel.

He didn't say anything as he watched her dry off. Then he finally shook his head. "Naw. You were right. You should enjoy this while you can because I did plan to leave early tomorrow." He turned, but she grabbed his hand. Despite the chilly night, his skin was warm and a bolt of heat traveled up her arm.

"You don't have to leave. You could join me."

He glanced down at their hands as if she was some type of alien about to abduct him. Instead of giving him time to think on it, she tossed the towel back to the branch and pulled him closer to the edge. "Vic." Maybe the warning tone was supposed to scare her. It didn't.

"Would hate to get your dry clothes all wet before our hike in the morning. You should probably take them off."

"Who said they're going to get wet?"

"Me. Just now." She gauged his somber face, felt guilty for pushing him. Letting go of his hand, she backed up into the water. "C'mon, Danny. Don't leave me in the wild all by myself. That's not very guide-like." Apparently, she didn't feel guilty enough to stop. She was such a bitch. "Think about it. You'll need to be able to tell potential clients about these hot springs. No better way than to try them for yourself."

His gaze narrowed. Probably because she was right and he didn't like it. She glided back into the pool, reveling as the warm water took away the chill.

He looked back toward camp and then at the hot springs and

then at her. Finally, he stripped off his vest, flannel shirt and T-shirt and Vic nearly hummed with satisfaction. She turned around, giving him her back in case he got shy, which she highly doubted. Still, staring at him like she might eat him alive—given half a chance—didn't seem the way to go either. She heard the splash of water as he entered and turned in time to see him come up next to her, shaking water out of his hair. His eyes were lit with the boyish charm she remembered from their first meeting. They stayed that way, facing each other.

"Nice, right?"

He nodded then glanced away. "Yeah. Nice." Water sparkled on the dark stubble of his square jaw.

"Can I ask you a question?"

He thought it over before giving her a sidelong look. "Depends on the question."

"When do you think you might start living your life again?"

He snorted and headed back for the bank, but Vic grabbed his shoulder and turned him enough to face her. They both had their footing in the soft wet floor of the spring, but she stood a little taller on the uneven bottom. Tall enough to almost look him in the eye, which *never* happened because he was so tall.

"Look, I realize this isn't any of my business, but—"

"Do you?" he cut in. "Because it doesn't sound like it."

She met his hard stare and held her ground. Granted, she wasn't a psychologist, but if he didn't get this off his chest, he'd never get past it. The wait-and-see approach hadn't worked so now...she pushed. "You never struck me as a guy who'd let himself get whipped. Yet, this...person...has you by the balls and she's not even around to see it."

He clenched his jaw, but she powered ahead.

"Personally, I don't think it's right to give someone—someone who's not even around anymore—that kind of power." She ignored the irony that she now lived her life without attachments because her last two boyfriends had cheated. This was about bringing Danny back from his self-imposed exile.

His gaze drilled into hers. "Why do you even care, Vic? You made it real clear in the beginning that you weren't interested. I don't know what's changed."

"*You've* changed. Look, I'm not looking for permanent. I'm not looking for happily ever after." Sometimes she hated the cynic she'd become.

"Why not? There's nothing but dating apps and ads trying to bring people together so they can have a happily ever after. Why don't you want one?"

Vic swallowed, felt her face heat with the question as the same ridiculous embarrassment flooded through her. "Fair question and I'll be honest." She took a deep breath and dove in. "I've been cheated on. Not just once, but twice. The first guy—his name was Evan. He was a real treat. We were together for four months. I fell hard for that man. He was everything I thought I wanted. He was a CPA, worked in his father's firm. A nice stable guy. He came over one night to watch a movie and he left his phone on the coffee table when he went to the bathroom. I sat down with the popcorn just as some text messages came through. *Hey, baby, can't wait to see you later. I hate your long hours. I miss your hot bod.*"

She didn't shy away from Danny's empathetic gaze. "You get the picture. I tried to rationalize that maybe someone had the wrong number except the last text said something like, *Evan, baby, I'm going to fuck you stupid tonight.*"

Danny had the courtesy to cringe.

"Needless to say, we never got around to the movie. I tossed Evan-baby out on his ass that night." She'd been completely crushed with his betrayal. "But, hey, I wasn't down for long. If at first you don't succeed, right? I dated here and there, and then a year later, I met Anthony. Nice man, good job at a bank, some kind of financial advisor. We dated for six months. I told him all about Evan early on, as we were getting to know each other. He commiserated. Agreed that guys could really suck, especially the cheaters. I thought, hey, I found a guy who gets it. He wouldn't ever cheat on me knowing what I'd been through, knowing how devastated I was. So what did I do? I fell hard for Anthony." She shook her head, gazing out to the lush trees and watching the steam rise from the water. "But you know what Anthony did?"

Shaking his head, Danny narrowed his eyes, clearly anticipating the worst.

"Anthony forgot he made a date with me. And when I went to

118

his apartment and used the key he'd *given* me to open his door, I found him fucking his neighbor on the sofa. The neighbor he'd broken up with because she moved out of the country."

"Sounds like she came back," Danny muttered.

Vic nodded. "Oh, she came back all right. I tossed his key on the table and left. Done. Finished. I'm out." She exhaled hard. "So, no offense, but I'm not in a particularly trusting mood."

"Sorry about all that. Really sucks. When did this happen with Anthony?" Danny asked.

"About a year before you and I met at *Write Your Ticket*. Look, I have no problem with the opposite sex as long as everyone understands the rules."

He nodded. "Okay, so you're not looking for permanent. What are you looking for?"

She shrugged off the memories of her past and took it as a good sign that he even asked. "Right here, right now? How about putting a smile back on your face, or taking some of that weight off your shoulders for a little while? It's not a crime, you know, to smile. It's not a crime to come out of this self-imposed mourning."

Despair crept into his hard stare and he scoffed. "Next you're going to tell me it wasn't my fault like everyone else. Maybe it wasn't. But I was the last straw. She killed herself because I rejected her."

"Did you promise her a relationship? A ring? What d—"

"No!" he cut in. "She knew it was just for fun. We got that out in the open first thing."

"Then you can't be so tough on yourself. You were honest when a lot of guys *aren't* honest. They say whatever gets them into the sheets then cheat because it's not enough."

He shook his head, huffed out a breath. "Great. I mean, don't stop now. Shrink it up some more."

His tone hurt worse than the words, but it was the devastating look in his eyes that hit Vic hardest. She moved in close, wrapped her arms around his neck and instantly discovered that Danny had come into the spring without a stitch of clothing. His hard gaze disappeared in a heartbeat, along with her breath. He was fully erect and now pressed up close to her stomach.

His heat seared her, stoked an internal fire that had been simmering for days. She worked to sound casual, but the words still came out in a whisper. "No boxer briefs?"

He shook his head and swallowed.

Exhaling a steady breath, Vic struggled to stay on topic. "Look, I apologize," she said softly. "I have no business telling you anything. It's not like I lead the perfect life. I want you to know that you won't break me. You have nothing to worry about from me. We're adults and neither one of us is looking for anything permanent."

He gripped both her wrists, one in each big calloused hand, as if he planned to pull her off him, but he just stayed that way as they stared at each other. Tension built between them and the heat of his hands felt delicious on her cool arms. She couldn't think straight with his erection against her stomach, and she ached to feel it deep inside of her. The old Danny knew how to make her panties—when she wore them—melt with one glance.

With a tactical move that could very well be the exact wrong thing, Vic pulled away from Danny all on her own.

DANNY TOOK A STEADYING breath as Vic glided back-flat on the surface away from him. No way to keep his gaze from traveling over the sweet curves of her body. She'd been taunting him all day, not that she knew it. Her moss green tank top had blended into the scenery, but it had fit her like a glove and showed off all the curves and cleavage the girl had to offer. Over and over he found himself watching her when she didn't realize it, only to look away when she turned in his direction.

He was so wrecked.

But that had been established long ago.

Still, he couldn't stop his physical reaction to her. It was like telling a caged eagle not to fly when the door opened. He might've been a loser and an asshole, but he wasn't dead. No matter how much he wished she didn't get to him, he couldn't control his physiology around her.

She floated for a minute then got her footing and sent a broad grin in his direction. She beckoned him over with an index finger, silently commanding he comply. Did he leave or stay? Meet her in the middle or keep his distance? His black heart told him one thing and his body told him something else.

It had been too many months since he'd had any physical release and the way his erection pointed right at Vic like an arrow to the yellow brick road didn't help his fogged up brain.

"C'mon, Danny." She said the words so quietly. "Just a swim. Doesn't have to be anything else." There she went with that index finger again. The fading marks around her neck showed up against all that pale skin and made it that much harder to deny her.

"The only reason I'm not getting out now is because I want to scope the place out."

Her eyes twinkled under the full moon. "That's fine. A great idea. My idea originally if you remember."

"I remember." He moved toward her, but kept going to other side of the small pool to get a sense of the depth. At least that's what he told himself. Vic just watched him from the middle of the pool, her smile almost gone, concern in her eyes.

"When's your birthday?" she asked.

"September sixteenth. Why?"

The smile came back, bigger than before. "That's cool. Mexican Independence Day. Bet you think all the drink specials at El Torito are for you every year."

He grinned for the first time in a long time because he always thought that exact thing. "Aren't they?" he replied. Her laughter went straight to his gut. He hadn't heard a woman laugh at something he said in a very long time. The last time had been... He lost the smile. Nikki's lifeless body flashed in his brain and he clenched his jaw to fight the nausea in his stomach.

"Uh-oh." Vic moved closer, but kept some space between them. "You had almost thirty good seconds, then poof." Water glistened in her long dark lashes.

"Yeah." He couldn't meet her gaze. She deserved someone who could focus on her and not a ghost in the past.

"You're about twenty-five, twenty-six?" she asked, changing the subject.

"Twenty-five. So is Eric for that matter. At least for a little bit longer."

121

"Irish twins?" She cocked her head to the side again, a soft smile back on her lips.

He should really quit looking at her lips. Soft. Plush. Kissable. "Yep. Irish twins. If you want to get technical, I'm also Irish twins with the twins too."

She laughed again. "That's very cool. A lot of twin shit happening in your house."

"Guess so." He was bringing it down. He knew it, but couldn't seem to stop himself. Just like he couldn't erase the tension sparking between them.

Vic eased close again and set her arms on his shoulders. His dick throbbed with want. She smelled like nature and hot springs and a touch of lavender. One whiff and fierce need arrowed in his gut.

"What if I kissed you right now?" Her voice—back to normal—was an aphrodisiac all by itself. Soft, inviting and enough to knock him on his ass if he hadn't been in the water.

But dammit he didn't want to cave to her. He could see himself moving too fast just like he used to and he didn't want to be that guy. "What if you didn't?"

She stroked a soft finger along his bristled jaw and the gentle touch only made him harder, which he didn't think was even remotely possible. He purposely hadn't touched her. Knew if he did that he'd crumble like a cheap building in a big earthquake because he was a weak son of a bitch.

That soft finger worked its way across his lips and he closed his lids. If he didn't look into her eyes, he wouldn't see everything she wanted. But closing his eyes was a mistake, because a second later, her lips replaced her finger and she smoothed that soft mouth across his in a feather-light touch that nearly stopped his heart.

He stayed stone still. Didn't move, didn't breathe. Nothing deterred her. She kept nibbling at his mouth, soft strokes, long glides with plush lips. The moment she brushed her tongue across his lower lip was when he lost the battle. He folded like he knew he would and he despised himself for it. Even as he took her kiss and gave back, he hated the mistake.

Still, he could survive this. Just a little longer. If he didn't touch her anywhere else, he could kiss her and get away unscathed. Well, not totally unscathed because he'd remember this kiss until the day he died. Jesus, lips this soft should be outlawed. He'd dreamed about kissing her. The whole fucking run of that bullshit reality show, she'd starred in his subconscious. None of those dreams came close to the reality. She was trouble waiting to happen. Hell, trouble happening now the way she licked into his mouth with shy forays, totally incongruous of her.

Until she got bolder and went in total attack mode. Take no prisoners, leave no stone unturned. Her tongue did an award-winning inventory of his mouth and he reciprocated. She tasted warm and faintly of chocolate. The s'mores they'd had after dinner.

He was breathing hard. He heard it in the quiet of the night. But still he refused to touch her anywhere else. He'd already crossed a line and couldn't, wouldn't continue to cross more. It was just a kiss, their tongues clashing, mouths nibbling. She lit him up like a fucking torch and if he didn't end this s—

An explosion of sound shattered the quiet night and Vic jumped away from him, breathing as hard as him. "What the hell was that?"

They both looked off in the direction of the noise, the direction of their camp.

"I don't know." Except he had an idea. He knew machine gun fire when he heard it. "C'mon. We need to get out of here." He pulled her with him up the stone steps and they dressed in seconds flat, the water soaking their clothes and making the cold hit that much harder. "Stay here. I'm going to check it out." He spun around.

She grabbed his hand. "Not on your fucking life. You're not leaving me out here. I'm coming with you." She trembled from head to toe. He didn't know if it was from the cold or fear. Probably both. But the absolute panic in her eyes did the trick.

As much as he wanted her away from whatever was going on, she also had a point. He didn't want to lose sight of her. "Stay behind me. Stay quie—"

Another round of gunfire blasted the air, but this time rounds whizzed past them, spraying bark, kicking up dirt and splashing water as bullets hit the hot springs.

Danny tackled Vic to the ground, protecting her from the gunfire, his pulse jacked up to new levels of crazy. "You okay?" he asked, when the bullets stopped flying.

She nodded. "Yeah." Her voice shook as much as her body.

Looking up, Danny eased to a crouch and pulled Vic next to him. "That came from camp." Where his brother and Zoe were sitting ducks in their tents. Danny's stomach heaved at the potential for worst-case scenario. As much as he wanted to run and rescue his brother, Vic's safety mattered as well, and taking her directly into the line of fire made no sense whatsoever. "Let's move downstream...get some distance."

"What about Zoe and Eric?" she asked.

Danny swallowed back bile. "If they were there, then walking into a trap does nothing but get us killed too. If they weren't, then we walk into a trap for no good reason." He took her hand. "Let's move."

She nodded, fast and silent, and Danny started out with Vic right behind him.

CHAPTER 13

MASKING ANY ODOR, ERIC kicked dirt over the puddle of urine near a bunch of rocks just as an explosion of machine gun fire erupted. Adrenaline surged in his system and his heart slammed hard against his ribs as he zipped up and spun toward camp.

Fifteen yards away, Zoe shot up from the dense brush where—like him—she'd just finished answering nature's call before crashing for the night. "What the holy hell was that?" She catapulted from out of the bushes, her eyes wide, face pale.

An automatic weapon if he had to guess. "Not sure. Whatever it is, it's close. Like at camp."

Zoe inched closer. "Should we—"

More rounds cut off her question and they stood completely still until the forest came alive around them. Pieces of timber flew through the air and pelted them from every direction. "Run! Run!" Even as Eric hissed the words, he grabbed Zoe and shoved her ahead of him. For once, she didn't argue and they raced farther from camp and away from the hell breaking loose behind them.

Eric caught up, snatched Zoe's flashlight and shut it down as they climbed the mountain at an unholy pace. Running in the dark slowed them down, but it was better than bringing whoever was out there right to them.

Grabbing Zoe's hand, Eric cut right, toward the lookout point Danny had indicated to earlier. If they could find it, he could scope out just what the hell had happened. Sweat glued his T-shirt to his back and his already tired muscles burned as he and Zoe scrambled up the rocks and weaved through trees. Zoe huffed for every breath and Eric kept a solid grasp on her hand. It took every bit of fifteen minutes to get to the spot, just as Danny had guessed. Although little bro hadn't anticipated doing this hike at an all-out run. Breathing hard, Eric slowed to a stop. Next to him, Zoe bent over, gasping for breath, her hand on her side.

"I don't think...anyone came after us," Eric said, panting hard. They'd been gone from camp for about ten minutes by the time the shooting started, plenty of time for Danny and Vic to get back from the hot springs, and plenty of time for them to be sitting ducks. His stomach knotted at the thought that they'd been gunned down. He pointed toward the edge of the platform about twenty yards away, dreading what he might find when he looked over at the camp. "Stay here. I need to take a look."

"No way. I'm in this too, Eric. Besides, four eyes are better than two. Let's go."

Despite wanting to protect her, he couldn't say no. She was right. One more quality about Zoe that he admired...even if it endlessly aggravated him. "Quietly," he whispered. When they neared the edge, Eric got on his stomach and motioned Zoe down too. They belly crawled to the edge and looked down, the view clear between two massive trees.

Four men paced in their campsite. One carried the automatic weapon that had nearly mowed them down. Even from this distance, it was clear he'd shot the hell out of the camp. No sign of any bodies, but that didn't mean Danny and Vic weren't in a tent. Dead.

Eric's stomach pitched again and instead of letting the possibility eat him alive, he focused on now and the next step.

Below, the men congregated near the shot-out lantern. Despite the full moon, Eric couldn't make out their faces because of their hats. He also couldn't hear their conversation. But he watched their body language, watched one guy point two men toward the hot springs and signaled the other man in a different direction and himself in another. He checked his watch and pointed to the campsite.

"They're splitting up to look for us," Zoe whispered. "And they're meeting back at the camp. I couldn't tell how long though. Do you think Vic and Danny got back to camp while we were gone?"

"Don't know. Those men looked pretty pissed, so I'm hoping not."

"We can't risk going back." She glanced at him. "It'll take too long anyway. They might be back in ten minutes or less. We don't know."

Eric looked at the massive trees right in front of him. The way the branches practically reached out to him. His mother always told him he was a monkey in a past life. "I was a great tree climber back in the day." All his brothers were. They used to challenge each other on every tree in just about every park. Drove their mom crazy.

Zoe would hate this idea. He glanced her way and her bugged out eyes confirmed his suspicion.

"I can scale down in a fraction of the time it would take to hike back. I can check the tents, grab some provisions."

"Absolutely not." Zoe shook her head so hard, her pony tail hit her cheeks. "It's too dangerous."

"We have no idea how long we're going to be out here, Zoe. They might even leave a man at the camp once they come back. We have to act now." Even as he said the words, the men split up and trekked out. Eric made an executive decision. "I'm doing this."

"No!" Zoe grabbed his arm. Sweat glistened on her skin. "You can't go back there. It's too dangerous. Please, Eric, you can't go back there."

"Trust me, it's the last thing I want to do, but I need to make sure Danny and Vic…" God, he couldn't even think about those bullets taking them down. His stomach knotted. "I need to at least check the camp and make sure they didn't get back while we were gone." Danny would do the same for him. He glanced down at their campsite again. This high up, the big moon seemed to light the area like a searchlight. "I won't be able to come up the way I go down. Stay here. You can keep an eye out. If you see one of them coming, toss a rock or something my way. I'll disappear and come back for you. Right here. Okay, Zoe? Stay here. Do this for me."

She grabbed his forearm. "Eric, you cannot leave me out here." No denying the unmistakable panic in her voice.

"Zoe, please." *Fuck.* "Don't argue with me on this. We don't have time. I promise to come back ASAP." The panic in her eyes cut like a knife to his chest. Instinct took over and he pulled her on top of him and rolled to his back, wrapped her tight in his arms. She fit perfectly against him, but he didn't have time to think about it. He bent near her ear and spoke softly. "Please believe me. I will be back as soon as I check it out."

She stayed in his arms for only a few moments before rolling away from him. Tears swam in her pretty eyes and she swallowed hard. "Fine. Go." She waved him toward their camp. "I'm going to be right here. I'm not moving a muscle. Probably."

What the hell did that mean? "Probably?"

"Well, if something happens and I have to run or hide or get eaten by a bear or a mountain lion, then I *won't* be here." She peered out over their camp.

She had worst-case scenario down pat.

He was more worried about the crazy humans out tonight, not the wildlife. The clock continued to tick and he had to go now or lose the opportunity. "Hang tight. I'll be back as soon as I can."

Instead of looking back, Eric took one last look below then searched for the nearest, healthiest branch that would support him.

ZOE GASPED WHEN ERIC leaped off the ledge and straight into the branches of the mammoth tree standing nearest them. He caught one branch above his head as his feet landed on a sturdier one. Like Tarzan, he made his way down in a matter of minutes as if he'd been born to it, and gave her a whole new appreciation for the man. He'd always been the uptight lawyer and suddenly he'd turned into this amazingly agile Tarzan he-man.

On the ground, he made his way toward the other tent. After a glance inside, he lifted a thumb's up sign. She took that for good. Vic and Danny hadn't returned while they'd been gone. Zoe released a breath she didn't know she'd been holding.

As Eric made his way back to their tent, she concentrated on the perimeter, scanning the area with sharp eyes. The moon lit up the center of camp while darkness blanketed the outskirts. She wouldn't be able to see a thing until it entered the light, just like she wouldn't be able to hear anything this high up. There wasn't a damn thing she could do to help Eric if those men came back.

Somehow the guys from L.A. had found them. That had to be it. Danny and Eric had been sure that getting out of town would solve the problem. Instead, the problem had followed them. But how? It didn't seem possible.

Something rustled in the bushes behind her and Zoe bolted to her feet and away from the edge. Blood surged in her veins as she slowly eased toward a giant boulder ten yards away. Fear made her lungs constrict. Sweat soaked her palms. She didn't have a weapon. Nothing to fight with.

Memories swamped her. Utter darkness and noises she couldn't identify. More panic bubbled up. Her knees buckled and she went down, grasping the boulder for support as she dropped.

CHAPTER 14

VIC'S HEART POUNDED LIKE clapping sticks at a playoff game. Danny had kept them near the river, but stopped a few minutes ago, his head cocked as he listened to the sounds around them. Aside from the rushing water, nothing moved, not a cricket to be heard. It was beyond eerie. The anticipation of waiting for the other shoe to drop only freaked her out more.

Hustling her into dense brush, he yanked her down and minutes later, two men walked by. Both held nasty looking rifles, neither of which looked like the machine gun that had almost shredded them. That meant at least one other man still lurked out here. One with an automatic rifle, the kind of weapon that shot things up in seconds flat and left nothing in its wake but destruction and death. Hunters carrying machine guns were only looking for one thing. And tonight that thing didn't move on four legs or have fur.

Danny picked up a hefty rock and weighed it in his hand before standing slowly. Silently, he rotated his arm, got a good stretch in, then threw that rock high and far on the other side of the river. The obvious crash through dense leaves had the two men splashing through the narrow part of the river and chasing after the sound. He motioned her to follow him.

No problem there. She planned to stick to him like her burnt marshmallow stuck to her graham cracker. Only now, he headed away from the water and back toward camp. Maybe he thought those men were the only ones to be concerned about.

Once they made it to the outskirts of their camp, Vic peeked over his shoulder and quietly gasped. The moon illuminated a gruesome scene. Their campsite was demolished. Their tents blown to bits. A fresh round of nausea rolled in her stomach.

Zoe and Eric could very well be dead in their tent right now. Bile rose up and Vic swallowed it back. Maybe they weren't here when these guys shot up the place. But where would they go? Tears pricked her eyes as she stared at their tent, looking for any sign of life.

Danny pointed at her, pointed at the ground and mouthed, *you stay.*

She shook her head and gave him wide, frantic eyes, but they didn't sway him and he shook his head adamantly. This probably wasn't the best time to argue since every second counted. She nodded. Fine. At least he'd let her come this far. If she'd stayed at the hot springs and those two psycho gunmen had found her, she'd be dead already.

After one last look around, Danny quietly snuck into camp. Keeping to the edge, he worked his way over to his and Eric's tent and looked inside. His chin hit his chest and he exhaled before continuing in. That had to be a good sign, right? The fact that he hadn't gone ballistic had to be a good thing. Minutes ticked by and Vic kept alert for any sound. The forest seemed to press in on her, quiet, but deadly. Something buzzed past her ear and she ducked and swatted. Damp clothes made her icy cold and shaky.

Danny came out of his and Eric's tent with a backpack and sleeping bag and Vic released the breath she'd been holding. He checked her tent next then looked around, noticed something and stopped. His gaze trekked up over the trees. What was he calculating? Finally, falling back into the cover of trees, he circled back her way.

He pulled her close. "No one in either tent. No blood," he whispered almost soundlessly in her ear, and she breathed out the panic constricting her heart. Taking a second, she rested her forehead against his chest, soaking up the safety she felt with his arm around her.

She heard the noise at the same time he did. Footsteps coming from across the campsite opposite where they were. Danny motioned her to follow him, heading back the way they'd come that morning.

Cold night air wrapped around her, and Vic could barely keep her teeth from chattering like a rabid squirrel. Her wet bathing suit beneath her clothes may as well have been an ice blanket. She knew they had to be quiet, but she desperately wanted information. She kept her voice whisper quiet. "Danny—"

"Shh."

She wanted to ask where they were going, did he see anything in the tent, what was he searching for when he looked up at the tree line, but the questions had to wait. With only the moon lighting their way, the midnight hike seemed to last for hours. Branches caught on her jacket and tugged on her drying hair. Breath billowed from her lungs and her legs tingled from overexertion by the time Danny finally stopped and turned to her.

"How are you holding up?" His low voice barely carried in the still night. It was as if the forest knew evil was in its midst.

She wrapped her arms around her middle, hoping to find a little warmth. "You know," she huffed. "Fine. F-for someone who's f-freezing to death."

"Sorry," he murmured. "Let's stop here for a few hours. I think we got past them and put some distance between us." He dropped the load on his back.

"What did you find in the t-tent?" she asked, keeping her voice just as soft.

"This," Danny said, indicating the shot-up pack on the ground. "I have no idea how they managed to get away but they did, and Eric left us this present. He packed it with food, water and some other stuff we'll need to get off this mountain."

"But what about them?" Vic sank to her knees, facing Danny. "Do they have anything?"

He nodded as he untied the sleeping bag from the pack. "Far as I can tell, he took another pack for himself. The problem is I'm pretty sure they're headed up. That means they'll have another three nights out here minimum without shelter or anyway to call for help since there's no cell service."

"Aren't we headed back the way we came? Why couldn't they?"

"Good question." Danny sat back on his heels. "There could be several answers. One, they couldn't get around the guys with the guns. Two, one of them is hurt and can't travel. Or three, they split up and Eric went back after he got provisions. *Fuck!* I didn't pack a two-way radio." He scraped a hand through his hair.

She hated seeing him beat himself up even more. "Cut yourself a break," she said softly. Dropping her voice lower, she leaned closer. "You hadn't planned on this trip. None of us did. It's a miracle you had as much food as you did. There was no reason for you to think we'd get separated to even need a radio."

His head shake dismissed her words. "The food was a fluke. I'd planned to taste test to weed the good from the bad. I should've bought a damn two-way and I *never* should've brought us up here in the first place. It was stupid. I should've gone to the cops and made them put us in a safe house." He exhaled a hard breath. "All I know is it's up to us to get down and bring help to get them back."

"Danny, the cops didn't seem like they were going to help us. You—*we* did the right thing." One big question remained. "How the hell did they find us? We left in the middle of the night. You got off the road a dozen times before we stayed on the freeway. No one was following us. You and Eric were sure."

"Vic, think about it. They knew exactly where all of us were after the meeting that never happened. A meeting no one at the DA's office made. They slashed your tires, they slammed Zoe's car with both of you in it. Hell, they threatened the cashier. They're either watching us or they've wired us somehow. For all I know they put a GPS on my Jeep. They wouldn't have had to follow us closely. They'd only need to access the signal and come straight to us."

The thought made her gut churn. It seemed inconceivable that they'd gone to all this trouble only to be found in the middle of nowhere. Vic's teeth started chattering again, but this time from fear. "Sometimes...I r-really h-hate technology."

DANNY DID HIS BEST to clear out the area so they could lie down for a few hours. Vic had grown unusually quiet as she soaked in everything he'd said. The temperature had dropped and it might not have been so bad if Vic hadn't started the night with wet hair and a wet bathing suit under her clothes. Though the hot springs were great, the cold seemed that much colder. His damp clothes didn't help, so he knew Vic had it worse with a wet bikini beneath her khakis. He needed to warm her up before her chattering teeth gave away their location.

"What were you looking f-for when you got out of the tent?" Vic asked him as he rolled out the only sleeping bag he'd grabbed. It was shot up, but still better than nothing. Hopefully the thermal blanket he had would help with insulation.

"Eric left a few signs," he said.

"You mean along with the present?" She gestured to the backpack and rubbed her hands along her arms. "That looks like Z-Zoe's red headband on the handle." Vic's face seemed extra pale in the moonlight.

Danny worked fast opening up the bag and discovered a big lump. "Yeah. It probably is. What the...?" He pulled out a small pile of rolled up clothes. "Looks like jeans, T-shirt...something..." lacy "...else. Uh...this doesn't belong to Eric, I can tell you that." He tossed it toward Vic.

She caught it. "They're Zoe's. She must have stuffed them in the bag before the shooting started." She unrolled the clothes. "Yes!" At his questioning stare she elaborated. "Sports bra. Better than my bikini top."

"Got it." He continued working and lined the bag with the thermal blanket. Luckily, it looked as if the bullets missed the blanket.

"So, Eric left signs?" she whispered.

"Yeah. When I saw the red band, I realized Eric was leaving me a message, so I looked for more."

"What else did you find? I mean, you knew the backpack was for you, but I'm still not sure h-how."

"When we were little, the four of us used to play a game." Danny glanced up as he worked, moving faster so he could get her warmed up. "Dad would put objects at the end of the yard and one would be designated with a red bandana. That was the object to win, but we couldn't tell which item was marked until we got there. We had to go through an obstacle course to get to the prizes. The one who came up with the marked item won the battle."

"Okay, so you knew when you saw the red marker on the pack that Eric was telling you to take it, but why did you think he'd leave other signs and what were they?"

"Did you notice the tent had shifted?" he asked while rolling out the thermal blanket inside the sleeping bag.

Vic knelt across from him and grabbed the edges. "I just figured the force of the bullets did that."

"Nope. Your tent was just as shot up and it was still staked in the ground. Our tent was lined up in a different direction."

"Meaning what?"

"I think it was the direction they ran. And if I'm right, it's in the direction of the ranger station up the mountain." Together they aligned the corners of the blanket with the sleeping bag. "Eric knows we can't get reception up here, but there might be a radio or spot device or even a ranger at the station."

"What's a spot device?" she asked.

"It's like an emergency beacon. Works off a satellite. Press the SOS button and local authorities get the info and send help ASAP."

"O-okay. And you really think that's where they're headed just because of the way he f-faced the tent?"

"Like I said, I won't know until the morning when I see the line of the station. But the path headed to our right, not up into the trees. There had to be a reason they didn't stay toward the path. Shit." He knew why. He sat back on his heels and pulled the map out of his back pocket. "I had this with me. Eric didn't know which way to go, so he took the direction where he knew he could find help. Dammit."

Vic took her edges and folded them toward Danny. "You can't beat yourself up over that," she said. "You didn't know lunatics were going to come shooting at us."

Danny stuffed the map back in his pocket and took the edges, closing the bag then zipping it part way. "Maybe not, but I should've made sure Eric, you and Zoe had your own maps. Stupid."

"Cut it out." She had zero sympathy behind the whispered words. "You're not a freaking psychic. You had no idea this was going to happen. Is that r-ready?" Her whole body shook with chills.

"Yeah. Sorry." She took off her shoes and started to climb in. "Wait," he said. "It's not going to do you any good to get in there with wet clothes. Strip 'em off." He began doing the same. He jumped out of the hot springs and right into his clothes so he'd been running in damp clothes too.

She only hesitated a second before following his lead. "This is going to be a very tight fit," she said. True words. The bag was intended for one and he was a big guy. "Vic got down to her bikini and started to get in, but Danny grabbed her leg and held her back. He felt the still damp strings on her back.

"Everything Vic. Take it off. It's wet. The point is to get dry and warm." For a lady who'd been all about seduction she seemed suddenly shy. Not that he was looking forward to hours of feeling all that soft skin against him and refusing to do anything about it. But just because they'd be naked next to each other didn't mean anything had to happen. "You can put on Zoe's clothes if you really have to, they're dry. But it's faster to strip and get in the bag. Go ahead. I'm closing my eyes."

Vic darted a quick glance his way then gave him her back. "I'm all for what's going to get me warmer faster." She yanked on the string and Danny shut his lids. He imagined a flash of pale, smooth skin as she scampered into the bag. "Oh my God, this is so freaking c-cold." Her teeth chattered harder.

"It'll warm up. Gimme a sec. I'll be right there." Danny stripped off his clothes in seconds flat. She huddled in the edge of the bag, her back to him as he scooted in next to her. "I know I'm a little chilly, but we'll warm up soon, I promise." After zipping the bag as far as he could, he wrapped an arm around her waist and tucked her tightly against him. He shouldn't have been shocked at the absolute smooth perfection of her skin. Shouldn't have been almost breathless as she curved along every inch of him like she belonged there.

He tried to keep it clinical. This was about getting her warm. Getting them both warm. Ha. Fat fucking chance of that happening. Although he was already pretty damn hot. There was no way for her to ignore just how hot either. His erection sprang up between them like a heat seeking missile ready to detonate. "Sorry about that," he murmured.

Her nervous chuckle sounded between clattering teeth. "At least I know you don't have anything against my body."

"At the moment, I have absolutely *everything* against your body."

This time a low, husky laugh arrowed straight to his dick and it twitched against her ass.

"See, that's the man I remember," she said. She paused as if considering something. "That's the guy I miss," she added softly.

Never shit a shitter. "You never knew me to miss me, Vic." No sense in avoiding the elephant in the forest. "Be honest, you never really *wanted* to know me at all. If you did, you would've called me. I didn't have your number. You had mine." He waited so long he didn't think he'd get an answer. Then it dawned on him that she might take what he said the wrong way.

"That's not all totally true," she finally said. "I mean, sure, I had your number, but do you think I just call guys because they give me their number?" She huffed out a breath. "If a guy wants to date me he has to put in a little effort, Danny."

He'd never considered that. Of course, he'd never had to put in much effort either. Most women made it easy for him and did the work. But he understood her point. He'd just never been into *hard to get*, and Vic definitely qualified as hard to get.

Something rustled in the bushes and they both froze. A few seconds later, a giant raccoon peeked out from bushes ten feet away and Vic sucked in a quiet gasp.

"S'okay," Danny murmured. "He'll go away." Danny closed his eyes and sent up a quick prayer. *Please let the large, sharp clawed rodent go away.*

After sniffing the air, the big guy decided to hunt in a new local and wandered off.

Vic shrank back against him and took a steadying breath. "All I was saying before is that you can't get mad that your *call me* line didn't work on me." She kept her voice whisper soft. "You just figured I'd come to heel because that's what you were used to."

Apparently, she'd thought about this for some time. Yeah, he was a dick and deserved everything she dished out. It wasn't anything he didn't already know, but the truth still slammed him hard. "Is this sleeping bag suddenly very warm?" he murmured. Because he was sure as hell hot around the collar. He would've run if he could, bolted into the brush to get as far away from Vic as possible, but under the circumstances, he didn't have that luxury. His job was to keep her alive and as comfortable as possible, so he rubbed his hand along her arm, trying to warm up her cold skin.

"Sorry." She turned her head toward him. "You're the one who wanted honest. And if I'm going to be even more honest, I hate that you've lost the sparkle you used to have. I might not have called you, but that didn't mean I wasn't interested. I just wasn't interested in being in a long line of forgotten women."

What? But earlier... "Weren't you the one tonight saying something about no pressure and no worries. That you aren't looking for anything permanent?" He couldn't believe they were having this whispered conversation buck-naked in the middle of the forest while being hunted by men with rifles.

"Yes, absolutely, but that doesn't mean I don't want to be remembered."

Women. So fucking hard to understand. "Let me get this right." He leaned up on an elbow and spoke softly near her ear. "If I'd tried harder, you'd have gone out with me. We might or might not have burned up the sheets for an undisclosed period of time and then gone our separate ways. We'd remember each other as a smokin' hot fling and continue to the next thing, *but*...we'd be sure to remember each other. Is that it?"

"I don't know. Maybe. I don't know." She shrugged a beautiful shoulder, but sounded seriously conflicted. "I just know I don't like feeling like I'm one of a hundred or a thousand or however many you have on your list. If a guy wants to date me, he has to work for me. He has to show me that I mean something other than just a warm body."

How the hell did he respond to that? He couldn't blame her for feeling that way. God knew she had a hell of a warm body right now. She didn't seem very chilly anymore and her teeth had stopped chattering. His hand still rested on her arm and he laid his head down next to hers, taking in the scent of hot springs in her damp hair. "Do you feel any better? Warmer, I mean?"

"Yeah. Thanks." Her soft-spoken words somehow made him feel as if he'd done or said something wrong. Again. "We should probably try and sleep."

"Yeah." Awkwardly, he lifted his hand and tried to figure out where to put it. Aw, hell, there was no place else to put it, so he wrapped her up against him in the name of warmth...and torture.

CHAPTER 15

TRY AND SLEEP. **YEAH,** right. Vic didn't actually see that happening for a couple of reasons. First, the hard body behind her made her acutely aware of every inch of Danny and second they were being hunted. Just another reminder how quickly life shifted in an instant. One minute she'd all but thrown herself at him in the hot springs and the next they were running for their lives.

She'd been seconds away from scoring a green light with him and now—despite the evidence pressing against her backside—the whole scenario was off the table. As it should be. They had too much to worry about to even think about sex. Every sound seemed to magnify in the wide open space making it nearly impossible to relax.

The only good thing to come out of this was the honesty. If she had to be even more honest with herself, she could admit that being open with a guy never even occurred to her anymore. How pathetic did that make her? *Maybe that's the reason you haven't had a date in almost a year.* The little voice in her head pissed her off and revved her blood.

How many times could someone bare their heart and soul only to have it thrown away, tossed aside like it meant nothing? She'd been down that road. Twice. Given her undying love to two different men who'd taken her feelings and squashed them like bugs on the sidewalk. But this wasn't love. This was clearing the air.

"Danny?" she said, quietly before she thought better of it—and instantly hoped he'd already fallen asleep.

"Yeah?"

Damn. Stuck. She could say *forget it,* or she could dive in with

139

that honesty she was so unaccustomed to. Swiveling—not an easy task because the bag was so damn tight—she faced him and shivered as she came into contact with the cold spots in the thermal blanket. "Look, I'm going to be straight because if I'm going to die tonight or tomorrow or whenever, I don't want any misunderstandings between us. It would've taken you all of twenty seconds to call Brendan and get my number from him or Casey. So it seemed clear to me that you didn't really care about seeing me again or not."

He rubbed his hand down her arm, warming her with his palm. Screw distance. She needed his heat and burrowed closer to him. "Truth?" His low voice vibrated near her temple and she caught the inference to their game the other night.

"Yeah, truth," she murmured into his neck. She ignored the fact that his strong legs tangled with hers and that his erection snugged up low against her stomach. New warmth spread from her center, the kind of sexual heat she'd gone too long without, but she forced herself to stay perfectly still.

"When I didn't hear from you, I took it a little personally. I actually waited." He paused, like he debated confessing more. "Then one night I went out with a few friends and that's when I met Nikki. I thought maybe meeting someone else, spending time with someone else would get you out of my head. But...didn't quite work out the way I thought."

The inference made her chest tighten. Adjusting, she tried to see his eyes in the dark night. "Wait a second. I know I didn't hear this right. You're not saying Nikki was—I don't know—a rebound date when I didn't call you, right?" Because that would make her feel like a hot pile of shit.

"I never thought of it like that," he replied. "I was just kind of let down when you never called and I fell back to my usual."

"Danny—"

"I know," he said, cutting her off quietly. "I'm an asshole. You don't have to say it."

"I wasn't going to say that." Vic stroked a gentle finger across the rough stubble on his jaw. She couldn't imagine dealing with what he'd gone through. "I could say I'm sorry for never calling you, but that wouldn't be a hundred percent honest and—"

Something else rustled in the bushes to their right and they both stiffened, not daring to take a breath. Danny carefully eased away from her as her heart threatened to pound out of her chest. A rabbit hopped out of the bushes and Vic's hard exhale sent a puff of air into the night. She was so past done with this whole thing. Danny returned and wrapped her up tight when he realized she was shaking.

"Are we going to get out of here?" she whispered.

He squeezed her closer and she breathed him in. Hot springs and Danny. "Yes," he said softly into her ear. "I'm getting you out of here."

He sounded so sure when she knew they couldn't be sure of anything. It seemed more important than ever to finish this conversation. "I'm sorry that you went through such a terrible time. With Casey and Brendan so tight after the show ended and things settled down, I thought for sure I'd hear from you. When I didn't, I figured maybe I didn't make a big enough impression."

He met her gaze. "You made an impression, trust me."

Vic moved in closer, tucking her arms against his chest, seeking the heat of his much bigger body, cuddling up as close as she could, skin on skin from top to bottom, and triggering a needy pulse between her thighs.

"I knew," he said, softly, grazing his hand down her spine and sending a wash of goose bumps in his wake. "I knew she was a mistake when I had you on my mind."

"Danny…" She didn't think she could listen to this, but he deserved an ear. It seemed the least she could do after everything he'd gone through.

"No, it's true." He continued to stroke his big hands down her back and her arm and the innocent gesture felt more emotional than anything Vic had experienced the last three years. "I knew when I saw her scars that she had issues."

Vic tilted her head. "Scars?"

He nodded. "I didn't see them initially. She had a ton of bangles on her wrists and up her arms. But when I saw them in the morning…and more in other places," he added quietly. "Jesus, I can't believe I'm telling you this."

"It's okay." She hugged him and a wave of fierce tenderness

crashed over her. A tiny little niggle in the back of her mind said, *shoulda called him.* But there was no going back now and she wasn't much for living in the past. "People make decisions, you know. And sometimes they're the wrong ones and they suck, but it's because they don't know how to cope." He'd coped by removing himself from his former life and forging something brand new. "You've recreated yourself and that's a great thing if you're happy." She tipped her head up and watched his face. "I just don't think you're very happy." And that made her sad.

DANNY SHIFTED THEM BOTH deeper into the bag, hiking the material farther up to block out the cold and muffle their whispered voices. He needed a few seconds to get his thoughts in order. He'd already spilled way more about Nikki than he had with anyone else and Vic was the dead *last* person he ever thought to share this information with.

Maybe he wanted to scare her away. Maybe he didn't deserve someone as brave, smart and beautiful. He'd purposely sabotaged his sex life months ago when he'd deleted dozens of numbers in his phone. This was just another way to go about the same thing…except she didn't seem thrown off by his ugly past. Instead she'd held on tight and listened.

"*Are* you happy?" she asked, shifting again to look into his eyes.

"I'll be happy when I know Eric and Zoe are okay, and I get us off this mountain."

"I think that goes without saying. You know what I mean." She cuddled close to him again, her voice muffled against his chest. Her warm puffs of air sent tingles down his spine and straight to his groin. "But that non-answer answered my question."

Frustration climbed up his sternum and thickened his throat.

"I'll bet you're thinking about how fast and far you could get if you took off right now, huh?" She spread her palms over his chest and smoothed her hands across his skin, sparking heat wherever she touched. "I think that you deserve however much time it takes you to work through this," she added. "But I also think you've done whatever penance you think you deserved and you should consider spreading your wings to encompass more than just work." She palmed his cheek, her hands still chilly. "I believe you that we're going to get out of here. And I won't push you for anything, Danny. Not a thing." With that, she tucked up close against his chest and exhaled a soft breath that wafted along his skin like a summer breeze.

Good thing she believed him, because he wasn't sure he even believed himself. Maybe it was her faith in him, or her hands on his chest and her warm breath against his skin, but more than ever, he needed to keep her safe.

Listening to every insect, every rustle in the bushes had him alert and ready to fight at any second. Getting off this mountain was going to be a supreme bitch.

Vic shifted against him and he stroked his hand down her arm. It wasn't as if he couldn't face the facts. He'd had an instant attraction to this woman and time hadn't changed that. The scratches and bruises on her hadn't changed it. If anything, seeing her beat up this way only made him more...fucking protective of her. He knew this trip was going to test him, but he hadn't planned on the extent. Not the emotional and certainly not the physical.

The good news: she said she wouldn't push him. More good news: that worked for him since he was fairly certain he'd fold as fast as he did when she'd kissed him. The bad news: he'd said way too much about Nikki tonight. The worse news: none of it mattered if he didn't get her off this mountain and to safety.

If Vic hadn't been stuck with him, she probably would've bolted in a fast minute. Or maybe she was right and he'd have bolted first given half a chance. Except she felt so damn good cuddled up next to him, smelling like nature and woman—two things he enjoyed most in life.

Karma was a bitch. So was lying on his side with her breasts crushed against his chest, making him hyper aware of her every breath and each tiny shift of her body. Took him right back to that second in the hot springs when she'd moved against him only to realize that nothing separated them but her teeny tiny bikini. Then she'd kissed him and his whole brain melted into a pile of mush.

She was like a drug and he wanted more. Craved more. He

wanted her breathless and moaning, begging for more and screaming his name when he made her come. The way things were going now, that might never happen.

He'd known last summer she'd be a handful, both in *and* out of bed. She'd never fallen for his lines or smiles and she'd kept her distance. He had to respect her for that.

He could analyze—until the day he died—all the ways he'd screwed up when it came to her, but he still couldn't figure out how to say yes to something he wanted so badly.

Now, more than ever, he needed to get them off this mountain and he needed to face his feelings for Vic once and for all.

CHAPTER 16

ZOE MANAGED TO CRAWL behind the cover of a few large rocks where she waited. Her heart thundered so hard it hurt and still she waited. Cold air seeped into her bones and made her shiver. Little creatures rustled in the bushes and kept every one of her senses on high alert. She waited until she was sure that something bad had happened to Eric. Vic and Danny too. She was going to be lost in the wilderness until either the men shooting at them found her or she faced a large four-legged animal that wanted to devour her. A very ugly death any way she looked at. She took stock of everything in her life. Her family would find out she wasn't what she claimed to be. Her true finances would prove she was a big fake, a giant failure.

Something rustled in the distance and she didn't dare dream that it was Eric finally returning. Barely there rays of moonlight shone through some branches and made for an extra creepy backdrop. It was scary how much noise the forest made at night, all the nocturnal animals that hunted for food and all the insects that buzzed to life.

But what if it wasn't a four-legged animal out there? What if somehow the men who shot up their camp, grabbed Eric and forced him to her now? No, no, she might not know Eric that well, but she knew he'd never give her up like that. He was quiet. Honorable. She knew that from watching him during the attempted robbery and the resulting meetings before the hearing.

Still, she listened intently, nearly stopped breathing altogether. The cold night clamped down on her bones like a vice. The temperature wasn't supposed to go lower than the forties, but she was a California softie, and cold affected her.

Vivid memories blazed through her mind. Nine years old and fighting the current in a rushing river, getting tumbled every which way and getting hit by debris in the water. Latching onto a fallen tree and hanging on, then slowly making her way—inch by tiny inch—to the slippery bank. Her relief at escaping the raging water quickly died on the heels of the realization that she was alone in the forest, possibly miles from her family. The tears had come hard and fast. When she finally stopped crying, she had screamed for help. She'd screamed until her throat was raw and she couldn't scream anymore. The sound of the river had probably drowned her out. Cuts and scrapes had burned along every inch of skin. She'd wondered if the animals in the forest could smell her blood in the air the way that sharks could in the water. Would the predators hunt her?

A snap sounded nearby and brought Zoe back to the present. She clapped a hand over her mouth to keep from making a sound. Terror swirled in her center and tightened her chest, wrapped around her lungs and squeezed out every molecule of air.

"Zoe?" Eric's low voice cut softly through the quiet night, and Zoe let out a rough breath then pulled in the air she so desperately needed to survive. But her heart was beating too fast and she couldn't get a rhythm with her breathing. The oxygen came in too fast and went out even faster. Her chest constricted and she couldn't control the tight fist on her lungs. Could barely see as the world went topsy-turvy around her.

A second later Eric was there, kneeling in front of her and dropping the pack over his shoulder and sleeping bag under his arm.

His big hands closed around her shoulders. "Zoe! Jesus! What's happening?"

She shook her head, couldn't get any words out.

He stared into her eyes. "Look at me, Zoe! Breathe! Slowly. With me. In." He took in a measured breath. "Out." He let it out just as slowly.

Zoe locked onto his gaze, tried to follow. Tried to keep his pace. His hands felt unusually strong and she concentrated on his warmth and the security he offered. After a couple of minutes, the vise around her lungs loosened up and she managed to match Eric's rhythm until finally she could breathe easier.

Eric sat on his heels in front of her, concern evident in his beautiful eyes. She'd never noticed just how beautiful they were before now. Sure, he had the same blue eyes as his brothers, but she'd never really looked at them before this trip. Probably because she hated seeing what he thought about her.

"Are you okay? Better, at least?" he asked quietly. He handed over a bottle of water and she took a grateful gulp.

She nodded and took in a last deep breath. "Yeah. I'm okay. Asthma attack." Better than admitting hyperventilating from shear panic. "Thanks for helping." She handed back the water.

His eyes narrowed. "That was an asthma attack?" He looked around the forest. "Are you allergic to the outdoors?" She heard the unasked question in his tone. *Why agree to this trip if it might kill you?*

If he only knew. She waved away his question. "I'm okay, really." And she desperately needed a new topic. "Did you find Danny and Vic?" God, even if they hadn't been at the camp, what if one of those wild shooting sprees had cut them down at the hot springs?

"No." Eric shook his head and stood, tugging her to feet. "No sign of them. I think they're in the same situation we are. They're just on the other side of it as long as they went back the way we came." He stuck the bottle in his pack. "C'mon. I want to get as much distance as we can tonight."

Zoe's million questions had to wait two hours until Eric finally found a stopping point that made him comfortable, both with distance and scenery. He found cover between some boulders and the mountain. Gave new meaning to being stuck between a rock and a hard place.

"I should've stayed with you. Then we might've found them...and hiked back together," Zoe panted as Eric handed her some water.

"No offense, but unless you have master tree climbing skills, it wasn't going to happen, because that was the fastest way down." Eric chugged water of his own. "I used ten minutes to pack a bag for us and one for them in case they made it back for provisions. That machine gun fire carried through the whole forest so if they were at the hot springs, they heard it. Danny would check it out. He'd see the tents and think exactly what I thought when I saw them."

Zoe pictured the camp riddled with bullet holes and swallowed back all that anxiety waiting to bubble over the top.

"I wanted to be long gone by the time the men returned," Eric continued. "I didn't want to take a chance they'd hear me."

"We saw them split up. What if they find Vic and Danny?"

Eric shook his head. "Danny's not going to let that happen. He's smart, smarter than me when it comes to survival. He'll take care of Vic and he'll get help. I'm going on the theory that we survived those random shots so they did too."

She didn't want to destroy his hope since he had an even chance of being right. "What did you bring? You were gone forever. I thought something happened to you."

"Sorry. It took me longer to get back. I've got food, a Jet-boil, bear canister. The essentials."

"So now what?"

"Remember the treetop building we saw on the way up? The ranger station?" She nodded and he continued, "That's our new destination. We need to call for help. I brought my cell phone, but it's useless up here. They could have a two-way radio, maybe some provisions up there. Not sure."

A shiver raced down here spine. "Do you think those men will find our trail and come after us?"

He only hesitated a moment before nodding. "Yeah. I do. They didn't come all this way…go to all this trouble only to leave after one try."

And who else would be after them so desperately besides friends or hired guns of the men they planned to testify against. "You think it's related to the robbery, don't you?"

He pinned her with serious blue eyes. "Don't you?"

It just didn't make sense to her. "How? We left in the middle of the night. How would they know where we are? It's just not possible."

"There are other ways to follow people. Or track them." He glanced at her as he set out the sleeping bag. "I'm thinking GPS."

"You mean like a LoJack? They bugged Danny's Jeep?"

"That's my best guess as of now. I mean they might've bugged all our cars. Vic's was stuck in the garage. Yours was totaled. Mine hasn't moved since it's been parked at my apartment. Process of elimination and boom, they know who to follow." He motioned to the bag. "C'mon, let's get a few hours of sleep. When the sun comes up, we'll hit it hard. The sooner we get to the ranger station, the sooner this nightmare ends."

Zoe kicked off her boots and scooted into the bag.

"You might want to take off your jacket and save it for when you're out of the bag. Besides it's going to be tight in there with both of us. I don't think you'll need it."

"Except I'm freezing," she said.

"I'll warm you up."

He didn't have the least bit of sexual innuendo behind the words and Zoe almost took offense, which made no sense whatsoever. He didn't like her and she'd do well to remember that. Fact was they were stuck together, whether they wanted to be or not.

Zoe unzipped her jacket, wadded it up and used it as a pillow. At least it was good for something. Eric slid in next to her, his mass taking up most of the space. Zoe ended up packed between him and the edge of the bag.

"Here, lay your head on my chest. It'll be more comfortable." Eric adjusted his arm beneath her and before she knew what happened she was nestled within the strength of his muscular arm with her head on his chest and her legs tightly against his. Her lungs threatened to erupt again, but this time because she'd never been next to a body this hard. "Zoe, are you breathing?" Eric adjusted to see her face.

She sucked in a breath of air and caught the smell of him. The outdoors, a hint of sweat, but mostly just Eric. Something elusive…macho. Sexy.

"Better?" he asked.

She'd be better when this whole thing ended and she got back to her life. No way was she falling into some weird fascination with Eric after all this time, especially knowing how he felt about her. "Yes, thanks," she murmured. "How long do you think it'll take us to get to that ranger station?"

He was quiet for a minute before exhaling a soft breath. "I'm hoping day after tomorrow, but I'm not sure. It's hard to tell and I don't know how rough the terrain is going to be. We're kind of off-roading at this point."

Any hope Zoe had about getting out of this hell, sooner rather than later, vanished faster than a quarter in a magician's hand. All she could do was hope and pray that Danny and Vic got out safely.

Pulling her closer, Eric exhaled a soft breath. "Look, I know you're worried about Vic. But she's in good hands with Danny. He'll get her off the mountain and he'll come back with help."

Zoe nodded, needing to believe him for Vic's sake, then burrowed a little deeper into his side. Because she was cold, that's all. Not because she needed to feel the protection he so willingly provided. Not that at all.

ERIC OPENED HIS EYES. Still dark. Carefully he checked his watch, hoping to let Zoe sleep for as long as possible before waking her. He'd only slept about three hours and wasn't sure if she'd been awake or not by the time he finally passed out. They both had a lot on their minds. Zoe was terrified. He completely understood, but there seemed to be something else happening, an element he didn't know about. Her *asthma attack* was his first clue. More like panic attack. His little brother, Blake, had told him about the first day he'd met his fiancée, Abbey. They'd been trapped in an elevator and Abbey's claustrophobia had thrown her into an anxiety attack. Blake had talked her through it. Eric was glad he'd paid attention to Blake's description of the experience. He planned to keep a solid eye on Zoe from now on. Something he pretty much knew she was going to despise.

A sliver of moonlight split the trees and lit the pale smoothness of her face. Without makeup she looked barely twenty and he was pretty sure she was a year older than him. He itched to touch her skin, just to see if it was as soft as it looked. He took a second to breathe her in. Even after everything they'd been through, he caught her vanilla scent. It always made his mouth water. At this particular moment it also sent a rush of blood to his groin. That annoyed the hell out of him since they got along as well as a feral cat and a junkyard dog.

In sleep, she'd cuddled closer to him, actually wrapping her leg over his thighs and throwing her arm over his chest. Her body warmed his side and he adjusted a fraction to get more of her heat. Turning on his side, he tucked her tightly against him as if that action alone could protect her during the next few days. She stirred but only to burrow deeper into him.

Eric vowed in that second to keep her safe no matter what. She'd been through enough already with these shitheads. She might be a pain in the ass, but seeing her struggle to breath earlier gave him a little insight he'd never had before.

Zoe wasn't the always tough, take-no-prisoners woman she made herself out to be. Well, maybe she was to a certain extent. She protected her little sister and best friend with the same ferociousness that he protected his siblings, but when it came to herself...

Get to know her. The dumbass part of his brain that thought with his hardening dick clearly hadn't received the message. Zoe was not his type. He had nothing against strong, but he needed compromise. He liked agreeing not arguing. He liked doing things together, not being ordered around. She made it hard to find common ground, but if they got out of this alive, he wouldn't mind discovering whatever drove her to that panic attack earlier.

Yeah that was asthma and he had a second home on the Death Star.

Eric waited as long as possible, but they couldn't afford to get caught. He rubbed his hand along Zoe's arm. She was toasty warm. "Zoe," he said softly. "We need to get up."

"Mmm." She adjusted closer, pressing all those soft curves against him and sparking a fire that had already—to his frustration—fanned to life with very little prompting. One minute she annoyed the hell out of him and the next she made him hard. He took a last opportunity to stroke his fingers along her arm, soaking in her softness before the chance disappeared.

"Zoe, wake up."

She tilted her chin up and Eric figured she was awake, just slow to open her eyes. When she lifted her head at the same time he adjusted to see her face, their lips brushed together.

Eric froze, not ready to dive in, but not smart enough to pull away. Zoe didn't seem to have the same problem. Her lips grazed his a second time, warm and plush and hella delicious. It was innocent as far as kisses went. Well, innocent until she rolled him to his back and took over the kiss. This kind of strength he didn't mind. Not for a second. He didn't mind as she licked his bottom lip then licked into his mouth. He didn't mind the way she rubbed herself against his now very hard erection. He stroked his hands into the mass of dark curls and groaned at the silky softness of her hair.

He didn't know where the hell any of this was coming from, but damn if he was going to stop her, at least not for another minute or two, just another minute to feel her weight on his chest, her tongue stroking against his. He should've known this firecracker would spark just as brightly in bed as she did out of it. She stroked a soft hand over the rough stubble on his jaw and a little purr vibrated in her throat. The touch, the sound, the way she continued to kiss him with devastating lashes of her tongue revved him hotter. She slanted her mouth over his and kissed him harder, deeper, until they both panted for air. Despite wanting more, wanting all of her, his conscience prodded him. "Zoe," he whispered when she lifted a fraction for breath.

Her lips came down and she licked into his mouth again before freezing. Every muscle tensed up tight before she slowly pulled away and opened her eyes.

"Oh my, God," she whispered. "What just happened?" She scrambled off him quicker than a hungry fox chasing hens, but the sleeping bag was so tight she didn't get very far. If he didn't know better, he'd think another panic attack was on the way. "Oh my God!" She breathed out in a fierce whisper. "Did I...? Was I...?" She covered her face with her hands. "Please tell me I didn't..."

The fact that she couldn't finish a sentence really only made matters worse. Apparently, he was *that* disgusting. Perfect.

"Zoe, it was no big deal, okay. We were both asleep and not thinking straight. It was just a kiss." More like a dozen of the hottest, sexiest kisses he'd had the pleasure of participating in, but that news he'd keep to himself. "It's not the end of the world. I can survive it if you can." Better to gently lob the ball into her court that way. He checked his watch and figured now was the perfect time to change the subject. "The sun'll be coming up in a little while. We should have a granola bar, then pack up and head out. I want to be long gone by the time the sun hits the trees." Eric unzipped the bag and hoped that his dismissal of the kiss snapped Zoe out of her misery.

Most women were happy to kiss him. Hell…a few women went so far as to chase him. Maybe not like Danny, but he didn't have a problem in the dating department. His problem was carving the time around his job and finding someone compatible. He wanted a woman with ambition. Someone with her own goals and drive to succeed. So far the only ambition he'd seen in his dates went as far as landing a husband. Thanks, but he'd pass.

Zoe had ambition and curves he craved, and a brain on top of it all, but she'd made it abundantly clear that any attraction he felt was very much a one-way street.

The more he thought about it the crankier he got, which meant he needed to push it aside and focus on now. Today's agenda was fairly obvious. Find help and don't get killed in the process.

But when Zoe finally looked at him and he saw the faint redness of whisker burn on her face, a bolt of heat shot straight to his groin almost as if he'd marked her. A primal instinct unfurled in his chest, and the urge to drive inside of her and mark her a different way made his blood pump faster. He didn't doubt his ability to seduce her. The right words, the right touch… Too bad the timing sucked.

CHAPTER 17

VIC SNUGGLED CLOSER TO the warm body spooning her. The pressure of a strong arm over her hip made her feel safe and she clenched her ass against the hard erection between her cheeks. Tingles between her legs spread warmth through her veins. Shifting the hand on her waist to cover her breast, she sighed at the way she fit into his palm. A fresh jolt of heat speared through her. Memories of hot water and even hotter kisses bubbled from her sleepy haze, then gunshots. Her eyes snapped open with terror. She froze. Hard ground beneath her. Harder erection behind her. Cold air on her exposed forehead and Danny's hand casually on her breast. She swallowed as her heart ricocheted in her rib cage.

"Uh...Vic?" Her hair muffled Danny's low voice.

Shit! "Yeah," she murmured, removing his hand just as smoothly as she'd placed it and feeling the loss more than she wanted to admit when he pulled away from her. "Sorry about that. I was half asleep." She hadn't even been overly horny. Just deliciously warm in Danny's arms. Although, *now* she was overly horny.

She hadn't budged all night. Well, at least not the hours they'd spent sleeping, which now that the sun was barely up wasn't really that long. Also, *now*, she couldn't be more self-conscious if she *wanted* to be.

Her thought seemed to put the man in motion because the zipper swooshed and the bag opened enough for Danny to move away from her, bringing in cold morning air. She burrowed deeper into the bag, taking the last few moments of warmth.

"Here," he said softly.

She turned her head in time to see him stuff her clothes into the bag. "Give them a second to warm up. They're pretty chilly, but I think they're dry." He stuffed Zoe's things in next. "In case you want to wear Zoe's..." He'd already pulled on his jeans, but showed no sign that the cold bothered him. Getting another glimpse of his chiseled chest made her mouth water for a taste. Those were ridges and valleys she wouldn't mind exploring. "Did you sleep okay?" He whipped his T-shirt over his head and slipped his arms into his flannel shirt and jacket. The guy dressed in seconds flat and she was still buck naked in the bag.

Fortunately, they were going to roll right over his-hand-on-her breast part, which under the circumstances made perfect sense and appealed to her in a thousand ways.

"Yes," she said, "I slept fine. Kind of surprised actually after everything that happened." She wiggled into her bikini bottoms, not ready to wear another woman's underwear, even if that woman was a best friend. The sports bra was a different matter. She struggled into the tight elastic and settled it in place. Much better than a bikini top. And she had thick socks for her hiking boots.

Vic finished dressing and Danny rolled up the sleeping bag with the extra clothes inside. She looked around the area. It wasn't as dense as she originally thought and she felt all sorts of vulnerable.

"Here," Danny held out half a granola bar, his gaze catching hers and holding it as he watched her. Vic took the offering and felt her cheeks heat. She probably looked like shit with the scratches on her face and her hair a giant mess. Danny broke the stare and searched for something in his pack. "Have a few bites just so you're not starting on empty." He chomped on his half.

Vic washed it down with a few slugs of water from the bottle he handed her. He didn't need to tell her to conserve.

"I'm going to move as fast as I can," he said, zipping up the pack. He stood and looked her in the eyes again. "Tell me if it's too fast and I'll slow it down."

She understood his urgency and didn't want to be the one to hold them up. Maybe she didn't hike on a regular basis, but she worked out. Not that she had any illusions about how tough this was going to be or how dangerous, considering they had armed gunmen following them with intent to kill. Yeah, that thought had her checking out the area again. She grabbed the elastic band around her wrist and pulled her hair back into a ponytail. After last night's dip, it had dried in a mass of uneven waves. Ugh, no wonder he kept looking at her funny. He'd only ever seen it straightened.

Danny heaved the pack over his shoulder. "C'mon, let's head out. Stay close, okay?"

Didn't have to tell her twice. "Like a second skin." That comment only reminded her of last night and this morning, and she felt another flush burning her cheeks. She blamed Danny. She had the old Danny pegged. In fact, she'd bet her last paycheck that the old Danny would've jumped on last night's invitation at the hot springs with the finesse of a gigolo. But this new guy...he seemed completely conflicted.

Their hike continued over rough terrain off the main path and Vic wondered if she was losing her observational skills. In general, she'd become fairly competent when it came to reading people. Her job demanded it. She had to be able to understand her clients and know when she could push and when to back off. She'd learned to interpret facial expressions, speech patterns and body language. Working in public relations meant evaluating people so she could figure out how best to help them. In all her years in PR, she'd never seen a more drastic change in personality than Danny. Sure, she had clients who got sober and changed a lifestyle to stay sober, but those people mostly remained the same at their core.

Dealing with the old Danny had been easy, because her instinct had been to stay away. He was everything she always wanted, and the things she always wanted usually hurt her the most. Now she had this new guy at her fingertips. A man who took time out of his day to talk to a lonely old neighbor. A man who risked his life for family and friends. A man who felt so much pain that no matter how hard he worked, he couldn't get past it.

For the first time in her life, Vic wasn't sure how to proceed.

WARM SUN BEAT DOWN on their heads and after three hours of navigating rough terrain off trail, Danny stopped for a break. Vic had kept up, though he could tell she was hurting. She'd found a thick stick and used it to negotiate and balance over big boulders and fallen logs. Still, covered in dirt and sweat with the scratches on her face and bruises on her neck, she looked like a model for an adventure magazine. Her long strawberry blond hair had gone up in a ponytail before they'd started and wavy strands escaped to frame her face. He'd only seen it stick straight and this natural version lit him up like wildfire. The way her thick hair had framed her face and fallen in soft crazy waves over her breasts this morning had made him itch to touch it, touch her. He'd purposely avoided looking at her for months, dreading anytime he got together with Brendan and Casey because he knew Vic might be along for the ride. Now he couldn't stop watching her. It was up to him to make sure she got out of here alive and that required his full attention.

He'd intentionally traveled away from the stream, so it took time to cut back for water, but if the strategy kept them safe then it was worth the extra time it cost. "I hear it," Danny said of the rushing water. "Should be right through those trees there."

He plowed ahead, concentrated on the idea of quenching his thirst and refilling and purifying the water bottles.

"Danny." Vic's voice didn't sound her usual confident self. In fact, she sounded freaked out and—

The distinct rattle stopped him in his tracks and his breath rushed out of his lungs in a single whoosh as he turned and saw the snake. If the brown and gray scales hadn't given it away, certainly the sound did. Somehow a giant rattlesnake planted itself between them on the narrow path. It slowly reared its head back while its tail rattled a warning. Vic's eyes widened in paralyzing fear.

"Danny," she whispered with both plea and panic.

"Stay still. It's okay." Frantically, he looked for a stick. Something to whisk the slithery beast far away, but nothing but pebbles and leaves surrounded him. The fucking thing slid closer to Vic, its tongue slithering out, tail rattling and head up ready to strike.

Danny did the only thing he could do. He kicked dirt behind the thing to get its attention. It spun and struck before he even blinked. *Shit!* He jumped back, felt the contact at his ankle. The fabric tugged as its fangs stuck on his jeans. "Shit! Shit!" Danny tried to shake the beast off and the reptile waved in the air like thick rope.

Vic screamed just as the rattler got its fangs free of his jeans and landed on the dirt, but it reared toward Danny again. Vic moved forward, swung out with her stick and sent it flying five yards off the path. The snake hit a tree, landed on the ground and slithered deeper into the brush.

Danny's heart chugged along like a bullet train. He glanced at Vic, who stood shaking, her eyes scanning the area, no doubt making sure the snake was long gone. As each second ticked by, she shook harder.

"Vic?" Danny took a step toward her and she spun, her eyes wide.

"It got you. Oh my God, sit down, we need to get the venom out. I read an article that the more time a snake has to strike, the more venomous its bite." She bent in front of him and Danny lifted her up by her shoulders.

"I'm okay," he told her. "I've got boots on." She didn't look too convinced and Danny crouched. "C'mere. Look." He pulled up his jean bottoms and showed her the two small indentations where the fangs had hit leather. His jeans had two small holes as well, where the snake got stuck after striking.

Vic sighed and closed her eyes, then cupped her hands over her face. "Oh my God. That was… I can't even…"

Standing, Danny set his hands on her shoulders. "Hey, it's okay. You did great. Glad you had that stick. That's what I was looking for before I distracted the stupid thing." Vic nodded, and a second later, she launched into his arms and wrapped herself around him like Cling Wrap. He felt the fine tremors that shook her slim figure. Danny refused to think about how good it was to hold her so close. Never in his life had he wanted more time—time to comfort, to learn, to be with someone—than he wanted right now with Vic, but her scream might've given away their location and he didn't want to linger in this spot too long.

"I saw it grab onto your leg and I…" Her mumbled words got lost in his shirt and he held her tighter.

"One for the books, that's for sure," he said quietly. He rubbed his cheek against the softness of her hair. She smelled like hot springs, sweat and forest. A total turn-on. The way she fisted his T-shirt made him feel even more protective of her. "You okay, babe?" *Shit!* The endearment slipped out before he caught it. He hadn't *babed* anyone in months. Swore he wouldn't do it again. It was as if the word itself acted like some kind of magnet. *Babe-ing* a lady somehow equated to exclusive.

But Vic didn't move, didn't act as if she'd even heard what he said. "Do you think we'll run into any more of those?" she asked.

"Sure as hell hope not, but anything's possible. Just keep hold of that stick you've got. It was a good find out here. I'm gonna look for one too. Definitely useful."

A minute later, Vic abruptly pulled away. After pinching the bridge of her nose with her eyes squeezed shut, she finally looked up at him. "You're sure it didn't get you…like through your boots?"

He couldn't help think there was something on her mind besides the potential snake bite.

"Scout's honor," Danny told her and gave her a rogue smile to help ease her worry.

A tentative grin barely curved her lush lips and a hint of sparkle returned to her warm brown eyes. "I'll bet ten bucks you were never a Boy Scout."

"I'll take that bet. In fact, let's double it. I could use some coffee money." He gently tugged her ponytail.

"No way. I don't believe you." She still stood right in front of him, and Danny couldn't help but breathe her in. The all-natural version of Vic appealed to him on every level. Hell, any version of her did.

"You can ask anyone of my brothers or my parents. I was a Boy Scout." He couldn't seem to disengage himself from her, still had his hands on her shoulders.

Her eyes narrowed. "For how long?"

"One meeting. I refused to wear the outfit so I got booted out pretty fast." He grinned again. "But I was a Boy Scout that whole night, so… You can't take it away from me." Vic shook her head, but her smile widened and Danny took some solace in changing her mood. "Seriously," he said, losing his grin and squeezing her shoulders. "You were amazing just now. Do you golf?"

She shook her head. "No, why?"

"Because that was a beautiful stroke you used to get that rattler out of here. I—" *might have to take you out for a round when we get home.* He just barely kept the words in his head because he wasn't taking her anywhere once they got home. But they *were* getting home. All four of them. He wasn't leaving this mountain without his brother and Zoe. He backed up, let her go.

"What were you going to say?" She cocked her head, her pretty brown eyes narrowed as if she saw right through him.

"Nothing. C'mon, let's get that water and keep going. We've got a lot of trail ahead of us." He held his hand out, not even sure where the impulse came from. He just knew he wanted her close.

She nodded as she placed her hand in his. The confidence she put in him humbled him. No one had ever relied on him before. Not for anything major. He was the wildcard, the free spirit, the guy always up for a good time. At least he used to be. Now he had to get this right, and he only had one shot. His brother—hell his best friend—and both Vic and Zoe depended on him. He wouldn't let them down.

CHAPTER 18

ZOE FOLLOWED ERIC UP the steep mountain toward the ranger station. Sun glared down on them, bright and hot, California's summer at work and not a breeze to speak of. She only hoped the heat translated into a warmer night when the sun went down. Had Eric thought to pack any of those bath wipes? If not, they were going be past ripe by the end of day.

Sweat trickled between her breasts and she heaved for every breath. They'd lost sight of the ranger station roof a while back and only tall sequoias and conifers filled her line of sight, but Eric promised he knew which direction they needed to go.

A couple of things kept her mind off the misery of this hike. The first was being happy to be alive to make it this far, and the second was the near constant replay of this morning in her head.

She still couldn't believe she'd kissed him. God, she'd done more than kiss him. She'd practically attacked him. Heat flooded her cheeks for the tenth time as she picked her way through the rocks and fallen logs that slowed them down. Eric had purposely stayed off any paths, hoping the trees and terrain kept them hidden.

"Need a break?" Eric asked with a glance over his shoulder.

"Nope," she huffed. Yeah, she was struggling, but damn if she was going to slow them down. Besides, she didn't want to stop because then she'd be forced to talk to him. Or look at him. And those lips. Heat infused her face again. Good God, when would this stop?

It wasn't as if she hadn't noticed how gorgeous he was before now. She glanced up, shaking her head, because damn he had one fine backside. They'd stripped off their coats a while back and he looked delicious in a gray T-shirt, jeans and boots. But it was hard to be attracted to a guy who looked at you as if you carried a disease or two. His feelings toward her couldn't have been clearer if he'd written them across his forehead with a black Sharpie.

Zoe Turner, you're a pain in the ass.

Besides, who wanted a guy so straight-laced and tight? He rarely smiled. She'd even joked with Casey about giving him the nickname Mr. Serious. As in, he was in serious need of stick removal from his butt.

Not that she was perfect. Far from it. But at least she knew how to cut loose on occasion. She'd been the ultimate rebel growing up. Sneaking out had been her favorite pastime. She'd needed the space from her overprotective, ever-repressed parents. Her actions had probably led to her sister's need to go the opposite direction and be a people pleaser. Vic had helped pull Casey out of her shell, and Zoe always appreciated that.

So, what would Vic say once she discovered Zoe had practically molested Eric in his sleep?

"Score!" Zoe muttered the word softly in her best impression of Vic and smiled at the silliness. A rock flipped beneath her foot and almost sent her on her ass before she righted her balance. Okay, maybe molested was too strong a word because it's not as if he fought her off. Nope, she'd woken up to his hands in her hair and his tongue stroking against hers and…

Zoe looked up at the midday sun. Was it getting warmer out here? She needed to go back to the other thing taking up space in her head. Her job. More like the job she wouldn't have upon returning home…provided they got home. She looked behind her for the thousandth time, making sure it was clear. There was no way the real estate agency would keep her on after this. The owners had been itching to get rid of her for over a year. All four of the homes she'd had in escrow the past eighteen months had fallen through. She'd spent a fortune on marketing and promotion, but nothing stuck. She never should've spent so much on her condo and a car when she'd originally sold her first house. Reality hit her between the eyes. Find a new job. Sell her dream house…and so much for replacing her car with another BMW.

How would she explain everything to her family?

Up ahead, Eric had stopped at a big boulder and shucked off his pack. "Here," he said, handing her a bottle of water when she got close enough. "Need to stay hydrated."

"Thanks." She took his offering and gratefully sipped the tepid water, purposely avoiding eye contact. Hell *any* contact! She was terrified of even touching him again. How the hell was she going to share the sleeping bag another night or *multiple* nights after this morning?

Eric stuck his own bottle in the pack, sighed and rubbed a hand over his bristly jaw. The scruff covered most of his bruising. "Look, can I talk to you for a minute?"

Uh-oh. Not a good conversation starter, but may as well pile on something else for her to worry about as they hiked. "Sure. Hit me." She braced herself.

He looked out to the trees. "You haven't said two words to me since this morning." When he met her gaze, she caught a vulnerability she'd never seen before. "I know we need to keep talking to a minimum, but you haven't said a word even when we take a break. This is going to be hard enough, but it's going to be impossible if we can't or don't get along."

Zoe nearly stepped back, stunned at his assessment of the situation. "I...I mean, we..." She exhaled and started over. "We totally get along, okay. I have no problem with you." With the tiny exception that she struggled to keep from staring at his amazing eyes when she had him in front of her and his gorgeous ass when she had his back.

"You don't act it. Look, if this is about this morning, I told you, it was no big deal."

She almost laughed out loud, but managed to keep her voice as quiet as his. "Sure, not a big deal to you. Did you ever think that maybe I'm a little mortified? I mean...to wake up with my tongue in your mouth..." *Dammit!* She spun and put both hands over her face. Sometimes she was so very good at putting her *foot* in her mouth. The idea was to *avoid* mentioning specifics.

She heard Eric move closer, then his big hands rested on her shoulders.

"Zoe. Did you hear me complaining?" He felt so strong behind her and so warm.

She wanted to lean into him just for a second, just to feel his chest against her back, but she stood her ground. "No." But she didn't see him overjoyed with it either. "I'm just embarrassed, Eric. I have no idea what to say to you after that." She faced him, sucked up her pride and looked him right in the eyes. "Put yourself in my shoes. You wake up one morning next to your future brother-in-law only to discover your tongue is in their mouth and you don't remember how it even happened." Except she did, kind of, remember. She'd been dreaming about him. Her subconscious got her into this mess.

He barely cocked his head. "So, you're not mad at me?"

"Why would I be mad at *you*? I'm mad at myself and embarrassed as hell, that's all."

Nodding, Eric studied the ground before meeting her gaze. "What if I even the score?"

"What does that mean? How would you even the—"

He kissed her. Just bent his head and set his lips on hers. He tasted warm and delicious, smelled like outdoors and distinctly Eric, something macho and elusive. She closed her eyes, nearly moaned at the contact, at the perfection of his lips molded to hers. At some point his arms came around her because she found her hands against his chest as he parted her lips with his tongue and snuck in for a taste. Something blossomed in her gut, a feeling, expectation, hope, and it grew into a ball of raging arousal. Just as the scrape of his whiskers burned a delicious heat onto her skin, Eric pulled back a fraction, leaving her wanting more. "We're even now," he murmured.

"Even?" she whispered. Her lids fluttered open as her lips tingled. What were they talking about?

"Yeah. We're even now. Except I think I want you to owe me, so…" He dipped his head and took her lips again before she processed his words. He was kissing her a second time so she'd kiss him a second time? Is that what he meant? Did it matter at this point? Good God the man knew how to use his lips. This kiss wasn't as gentle as the first. This one wanted more. Hell, demanded more. He hauled her closer, close enough that she felt the growing iron bulge in his jeans. Talk about burning her up from the inside. Zoe gave in to the bliss of his mouth against hers and sank deeper into the web of seduction swirling around them. One of his hands speared through her hair, just like this morning, while the other held her hip and kept her tightly against him. Their tongues dueled, danced, mated, separated and mated again. Hormones. Pheromones. Hell, lightning. Whatever the hell was happening between them had never happened to her like this before. His whiskers burned a path around her mouth and she didn't give a damn.

Eric was neither shy, nor hesitant. He acted like a man who knew exactly what he wanted. The hand at her hip curved over her ass and the low groan vibrating between them might've belonged to her. Zoe didn't know how much time ticked by, but when Eric finally pulled away she was breathing hard and more turned on than she'd been in years.

Staring into her eyes, Eric seemed just as bowled over. "So, yeah." He stepped back. "No reason to be embarrassed." He backed up more. "Just a kiss. No harm, no foul." He turned away and focused on his pack so quickly that Zoe blinked. What the hell had just happened?

She put her fingers against her still tingling lips. She'd never be able to look at him the same way again. It was one thing to kiss him from a dream...

But now? It was something else to kiss him when they were both wide awake and thinking straight.

Seriously, had he only kissed her just now to make her more comfortable? Or did he...*like* her? She didn't see how that was very possible. One thing she did know...her lips still buzzed and— whether she wanted to or not—and it couldn't have been worse timing—she craved more of him.

WHAT DID YOU DO? The same four words kept pounding in Eric's head like a never-ending drum as they continued their trek up the mountain. Temporary insanity? It would never hold up in court. Random spontaneity? Definitely, but why? He was the guy who thought everything through, the brother who deliberated before deciding. And he'd gone totally off-road with that kiss. He'd come up with a half-baked reason on the spur of the moment and

Zoe actually seemed to buy it. Even the score. Yeah, right. It might've worked—might've—if he hadn't gone back for seconds. I want you to owe me. So frickin' stupid. And while they were literally running for their lives.

But he hadn't liked the cold shoulder from her all morning. Maybe they were expending a ton of energy during the climb up the mountain, and yeah, under the circumstances a lot of talk probably wasn't a great idea, but a little conversation wouldn't have killed her. Instead they'd moved for hours without a single word between them. It'd driven Eric insane. Especially after that high-octane kiss this morning. The kiss that totally jacked him up and put Zoe in a brand new light. He wasn't exactly sure how to process this new information either.

He checked his watch. They'd been on the move for hours. Time for a meal. They needed energy if they planned to keep this pace to the ranger station. He found a shaded spot with a few big boulders, enough space to sit for a few minutes and regroup. "Let's stop here," he said, pointing to the spot and shucking the pack off his sore shoulders. He'd split the food and water between his pack and the one he left for Danny. Extra clothes didn't make the pack for anyone. It was strictly survival gear. "You want to pick lunch?" he asked, unzipping the pocket holding the bear canister with the meal packets.

She shrugged and sat on a nearby rock, sighing as her ass hit the stone. "You can choose. I'm so hungry I could eat your boot, so anything works for me."

Eric couldn't help the grin kicking up his lips. He never would've expected that answer from Zoe. He pulled out the pack on top. "Fettuccini Alfredo with chicken. Sounds good to me." He checked the back. Eighteen grams of protein. Perfect. "You okay sharing out of the same bag? It's two servings in here, but I don't have any bowls, so…"

"I think sharing out of the bag is the least of our problems right now." She kicked off her shoes and peeled off her socks. Her toenails were painted bright pink. A girly girl 'til the end. Something close to guilt shot through his chest. If he'd grabbed her sleeping bag instead of his, she would've had clothes to change into, but he'd been so bent on getting away from the campsite, he hadn't thought about it then. Hadn't realized that the lump in the sleeping bag he'd left for Danny was Zoe's clothes. He should've grabbed her pack in the front of the tent too, but he'd been so concerned about leaving Danny gear that he hadn't thought about that either.

Sweat gleamed on her skin and damp spots darkened the blue cotton T-shirt she'd slept in. He doubted she'd want to sleep in that tonight. But the alternative was nothing and…he needed to absolutely stop this train of thought.

Eric concentrated on the bag and found the Jetboil. Thank God Danny had purchased two of them. The container housed the fuel that connected to the bottom of the cup and made it simple to boil water. Danny had figured to get ten boils for each liter container and he'd brought along two extra small fuel tanks just in case. Eric had stuck one in each pack along with the extra fuel. He had enough water to boil for the meal and leave each of them with another cup to drink. They'd have to head toward the river for a refill and purify before they continued up, but he felt safer off the trail.

Twenty minutes later, after boiling the water, pouring it in the pouch, mixing up the contents and letting it sit for thirteen minutes, they took turns digging into the food.

"This isn't half bad," Eric said around a bite.

Zoe sat next to him on a big boulder, every molecule of attention focused on the steaming bag of food. "Mm, it's great." She shoveled more into her mouth. "No complaints."

He forked more pasta then tilted the bag toward her. "This from the lady who'd have been happy with a leather boot."

She nodded. "True." Then dug in for more. He didn't know if the mountain air or the exertion the last few days, but her scrapes had almost completely healed, leaving faint pink marks where the scabs had come off.

They ate in silence for a bit as they killed their hunger. Zoe had gone off into the woods with the handi-wipes to commune with nature while the pasta soaked, so they still hadn't said too much to each other. After today, he admired the hell out of her. She hadn't bitched or moaned or asked for any breaks. She'd simply kept up with him with a single-minded determination. Nothing had gotten her down. Sure, she'd recovered from the shooting a long time ago, but in the last few days she'd had not only a severe car accident, she'd been attacked and had shot a man. This girly-girl was a major fighter...and he liked it.

Eric figured he'd dive into safe territory conversation. "How's Casey doing?"

Zoe smiled around her bite then swallowed, clearly proud of her reality show winning sister. "She's good. Working hard. Writing new songs. She said she's working on something with Brendan, but they're going to hold onto it until she's out of her current contract."

Eric lifted an eyebrow. Brendan had told him that writing a song with Casey while she was under contract meant that her producer would see the majority of the royalties. "That could take a while." Like ten years if he remembered right.

"Ha. Trust me. We know." Zoe licked her fork clean and stuck it in a plastic baggie for the next time. "Sometimes I wish she hadn't been a part of that stupid show. I mean I'm happy they found each other and all, but... I think Brendan definitely got the better deal now that he's working with Seger."

Eric still couldn't believe his brother hadn't shown his mega-famous boss his music before trying out for the reality show that changed his life. Reality television was bad enough, but add in several attempts on your life on national television and it made for a hell of a clusterfuck along with crazy ratings. "I hear what you're saying, but trust me, the guy was crushed. He called after it happened and... Well, let's just say I'd never heard him sound that devastated before. Although that was before he talked to Seger and everything turned around."

"It's kind of weird having a famous sister all of a sudden," Zoe said.

Nodding, Eric finished the last of the meal and folded up the empty bag. "I totally understand that. First my sister hit it big, now little brother is making waves." He shook his head and felt that all too familiar strangle of failure tighten his chest. All of his siblings had found their passion if he included Danny with this adventure business and Blake earning his PI license. Just because he made a healthy living as a lawyer by no means translated to success for him. Success meant doing something you loved. Something meaningful. Eric had neither of those things. The pasta turned in his stomach.

"Yeah, Casey told me about your sister. I wouldn't have made the connection otherwise. She had success out of the gate. Personally, I'd just as soon not go through what you and your family went through to get it."

"Yeah, well, we weren't thrilled about it either." Sometimes the kidnapping felt like a million years ago and sometimes it felt as if it happened last week. Sometimes his dreams were so vivid, the whole thing could've been happening a second time. He still relived the beating he took after coming home and being attacked by the men who'd invaded his house. Still heard the sounds of his parents being beaten when they got home. To this day he got sick to his stomach remembering it all. He didn't especially like talking about the kidnapping. None of his brothers did. Of course, his sister had worked through her anguish by writing it all down. That little endeavor had turned into a critically acclaimed sleeper hit that not only launched her directing career, it had skyrocketed her to stardom. Talking about his siblings didn't bother him at all, hell, he was crazy proud of all of them. He just didn't like his own physical reaction when it came to comparing success or happiness.

"Out of the gate is relative," Eric added, needing the change of subject. "Jess struggled for six years before making that film. She lived in a hole-in-the-wall studio apartment in Hollywood and barely made ends meet working eighty-hour weeks. She deserves all the success she can handle."

"It's sweet that you're so proud of her. Sometimes I see Casey's success and..." Zoe trailed off, shook her head. "Well, I feel the same way. She deserves all she can handle too. It's almost intimidating to have such successful siblings, ya know?" She canted her head a fraction as she studied him. That laser vision of hers seemed to see right through him, because he sure as hell *did know*. She put her socks and shoes back on.

He snorted. "Not like you're not as successful in your own business." He knew the neighborhood she lived in and the car she drove... Well, at least before the accident. Her commissions as a realtor for even one upscale property earned her enough to last a lifetime if she invested right.

"Yeah." She hopped off the boulder. "Can I help you with anything?" she asked, ending that topic in a quick second.

Eric eyed her, sensing he'd somehow pushed a button, but he dropped the subject. "Not much to do." He stuffed the trash into his pack. "We need to head toward the stream and refill. I'm worried they'll be searching for us closer to the water. They know we need it."

"You really think they were able to track us this far?"

"They found us last night, didn't they?"

She nodded. "Yeah, but we weren't hiding our tracks. It's not like we thought they'd follow us up here."

"Well, now we *do* know." Which meant they had to count on being followed from here on out. Eric was sure they'd left tracks last night during their race to escape the bullets, but there'd been no thought of anything but staying alive then. What if the men saw the ranger station too and figured it to be their destination? "Bottom line, we have to be extra cautious."

Zoe nodded again, her eyes downcast. The nod turned into a headshake. "I can't believe this is even happening. Makes me so mad."

"If it's any consolation," Eric said, "I know exactly how you feel."

She met his gaze, her cool eyes assessing like they always did. This time Eric didn't feel any judgment, he felt a kinship, almost a friendship. "I guess we should go," she finally murmured.

He agreed. They still had a long way to the ranger station. Eric hefted the pack and they trekked about a mile back toward the stream and right along the main path. He put his finger to his lips to remind Zoe to be extra quiet. She nodded and followed him to the water's edge.

While Eric refilled the bottles, Zoe splashed some water on her face and cleaned up with a bath wipe he'd thrown into the pack.

A noise on the path downstream had them both jerking toward the sound. Eric motioned Zoe back toward some brush and they tucked behind a fallen log and waited. When they didn't hear anything, Eric peeked up and sighed.

"It's a deer."

Zoe lifted her head and peeked too, and a smile broke out on her face. It transformed her features. Her blue-gray eyes sparkled. "There's a whole family," she whispered. "Look."

Eric was more interested watching her reaction to the deer, but he forced his gaze to the stream. Two adult deer and three babies were drinking from the water. The picture could've been a postcard. The serenity almost made him forget why they'd hidden in the first place.

A second later, the deer scattered back into the forest. Birds flew en masse from the treetops and leaves rustled from their sudden departure. Heavy footsteps crunched through the brush.

Eric yanked Zoe behind the log and tucked her up close. Her breathing turned erratic and he put his hand over her mouth. He leaned right next to her ear and whispered softly, "Breathe deep. Hold it. Let it out slowly. You can do it." She nodded and held onto his wrist with a massive grip.

CHAPTER 19

DANNY STOPPED IN HIS tracks and Vic nearly ran into his back. "Did you hear that?" he asked.

She looked out at the surrounding trees. Sunlight blasted through the branches in long rays. Birds chirped and bushes rattled with little woodsy creatures she didn't necessarily want to see. She'd been so concentrated on following him that she hadn't heard anything out of the ordinary. "What?"

"Not sure. I thought I heard something."

"Maybe it was my stick on the rocks?"

"Maybe." But he didn't sound so sure. "C'mon, let's move." He started a fast jog...quiet enough to avoid detection, but fast enough to cover distance. Vic barely kept up. After twenty-five minutes, she thought her lungs might burst and her thighs and calves might rupture. Maybe it was the altitude or maybe it was just negotiating the uneven terrain. Danny glanced a look over his shoulder and slowed to a stop. "Let's take a breather."

Bending over, Vic sucked in air. "Thank God. I need...a minute." Every muscle screamed in protest and her lungs burned for air.

"Sorry, ba—Vic. Sorry."

There it was. He'd almost called her *babe* again. She hadn't minded it the first time, which completely shocked her since she usually hated that word. Casey's ex had called her *baby* or *babe* and Vic had cringed every time. But hearing Danny say it somehow made her a complete marshmallow. Maybe it was the tone or just hearing...*something* in his voice she couldn't pinpoint. But obviously he was making a concerted effort to avoid saying it, which didn't bother her one way or the other. She just found it interesting. What did the word mean to *him* if he had to keep correcting himself? Or maybe he was worried about the definition of the word in her mind?

Still, her brain wanted to know what it meant that he used the word a second time and tried to cover it. Was it because they'd shared the sleeping bag last night? Or had their kiss in the springs affected him more than she thought? She seriously doubted it.

Although, it had been a hell of a kiss. Every time she remembered it, she literally tingled. As if all her senses craved the way he made her feel.

This was Danny. The player. Yes, he'd changed, but the fact remained that the guy had a track record a mile long. She knew. She'd researched him. Well, as much research as one could do considering her best friend was engaged to his brother.

"C'mon over here," Danny said softly. He led the way to a massive sequoia and dropped the pack.

Vic sat at the base of the tree and took a few grateful chugs of the bottled water she'd been carrying. "Any idea how much farther before we get back?"

"We still have another night out here, if that's what you're asking." He gulped his own water and wiped his face with the bottom of his T-shirt, baring all those amazing abs that made her mouth water. Good God the man was ripped. She loved his habit of wiping sweat with his T-shirt. It was almost the equivalent of a free Chippendale's show. "We might make up the extra miles we're going because we're moving faster, but I can't guarantee it." His Adam's apple bobbed as he sipped more water.

She didn't even want to know how far out of the way they'd gone to dodge the trail and anyone hunting them.

Hunting. The word gave her shivers. It also pissed her off. Made her more determined than ever to keep up with Danny and get the help they and Zoe and Eric needed.

Her stomach rumbled, needlessly reminding her that she was hungry. "Any snacks?"

Danny pulled out a bag of almonds and dried cranberries. Vic took a handful, her eyes glued to the strong forearm stretched toward her. Remembering that arm wrapped around her this morning, the way he'd warmed her from head to toe—inside and out—sent a burst of heat into her face. Her pulse thumped faster and she looked away. Every inch of him attracted her, always had, but keeping him in one box in her head was getting harder and harder the more they talked.

Vic munched on the nuts, and let her aching feet take her mind off Danny. A fly buzzed her head and she swatted it away.

"Let's say we get back to the visitors center after another night out here," she said. "How are we going to find Zoe and Eric when they're headed in the opposite direction?"

"Helicopter." Danny said the word with such conviction that hope spread in Vic's chest. Maybe all of them would get out of this mess alive.

"Do you think we'll make the hearing on Monday morning?" she asked.

"Damn fucking right we will." The anger in his voice matched the jerky movements he used while shoving the water and snacks back into the pack. He shut his eyes and sighed. "Look, even if we don't make it back by Monday, they'll just postpone the hearing." Danny shot her a sympathetic grin. "Ready? Or do you need another few minutes?"

She sure as hell wasn't going to slow them down more than she already had. After wiping dirt off her ass, she grabbed her stick. "How many camping trips like this have you done?"

He started out and Vic followed. "This is the first one here, but I've gone out with friends to other spots, mostly local to L.A. We never did anything more than a weekend."

They trekked for another fifteen minutes and Vic wanted to do something to get Danny's mind off the weight of the situation. "How is your adventure company coming along?" she asked quietly.

Danny glanced back at her with questioning eyes, but he answered. "So far so good." He held a branch back as she walked past. "I had the idea to approach big corporations and pitch the concept of using an outing as a team building exercise. It's worked better than I thought it would. I've been slammed with water sports dates for months. Had to hire some guys to take on the overflow."

"Wow, good for you." So how big did he want to grow his business? "Have you thought about promotion on a larger scale?"

"Like how large?"

Vic shrugged. "Like using-a-PR-firm large."

Danny smirked and rolled his eyes. "I thought your firm mainly handled famous people."

"We handle anyone who pays our fees. Imagine how big you could grow with some well-placed promo. We could get you into some major events, bring you into contact with even more companies who want that same team building experience. When we make you famous, we make your business famous."

He considered that for a minute. Then from out of nowhere, he smiled. A smile she hadn't seen in many, many months. Danny was already gorgeous, but the flash of straight white teeth and the way his to-die-for blue eyes crinkled in the corners made Vic's heart skip a beat. He was simply breathtaking when he grinned like that. "I see you're going all out with the phrasing. '*When* you make me famous.' I don't remember saying I wanted to be famous. I'd be happy with a successful business. I'll have to think on it. It's an expense I hadn't planned on. If I grow really big, the tours could lose the personal touch, and quality control becomes an issue.

"I have a question for *you*," Danny said, giving her a sidelong glance. "Why did you go into PR work?"

Vic liked that he wanted to know. "No one's ever asked me that. I guess I like the idea of helping people realize their full potential. Most people don't see a big picture or end goal."

"So, you think everyone has an end goal that's worth hiring a PR firm?"

"Not everyone, no. But there are special people." She lifted an eyebrow indicating she was talking about him. He was special, he just didn't see it because he was too busy beating himself up.

"Most big pictures cost a chunk of change," Danny replied, avoiding her silent insinuation."

"You've heard the saying, you've got to spend money to make money." The path opened up and they walked next to each other.

"Exactly. And I'm not sure I have the money to spend. I've already had to buy more equipment, which means storage space, hire more guys, yada, yada. The list goes on." He gave her an assessing look as they continued to move. "But I'll think on it."

She chucked his arm. "You do that. I'll be waiting for an answer." Her boss would love Danny. They could do so much with a face like that. She saw the campaign already. They could package him as the next incarnation of Bear Grylls. He could charge extra for personally guided tours. They could probably pitch a reality show to the networks too. A face and body like Danny's deserved screen time. Yep, she saw the whole thing. Now she had to make Danny see it.

As soon as they all got safely home.

ZOE COULDN'T REMEMBER THE last time she'd been this uncomfortable. Every muscle protested being still for so long. Eric and she had been stuck for hours behind the huge fallen log upstream. They hadn't moved an inch, barely even breathing as the men settled in thirty yards downstream.

The first few minutes of panic, of thinking these men would find them and shoot them at point blank range, had robbed her of breath. Somehow Eric knew that setting his hand over her mouth would center her, get her focused on something besides sheer panic. She'd concentrated on the smell of wood and man, the outdoors mixed with his particular scent. It was the second time she'd fallen apart in front of him and the second time he'd come through for her.

She wanted to be stronger, wanted to prove she wasn't a big sissy, but every time she turned around, it seemed she cracked under pressure.

The men talked, their voices too low for Zoe to understand. For some reason they'd settled right in that spot.

Now, after lying on her side for so many hours, the whole right side of her body had fallen asleep and every other muscle screamed in agony. Her empty stomach growled and her parched mouth craved the water that was just yards away. She turned her head the slightest bit and locked gazes with Eric. The sympathy in his eyes killed her. She didn't want it, except she knew everything she was feeling was on her face. He squeezed her arm and kissed her temple, not making a sound, but letting her know he understood.

Instead of the pain, she concentrated on Eric. The feel of his hard body behind her, the knowledge that he'd already saved her once and together they could handle anything. She took comfort in the solid beat of his heart at her back, the way his palm flattened against her stomach centered her. She just didn't know how long she'd last.

How long would they remain trapped? They had no way to move without the guys with guns hearing them. More time ticked by and Zoe didn't think she'd make it.

What were these guys waiting for? What were they doing in one spot for so long?

Eric adjusted, his lips next to her ear sent an arrow of sexual awareness straight to her gut. "You can do it. A little bit longer."

She barely heard his whispered words, but she still didn't understand how he planned to get them out of there. Until a few minutes later she heard the men moving farther into the forest.

"Now," Eric whispered in her ear. "Follow me. Take every step exactly where I take it. Understand?"

God, she didn't know if she could even move at this point. Her whole body had fallen asleep. But she couldn't stay here all night either. She nodded.

Eric sat up, moved into a crouch, looked over the log and motioned her to do the same. Zoe forced herself up, and pinpricks of pain shot through every nerve. The sun would be down soon, but plenty of light still made them giant targets. Eric walked along the tree line where big rocks softened their steps. Quiet was good. Being in their line of sight if those guys came back wasn't so good, but she understood the problem. Walking in the forest meant a greater chance of breaking twigs and branches. Staying on the rocks gave them a softer exit. They just need to get far enough away before they ventured into the woods again. Luckily the stream got louder as they followed it up and a slight bend gave them natural forest cover.

Twenty minutes after they started, Zoe grabbed his arm and pointed to her bladder. Eric nodded and gestured toward some brush a few feet away.

She widened her eyes. He expected her to go *that* close?

Eric read every unuttered word on her tongue and nodded before turning his back.

Well, fine. At this point she almost didn't care anymore. So, with no toilet paper or handi-wipes, Zoe took that few steps into the brush and answered nature's call. Her relief nearly brought tears to her eyes. She heard the telltale sound of Eric answering the same call. A couple fallen leaves did their job and Zoe was back on track.

One thing down, now they needed to disappear a little bit more, eat something, then catch a few hours of sleep.

Zoe couldn't guess how far they trekked before Eric finally cut into the forest. She took the last opportunity and knelt at the rushing stream. Rinsing her hands in the freezing water made her fingers numb, but who knew when they'd get back to it.

Even in the forest, Eric kept his movements precise. It felt as if they'd been moving for hours when he finally stopped near a mass of gnarled trees.

"We'll sleep here," he said softly already laying out the sleeping bag.

"Do you think we're safe here?" She looked over her shoulder into the growing darkness. Giant trees loomed overhead like monsters ready to swallow them whole. She kept alert for any sound. They couldn't be more than a few miles from their starting point.

"I think those guys are down for the night and if we don't rest we'll pay for it tomorrow. Besides, I don't want to lose my way and head the wrong direction. That ranger station is our only hope at this point." With the sleeping bag out, he sat on top and pulled the pack between them, motioning her down across from him. Eric handed her half a granola bar and a half full bottle of water. "We're as safe as we can be for now."

"Why do you think they stopped in that spot for so long?" she asked, taking a small bite. Her stomach growled, demanding she eat the whole thing in three bites, but Zoe planned to make it last. She opened the pack to see what else he'd brought.

"Not sure. Maybe they're waiting for a sign, or maybe they thought they'd catch us. Either way, I think they're going to wake up in the morning and head up." Eric bit into his bar, his strong jaw chomping the nuts and honey.

"You think they've figured out we're going to the ranger station?" Zoe spotted a pack of bath wipes and breath strips. Her heart soared at the simple pleasures.

Eric nodded. "I do. And if we don't get there first and call for help then we're screwed."

UNDER THE COVER OF darkness, Danny came back from a one-man excursion. He'd circled a wide area of their camp, making sure they were safe for the night. He'd found a small clearing within a circle of massive trees and felt confident it would hide them well enough while they slept. Clouds blocked the moon and despite the heat during the day, the temperature dropped a few extra degrees. A symphony of crickets welcomed him back. "It's just me," he whispered, headed toward Vic who was already tucked away in the sleeping bag. Danny shucked his jeans, boots, jacket and T-shirt and slid in next to her. She'd rolled up her clothes and used them as a pillow. Which meant. Shit. She only had on her sports bra and bikini bottoms. He should've expected it, but the shock of all that smooth skin shot his dick to immediate attention.

He knew better than to touch her. Last night had been a lesson in self-control, one he'd barely passed. Tonight he didn't have an excuse. It might've been cold, but it didn't compare to cold on top of wet clothes. Last night, they'd needed each other's body heat. He could rationalize getting up close and personal for survival. But now...

She faced him and all he could do was think about touching her. Shit. He had to get over this fascination with her.

"Aren't you tired," he asked, zipping up the bag. He followed her lead and rolled up his jacket to stick under his head before lying on his back. His whole right side connected with every silky inch of her. He didn't trust himself to face her.

"Yeah, but I'm nervous too," she said softly. Not once had he needed to remind her to keep her voice low. It was just one more thing to like about her. "Been trying not to think about why we're in this situation. Praying my brains out that Zoe and Eric are okay wherever they are." She needed reassurance and that was one thing he could provide.

"Eric's smart. So is Zoe. I'm sure they're doing fine." He had to believe that. Thinking anything else would break him. His whole family was close, but Danny didn't take for granted the bond he shared with Eric. The kidnapping had taught them the value of every minute and every family member. Just as Danny knew Eric would die trying to save him, Eric knew Danny would do the same. His gut tightened with Vic and Zoe's lives in the balance as well.

Danny dared a glance at Vic, just then realizing something. "Thanks for trying to take my mind off everything today. I appreciated the distraction."

She lifted up, rested on her elbow with her head in her hand. "I wasn't kidding, you know. We could build you up, build your brand, your business to epic proportions. One day, you'll find yourself sitting on an empire."

He turned then, couldn't help himself. "How come I don't see it quite that big?"

"Because you need vision." Her smile gleamed in the darkness and a dimple peeked out on her cheek. "Let me guess... You only saw you and your brother leading the tours. Maybe a couple extra guys here and there like the ones you've already had to hire, but basically a two-man operation, maybe a van to accommodate bigger parties, equipment expense, but other than that, something manageable. *I'm* talking about growing to the extent of running the business from an office. Having enough guides, beach kiosks, equipment and transportation so that you're making the money without having to do every expedition yourself."

He hadn't ever pictured it that way. "I don't know that I'm an office kind of guy."

She shrugged a shoulder. "That's fine. The point is to do the tours you want because you want to, not because you have to. The point is to get business booming enough so that you can do whatever you want with your life. You can expand to merchandising with T-shirts, hats and other accessories. Maybe even get sponsors. The idea is to make money while you vacation or sleep or whatever."

Yeah...that didn't sound half bad. He nodded. "I told you I'd think on it. I mean it."

Danny wiped his hand down his face, rubbed at the bristles on his cheek. They should hit the visitors center by late afternoon tomorrow at the latest. Keeping a good pace had made up for the extra miles, and he intended to stay clear of the main trail in case the men hunting them had it staked out. Eventually they'd have to show their faces, and Danny hoped like hell they didn't nearly kill themselves getting through the forest only to be killed as they emerged for help.

"Danny?" Vic's voice was so soft, he barely heard her and with the moon hiding behind the treetops, her face stayed hidden in the shadows. Something in the way she said his name made his gut tighten more.

"Yeah?" An owl hooted in the long pause before she spoke and Danny breathed her in. Her hair still smelled like the hot springs.

"I know last night we were wet and cold and needed to keep warm, but…do you think you could hold me tonight too?"

The ballsy chick had suddenly become shy. Hell, like he could say *no* to any version of her? Didn't matter that he was in for another long ass night of fighting his libido. She was scared and cold and he didn't have a choice.

"Sure. C'mere." He lifted his arm and she cuddled into him. No way to avoid all that smooth skin now. Her thick hair draped over his arm and her hand rested on his chest. He forced himself to keep his hands to himself.

Torture.

Absolute fucking torture.

"Do you think they'll be waiting for us when we get off the mountain?" The quiet seriousness of her tone hit him like a punch. He'd been stupid to think this hadn't scared her as much as it scared him and if nothing else he owed her honesty.

"Yeah. I think it's a real possibility and we need to be prepared for it."

She wrapped a spectacular leg over his thigh and Danny took a steadying breath to calm his suddenly racing heart and slow all the blood rushing to his dick. She was absolutely killing him.

"Do you believe in living life to the fullest? In taking advantage of every minute because you don't know what's going to happen next?"

He of all people knew how quickly life changed. He'd made it a point to do the things that made him happy, but doing that had led to someone's death.

"Yeah, living life to the fullest can sometimes be a double-edged sword, but I know what you mean."

Vic lifted up and eased over him, her face inches from his and all the lust Danny had been trying to keep at bay showed itself in the continued hardening of his dick. She placed one hand on the top of his head and the other against his jaw. Stars twinkled overhead and the sudden intimacy of the caress hit him like a club.

Danny had never ever been terrified of a woman, but Vic scared the shit out of him. A year ago, he'd been all over the idea of getting together with her. He'd waited for his phone to ring for weeks after giving her his number. And she'd never called. He'd bounced back with Nikki.

Now Vic was on top of him and he knew exactly what she wanted.

"Vic…" He wasn't sure what he meant to say, but she didn't give him a chance anyway. Her lips brushed over his whisper soft, like the fucking best dream he'd ever had in his life.

He could've stopped her, could've moved her off him, but he tasted her hesitancy…and her need. So, he let her kiss him. Let her tongue slide into his mouth and mate with his. She tasted minty, must've found the breath strips stowed in the bear canister. He hadn't touched her in the hot springs and now he let his hands grip her waist and run up the expanse of her smooth back. He craved her like air, like a parched man needed water.

"You are the best kisser," she murmured.

Jesus, Nikki had said almost the exact same thing and suddenly all he saw was a bathtub of blood and Nikki's sightless eyes. Breathing hard, he cupped Vic's head and pulled her off him.

His heart slammed against his ribs. He didn't know what to say or how to say it. She deserved honesty. "I'm not sure I can do this." Just because his lower half was in the mood didn't make his brain on board.

She didn't shy away. Her gaze locked onto his. "Okay… Not sure what just happened, but I'm not her," she said softly, stroking her thumb along his whiskered cheek. "It's okay to live your life even if she chose not to live hers." She watched him like she could read his mind. Maybe she could. "You won't break me, Danny. I'm strong. But I'm scared as hell and I could really use some comfort tonight. I won't ask anything of you that you're not willing to give. I promise you that." She waited for him, watching him with serious, hopeful eyes. The most beautiful dark eyes he'd ever seen.

There was definitely a reason they couldn't do this though. "I don't have any condoms, Vic. I won't take a chance like that."

"Even if it's a chance I'm willing to take?" A sad smile lifted her lips. "Does it make a difference if I tell you birth control is covered?" She lifted her arm like she was showing off her bicep. "It's a little implant. Handles all those pesky hormones." Putting her hand down, she stroked her fingers against his scalp and revved his pulse faster. "I will admit, I've never had no-condom sex before, but if I'm going to die tomorrow then I don't really care."

Everything she said pretty much blew his mind and it took him a minute to process the information. "Well, we're even there. I've never gone without a condom." Jesus the thought made him even harder. He never thought he'd go bare, mainly because he never saw himself having kids, much less settling down.

A smile crept across her face and she adjusted on top of him, rubbing along his erection and making him suck in a rush of air. "I see the idea isn't dimming your interest." She kissed him before any semblance of a reply hit his tongue. "I just want to forget for a little while," she whispered at his lips. "That probably makes me a bad person, but—"

This time he kissed her. She wasn't bad at all. She'd been busting her ass to keep up with him all day and he respected her for it. He never would've pegged her as tough, but she was. All those times he'd seen her in dresses and heels, he never imagined she'd handle the rough terrain without some serious TLC. His planned five-day semi-easy hike had turned into a life and death survival of the fittest.

He wouldn't fool himself into thinking this was for Vic, because he wanted her too. He'd wanted her from the first day he'd laid eyes on her. Time to take her at her word. She wasn't asking for anything he wasn't ready to give. Plus, the lady had a point. They had no clue what tomorrow would bring and if his parents—and the kidnapping—had taught him anything, it was live for now.

CHAPTER 20

VIC MADE A POINT to stay quiet when she really wanted to sigh and moan and let Danny know that every kiss and every stroke made her that much hotter for him. The way he palmed her head and owned her mouth shouldn't have surprised her but it did. Probably because the guy had dodged her for so long. Amazing how the tables had turned with them.

Nikki still messed with him from the grave, and Danny didn't deserve that kind of haunting. Vic wanted to free him tonight. Not that she wanted him to go back to his old ways, but a happy compromise couldn't hurt.

She meant what she said about needing to forget, about needing some comfort and distraction to the reality of what lay in front of them.

Danny clearly excelled in distraction.

His calloused hands ran across her skin, pebbling every inch as he stroked and caressed. He pulled her thighs apart so she straddled his hips and every time he pushed against her, she swallowed back the gasp in her throat.

Finally, *finally*, she was about to be with the man she'd dreamed of for months. He'd been in her head since the day she met him, all cocky smiles and twinkling eyes. Adorable, sexy and chivalrous. She just couldn't fall for him. Shoving the thought aside she concentrated on now. On his searching hands and voracious mouth.

She needed to get her bikini off and his boxer briefs off. Yeah, she'd checked him out. What red-blooded American girl wouldn't? The man belonged on the cover of a magazine or in a boy toy calendar.

Breathing hard, he held her head and lifted her a fraction of an inch. "You're sure?"

"God, yes." She didn't think she'd ever been *surer* of anything in her life. She wasn't one to get mushy or emotional because of sex. She didn't sleep with every guy she dated, but she also made it a point to keep herself happy. She was an adult and adults had sex. Simple. And mutual.

She just couldn't remember a guy who lit her fuse quite the way Danny was doing now.

Just by staring at her with those amazing blue eyes, all that male intensity focused on her, he made her hotter. He didn't go in for another kiss immediately. He watched her as he adjusted her position, hooked his thumbs into her bikini and pulled them down inch by tiny inch.

Her breath caught as his warm calloused palms glided over her ass and a low rumble vibrated in his chest. Every gentle caress sent more heat flooding through her and they'd just barely gotten started. "Don't forget the top," she breathed the words at his lips, so glad Eric had thought to toss in breath strips to the pack he'd left for them.

"Hell no," he muttered. "Can't forget that." He hooked the tight elastic in his thumbs and stripped it over her head, sending her mass of hair in every direction. "God, your hair is gorgeous. I had no idea it was so wavy, so soft." He speared his hands along the sides and took her mouth in a searing kiss, stroking his tongue past her lips and revving her hotter and faster than any man before him. She sucked on his tongue, couldn't get enough of him in her mouth and he held her head as he slanted the angle to get more of her. Breathing hard, he finally pulled back and stared into her eyes. She thought he might say something, but he just watched her until bringing her mouth back to his. This time, he slowed it down. Way down. Slow, sexy, deep kisses that made her crazy with wanting him.

One big hand cupped her breast and she arched into his palm. "Just like that," she whispered, lashing his ear with her tongue. His erection twitched beneath his boxer briefs. Those needed to go. Pronto.

"Your turn," she whispered, hooking her fingers into his

waistband and tugging off his underwear. He helped. Damn, this sleeping bag was tight. Gliding her hand slowly up the inside of his bare thigh, Vic took immense pleasure in his unsteady breathing and the way his hot gaze never abandoned her. She'd been watching his ass for days now, enjoying the view and the way he filled out his jeans with an amazing butt and muscular thighs, but feeling that power now, beneath her, almost scared her. The man was every bit as lethal as she knew he would be.

Though it was crazy cold outside, their combined heat had them sweating. They teased each other with small nips and quick tastes that turned into breathlessly long make-out sessions before starting all over again. A quick gasp caught in her throat when he pinched her nipple. She returned the favor, flicking a nail over his nipple and feeling the resulting drop of precum against her stomach.

Foreplay was highly underrated.

When she eased her hand over him, when she finally took him into her palm, he tensed and sucked in a rough breath. She wanted to see him so badly, taste him. But the only way to make that happen was to unzip the bag and no way was she losing her warmth to cold outside air.

Still, she gripped him tighter, saw his gaze get hotter in one fleeting shaft of pale moonlight. "If it wasn't so crazy cold outside, I would be crawling off you just to see if what's in my hand isn't a figment of my imagination." The man had a serious package. Serious. He twitched in her hand and she stroked up and down in a slow glide.

"Not so fast," he murmured, easing his hand between her legs. He groaned when he discovered how slick she was. She sucked in air when he found her clit and circled it before slowly pushing a blunt finger inside her.

They continued to tease each other, mixing it up with soft kisses, desperate kisses and none at all, just breathing each other in while their hands did all the work. Nerve endings fired to life in a dizzying rush of colors behind her eyes. She rode his fingers, pushing down, searching the perfect rhythm. His lips caught hers again, fanning the flames that threatened to take her out. So good. So close.

"I need—"

Before she finished the sentence, he positioned himself right at her entrance and they both froze. He was huge and hard and Vic's breath seized in her lungs.

Danny slowed it down with a soft kiss and pushed a fraction inside her. Vic gripped his shoulder, breathing through the fullness. "Easy," he whispered. "You got this." He grinned against her mouth and Vic bit his bottom lip, feeling a crazy euphoria that had nothing to do with sex and everything to do with his smile. Knowing she got one out of him a second time felt like crossing some invisible finish line as the winner.

She pushed down a fraction, taking him at her own speed, lifting up and dropping down inch by slow inch. "Oh my God," she breathed. She chalked it up to too many months of celibacy. The only action she'd seen in almost a year was the purple vibrator in her night table drawer.

Danny gripped her hips and pushed up inside her, hit a bundle of nerves that sent a hot spark of electricity arcing up her spine. "Jesus." He stopped moving and closed his eyes.

"What? What's wrong?"

"Nothing. You. This. *Shit!* Sorry. Give me a second or I'm gonna come like a fucking teenager." He pulled her mouth down and kissed her again, distracting them both with the brilliant play of his tongue against hers while he held her hips completely still.

Just because he stopped her moving didn't change her velocity to a long overdue orgasm and every heart-stopping kiss took her closer to the edge. Every heartbeat throbbed between her thighs and prolonged sweet agony. Long minutes ticked by and every cell screamed for release. "I can't wait," she huffed softly. "Need you. Need to come." She moved then. A quick series of strokes that hit a spot deep inside, and she balanced on the line of total meltdown and unprecedented bliss.

"Vic, shit, so fucking good."

His guttural words set her off. Her muscles tensed and she reached that perfect place before the free fall happened. One more slow motion stroke took her there. The internal explosion rocked her like a mushroom bomb. Waves pounded through her with mind-numbing euphoria. She bit his shoulder to keep from screaming, felt the hot stream of his orgasm fill her as her internal muscles clenched around him. The waves hit over and over until finally subsiding to small ripples.

Small aftershocks shook her limbs as she lay—deadweight—on Danny's chest. Night air cooled the sweat on her face and shoulders. One strong hand cupped the back of her head and his arm wrapped around her waist and held her close. His racing heart matched the beat of hers.

Neither one of them said anything.

What the hell did she say after that kind of sex? She didn't want to move a muscle. Just wanted to stay right here on his chest, breathing him in, feeling his strength all around her.

"Danny?" she mumbled into his shoulder. "Think I can stay here for a while? Just like this?" He was still semi hard inside her and she didn't want to lose that feeling either.

He nodded, stroking his warm palm up and down her back. "Yeah. I'm cool with that." His low voice vibrated in his chest. One hand stroked into her hair and he rubbed her head in a scalp massage that would've made her purr if she dared to utter a sound.

She was in trouble. She recognized the emotion squeezing her heart. She'd sworn to herself that she wouldn't go through this again. She'd vowed never to trust a man and yet all it took was twenty-four hours and she trusted Danny with everything she had. Fear and panic had a way of opening doors better left closed.

DANNY COULDN'T THINK. NOT with Vic on his chest and not because she was heavy. Nothing had actually felt more perfect then having her on top of him. Her soft curves meshed right into him like puzzle pieces. Her warm breath wafted across his neck and her heart beat in time with his. Her soft hair sifted through his fingers as he stroked through the long strands.

Bright stars twinkled overhead in the clear half of the sky, and a barely-there breeze rustled the leaves high above. If he had to describe *perfect*, this moment might rank as that. He was still semi hard inside her, still coming down from his high, and having her breathing steadily on his chest brought him a peace he hadn't experienced in… He couldn't remember how long. Maybe never.

She'd made him forget everything and he hadn't thought that feat possible. All he'd wanted was to feel her, taste her, sink inside of her until everything disappeared, but he hadn't thought that might really happen. He'd been wrong.

"Can I ask you a question?" Her soft words puffed warm air across his skin.

"You mean *another* question?"

He felt her smile. "This is an easy one." When she shifted and playfully bit his jaw, his dick twitched inside her. "What's it like being in a big family?"

Danny hadn't expected that. He shrugged. "It's good. It's great. It's nice knowing there are people who have your back no matter what." Damn. He forgot she was an only child. "Bet you had it good though. You didn't have to share anything. I had to share everything, and not just with one kid, but with four."

She nodded, and slowly ran her hand along his side as if she might memorize him by touch. If she kept doing that—hard ground or not—he was going to roll her over and make love to her the way he really wanted to. Except, holy shit…make love? When had sex become *making love* with anyone?

"I don't think I would've minded sharing," she said, bringing his thoughts back to the topic. "I don't know. That's probably a lie. I can be a little selfish sometimes." She shifted and looked at him. "Let's keep that our secret, okay?" Her smile slayed him.

"My lips are sealed." He pulled an imaginary zipper across for good measure.

"Not so fast." She unzipped his lips. "These are too good to keep closed." She brushed her mouth across his, slow and sinful, before pulling back and resting her head on his chest. Crickets buzzed and another breeze ruffled her hair.

With so many siblings, Danny couldn't even imagine what it would be like to be an only child. "Okay, so you didn't have siblings, but you probably had a ton of friends."

It took her a few seconds to answer. "Not really. Not until college," she murmured. "Both of my parents worked, which meant I usually had a babysitter pick me up from school." She shot him a fleeting glance with a smile that was more cover up than genuine. "I was the poor kid in a rich school and somehow everyone knew it. That made me tainted goods, I guess. I was invited to just enough parties to know that none of those kids were ever going to see my tiny house." She glanced up and lifted her eyebrows. "Wow. TMI, right. Hey, well, me and my computer…we were like *this*." She crossed two fingers together, then shrugged a shoulder. "I'll admit it. I was weird. Probably why I grew up to be weird."

Their upbringings couldn't have been more opposite. "I would never describe you as weird." Danny stroked his hand down her bare back, amazed at her softness. He'd never had a conversation while actually inside a woman. By this time, he'd be in a bathroom, disposing of a condom and cleaning up so he could get the hell out.

"How would you describe me?" She rested her chin on his chest, gazing at him with dark eyes as if this were any other random conversation.

He had to quit thinking about the tight clasp of her body and focus on answering her. He remembered that night in the market and it made the first two easy. "Bold. Fearless." Right now in his arms. "Beautiful." He couldn't forget how hard she worked in a high-pressure job. "Ambitious." He could probably come up with more, but didn't want to get in too over his head. "Should I keep going?"

"Oh my God, no. It'll probably be all downhill after that." She chuckled softly, stroking a gentle finger along his jaw. "But thanks. I like all those words. I thought you were going to say something more along the lines of…obnoxious, adolescent or the ever-adorable ball buster. One of Zoe's favorite words, I might add."

A grin kicked up his lips.

"See," she said, her eyes sparkling with a smile. "Now you want to start over, don't you?"

He shook his head, ran his fingers through her hair. "Nope. I stand by my original assessment." His grin faded. All those wasted months during the reality show of thinking she'd come to him like every other woman. But she wasn't like every other woman. She stood out. He'd known it before the attempted robbery, but her bravery continued to bowl him over.

He adjusted the sleeping bag to better cover her shoulders and the movement pushed him deeper inside her. Sucking in a breath, he clenched his jaw to fight the blood rushing south. Should've known this might happen. She was too tempting, too soft, too damn delicious. God, what he wouldn't give to really taste her, open her legs and lick her until she screamed his name, begging him…

Fuck.

She was so wet and warm, so unbelievably tight that his brain was turning to mush. He wanted nothing more than to drive so deeply inside her that the world simply disappeared.

She shifted, clenched internal muscles and made him harder in the process. "Mmm." The small rumble in her chest vibrated straight to his balls and she adjusted to take him deeper. She burrowed into his chest and bit his clavicle. Not hard, but with enough force to seriously wake up his whole system. She licked the spot as she lifted a fraction and dropped down on him. Every nerve fired to life a second time. Only a few minutes had passed, but it was long enough for him to recover and go another round. A round he hadn't been planning on mainly because the distraction made them vulnerable.

But no one told Vic, and she continued to move over him with long, slow glides that ate away at Danny's thought process and made him focus completely on her. The way her hard nipples pressed into his chest, how her hair tickled his skin and her soft lips brushed over his, before opening for his tongue. Over and over she rode him, her warm breath wafting along his cheek, her lips grazing his in a barely-there touch.

She slayed him and he went down without a fight. He couldn't touch enough of her soft skin, couldn't drive deeply enough inside of her to quench the hunger. He'd never burned like this before, never needed like this. He couldn't even pinpoint what he needed most, but it was there, eating at him as her internal muscles clenched him harder with each thrust.

"Feels so good," she murmured at his ear, her voice husky. The sound spurred him on. When she licked the shell of his ear, he nearly lost it.

Possession.

He had to have her in the most basic, elemental way. It went soul deep.

A groan rumbled from his chest as he rolled them over, bag and all, until he had her under him. Cupping her head in his palm, he took her lips in a kiss hot enough to set the sleeping bag on fire.

Then he moved, pumping deep and hard into her welcoming heat, looking for sanity when everything was so crazed. She wrapped her legs around his hips and locked him in tight, moved with him in a perfect combination of rhythm and energy. Buzzing started in his balls and sizzled up his spine and every consecutive thrust drove him closer to release. She froze and the tiniest squeak sounded in her throat as he continued to take her. Pressure mounted and his balls tightened, signaling his impending release. Her internal muscles clenched around him, milking him as she came. Danny didn't hold back as his climax exploded, pounding in utter perfection as he continued to move inside her, until just the tiniest ripples ran through him. Instead of collapsing on her—which he nearly did—he rolled back to his side, taking her—and the bag—with him. *Jesus.* When had anything like that happened before?

Uh…never.

Breathing hard, they both lay still, sweaty and satiated.

"Wow," she said against his neck. "That was… Wow."

Fuck. It *was* wow. And that couldn't be a good thing.

CHAPTER 21

DARKNESS HIT FAST BENEATH the clump of trees, and a pang of remorse hit Eric over the head. He hadn't intended on being so blunt, but he didn't want to sugarcoat the possibilities. Fact was they had no clue how many people were hunting them or where they were. He didn't even know for sure if Danny and Vic were safe or if Danny managed to get the pack Eric had left for him in their tent. What if Danny and Vic were already dead?

Nausea twisted his empty stomach. He couldn't think that way. He had to stay positive. If anything, the other two were safer because Danny was the more experienced outdoorsman. It wasn't as if they'd heard any other gunshots after the initial rounds that destroyed their campsite. Although he had no idea how far sound carried or if he'd even hear any other shots miles away. Or if they'd used a silencer.

Stupid fucking thoughts. He needed to focus on now. On doing what he needed to do to keep Zoe safe. Keeping Zoe safe entailed that he stayed strong, so even though his stomach twisted into tight knots, he forced himself to have the other half of the granola bar he'd split with Zoe.

She came out from a cluster of bushes ten yards away and Eric continued where their conversation left off.

"We can't afford more than a couple hours sleep," he told her softly after swallowing a bite. "We need to stay ahead of them." He hated the shadows beneath her eyes, hated the furrow between her brows. She didn't deserve the stress after everything she'd already been through.

She nodded, sucked on that lower lip then took a sip of water, her gaze bleak. "What happens if we get there, but there's no way to call for help?" She took off her shoes and set them next to the sleeping bag.

Eric appreciated the question, but had to believe there was a way to call out. They wouldn't build those stations then not give them any communication. Didn't make sense. "There'll be a way," he said. "There has to be."

He opened the sleeping bag and motioned Zoe inside before taking off his boots and following in behind her. They'd been lying down for hours without moving an inch, but the fear of getting spotted, the mental stress and the physical exhaustion of quietly bugging out of the area had wiped them both out. Eric put his arm out and Zoe cuddled close. She smelled like lemons. The pleasure on her face when she'd found the citrus bath wipes was the best thing to happen all day. She fit against him as if she belonged there, and Eric wrapped her a little tighter.

"Thank you," she whispered, her grip firm around his waist. The soft sincerity in her voice had him adjusting to see her face.

"For what?"

"For centering me out there. For somehow knowing what was going to calm me down when *I* didn't even know what would." She looked up at him, her stormy blue eyes full of uncertainty. "For packing bath wipes and breath strips and...I don't know...for being so calm during this whole thing."

Eric adjusted on his side, stroked a few curls off her cheek. He didn't know what to say to that. He sure wasn't feeling especially calm. Before anything witty or intelligent came out of his mouth, her gaze roamed to his lips and he decided he didn't need words at all. Leaning closer and slanting his head, he brushed his lips softly across Zoe's. She pressed against him harder and the hand around his waist, curved up around his nape and held him tightly in place.

She tasted warm. And minty.

He opened his mouth wider to get more of her, to inhale her and she met every stroke of his tongue with her own. It only took a few seconds for his tired body to rev into action. His dick sparked between them, hard and heavy. Zoe threw a leg over his and rubbed against him, setting off rockets of need behind his closed lids. As much as Eric wanted her, there was one thing he hadn't packed for this trip.

He pulled back, breathing hard, holding her head steady as she blinked open heavy eyes. "As much as I'd really love to continue this—" He shook his head, stroked his thumb across the soft skin of her cheek. "I'm not sure now is the best time."

She gave him the tiniest quirk of a smile. "Casey's always said my timing sucks."

Eric leaned in and kissed her again. Soft, sweet, just a few more nibbles because she was so damn delicious, before finally pulling away. "Zoe, if we didn't have to be so quiet, if I had even just one condom in that pack, you'd be in serious trouble." He rolled to his back and took her with him so she rested, again, in the crook of his arm.

She leaned up, dragged a gentle finger over his bottom lip and his dick responded to the touch like a rocket launcher ready for takeoff. "Really?" She seemed honestly surprised with his words when the evidence was clear behind his zipper.

"Yes, really." He brought her head closer and kissed her again, just to prove his point. One last sweep of his tongue in her mouth, one last taste of her before they got a few hours of sleep.

When she pulled away and tucked up tight next to him, Eric felt a whole new wave of need to protect her.

Although he didn't know how the hell he was going to sleep with his dick as hard as the trees surrounding them.

"Zoe," he said softly. "Tell me something about you I don't know."

She adjusted to see his face. It took her a second to come up with something. "When I'm stressed, I like to soak in a hot tub with a glass of wine." She sighed. "What I wouldn't give for those two things right now. What about you?"

"What do I do for stress?" When she nodded, he scratched his itchy jaw. "The gym. Definitely the gym. A game of basketball with my brothers is good too."

A coyote howled far away and Zoe clung tighter. "Tell me something else," he said, hoping to distract her. "Like...what's your favorite meal?"

"Favorite meal? Hm." She thought about it and yawned. "Okay,

I don't know about a favorite meal, but the best meal I had was actually at your parents' house when they had that barbeque before the holidays. Obviously, Casey was going to be invited because of Brendan, but I thought it was really nice of them to invite our whole family. Anyway, your dad grilled a salmon. Oh my God, best dinner ever."

Eric remembered that night. It had been hard to keep his eyes off Zoe. "You wore a pair of black jeans and heels with a red sweater."

She lifted her head. "You remember that?"

"Yep." Hard to forget the way she filled out those clothes. Shit. This talk was supposed to be getting rid of his hard on, not making it worse. Rubbing a hand down her arm, he resettled her against his side. "Goodnight, Zoe," he said softly.

She yawned again. "G'night." Her breathing evened out within a minute.

Too bad he couldn't knock out as fast.

Stars glittered overhead next to a cloud-covered moon. Crickets chirped in a never-ending insect chorus. The beauty of nature had taken a backseat to the drive to survive. Eric didn't think the men hunting them had any plans to keep them alive if they found them. They sure as hell hadn't wasted any time shooting the hell out of the campsite and that was without checking if anyone had been in the tents. He hadn't been gone that long or been that far away when the bullets exploded. He'd have heard someone call out. But no. The devastation at their campsite wasn't accidental, wasn't just some crazy lunatic sitting on a trigger for fun.

Eric finally wound down enough to relax and close his eyes. Zoe had locked herself around him again in her sleep, throwing her arm around his chest and her leg over his thighs. A half smile curved his lips. He hadn't expected the heat they sparked when they came together. It made him wonder how hot things could really get if they took their time and focused solely on each other.

DANNY OPENED HIS EYES to discover dawn was just breaking through the trees. Shards of light cut through the branches and barely illuminated the area. The peaceful morning twilight did nothing to ease his worry about the day ahead. Taking a minute to enjoy the softness of the woman in his arms, he breathed in the undeniably intoxicating scent of Vic as she slept, spooned up next to him just like yesterday morning. She had her hand over his, cupping the fullness of her breast. He itched to slide his fingers over her silky soft skin.

It was wrong that one of the best nights of his life with one of the bravest and most amazing women he'd ever met had to be on the hard forest floor in near frigid temperatures. A hell of a way to break his self-imposed celibacy. He never would've done it if she hadn't phrased her worries out loud. Just like Vic, he was only human too. Denying either one of them hadn't made sense.

But, holy shit, he never imagined that going bare was going to be the extreme high that it was. He'd nearly come the second she'd adjusted on top of him and every inch farther inside her had him struggling to hold it together.

Although, if neither one of them had participated in no-condom sex until last night *and* Vic had an implant, then the chances of STDs or pregnancy dropped to miniscule proportions. Which meant he could do this again with her and not have to worry about two of the things that scared him most.

It didn't, however, protect him from the first thing that scared him most.

Yeah, he'd heard her tell him she wasn't out for anything permanent. No promises, no attachments, but Nikki had said the same thing too, that first night.

"Sure, baby, just for fun. I'm not looking for a mister." But she'd attached herself to him like Velcro on felt. Her words had been a line to get under the sheets and he'd fallen for them.

The analogy brought his brain back to last night and the way Vic destroyed his composure with the absolute best sex of his life. He couldn't remember the last time he'd come so hard.

Thinking about last night gave him morning wood that screamed for relief. Too bad they didn't have time. He'd love morning sex with Vic. He'd love to watch her sleepy, sexy eyes fill with heat and desire as he pushed inside her hot core with long, gentle strokes, working her up until she begged him for more. For harder, faster, deeper.

Shit. He was *not* doing himself any favors right now.

He killed the urge to kiss Vic awake. He couldn't undo last night and didn't especially want to, but that didn't mean he intended to continue where they left off. All he could do was take her at her word. She needed him last night and, yeah, maybe he needed her too, but it was a new day and they had shit to do.

Fighting the urge to squeeze the softness of her breast one last time, Danny eased his hand away, stroking down her midsection over creamy skin. Jesus, she was so fucking soft.

"Vic," he whispered in her ear. "We need to get going."

"Mmm," she moaned softly, turning on her back then promptly cuddling up close to his chest.

Damn she was pretty. Her hair curled into a mass of strawberry-blond waves that slid through his fingers like silk. He'd never seen it anything but straight and it made him realize there was a lot he didn't know about her.

The qualities that stuck out most: Unpredictable. Adventurous. Sexy. Brave. Not a bad list to start with.

"Vic." He squeezed her shoulder and finally, because he couldn't help himself, he stroked some hair out of her face and brushed his thumb along her cheek. "Wake up, ba—" *Dammit!* "Wake up."

She opened gorgeous brown eyes, eyes that immediately turned hot and liquid when they met his gaze. But she blinked and when she looked at him again, she was the cool, in charge female he'd originally met last summer.

"Hi," he said softly, fighting the urge to touch her again. "Sorry to get you up so early, but…"

"S'okay." She stretched next to him and Danny took the opportunity to scrounge for his boxer briefs near his feet in the bag. He came across her bikini and handed it over. Brushing up against all her creamy skin was a lesson in temptation, one he barely passed.

He sucked it up, opened the bag all the way. Cold air hit his skin like a body check on the hockey rink and he dressed at lightning speed, rubbing his hands together for warmth after getting his boots on. He pawed through the meal pouches Eric had left and found an organic cinnamon apple oats and quinoa breakfast that looked promising. He heated up some water in the

Jetboil and poured it in the pouch. As the meal readied itself and Vic dressed, Danny packed up the sleeping bag and got organized for the day.

"You okay," Vic asked. She'd been watching him, but he avoided her eagle eye.

"Yeah." He glanced up. "You?"

She nodded. "Fine. I'm good." She cocked her head a fraction and he'd have sworn she had X-ray vision by the way she looked at him. Birds twittered and bushes rustled, but apparently neither one of them had much to say. Vic took a few minutes in the bushes for some privacy and Danny dropped his chin to his chest. The dreaded *uncomfortable* morning after. Why the hell hadn't he thought about that possibility last night? Maybe because they were being hunted down like animals and his regular thought process was as jacked up as this whole situation. Shit.

"Breakfast is ready," he said five minutes later. "We're going to need energy for today. I hope to get to the visitor center in four or five hours."

"Got it." She stuck her fork in the pouch he offered and took a bite of breakfast. "Not bad," she said around a mouthful.

He agreed. They ate the rest of the meal in silence and there was something way too intimate about sharing a pouch of breakfast after their night together. Like sharing a toothbrush or a razor…or a sleeping bag. Just one more thing that connected them. Danny took one last bite and handed the pouch to Vic. "Finish it off and we'll get going. I'm going to make a quick pit stop."

"Okay." She eyed him again with those huge brown eyes. "I'll be here."

Shit. He felt like some kind of experiment under a microscope and had no clue what to do about it. She wasn't doing or saying one fucking thing that should make him feel this way, but he couldn't shake the thought that he was being analyzed on some cosmic scale.

When they finally vacated their small camp after making sure they hadn't left any telltale signs of being there, Danny shook off last night and concentrated on the hike. Vic still used her staff to help negotiate tough terrain and she hadn't complained about one single thing all morning. He admired her that much more.

"Have you done any more thinking on my proposition last night?" she asked.

His brain immediately went to the moment she straddled him in the sleeping bag and he felt his cheeks heat with an uncharacteristic blush. "Your proposition?"

She lifted strawberry blond brows. "Hiring the PR firm I work for?"

"Right." Shit. He focused on the uneven terrain. "Can't give you an answer yet. Let's make it out of here and I promise to give it some serious consideration."

"I can live with that." They walked a few more paces. "Danny, last night was great, but don't worry about it, okay. I'm cool. You're cool. It's all good."

She was the female version of his old self and he wasn't sure how he felt about that. Especially since last night mattered to him. Holding her had been about more than sex. Hell if he knew why, either. Keeping her safe had already been his first priority, but now it seemed even more imperative. Maybe it was her bravery, or her fortitude. Or maybe it was her gorgeous smile when she might otherwise be freaking out. Whatever it was, Danny realized something had shifted in him when it came to Vic. Something that scared the hell out of him.

CHAPTER 22

SWEAT DRIPPED BETWEEN ZOE'S breasts, adding to the dark spot on her T-shirt. With every mile, the rocky trail got steeper and Zoe had to admit—at least to herself—that she was nowhere near the shape she thought she was in. Apparently working out three days a week on the treadmill was just a ploy to make her think she was living a healthy lifestyle. She chugged for every breath and concentrated on one foot in front of the other.

And man, did she stink. She couldn't wait to get her hands on those bath wipes again.

Under normal circumstances, she might've enjoyed the panoramic view or the fresh air, but right now she focused on the ground in front of her. The path they walked couldn't even be called a trail. More like a ledge on the side of a mountain with a fifty-foot drop on their right. Eric had hesitated taking it, but with a look behind them, he'd motioned her forward. "We don't have a choice," he'd murmured.

Zoe's skin had crawled with that declaration.

Things had only become more precarious, as the higher they climbed, the more the path narrowed. Eric had even taken off the backpack because it was too thick to stay on his shoulders. He held it in front of him as he slowly picked his way forward.

She had so many things on the tip of her tongue. *Maybe we should go back? This doesn't seem like it's leading anywhere. What if we get to a point where there's no more trail?* Hell, since when had she ever been shy?

"Eric, maybe we should—AHH!" The ground crumbled beneath her feet and a terrifying fear of imminent death ripped through Zoe as she slipped down, scrabbling for a hold on anything. She barely grasped a protruding rock.

Something tumbled next to her and for a half second, she thought it was Eric until an iron band wrapped around her wrist before she lost her hold. Dangling off the side of the mountain, she dared a look down.

"Don't!" Eric said. "Zoe, look up. At me."

Too late. The height made her dizzy. Her heart pounded like it might bust a rib. Sweat slicked her wrist and Eric's hand, and she slipped a bit.

"Hang on, hang on. I'm not lettin' you go." Eric uttered the tight words through gritted teeth and she reached for another handhold only to have that chunk fall away with her weight.

Zoe bit back a scream as Eric's grip tightened. She turned her head again to see the distance below her.

"Do *not* look down," he ordered. "Look at me. Look at my eyes."

Fear practically oozed out of her pores as Zoe glanced up. The confidence and determination in his beautiful eyes should have allayed her fears, but nothing short of solid ground was going to do that. She saw every one of his muscles straining as he pulled her up one-handed. When he got her up to a certain point, he was able to grab the waistband of her jeans with his other hand, and drag her on top of him so they both lay flat on the tiny trail.

Bone-melting relief made her lightheaded and Zoe could only gasp for air as she clutched his shoulders with white-knuckled fists. The fall replayed in her head, she tensed and squeezed her eyes to get rid of the picture. Something had fallen next to her and if it wasn't Eric, then that left only one other option. All their gear.

Eric held her close, his hand cupping her head, his chest heaving and heart pounding hard beneath her ear. A soft breeze cooled the sweat on her face and birds chirped as if nothing out of the ordinary had happened. She couldn't stop the tremors that racked her body.

"You okay?" he asked.

Her whole left side buzzed after being shaved by the mountain during the fall, but that didn't compare to the other possibility. Breathing hard, she swallowed, furious that she hadn't been careful enough. Botching her life was one thing, but this misstep cost too much, their food, water…even those bath wipes that made her a little less ripe. "We lost everything," she whispered. "It's all gone."

He lifted his head and cupped her face so they were nearly eye to eye. "No, we didn't," he said softly. "We have you." The sincerity in his gaze, the tenderness in his touch, had her swallowing back tight emotion. He grazed his thumbs across her cheeks in the softest, sweetest caress, before palming the back of her head with a strong warm hand. Then he pulled her face to his and kissed her.

Maybe she should've seen it coming, especially after last night, but Zoe was so shocked by the contact that she didn't fight it. She tasted the relief on his lips, and pushed a hand through his hair to hold his head steady. Not that he seemed to be going anywhere. On the contrary, his grip tightened as he wrapped a muscled arm around her back. Happy to be alive, she took it a step farther and stroked her tongue into his mouth.

He groaned, the sound rumbling in his chest, and tightened his hold on her. Zoe sucked the air out of his lungs, needing to thank him, take him, needing to find a tiny fraction of control over a situation completely *out* of her control.

A minute later, she pulled back and laid her head on his chest. His heartbeat slammed against her ear and she gripped his sides, not ready to leave the safety of having him so close. Of course, she didn't know how the hell they'd get out of the particular situation. To her immediate right was a steep mountain and to her left, a sheer drop off. She faced the wrong direction.

Still, it wasn't as if they could stay here much longer. "You know it's going to be a trick to get up now, right?" His chest shook and Zoe looked up. "Are you laughing?" She didn't know if she should be angry or laugh with him.

"I guess so. I have no idea why." Except maybe he did. He took a deep breath and lifted his head. Something in those deep-set eyes said more than his words. They'd gone completely topsy-turvy on the trail. "Okay, you need to inch backward and get to your feet and turn around. You're going to be in front. I'll bring up the rear."

It was either that or crawl over his face and that didn't seem any easier. "Okay." Zoe inched backward, thoughts flying. They'd kissed, but a kiss didn't really mean anything. It was more accidental. At least the first one was. The second one…that was just to relieve stress, and last night and this last time… Fear? Adrenaline?

Okay, she was completely out of excuses. Unless she tacked on attraction or lust.

Once Zoe cleared Eric's boots, she eased up with her back plastered against the mountain. Eric stood too and took her sweaty hand in his strong one.

"What are we going to do without all our gear," she asked, trying not to let the hopelessness invade her tone.

"We're going to improvise." He didn't sound the least bit worried and Zoe looked up at him. The smile he gave her absolutely did not match their predicament. "I'd rather have you than the gear, Zoe, so I'm okay with the choice I made." He squeezed her hand for emphasis. The honesty of his answer melted her heart and that was the last thing she wanted.

"Stop it or I'll tell Casey you were flirting with me." It was possibly the lamest thing she'd ever said in her life, but the more time she spent with Eric the more he flustered her. And that made no sense whatsoever. She didn't fluster.

"Wouldn't want that." He squeezed her hand again and gestured to the trail. "Let's get off this mountain. We need to make our way toward water. Can't veer too far away from the stream without any gear." Water they could no longer purify without a Jetboil or iodine, which had both been in their pack. Chalk up one more thing going against them.

Zoe started moving, but she kept her hand tightly clenched in Eric's.

ERIC DIDN'T NEED TO mention the obvious. With no gear they were in shit shape. They had to reach the ranger station today and now more than ever, they needed to push to make that goal.

Their tiny path finally opened up as the terrain widened, and Eric breathed a sigh that, hopefully, the worst was behind them.

Zoe hadn't removed her hand from his and he wasn't sure if it was a conscious decision. Didn't bother him either way. He was a lot bigger than her, but somehow they fit. It didn't make sense, because he never noticed it before, but when he pulled her from the mountain's edge and she'd sprawled across his chest and tangled her legs with his, she'd just fit. There was no other word for it. Her body fit against his. Her hand fit in his. Somehow, they even walked in sync.

Yeah. It was weird. It was also time he got his head out of his ass and got them to shelter. The ranger station was bound to have some provisions. Even if it didn't, they could wait it out until help came. They just had to send out an SOS.

"We have to get out of here today," Zoe said, voicing his thoughts. "We have to show up at the hearing Monday morning. I swear if we don't make it and the judge calls for another continuance, I might jump off this damn mountain."

He squeezed her hand. "Don't even joke about it. I'd rather stay alive and risk a continuance than make a wrong move out here and miss the hearing because we're dead."

Zoe took a whole two seconds to let that sink in. "I know. I'm just…" She sighed. "Good point." But then her eyebrows slammed together and eyes turned hard. "You know what? I'm seriously pissed now. Those assholes are not going to stop us *or* kill us. We're *going* to make it to that ranger station, we're *going* to get help and we're *going* to testify, or so help me God, I'm going to die trying."

He liked everything…right up until the last part. "Look," he said, pointing farther up the mountain. They barely caught a glimpse of the ranger station. On the off chance that an unfriendly made it there first, he didn't want Zoe in the vicinity. "Stay here." He stopped behind a cluster of trees and brush. "I'm going to check it out. Make sure there are no surprises."

Zoe's wide eyes warned of trouble and she grabbed his arm. "No," she whispered fiercely. "You can't leave me. I swear I'll be quiet, but Eric, you cannot leave me here." She was already hyperventilating with choppy breaths.

"Zoe, Zoe." He took her shoulders and bent to her level, looking her in the eyes. "It's okay. You're safer here."

She shook her head adamantly and lost nearly all color in her face.

"Breathe. Zoe, breathe. Look, you're scared, I understand, but I just want you to be safe." She shook her head again, her face as pale as the full moon the other night. This wasn't helping at all. "Breathe. In. Out. Slow. With me. You can do it." It took a few minutes and a concerted effort, but her breathing finally leveled out. When he thought she had it under control, he pulled her close, surprised how strong her arms wrapped around his waist and more surprised how right it felt.

He had to check out the ranger station, but couldn't leave her like this, so he sucked it up and carved out the time she needed. "You going to tell me the real problem? Because that's no asthma attack." He kept his voice soft, didn't want her to feel cornered.

She was quiet for a long time, but didn't let go of him, so Eric waited. "I have an issue with being alone in the forest." Her mumbled words nearly got lost in his chest.

He pulled away enough to see her face. "Why is that?" He brushed a few dark curls off her cheek.

She swallowed hard and avoided his gaze. "Because when I was little, I got lost in the woods."

Shit. She never said a word this whole time. He kept his surprise in check. "How little were you and for how long?"

She pressed her lips together before exhaling hard. "I was about nine. Casey was playing by a river. The current was really strong and she slipped. I barely caught her before the water took her out, but when I heaved her onto the embankment, I lost my footing and slipped. The current carried me over a mile downstream. I finally caught a fallen log and pulled myself out, but I was cold and scraped up and so...so lost. I screamed until my voice was raw." The words came out lightning fast. As if they'd been waiting for years to be spoken. When she met his gaze, her eyes brimmed with tears. "The search party didn't find me until the next day. I was lucky it was summertime and I didn't die of hypothermia." She pulled away from him and swiped at her eyes. "I know you think I'm tough, but I'm not. Everything I do in my life is about battling that feeling, that loss of control. Look, I know you think you're protecting me, but I can't be alone out here again. I can't. Okay?" She swallowed and stood tall in front him.

He cupped her face in his hands, saw the determination in her pretty eyes along with the panic. And that was something he couldn't stand. "Okay," he said softly. "We stick together. But you do what I say when I say it. If something goes wrong, if there's any sign of trouble, you run like hell, hear me?"

"Run where?" She studied his face. "There's nowhere *to* run. We've got no food, no warmth. We have to make this work. If we run into trouble, we fight. Together."

Together. Something about the word knocked him off balance. Shit, he hated that she had a point. But she was wrong about one thing. She was so fucking brave. He kissed her. Didn't think about it, he just did it. He brushed his lips over hers softly until she opened for him, then he tangled his tongue with hers, breathing her in and getting lost in the way she gave so freely when she was so damn scared.

She matched him, didn't run, didn't hesitate and the bond between them strengthened. It might have been unspoken, but it was there. Blood rushed hot and fast through his veins, coiling where Eric least needed it. The urge to touch her everywhere, to sink inside her, rose up like a compulsion.

Worst timing ever.

Eric forced himself to pull away. They'd become a team. A unit. A duo. "You ready?"

She nodded, her gaze focused. "I can do anything as long as you don't leave me alone."

Eric knew what she meant, but the way it sounded cut into his heart in a way he didn't expect. The longer he spent with Zoe the more connected he felt to her. "Okay, we'll do this together. C'mon." Taking her hand, he started toward the ranger station, staying among the trees and watching for any movement. The forest seemed too quiet, too still and Eric didn't like it. They circled toward the back where the building butted up against the mountain. The two-story wood-and-stone structure had one entrance on the second level with a wraparound porch that served as a lookout over the valley below. Someone could be up there right now, watching them.

CHAPTER 23

BRIGHT SUN PICKED ITS way through the overhead leaves as Danny and Vic hiked the last mile to the visitors center. Vic swiped at a drop of sweat trickling down her temple. She still didn't know what came over her last night and why she felt the need to tell Danny about her lonely childhood. Her upbringing wasn't newsworthy although it had made her more ambitious, more focused on the things she wanted in life.

She used to want a man. Someone she could trust, someone to listen to her rant on bad days and laugh with her on good ones. Going through back-to-back cheaters had changed her. Turned her into someone she wasn't especially proud to be. Maybe that's why she hadn't had sex in so long. Meaningless sex ultimately left her just as lonely as no sex at all.

Time with Danny had all but crumbled the walls she'd erected. He made her hope. Made her wish for things she'd given up on.

Mutual trust.

Unconditional love.

Two things she'd eluded to Danny that he wouldn't have to worry about from her. Now she had feelings for him that she couldn't let him see, feelings she swore she'd never have for any man.

She blamed the off-the-chart sex...and his compassion. And bravery. The guy had faced a snake head-on to protect her. How did she stay immune to all that?

Danny pulled her down next to him behind a thick grove of bushes and yanked her out of her thoughts. "Why are we stopping?" she whispered. They could see the visitors center through the trees. They were practically there.

"Because I don't know who might be out there waiting for us and I don't want to walk into an ambush." He faced her, keeping his voice low. "Let me ask you something. Has it occurred to you why we haven't seen any people out here?"

"What do you mean?"

"I mean, it's been empty of other hikers. No one."

"I thought maybe it was because this trail was so new. Isn't that the reason you choose it? Because this part of the mountain was just opened up to the public?"

He nodded. "Absolutely. But there's no way I'm the only one who had that idea. Don't you remember when we started out that there were a few other people getting ready to hike? We got off first, but it's not like we've seen one person since we began."

A chill raced down Vic's back. "You think someone's down at the visitor center warning people away…just so there aren't witnesses when they kill us?" She liked the guy, but that seemed like a stretch. "You're reaching, Danny."

"Maybe so. Trust me, I'd love it if I was wrong, but I'm not taking a chance. We got this far and we're not getting killed now. Not when we're so close."

"We can't just stay here. We have to go in eventually."

"Actually, I'm thinking we hop in the Jeep and haul ass to the next visitor center. They'll be expecting us to walk into this one—" he gestured over his shoulder, "—so we'll do something they don't expect. At this point, we're only tacking on another half hour max before we find another visitor center. We just have to get to the Jeep." He'd parked on the long side of the building, a one-story concrete structure with windows in front but not along the sides. "Stay here. I'm going to jump in and start it up. I'll swing by and pick you up. I want you to stay out of sight for as long as possible." She shook her head to argue and he cut her off. "Don't bother. I'll be right back." He looked at her and for a second, she thought he might kiss her, but instead he bolted toward his Jeep, reaching into his pocket for the keys. He wasn't there long before he sprinted back toward her. "Okay, yeah, we're fucked. Two of my tires are slashed."

"There are three other cars in the parking lot. Were their tires flat too?"

"No, not that I could tell. So maybe those cars belong to the guys tracking us. Maybe they blocked off the entrance from the main road. It would explain why it's so quiet."

"Now what? We have to get in there."

"I know. I know." He scrubbed his hands over his head.

Vic exhaled a frustrated sigh. Time to do what she did at work when trying to promote someone or something. Throw out ideas and see what stuck. "Okay, we know there were two guys following us. We have to assume there was at least one or two following Zoe and Eric. Which means *maybe* there's only one person here manning the building."

"You mean waiting for us," Danny said.

"Exactly. So now, we lure him out."

He nodded. "Okay, okay. And he blows us away with his rifle. Then what?"

She smacked his arm lightly, pushing aside her frustration. "Don't be so pessimistic. The entrance to the building has that big walkway under the roof before the front door. If we can get the guy to come out, we can surprise him. He won't see us until it's too late. You jump him and I'll run in to the phone and call for help."

"What if there's *two* guys?"

"Then I guess I'll be seeing if my kickboxing class paid off."

He shook his head. "No way. I don't like it. Besides what would we do to draw him out and still surprise him at the same time?"

"What if you point the Jeep in the right direction, put it in gear and rig it to head straight for the road? Anyone inside is going to come out like a bat outta hell."

Danny stared at the Jeep, his eyes narrowing. "I do have some bungee cord I could use to hold the steering wheel straight."

Yes! She loved that he considered it. Vic picked up a nearby rock that weighed eight or ten pounds. "You can put this on the gas."

"Damn, I'm gonna have more than two flat tires after this." He took the rock from her hand. "But it's worth a try. We have to do something." Hefting the stone in his palm, he seemed to weigh it. "There's only one thing that's not going to happen in this plan of yours."

"What's that?"

"You're going to stay out of sight. Completely. Because if something happens to me, I want you to run far and fast back into the forest and lay low until the sun goes down. Then make your way to the main road and the next closest structure. Stay alert and do whatever it takes to survive."

When was this man going to understand? Vic moved up close and personal, laying her hands on Danny's chest sweetly before grabbing chunks of his T-shirt. "You and me...we're in this together. I'm not leaving you, and we don't have time to argue about where I'm going to run and who I should trust. I'm staying with you."

"Vic, don't arg—"

She tugged him down and kissed him. It wasn't soft, it wasn't sweet, it was full of terror and panic and fear, because the next few minutes might take away one of the best things to ever happen to her. Danny jumped on board, taking her mouth with a savage possession that only made it harder to let him go. When she finally pulled away, she worried that everything in her heart might show in her eyes and she didn't want to freak Danny out. She'd told him she was strong and she was, but she'd come to care for him in the last two days. More than she would've thought possible.

Danny's gaze smoldered into hers. "As mind-boggling as that was, I'm not changing my mind. You stay here and run for cover if you see trouble. I need to get my Jeep ready for demolition." The pained look on his face had her cocking her head in empathy. Poor guy.

She nodded and turned him around, with no intention of sitting this out. "Go set up the Jeep. I'll wait until you're done." Not a lie. Just not especially clear either.

He ran to the Jeep, grabbed some bungee cord from the back and took a minute to arrange it in front of the steering wheel. He cranked the engine, and Vic held her breath, hoping the sound didn't carry inside the building. Danny backed up, the Jeep lurching on the flat tires until it was in place. Once in position, he secured the cord to the steering wheel. He lifted the rock to show her it was go-time. As soon as the rock hit the pedal, the Jeep would shoot toward the exit. At least as fast it could with a ten pound weight on the gas pedal and two flat tires. Danny motioned her back into the forest and Vic ran that way. With a glance over her shoulder, she saw the Jeep moving in the right direction and Danny running along the building to get into place.

Vic took off for the other side of the structure. Nothing said *surprise* like a two-person ambush. Danny meant well, but no way would she let him face this danger alone. She sprinted along the back of the building, flying past the solid cement back door then rounding the corner to haul ass along the side. She ran faster, arms and legs pumping, hoping she wouldn't be too late. She rounded the corner as the barrel of a gun come into view from the inset doorway, just as bullets fired into the moving Jeep. She saw Danny right there at the wall, a sitting duck since the gun was already aimed and firing.

A man came into view, walking as he fired. Husky guy, jeans, baseball cap, about six feet tall.

"Hey!" Vic yelled. She didn't get a chance to say anything else because he turned and fired, but Vic was already moving back toward the cover of the building. Danny tackled the man just as a hot slap of fire sliced below her hip. In a split-second decision, Vic changed course and ran toward the front door as the Jeep crashed into a tree. She didn't see how she could help Danny as the men battled, the gun under them as they scuffled and threw punishing punches. Getting help to Zoe and Eric required a call and that had to be her first priority. Danny would insist on it.

Hauling ass through the glass door, she spotted a ranger crumpled up in the corner of the front lobby. Dead or alive? She didn't know and didn't have time to check. Her racing heart beat faster. She jumped the low counter separating the few desks from the main lobby and saw a second ranger tied up and unconscious behind a leather chair. Shaking, she picked up the phone.

The dial tone nearly made her weep and with trembling hands she punched 9-1-1. Her heart slammed against her ribs as the phone rang and finally a dispatcher answered the call. Vic's voice cracked as she quickly explained the situation. Moments later a front glass panel shattered and both men fell through, landing hard on the wood floor as they continued to struggle with each other. Vic saw no sign of the gun. Maybe it was still outside. She dropped the receiver on the desk as the man landed a vicious fist that snapped Danny's head sideways and sent him to the ground. The man turned to her, and stomach-churning fear roiled inside Vic. She sprinted for a door farther into the main room, her lungs bursting for air. His footsteps pounded after her. Her momentum swung the door wide—into an employee lounge—and she turned to slam it shut. Somehow he was there and burst through before Vic got it closed. The force threw her back, pushing her to the floor in a hard bounce. Air whooshed from her lungs and pain shot through her hip. He pounced on her, his weight crushing, and wrapped his hands around her neck.

Déjà vu.

Vic's scream stuck in her throat as air refused to go in or out. Her heart pounded loud between her ears. She'd learned from her mistakes and intended to wipe away the victory lurking in his dark evil stare. Instead of trying to release the meaty grip he had on her neck, she went for his eyes. He dodged to one side to avoid her nails, so she reached down with one hand and grabbed his crotch. When he doubled forward she went for his eyes again and this time he lost his grip on her neck when he shied away.

Vic gasped in a lungful of air as he toppled sideways and off her. Before she scrambled up, Danny landed on top of him, fists flying, hitting the son of a bitch over and over until he wasn't moving.

Danny finally stepped back, wiping his bloody lip with the back of his battered hand and Vic sat up, not trusting her shaky legs to hold her. At least not until Danny pulled her up and dragged her into his arms. She held on tight, drinking in his strength and the security he offered. "Jesus, Jesus," he muttered, cupping her head and holding her tight. After a minute he pulled back and studied her face. "Are you okay?"

She nodded, because she wasn't sure she had working vocal chords yet. His lips crashed down on hers and Vic didn't shy away from his kiss. She wanted it, wanted anything he felt inclined to give her. Not her usual style at all. What the hell was happening to her?

But when he pulled away again, his magnificent blue eyes were dark and stormy. "Are you crazy? I told you to stay out of sight!" He hauled her against him again.

Vic cleared her throat. "So you could get yourself killed? No way!" she finally answered, her voice a ragged whisper. Even as she said the words, her body reminded her of the beating it had taken in the last few minutes. Her hip especially burned. She must have landed on it harder than she thought. Actually, the longer she stood, the dizzier she got until her legs gave out completely.

"Whoa! I've got you. What was that?" Danny picked her up and carried her to a nearby sofa before scanning her from top to bottom. His eyes widened. "Holy shit!" Vic looked at her sore hip and the blood soaking her khakis around the wound just as Danny said, "You're bleeding. Gunshot."

"Oh my God." She hadn't even realized it. That sure as hell explained the sting. No wonder she was so wobbly. Just seeing the blood made her stomach queasy.

Danny headed to a wall of cabinets where he began opening doors. The room contained a small kitchenette to the left with a fridge, vending machine and microwave oven and a lounge area where she sat on a sofa with chairs around a circular coffee table.

"What are you looking for?"

"First aid kit and rope. Need to patch you up and make sure that guy's not going anywhere when he wakes up." He pulled a dishtowel from a drawer under the microwave and tossed it to her. "Put pressure on it with that." Then he glanced out the door. "Hang on. I want his gun. Those shots he fired were bound to draw his buddies in." He returned a couple minutes later, carrying the unconscious ranger. "The ranger by the door didn't make it. But this one's still breathing." He set the man down on another couch against the far wall and Vic spotted a gun tucked in the back waistband of Danny's jeans. Next he rummaged for a first aid kit in a storage closet.

Vic swallowed back emotion. It could've just as easily been one or both of them dead.

Danny found rope in a lower cabinet and tied up the unconscious man on the floor. Then he returned, crouched in front of her and scrounged through the first aid kit.

Watching him do half a dozen things at once made her feel

fairly useless, which led to the one thing she did do. "Shit!" She pointed to the main lobby. "The dispatcher was on the line. See if she's still there. Ask how fast she can get police here and to that ranger station."

Danny didn't budge, but his eyes darkened to an impossible blue. He leaned forward and kissed her hard and long, sucking the wind right out of her and making her dizzy for a whole different reason. After taking her mouth in the most obscene way, he rose and stalked out of the room. Vic licked her stinging lips and felt a full on blush heat her cheeks.

Hopefully they'd be in time to save Zoe and Eric.

GIRLY, SWEET, SEXY, SINFUL and brave. Danny had a ton of words that described Vic, but the last one was the most surprising. She was bleeding from a gunshot wound, but making sure her friend and his brother were getting the help they needed.

It was enough to make a guy want to fall and Danny had never fallen in his life. He'd just made a promise to himself and watching that resolve crumble set him adrift. Now was just the worst time to think about it. Not with Vic bleeding, two unconscious guys and a dead ranger on the floor.

He'd covered the ranger with a coat from a nearby rack, but glancing at the body twisted his gut tight and nausea made him queasy. He spoke to the dispatcher who was still on the line, but only long enough to give necessary information about their current situation and his hunch about Eric and Zoe's target location. Minutes later, he returned to Vic's side. "You doing okay?"

"A little shaky to be honest," she whispered, holding bloody gauze against her wound. Her raw voice made him angry all over again. The asshole waiting for them would've snapped her neck given another few seconds. "You're bleeding too." Vic's words brought him out of his haze.

He wiped his lip again and discovered a smear of blood along the back of his hand. She tapped her cheekbone. "Here too."

Yeah, Danny not only felt that one, but he saw the swelling under his eye. "I'm fine. Let's get a look at this." There was no way to pull her khakis off without making the injury worse so Danny took his knife out of his boot.

"What's that for?" Vic asked, her eyes wide.

"Need to slice the material around the wound."

"Oh."

"Trust me, as soon as paramedics get here, they're going to cut these totally off."

"They are?"

He nodded. "Oh yeah. When I—" He'd never talked about the kidnapping to anyone other than a professional. The whole family had gone through extensive counseling separately and with each other, and they all harbored similar issues. But sharing with someone outside the family hadn't ever been a consideration. Sharing the most traumatic experience of his life was opening his soul to inspection.

"When you what?" Vic prodded.

Danny cleared his dry throat. After everything Vic had gone through, it seemed lame to leave her hanging…and for some reason, he wanted her to know. He wanted to let her in. "After the kidnapping when paramedics took us to the hospital, they cut off my T-shirt and jeans. Just slit everything apart like butter. Nothing more efficient than a sharp knife."

"You had that many injuries?" she asked.

Nodding, Danny took out some fresh gauze. "I wasn't as bad off as Brendan—one of his broken ribs punctured a lung—but I wasn't in great shape, either. I could barely move with two broken ribs. Then there was the hematoma on my thigh. It was so swollen from continuous kicks that I needed surgery to drain the blood." He couldn't look at her as he relayed the details, didn't want to see the horror in her eyes. "The point is, they stripped off my clothes in the ambulance to see what they were dealing with. Good thing I was never shy."

Softly, she stroked her hand across his cheek and he finally met her gaze. Her empathetic eyes said she read through every word, understood the pain and violation he felt. Maybe he wasn't as good at hiding his emotions as he thought. At least not from Vic.

"I also happened to be blessed with a great plastic surgeon who minimized the scars on my face." The one on his forehead blended into his eyebrow just as the one at his mouth outlined his lip line. Practically invisible. Same with the one by his eye.

"Right, I remember that talk we had about scar cream when we took Zoe home from the hospital." She traced the tiny *laugh line* at his eye, her touch soft, almost reverent and his heart took a little tumble.

Danny peeled back the material to see the wound. "Hope you weren't in love with that bikini, because the bullet sheared right through it." It had also taken a chunk of her skin, but a surgeon could piece her together well enough.

"I don't think I want to see." She never took her eyes off his. "I'm not really good with blood."

He met her gaze again, falling even harder and struggling not to drown in the compassion he saw. "My sis isn't either. It's okay. Let me clean it up with what I have until paramedics get here."

"Do you think the men following us will get here before the police do?"

A good question that scared the crap of him. "I hope not." He looked around the room. "But in case you're right, maybe we should close the door." He not only closed it, he locked it, then came back and put pressure on the wound with a wad of gauze. Vic gritted her teeth, but didn't utter a sound. The woman was a warrior. After a few minutes, he taped fresh gauze to her hip. "That should hold you for a little bit."

"Wait a minute," she said when he started putting the supplies back in the kit. "Let me fix you up. You could use a little TLC too."

Danny let her tend to the bloody gashes on his face, never taking his eyes off hers. She had amazing eyes. Eyes that sucked him in faster than a riptide. *You're my—brown-eyed girl.* The lyrics to one of his dad's favorite songs played in his head. Sometimes, growing up, he'd catch his dad singing the words to his mom. He hadn't paid much attention, mainly because his parents were good at embarrassing all the kids while they were growing up. The kissing, the touching. None of the other kids' parents did that.

Only as adults did they all come realize the importance of such a strong bond.

Vic finished cleaning his cuts and Danny promptly leaned in and kissed her.

"What's that for?" she asked.

"Services rendered," he whispered.

Her playful grin said everything he needed to know. "Maybe I'm not done with my services."

Damn, he liked the sound of that. "Maybe I'm not done with my payment."

They stayed that way for many long seconds. Just watching each other and smiling, and Danny sensed something shifting into place for him. Finally, finally, he understood what all the fuss was about. What the hell did he do with that information, though, especially when she'd made it clear she wasn't in the market for anything serious?

For the first time, he could see hanging out with the same person for the foreseeable future...and the not so foreseeable future, if he wanted to be honest with himself. He'd woken up next to Vic two mornings in a row and this morning, all he'd wanted to do was begin where he'd left off, which entailed stroking every inch of her soft skin to thrusting hard and deep inside the velvet clasp of her smokin' hot bod.

He dug her sass as much as her smarts. He liked that she seemed as interested as he was in making his business a success. She just had different ideas on how to do that. Ideas he hadn't considered until she brought them up.

That's what he'd do! He'd say yes to her proposal, then she'd have to see him. He'd turn her around, and he'd give her the fucking moon if that's what it took to get her onboard with a relationship.

Jesus. *Relationship*. Was he really prepared to do this now?

"You okay?" she asked, her head canted to the side and her eyes narrowed a fraction.

He stroked his thumb across her cheek, so damn glad that they'd made it this far together. "Yeah," he said. "In a way, I don't think I've ever been better."

CHAPTER 24

A COOL BREEZE WHISTLED through leaves overhead and a pair of squirrels played tag around a fallen log to Zoe's left. She waited thirty yards away in the circle of trees surrounding the ranger station while Eric checked out the stone-and-log A-frame building. As long as she had him in sight, she didn't mind the separation. The main reason she'd agreed to let him go alone was because she liked the idea of being a lookout in case the men tracking them showed up. She kept alert for any sounds and continued scanning the area. When she glanced back at the structure, she no longer saw Eric. He must've gone around the far side on the second story wraparound porch.

The sound of glass breaking jerked her attention back to the building, but she didn't see anything. Her heart raced faster the longer she didn't have Eric in her sight.

Tired of waiting, she crept forward, pushing her pace until she was at a full sprint, closing in on the stairs off to the right side.

"Psst."

She looked up and Eric waved her forward from the second level door. Zoe took the stairs two at a time and rushed inside. Eric closed the door behind her and locked it.

The large space seemed like a barren office with an out of place five-by-eight-foot abstract, red, orange and brown area rug in the center. A long built-in wood counter ran the length of the far side with several wood chairs tucked neatly beneath it, and a small portable fireplace at the end. Against the left wall sat a cot and next to it a wood storage chest, bolted closed with a padlock. To the right, broken glass littered the floor under the window near a desk and another chair. Eric's point of entry. Two rows of built-in cubbies on the right wall housed an array of items from kitchenware to first aid.

"I never would've pegged you for the breaking and entering type," she said as Eric went behind the desk.

He lifted an amused eyebrow. "That makes two of us." Then he was checking drawers and cubbies for anything that might help them.

Zoe headed for the wood chest and stepped on an uneven part of the carpeting. Lifting the corner, she found a hatch in the floor. She grabbed the handle, surprised at the weight. Maybe it was locked from the other side somehow, but that didn't make sense. There wasn't any other entry to the bottom level so this door was probably the only interior pass through for the structure. Flipping the carpet back into place, she knelt at the wood chest. "Something worth locking is in here," she said, tugging on the padlock. It didn't budge. "You think someone hid a key up here? Wouldn't make sense to take it away, right? Different people must take shifts. What if someone needed to get to whatever is in here?"

Eric looked up from his search at the cubbies. "Let me know if you find any false sprinkler heads."

A sense of humor lurked under there after all. She grinned at the reminder of his boss's house, then abruptly lost the smile when the rest of the night flashed in her head. She sat at the wood counter and stuck her head in her hands. She took her first deep breath in what felt like days. Her stomach growled as Eric took the seat next to her. The warmth of his hand rubbing her back soothed tense muscles. "On the bright side, we have shelter," he said quietly. "I'm sure Danny and Vic will get to the visitors center. They'll send help."

Zoe turned her head and read the worry in his eyes. "You think they should've reached it by now?"

He nodded then shrugged. Ran a hand across his jaw. "I don't know. I would've thought so, but I don't know what they came up against." Psychos with guns. Wild animals. Those just topped the list.

Zoe kept it positive. "You said it yourself. Danny is the most prepared of all of us. I'm sure he's keeping them safe."

An explosion of gunfire ripped through the quiet moment and shattered the window in front.

Zoe's pulse tripled as they both ducked and Eric swore. "Now what?" she whispered, knowing she sounded as piss-in-the-pants scared as she felt.

"What was it you found under the carpet?" Even as Eric asked the words, he lifted the corner of the area rug and took stock.

"It's heavy. Or locked. I couldn't open—"

Eric put his considerable muscle into the job and the door creaked open. "Hurry up. Down you go." He hefted the door higher, his bicep bulging with the effort.

"We have no idea what's down there." But that didn't stop Zoe from descending the slanted steps to the lower level as quickly as possible. "Pull that rug farther over so it covers the hatch more."

"Got it."

Zoe hit the bottom and promptly tripped on something. She went down, palm first and caught herself. Pain sliced up from wrist to elbow. Dammit! She shook it off and looked up. The interior was going to be pitch black when that door closed over them. It smelled dank and old, as if no one had been down here in years. Meager light from above shone on the coil of rope she'd stepped on. Stacks of boxes lined one wall next to a tall wood pile in the corner. Cob webs weaved between boxes and the rafters, sending a fresh wave of chills down her arms.

Spiders.

Eric wrestled with the rug overhead, tugging it over the hatch then hurrying in behind her.

Zoe took the length of rope at her feet and handed an end to Eric. "Here! Wrap this on the handle on our side. If they find the door maybe we can tug on it hard enough that they'll think it's locked."

Eric slipped the end through the handle just as more bullets riddled the room above them. He hit the floor and they huddled off to the side, both of them holding onto the rope and keeping the tension tight. Zoe worried they could hear her pounding heart through the floorboards.

The door busted open above then eerie silence before footsteps trekked across the floor.

"You said you saw someone." A man's voice barely carried through the thick wood flooring and Zoe forgot to breathe.

"I said I thought I saw *something*. I told you not to fucking fire unless we knew it was them," a different man said. "Must have been a shadow. I don't know." Another gunshot made her jump, followed by eerie silence that raised every hair on her body. Boots stomped toward the door above them and the sudden stillness warned of the worst-case scenario. Had they found the bulge in the carpet? Were they signaling to open the hatch? She couldn't say how long they stayed up there, but an eternity might've described it best.

Bullets rained down from above, splintering wood overhead. Zoe jumped a mile, clamping a hand over her mouth and muffling a near scream at the same time Eric threw himself in front of her and pushed her against the cool stone wall. More gruff words were exchanged above before the stomping echoed farther away and new silence descended.

Eric dropped the rope and pulled her tighter against his chest. This wasn't about protection anymore. It was something else. Comfort? Reassurance? Both of those and maybe more she didn't want to label in case she was wrong. Didn't really matter why because Zoe didn't fight it, didn't want to. She wrapped her arms around his waist and held on tight, her wrist burned in agony. "I think they're gone," he whispered in her ear. The incidental brush of his lips gave her comfort she desperately needed and sent a sweet tingle down her spine.

"What if they come back?"

"We stay here for a while, that's all." He didn't let up on his grip and Zoe soaked up his warmth and strength. "Good thinking with the carpet," he murmured.

A compliment. She almost smiled. They'd come a long way. "I wasn't too bossy?"

His chest huffed and his lips curved against her cheek. "Well, yeah, you're always bossy, but...I'm getting used to it." Before she came up with a suitable reply, he shifted his head and set his lips against hers.

Maybe because her senses were on fire—every nerve buzzing with tension—maybe that was why his kiss rocked her so hard. Celebration. Survival. Kindling.

Fireworks. That was the only way to describe his kiss.

Lights. Explosive. Beautiful.

Zoe kissed Eric back with equal hunger. Their tongues mated in a slick dance. It could've been a combination of fear or certain death, lust or longing, definitely relief and attraction. The only thing she knew for certain was that Eric St. John knew how to kiss. Heat radiated off his body as she fisted the material of his flannel shirt. His mouth crushed hers with stunning ferocity. He was all male, all testosterone and hard muscle, taking everything she gave and demanding more. Zoe did her best to comply.

Finally, long minutes later and breathing hard, Eric pulled his lips off hers long enough to hold her tightly against him. The evidence of that kiss was wedged between them, low against her stomach.

Zoe's fogged brain struggled to make sense of the situation because she seriously had no clue what was happening between them. She just knew she wasn't ready to let go of him or have his arms anywhere but their current position...around her.

ERIC WANTED TO BE anywhere, but this dark, dank room that smelled like petrified mouse. It really wasn't the best time to kiss Zoe. He'd just reacted to having her safe and in one piece. And in his arms. After the stress of the last two days, running for their lives and narrowly missing the barrage of bullets, it seemed as if the moment—like last night—required a celebration of life.

Getting to know her, to see her outside her normal routine, had given him a different perspective. Under the circumstances, the woman was fierce in a pixie sort of way. A mix of fearless and scared shitless, wrapped up in sweet curly-haired package with curves to kill for. That little hint of possibility between them from months ago had blossomed into an all-out probability.

His feelings for Zoe had changed. In a big way. Big enough that he was ready to see if this sizzle between them could ignite into something hotter and heavier. Provided they survived this clusterfuck.

Sobered by reality, Eric set her away from him. "I need to go up there." He couldn't see her face, but felt the instant stiffness of her muscles under his hands.

"Why? What if it's a trap and those men are still up there? No," she whispered fiercely.

He bent his head low, right in her face. "Zoe, staying down here is the same as being lost in the forest. I need to put up a sign. A flag. Something. If help comes this way, they need to know we're here."

"What if those men are outside watching? Then they know we're here, too, and they'll come back. You can't go."

"I think they'll probably backtrack thinking we haven't made it here yet."

"No." She shook her head. "What if they're waiting on the outskirts like I was when you first checked the place out. Then they'll see you—"

"Zoe." He squeezed her shoulders, appreciated the concern, but if she thought to boss him around on this point, she was one hundred percent mistaken. "I've got to do something. I can't wait down here."

Her silence didn't last long. "*We* can't wait down here. Fine. Then I'm coming with you."

Dammit, she made everything an argument. "You're safer here."

"No. Absolutely not. We started this together and we end it together. That was the deal."

Eric tamped down the anger building in his blood. "You are *such* a ball buster," he groused.

"Absolutely. One hundred percent ball buster. It's my middle name. You can ask my sister."

There it was, that sense of humor that appeared out of nowhere. He might've laughed under other circumstances, but now his gut twisted with worry and fear for her safety.

She stroked a thumb across his bristly cheek, her hand cool on his face. "Eric, you're not my protector in this. You're my partner. We're stronger working together." Her soft touch, her quiet words, hit him soul deep. She had an equal stake in this, a right to face anything head-on.

"Fine." Eric kissed her palm before bending and taking her lips in another soft kiss. He needed the connection. Needed some of that fire she exuded so often. "Stay close." He turned toward the ladder and kept her hand in his as he moved.

They'd heard the footsteps pounding outside and the gruff voices moving farther away, but lifting the hatch still had his palms slick with sweat. Using all his muscle, he forced the hatch up and cringed at the squeak. Then he eyed the empty room before lifting it higher, fighting the weight of the carpet.

Once emerged, they stayed low and adjusted the carpet over the hatch. "Now what?" Zoe asked. Like him, she took in the damage with the new bullet holes. They'd shot up the cubbies and the lock on the wood chest. Blankets and a two-way radio—now splintered apart—spilled out from the opening. Zoe picked up the busted radio that might've saved them, despair clear in her eyes. "Now we know why this thing was locked." She tossed the shot-up blanket onto the cot and dug farther into the chest. "Nothing but more blankets," she said, rummaging through one-handed. After pulling out the contents, she shoved everything back inside. Something fell from within one of the quilts and clattered to the floor.

"What's that?" Eric reached the small device first and turned it in his palm.

Zoe saw the letters SOS at the same time he did. "Oh my God. Do you think…"

Did he think this little thing could save them? Absolutely. He opened the small lid and a beautiful red button with another SOS stared up at them. He pushed it. Nothing happened. He tried again, keeping his finger on the button. A few seconds later, a green light flashed on the outside of the device. For the first time, good news had his adrenaline racing. "Holy shit. I think this is working." He glanced at Zoe, who had two fat tears running down her cheeks. Pulling her close, he rubbed his cheek against her head, totally thrown off by the emotion in her eyes.

After a minute, she pulled away, wiped at her eyes. "Now what?"

"Now we stay away from the windows, keep an eye out and wave like hell when the cavalry shows up." His stomach growled. "Maybe if we're lucky, we find something to eat or drink in here." He continued rummaging through the cubbies.

"Maybe there's something else hidden in this chest." Zoe lifted the top blanket and gasped, gingerly pulling back her right hand.

"Hey, what happened?" He stepped close, lifted her right arm and pulled the sleeve of her coat back. Her wrist had ballooned twice its size. That had to hurt like a bitch and she hadn't said a fucking word.

"Dammit. I tripped and caught myself down there. It hurt, but I didn't realize it was so swollen."

"We need to wrap it." He looked around, spotted the blankets from the chest and cut up two sections of one with his knife. "C'mere. Can you move it at all?" She tried and grimaced. "Stop. You might've broken it. Best to stabilize it until we get you to a hospital." The amount of swelling worried him. Zoe clenched her jaw tight as he wrapped her hand and wrist.

Forty minutes later, they sat at on the floor with their legs in front of them. How long would they have to wait for help? What if Zoe's wrist got worse? "This isn't good," Eric mumbled.

"You already said that." Zoe tried to move her fingers and grimaced. Then her stomach growled in an almighty roar. "Sorry. Just ignore that."

He was hungry, too, and his stomach growled a response. A very long response, until he realized the sound wasn't coming from him.

Zoe's eyes widened. "Do you hear that?"

He did. An engine. Overhead. Like a plane engine. They both bounded to their feet. "Stay here," he said, grabbing a red-and-white checkered dish towel from one of the cubbies. "I'm going to go out and flag it down."

"I'll come with you."

Eric caught her good hand. "Zoe, please." He pulled her close. "Please stay inside. Let me do this and come right back. Hang tight here. Stay low."

"I do *not* like that idea. I thought we were sticking together."

"We are. But right now, one of us needs to flag down a plane." The engine noise got louder. "You need to keep your wrist elevated and keep your pulse rate low." His version of: there was no way in hell *she* was leaving the safety of the ranger station.

"Eric, no. I don—"

"Zoe. Stop. You aren't going to win this time. Look at your wrist. I don't know if it's broken or sprained, but the swelling is scaring the shit out of me. Cut me some slack and just nod your head."

Her posture folded a fraction and after glancing at her ballooning hand, she nodded, but looked unhappy. The compulsion to protect her doubled. It wasn't a new feeling, he realized, but something that had been steadily gaining traction. Keeping her safe went beyond the fact that they were friends. During the last few days, he'd grown to care about her more than he'd cared for anyone.

Before he thought about it, Eric leaned in and bussed her lips. Just a quick, hard smack to let her know he appreciated her need to watch his back. Creeping toward the windows, he viewed the trees outside. Everything looked quiet enough, but he doubted those men were far away. "If they come back," he said, scanning the area. "You open the hatch and hide again."

She shook her head. "No way am I strong enough to get it opened and closed with that carpet on top, much less with one hand." She looked around the space and pointed to the old trunk. "They've already shot that. I'll hide in there."

Eric wasn't sure he liked that idea, but unless he stowed her away now, then they didn't have any other options. "Okay. Just be careful."

"I was going to say the same thing to you." She lifted an arched brow.

Eric winked then slid out the door, keeping a careful eye on the area. A little higher up the mountain, the trees thinned out and it seemed the best spot to be seen. He ran up the hill as fast as he could, watching as the small plane got closer.

Waving that damn towel like a lunatic, Eric tried to alert the plane, but the stupid thing kept right on going. As he watched it get smaller in the sky, he heard a click behind him. *Fuck!* Every molecule in his body came to attention. Pulse pounding, Eric turned.

Two men stood about fifteen yards away. The plane engine must have drowned out their approach. One big dude with a hunting rifle and anther a few inches shorter with a machine gun. Eric recognized the smaller one from the original robbery. The cashier had identified him as the driver. The police had arrested him after a brief car chase.

"You're a tough man to track down," the big guy said, pointing the rifle at his chest.

The man next to him grinned. "Where's your girlfriend?"

Eric swallowed though his parched mouth fought the involuntary action. "She fell. Slid down the mountain. I tried to catch her, but..." He shook his head. They'd kill him for sure if they thought there was no point in using him to find Zoe—if she was dead. At least she'd be safe at the ranger station. "You might've seen all the gear that went down with her." Or not depending on how they got up here. There had to be an easier route than the one they'd chosen.

"Didn't see shit," the second man said. "And I think you're lying to protect her." He pointed his gun higher and took Eric right back to the grocery store when he'd stared down the barrel of a different gun. His stomach twisted in a knot of fear. "If I shoot your leg, you won't be able to walk, so that doesn't work. Maybe I'll save my shots to bring your girlfriend out of hiding." He nodded. "Yeah, I like that plan better."

The first man waved his rifle. "Walk. Back to the ranger station. My guess is she's waiting for you there. Move."

There had to be something he could do to stall.

Tree bark exploded near his head as he shied away from the bullet that blew past him.

"He said move. Or the next one is in your kneecap and you'll crawl back to that ranger station."

Eric clenched his jaw and set out, the men close behind him.

"Watch out for that log," the man behind him said. Just as Eric stepped over the fallen tree, something smashed into his shoulder and took him down. Pain erupted like fire all the way down his arm and he fell, sprawled over the log, like two hundred pounds of dead weight. He looked back at the men behind him.

"Oh, were you under the impression that I was going to make this easy for you?" the smaller man asked. He held up the butt of his rifle and shook his head. "Cuz I'm not."

CHAPTER 25

VIC AND DANNY HAD done all they could for the unconscious ranger. She'd worried about Danny moving him, since they didn't know his injuries, but leaving him on the floor seemed cruel so she was glad he'd set him on the other couch.

Knowing a bullet grazed her increased the throb factor in Vic's hip, but it didn't compare to watching Danny's eye swell shut and his lip balloon up. She'd insisted he put ice on his face and he'd waved off her concern and focused on her. The more attention he paid her, the harder she fell. A huge mistake, she clearly realized. He'd insisted on changing the gauze bandage when it got too bloody and she'd held her breath when his strong fingers had brushed her skin.

"How long did the dispatcher say until someone would be here?" she asked, mainly to distract herself from thinking about Danny's hands on her.

"The nearest visitor center is thirty minutes away, so...we need to be ready for worst-case scenario." He tossed the rest of the gauze into the nearby kit.

"You mean in case the assholes hunting us get here first." No sense in making it a question, since that's obviously what he meant.

"Pretty much. Yeah. I want to stake out the front door. No way to lock it since we busted through that glass window. Too bad that creep went through all his rounds or we would've had a gun on our side." He stood. "You stay here. Keep the door locked."

She shook her head. "I don't like that idea. It makes me useless. We need to devise a plan just like they did. We've been a good team so far. No reason to break it up." Now if she could figure out what that plan was. She grabbed Danny's hand and the arm rest to haul her ass off the sofa.

"Where are you going?" Danny asked, following her. He was all testosterone and male, his eyes narrowed and jaw set.

"Just need some water," Vic said, heading to the small sink across the room. She found a glass in a cupboard and after rinsing it, she swallowed a long cold glass full.

"I could've brought you water," he said.

She refilled the glass and took another swallow. "I'm okay, Danny. Besides, we're not safe until we're either free and clear from this place or backup gets here, so you may as well be prepared to deal with me as an equal partner in this."

Yes, they'd been a great team, for survival's sake, but did Danny see it in more than that way? He hadn't mentioned anything about his feelings regarding her *or* the sex so she had no clue where she stood with him. She'd really done it to herself this time. She'd totally fallen for the guy. Dropping her chin to her chest, she sighed her frustration.

Seconds later she felt Danny's presence behind her. He wrapped an arm around her waist and brought her up against his chest. Vic's pulse picked up and she leaned against him, taking the comfort he provided, soaking it in, knowing very well it wouldn't last.

His lips hovered over her ear and sent goose bumps across her skin. "I swear, I'll keep you safe, Vic. You can trust me."

Before Vic thought about what she was doing, she set the glass down, turned and wrapped her arms around his neck. "I know. I do." She desperately wanted to kiss him—swollen lip and all—but she needed him to initiate it. Needed him to want her, so she knew where they stood. Staring into his eyes, she watched his struggle and it nearly broke her heart. "You don't have to be afraid," she whispered. "I'll keep you safe too. You can trust me."

He stroked his thumb across her cheek and barely shook his head. After long seconds ticked by, Danny finally bent his head and closed the distance until his lips brushed across hers.

Vic adjusted, careful of his cut, and opened her mouth in an invitation he didn't decline. The long, slow kiss melted her bones. Their tongues tangled in a sweet two-step, coming together and breaking apart in a rhythm they'd perfected in a very short time.

She ran her hands over his shoulders, dug her fingers into his nape and kept him sealed to her. The tender kiss deepened, turned into something more than just comfort. His arms tightened around her, sealed them together more, and the sweet tide of emotion took Vic along for the ride.

Her chest tightened. As much as she tried to keep from having any feelings for him, she'd absolutely failed. He'd busted his ass to keep her safe and shown her the kind of consideration she'd always wanted from a man. They bounced off each other in an equal give and take and most of all, he treated her like she mattered. He meant so much to her. God, she might even love him. How could she have let this happen?

She'd promised not to get into anything too deep, so all she could do was show him in her kiss.

She loved the burn of his stubble against her face. Loved the—

Glass crunched in the main hallway and they both froze.

"Shit!" Danny hissed, pulling away. He tilted his head listening harder. There it was again. Someone was inside. The fact that they hadn't heard sirens or anyone calling out made it easy to deduce the bad guys had landed first.

Danny pointed to the unisex bathroom and pushed her toward it, waving her forward as he moved to the door, grabbing his knife off the table as he went.

Vic's palms sweated and her heart knocked against her ribs like a pinball. Wouldn't do any good to argue at this point. They didn't have time. Silently, she opened the door, slid inside and with a last glance at Danny, closed it behind her. Nausea turned her stomach and she took a deep, quiet breath to calm her nerves. Yeah, like that could happen. Standing with her hand on the knob, she listened with her ear to the door.

Nothing.

Absolutely nothing for the longest time.

When she thought she might go out of her mind, she heard a gunshot and jumped back. A door slammed hard, and grunts and groans that went with a fight bled through the wall. Her heart knocked behind her ribs. How the hell was she supposed to stay here when Danny was fighting one—probably two—men at the same time?

The knob turned in her hand—from the other side—and Vic didn't have time to think. Fresh adrenaline pounded into her system and she did the same thing she'd done at Eric's boss's house. Surprise was the only thing she had going for her. Putting her shoulder into it—and all her weight, she pushed the door open hard, smashing right into the man on the other side. He fell back, tripped on a chair and landed on his butt. His gun clattered behind him and Vic ran for it. The guy caught her ankle, tripped her up and she fell forward, reaching for the weapon even as the man tugged her back.

A roar emerged from her throat as she snagged the handle and secured the gun in her hand. Spinning onto her back, she aimed at the man who knelt at her feet, his face a mask of rage and violence as he wrapped a hand around her ankle. "Don't!" Vic ordered, shaking like a tree in a hurricane. On the other side of the room, Danny still brawled with another man.

"Get off me." He didn't budge. Seconds ticked by. She tracked his gaze to the broken leg of a chair right next to his hand. "Don't!" she told him again. "Let me g—" The muscles in his neck tensed and he scooped up the hard plastic. Vic fired two shots into his chest. She might've fired a third, but he fell so fast, all she could do was try and dodge the heavy weight of his body as he crashed on top of her with dead eyes.

VIC'S SCREAM AND THE gunshots sent another surge of urgency through Danny and he elbowed the guy who had him in a chokehold, before flipping him onto his back. The guy kept hold of Danny's arm and momentum took him down. *There.* Danny saw his knife on the floor and reached for it as the guy leveraged himself up. Danny didn't try to get the knife into his dominant hand, he just pushed the blade into the guy's side at an upward angle and pulled it out, ready to deliver more.

The guy paused long enough for Danny to land a hard right punch to his jaw and scramble up. The man grabbed for his side and gasped for breath. Blood spewed from between his fingers in a gushing red flow.

Glancing up, Danny saw a man sprawled over Vic and weighed

the chances of the guy he'd just knifed getting to his feet. Fuck it. He sprinted for Vic and grabbed the man on top of her, hauling him off with one hard yank and expecting a fight. The guy rolled over, sightlessly staring ahead. A gun clattered on the floor next to him.

Blood covered Vic and panic roared through Danny. She scrambled to get distance, slipping on the blood that covered her hands and clothes as she tried to crawl away. Danny jumped the body in front of him and skid to his knees next to her. He grabbed her shoulders and she screamed, striking out with her arm and landing a solid blow to his chest.

"Vic, it's me! It's Danny!"

She wouldn't stop screaming, her voice raw, her breathing choppy as she kicked and clawed for space.

"Victoria!" Danny got to his feet, grabbed her around the waist and lifted her, spinning her around and getting in her face. "Vic, look at me! It's Danny!"

Her wild-eyed gaze landed on him and her screams stopped. A second later, her face crumpled into pure emotion, and tears flowed down her cheeks. He pulled her closer, but she shook her hands in front of her. "Get it off, get it off! Danny get it off of me."

For a second he didn't understand, but then she was clawing at her shirt, trying to get it off.

The blood. She wanted the blood off her.

Danny grabbed the bottom hem of her top and ripped it clean in two. He wiped what he could off her neck and arms with the back of the shredded shirt and she stood there in her sports bra with her eyes tightly shut and her body shaking so hard he thought she might be having a seizure. Yanking off the flannel shirt over his T-shirt, he put her arms through the holes and buttoned it up. The whole time he spoke to her in low tones. "You're okay, you're okay. I've got you. It's going to be all right. You're okay." God, he hoped she was okay. He honestly wasn't sure. He'd never seen her like this before.

Danny looked across the room at the man he'd tangled with, relieved to see him unconscious. Then he glanced at the dead man on the floor next to him. Brown hair, angular face. No one he recognized. Danny exhaled. At least the guy was dead. Not terrorizing anyone else ever again.

Finally, Vic opened her watery eyes, still red and swollen. This time, when he went to hug her, she latched on tight and didn't seem like she'd ever let go. He was cool with that.

Sirens wailed and Danny closed his eyes, thankful to have her in one piece.

"I'm sorry, I'm so sorry," she whispered at his neck.

What? Truly baffled, he pulled back far enough to see her tear-streaked face. "What are you apologizing for?"

Her brows pulled together in uncharacteristic worry. "I kind of lost it for a minute. I don't know what happened. I've never done that before."

She'd never shot anyone dead before either. "It's okay." He pulled her close again, rocking them gently and gauging the tension in her body.

"Are you okay?" she asked, still holding him tight.

He swallowed hard. He hadn't been okay when he'd thought that blood was hers. "I am now," he assured her. God, he didn't want to let her go. Ever. Strong, brave, full of fight and so damn resourceful and beautiful. She was everything he didn't even know he wanted.

"Oh my God," she said, moving away from him. "I'm still covered in blood. I need to wash this off before the police come and I don't get the chance. She moved to the bathroom and left Danny standing there alone, when what he really wanted was to stay by her side. What happened if she went back to her life and they hardly ever saw each other? Worse, what happened if she showed up at Brendan's next New Year's Eve party with a fucking date? How did he tell her what he felt for her when she'd been so clear with what *she* wanted? Nothing permanent. No emotions. For the first time in his life, he wanted the attachment. He wanted everything that went with being with Vic.

Sirens blared louder, then stopped outside the building and Danny's thoughts turned to the urgency for his brother as he headed toward the lobby. Time was ticking and they needed to get to Eric and Zoe.

"**Zoe Turner, show your** face or your friend here will die a very slow and painful death."

Zoe spun around at the sound of a man's voice calling from outside the ranger station, another burst of adrenaline rushing through her veins. *They had Eric.* She'd heard the shot minutes ago and her heart had stalled.

"She's not there!" Eric's voice loud and clear. "I already told—" A dull thud and groan cut off the sound.

Panic and fear churned in her stomach. In that moment, all the feelings she had for Eric blindsided her. He was too important to her. She couldn't lose him. She never should've let him leave and she had absolutely nothing to bargain with.

"C'mon out," the voice called again.

"I told you she's not in there." She barely heard Eric utter the words as he tried to protect her.

Shit, shit, shit! What did she do? They were going to kill them either way. The question was whether they went down with a fight.

"You got about thirty seconds before I start putting bullet holes in your friend. Starting now."

Zoe swallowed back bile. She had to do something to buy time. If she could at least distract them, maybe Eric could fight them off long enough for her to get closer and help.

She didn't have much of a choice.

"Ten, nine…" The man counted down and Zoe looked out the side window Eric had busted to gain entrance in the ranger station. She barely saw Eric's feet. He must have been on his knees in front of the man holding him.

"Six, five…"

Zoe opened the door and stepped out onto the porch, her stomach knotting. "Stop! I'm here. You don't have to do this."

"No! Zoe, run!" Eric yelled, panic clear in his eyes.

"We won't testify!" Her clear voice rang through the quiet forest. "I swear, we won't show in court and without our testimony, you walk."

"Hey," the big guy said, facing his partner. He had a rifle slung over his shoulder and a gun in his hand. "What the hell is she talking about?"

BAM!

The smaller man had pointed his rifle and fired, blowing the other man back into the dirt, nearly cutting him in half.

Zoe jumped, her stomach dropping at the gore. Not wasting a second, Eric twisted and lunged from his knees, wrapping his arms around the shooter and knocking him to the ground. She flew down the stairs, headed toward the gun the dead man had dropped when he fell. Eric fought over the rifle with the other man as Zoe picked up the gun. Holding it one-handed, she tried to aim, but the fight made it impossible to fire for fear of hitting Eric.

The men rolled, back and forth, vying for the upper hand. Eric ended up on his back and the man released the barrel long enough to slam his fist into Eric's shoulder. His roar of pain spiked Zoe's adrenaline higher as the man wrenched the rifle from Eric's hands. Before he got to his feet, Eric grabbed a handful of dirt and threw it at his face. It gave him the second he needed to lash out with a hard right punch that knocked the man off him and to the ground, face first.

The man stilled. Zoe moved closer and kicked the rifle away as Eric staggered to his feet, holding his left shoulder. With her gun still trained on the man, she rushed to Eric's side.

The guy on the ground shifted groggily and a second later, he flipped over, a smaller gun in his hand. Zoe didn't think. She fired two rounds that somehow landed right in his chest. He bucked at the impact, the gun flying from his hand, then he lay still.

Only their heavy breathing sounded in the silent woods, and Zoe's pounding heart beat like a bass drum between her ears as she kept the gun trained—with shaking hands—on his lifeless body.

"It's okay," Eric murmured. "I don't think he's going anywhere."

Trembling, she dropped the gun. Eric took a staggering step and she wrapped her arm around his waist as much to steady him as herself. The hot sting of tears burned her eyes as relief nearly took her to her knees.

The beautiful *whap, whap, whap* sound of an incoming helicopter had them both looking skyward.

"Think that one's for us?" Zoe asked, taking a step back and shading her eyes from the sun.

The red and black helicopter hovered over them high in the sky. "Yep. Finally," Eric muttered, wiping a hand across his bloody lip.

"Thank God." A second round of relief poured through Zoe's tense muscles in a crippling wave. It was over. They'd survived. She did something very un-Zoelike when she threw herself into Eric's strong welcoming arms.

CHAPTER 26

EARLY MONDAY MORNING, THANKS to a police escort, the foursome made it to court on time. The parent reunion was as emotional as any Hallmark commercial with three moms fawning over four adult children. Although, Danny was proud of his mom for being a little fiercer than the other two, with hard hugs and determined eyes. Zoe and Vic's parents didn't seem as if they'd let them go long enough to walk into the courtroom. Blake, Brendan and even Jess and her husband, Tanner, showed up.

Danny hoped the judge got the message as to why they all looked as if they'd come from a barroom brawl. Eric and he especially looked like they'd been in a cage fight. Felt like it too. They'd all spent the end of Saturday and most of Sunday at the park's urgent care. Then they'd spent hours talking to multiple divisions of law enforcement. Several park rangers had packed up what was left of their camp and brought their things. Eric wore a black sling on his arm because of a fractured collarbone. Danny had fresh stitches along his cheek. Vic had six stitches of her own patching the wound on her hip, and Zoe had a black splint on her badly sprained wrist.

As motley a crew as they made, they came into court with a distinct advantage. The one man who'd been set on killing them was now dead, along with the two local hunters who'd helped him last week. Two new suspects faced charges including the one who murdered the park ranger. The surviving ranger—who regained consciousness on Sunday—would testify against him. The bailiff led the suspects, including the man who'd originally shot Zoe into the courtroom. Danny felt a certain satisfaction at seeing the men in lime green jumpsuits and shackles, more so after the last few days.

The judge entered the courtroom and the bailiff called the court in session. As the judge looked at some papers in front of him, an older man walked toward the bailiff and motioned him closer to the wood partition that separated the visitors and upcoming cases from the lawyers.

Danny glanced toward the judge just as two pops sounded and the bailiff fell backward. The man who'd been talking to him had a gun in his hand and fired off two more rounds at the officer. Had to have been the bailiff's gun because everyone went through a metal detector on the way in. Chaos erupted. People screamed as the man turned the gun on the crowd.

Danny's stomach hit the floor even as adrenaline spiked in his veins. As Eric pushed Zoe to the floor, Danny grabbed Vic and shoved her down, hoping his body and the table were enough to protect her. The judge ducked and ran for the door behind his bench with two of his staff right behind him. The man turned and fired more rounds at the retreating court officials until they disappeared, before facing front again. People rushed to get out of the courtroom through the double doors at the back, causing a disastrous bottle neck. The rest of the family ducked behind the seats in front of them.

The man waved the gun between the four of them and the suspects, but it seemed like involuntary movement. "You," he said, talking to the suspects. "You're the ones who caused this mess." He fired the gun, and hit one of the men. The other two cowered in fear against the wood panel. "You're one of the reasons my son is dead." He fired more rounds, which hit their mark and both men slumped over, while their lawyer cowered beneath the table.

The gun swerved Danny's way.

The side door busted open and officers rushed the room. "Drop the weapon!" one yelled.

The gunman turned, spraying bullets as he moved and the all the officers opened fire. He jolted back, took a last gasp of air and dropped to the ground. Crying in the back of the courtroom ended the short tense silence.

"Oh my God, oh my God. Is it over?" Vic whispered, her limbs trembling under him.

Blood pooled beneath the dead man and Danny's gut roiled. "Very over."

"Is everyone okay?" She got to her feet, holding on to him as she stood. In the back of the courtroom, their family members seemed unhurt and a few waved.

Vic turned toward the man on the ground. "Who was *that?*" she asked, her eyes still wide and panicked.

Danny wanted the answer to that question too.

ERIC KEPT ZOE IN front of him as he guided her into the hallway. No one needed to see the carnage behind them. His shoulder throbbed like a bitch after all that.

The hallway buzzed with dozens of people and almost as many cops. EMTs made their way through the crowd looking for any injured people. The whole St. John family, along with Vic and Zoe and their parents, congregated near the corner, waiting for the inevitable questions from the authorities.

What pissed Eric off most was having all of thirty fucking seconds to say goodbye to Zoe before officers escorted them all in different directions. They still hadn't had the conversation that mattered most.

Last night the local police had put them up in a small hotel and, instead of the guys taking one room and the girls taking the other, they'd split up into pairs. Despite being less than a hundred percent, Eric had purchased condoms in the small sundry shop, sure that Zoe and he would finally have a few hours of uninterrupted time together. He'd debated walking in on her shower, but figured soap, water, her arm in a splint and his in a sling didn't make for very good odds.

When he finished in the bathroom, he'd come out to discover her fast asleep in the middle of the bed. Smiling, he'd eased in next to her. She'd fit herself against him as she had the past few nights in the wilderness and slept in the crook of his good arm. Exhaustion had sucked him under in minutes. They never had a decent chance to talk to each other this morning either. Now, she was simply gone and it seemed weird to be without her...as if a vital part of him was missing.

After hours of rehashing the Monday night attack at his boss's house, Eric was finally released. He found his parents and Danny waiting for him in the front lobby of the building.

Danny met him halfway. "How'd it go?" With dark circles under his eyes and bruises on his face, he looked as wrecked as Eric felt.

Shrugging, Eric wiped a hand over his scruffy jaw. He needed to shave this beard before it drove him crazy. "It was endless. What about you? Been out long?"

"Nope. Just got here."

"What about Zoe and Vic?" Eric asked, looking for either one of them.

"Mom said they left about an hour ago. Did the cops grill you about Monday night?"

"Yeah. From the sound of it, there won't be any charges against us. At least not against you guys. I don't know if my boss is going to press charges against me for the damage to his place." Eric's stomach rolled at the possible legal trouble of that mistake. They headed toward their parents. "Do we know who the shooter was in the courtroom? No one had any information during my interrogation."

"I found out," his dad said, lifting his cell phone before shoving it in his back pocket. "Guy's name was Liam Collier. His son was Trevor, the one—"

"The one who decided to track us," Eric said.

His dad nodded. "Police found a note at his office. He never intended to come out of that courtroom alive."

"Suicide by cop," his mom added. "He'd been diagnosed with Parkinson's and the police said it was his way dealing with the loss of his son and declining health."

Eric closed his eyes, a mix of relief, sadness and anger swirling in his chest. He remembered what the detectives had initially told them about Liam Collier. Whether the man was guilty of anything or not, clearly the idea of losing his son had triggered his reaction.

"I'm ready to blow this place," Danny said. "I didn't sleep at all last night. I don't know how I'm still standing."

Ready to put this whole thing behind him, Eric couldn't agree more. His mom hooked her arm around his good one. "You guys hungry? Feel like a meal? My fridge is full." She knew them too well, but Eric didn't think he could eat.

"Honestly, Mom, I'd just rather head home. Haven't slept much lately."

"Of course."

Their parents drove them back to their apartment and insisted on walking them up.

"I know you're both grown men and you don't need your mother telling you what to do..." At five feet two and barely a hundred and ten pounds, Terry St. John might've been the shortest in the family, but that never stopped her from speaking her mind. "But the next time you're in a situation like this, you had better come straight to us." She glanced at their dad.

"We didn't want to make you guys targets too," Danny said, voicing Eric's thoughts.

"Daniel St. John, after everything this family has been through, you should know by now that we stick together no matter what. We face the good and bad as a family." She shot her stern-mother-face at Eric next. "And you. You're the big brother. You're supposed to keep your siblings in line." Eric couldn't help the half grin curving his lips. "And don't you give me that smirk, young man." She opened her mouth to say something else then thought better of it. Instead, she walked over and gave him a hug before giving Danny one as well. "Get some sleep, both of you." She headed toward the door, their dad following behind. "I used your extra key last night and put some enchiladas in your fridge for later. Call us if you need anything." The door closed behind them.

Alone, they both took a breath. Eric sat on the sofa and closed his eyes. He wasn't ready to deal with anything else at the moment. Not when he felt as if he'd been run over by a steam roller. The worst ache wasn't even his shoulder, it was the organ beating behind his ribs.

"So, you and Zoe...?" Danny asked, not waiting a full minute to tackle the gorilla in the room as he dropped into the brown leather recliner.

Eric cracked an eye open. Sure, he'd kissed her, but it wasn't as if they'd had sex. Although he would have in a flat second last night if Zoe had been awake. God, just remembering how sweet and sexy she looked last night started the blood rushing south. "It's probably not what you're thinking." But Danny on the other hand… Eric knew his little brother well enough to know something had happened on his end. "So, you and Vic?"

Leaning forward, elbows on his knees, Danny nodded. "She said early on she didn't want anything permanent." He dropped his head in his hands and rubbed his forehead. Like he was giving up?

Not the reaction Eric expected. "What do *you* want, Dano?"

"I don't know." He shook his head, then stood and paced the floor. "I don't fucking know." He paced some more. "Okay. Yes, I know. I want her. She's brave, strong. She's funny. Gorgeous. Smart. Why wouldn't I want her?"

Eric shrugged his good shoulder. Seemed simple to him. "Tell her."

"Tell her," Danny mocked. "And have her slam the door on my face? I don't think so."

"Maybe you grew on her, just like she did with you. Won't know until you face it."

"What? Just go over there and say, 'Hey, Vic. How's everything. I'm ready for a relationship.' That'll go over well."

"You won't know if you don't try."

"Look who's talking. I don't see you rushing to tell Zoe how you feel about *her*. Don't give me that look. She never left your side in the hospital, and the looks you two were giving each other since Saturday had more hidden messages than a double agent's email."

Eric shot to his feet and the move sent a sharp stab of pain down his arm. "*Shit!* Dammit, Maybe I don't know exactly how I feel about her, okay?" He went to the kitchen and cracked open the only thing in the fridge. Ginger ale.

Danny watched him. "I think you do and I think you're scared to admit it."

"All of a sudden you're Mr. Insightful." Eric eased back down to the couch and set his drink on the coffee table. "It was only a week," he muttered. How could he feel this strongly about her in only a week?

"Maybe." Danny sat on the other side of the sofa. "But it was a week where we learned a lot about them. Ourselves too."

Eric watched his brother. In the last twenty-four hours, he'd seemed a little more like his old self, but at the same time, he'd changed. Grown up. That was it. Danny had finally grown up. A mix of happiness and pride jolted through his chest. "Can I take that to mean, you're back among the living?"

Danny scowled. "I was never dead."

"Your heart was," Eric said softly. "You tuned everything out but your own pain. I think Vic helped you find a way through it. You should go tell her that."

Running a hand over his head, Danny nodded and stood. "Yeah. You're probably right. I will." He got to the front door and turned. "Can you give me a lift on your way? My Jeep is totaled."

Eric got to his feet—a little gentler this time. "Sure." He stopped. "On my way where?"

"On your way to Zoe's to tell her how you feel about *her*."

ZOE UNPLUGGED HER NEWLY charged phone and scrolled through all the messages she'd missed during her week in the forest. An even half a dozen voice messages from her boss waited for her along with dozens of texts from everyone from her sister and co-workers to clients.

Taking a fortifying breath, Zoe hit play and listened to the last message. Tears stung her eyes at her boss's build-up. It didn't take long to get to the main point. *We've replaced you at the office and your desk is now occupied by a new agent. We've boxed your belongings so you can pick them up at your convenience. Sorry it had to happen this way, Zoe.*

She missed the rest of the message because a call came through. Vic.

Zoe took a deep breath, wiped her nose and accepted the call. "Hey, girl. How are you doing? Get home okay?"

"Yeah." There was a pause. "You okay? You sound...off."

Exhaling slowly, Zoe pushed through the emotion clogging her throat. "I'm just tired. It was a long week." And she wasn't ready to share her bad news. "You better be calling to tell me what happened with Danny." Every time they found a minute alone after the rescue, they were interrupted, if not by police or medical staff at the hospital then by Danny or Eric. Zoe knew the hot springs seduction had been busted up, but obviously along the way, Vic and Danny had found time to get close. "Strictly from an observational stand point, Danny was looking seriously whipped the last twenty-four hours. Dare I add…you were too," Zoe murmured.

Vic groaned. "Don't… Look, I promised him no emotion. No commitment."

"But now you feel differently." Zoe didn't bother making it a question.

"How do you know that?"

"Like I said, it was written all over your face. You couldn't take your eyes off that man and he pretty much had his glued to you. I wasn't about to get in between you and ask what was up."

"So what do I do?"

"About what?" Zoe looked at the small note pad on the counter with the real estate logo and her picture. She flipped it over and blinked back the sting in her eyes.

"About Danny. Are you even listening to me? I can't tell him how I feel because I told him I wouldn't feel *anything*. Besides, I don't *want* to feel anything."

Zoe sighed. "Definitely a tough spot. All I can say is, if he calls or comes around, then you need to make every effort to find out how *he* feels so you can be honest with him." Vic didn't answer so Zoe cut her some slack. "It's your future and it's in your hands."

Vic let out a huff of air. "What about you and Eric? You two didn't mind sharing a room last night when Danny and I asked to bunk together."

Zoe rubbed her forehead, frustration climbing up her chest. "Yeah, that didn't really go as I had planned." She really didn't want to expand on the matter.

"I'm waiting," Vic said.

"Jeez, fine. I fell asleep, okay? I hadn't planned on it. Eric took his turn in the bathroom and by the time he got out I was probably already drooling on my pillow. I'm not proud."

"So, you two never—"

"No," Zoe said, cutting Vic off before she threw out one of her crude euphemisms.

245

"But you kissed him. Obviously, you kissed him. How was that?"

Zoe closed her eyes and imagined Eric's lips on hers. The way his touch made her feel wanted and protected. Sexy. "Pretty damn spectacular," she admitted softly. It didn't seem possible that after one week she'd grown to love the man, but even the few hours of separation since the courthouse seemed like forever. She loved the way he stroked his jaw, always grimacing when he came across the beard. She loved the way his blue eyes gazed on her with so much appreciation. Zoe blinked, realized Vic was waiting for her. "Look, it wasn't like we talked about anything—you know—continuing once we got home. For all I know he's back to giving me the stink eye."

"That's bullshit and you know it. You should call him."

"The same way you're going to call Danny?"

"Two different things and you know it," Vic argued.

"Maybe so," Zoe grumbled. "Ultimately, I don't know where we stand." And she had too much to worry about to go chasing after Eric anyway.

"I'm about to dive into a pint of ice cream. Want to come over and join me?"

Something sweet sounded good. Zoe got up and opened the fridge. She needed... There, waiting for her in the side door. Chocolate. "How about a raincheck on that offer?"

Vic's invitation didn't sound half bad, but if she went over and got lost in ice cream—and probably wine—she'd end up telling Vic about her non-existent job and she wasn't up for any of her friend's outrageous ideas for either A) revenge or B) retaliation. Vic had no idea that Zoe had only sold one house in two years, the one sale that got her in the agency to begin with. Then Vic would grill her on Eric, and she had feelings she didn't know how to categorize when it came to that man. Love seemed too strong a word. It just didn't seem possible to love a man after one week.

CHAPTER 27

DANNY LOOKED OVER HIS shoulder and watched Eric drive away. If Vic didn't let him in, he'd be stuck with the most humiliating Uber wait in history. He lifted his hand to knock, then held it there, waiting for... He had no idea. She'd never specifically said *no strings.* Her exact words had been *you have nothing to worry about from me.* Attachment had always been his biggest fear, so his brain had interpreted her words the way he used to want to hear them.

For once in his life, he *wanted* strings. He wanted attachment. He wanted one woman to call his own, but only if that woman was Vic. He moved his hand to knock and the door opened before he connected.

"I thought I saw someone out here."

Seeing her sent his heart thrumming and a mass of butterflies took flight in his stomach. That sure as hell never happened before. Barefoot, wearing skin tight jeans and flowing white shirt with a neckline low enough to tease the eye with soft round cleavage, she looked like a model. She could've been Quasimodo and he wouldn't have cared. She'd gotten through to him when no one else could. She'd pushed him into seeing what mattered. She pushed him into living life instead of letting life rule him.

Everything hinged on her reaction. Was she tired of him or willing to give him more time?

Vic's curious smile faded and her brows pulled together. "Is something wrong?" He didn't know where to start and she pounced on his silence. "Please tell me everything's okay. Come in." She grabbed his hand, tugged him through the door and the contact shot through him like a high voltage current.

"Everything's fine," Danny said, walking into her apartment. A large living space melded into a small, but updated kitchen. A hunter green accent wall set off a colorful area rug and red upholstered chairs. Spacious, eclectic and colorful. Just like the woman who lived there. "Nice place." Albeit a little sparse on furnishings. He hadn't paid much attention last Monday when he'd brought her home to pack. He'd been too busy texting Eric about the whole plan. He faced her, not ready for the hot arrow of need that pierced his gut. As if the last few hours without her had sucked his soul dry of light and just the sight of her filled him up again.

"Thanks. It's a little bare at the moment. My roommate moved out a couple of weeks ago and she owned most of the furniture, so…" She shrugged. "I need to put some feelers out for another roomie soon, but I like having the place to myself for a little while. At least I did before the last week. Not sure how much I'm going to like solo living. I'm already jumping at every sound and I've only been home a few hours." Her face heated in a pretty blush. "What's up?"

"I just wanted—needed—to talk to you."

"Oh. Okay." Her inquisitive brown eyes watched him and Danny's heart started an unholy beat. Flashbacks of her moving on top of him—whispering his name as she came, holding on tight as he pumped deep inside of her—flipped through his mind like a film on fast forward. He didn't want that to be all there was. He wanted more. He wanted everything. She rubbed the side of her nose, her gaze now everywhere but on him. "Have a seat." She indicated one of the two red chairs in front of the flat screen and he sat as she took the other one.

He ran a hand over his hair and jumped to his feet. No way could he do this sitting.

"Danny, you're scaring me. What's wrong?" Vic stood too. Her brows pulled together like they'd done so many times before during the last few days when she'd been terrified.

He exhaled hard. "Okay. Here it is. You know how people change, right? People can change when life gets, you know, crazy… When you get shit thrown at you and you don't know how to cope so you just do the best you can to get through every day."

"Yes." She sounded hesitant and hopeful in the same breath, but looked so confused and worried that Danny wanted to pull her close, attach his lips to hers and never let go. And she'd been very clear that she didn't want *permanent. I'm not looking for happily ever after.*

So many things she'd said that had been things he'd always wanted before… Before he fell in love with her.

"Danny?"

Shit. She was looking at him with wide eyes as if he'd completely flipped out. Maybe he had.

"Yeah, so… Here's the deal." What if he said something and wrecked the chance of even having her in his life? What if she didn't feel the same way? At least with time, he could potentially change her mind. So where did he buy time? With business. "I definitely want to do all that stuff you mentioned before, you know, on the mountain. The PR stuff," he clarified. It was official. He'd turned into a bona-fide loser with glass balls. Hell, non-existent balls.

Her face fell a split second before she smiled. "Oh, that's great. Okay. I'll let my bosses know. They'll be really excited."

"But I get to work with you, right? I'm not doing this if you're not on my team." At this point, he didn't want to do *anything* without her. He wanted to see her face first thing in the morning and last thing when he went to bed at night.

"Sure. Whatever you want. That's fine." She anchored a chunk of hair behind her ear and Danny itched to touch her so badly his fingers tingled. He remembered the thick, soft locks wrapped around his hand, the way they sifted through his fingers when she slept on his chest.

"Okay then. Good." He stood there like a dope, hands on his hips, aching to touch her, his heart pounding a beat in his throat.

"Was there something else?" Her voice sounded unusually high, but that was probably because she wanted him out.

He needed a reason to stay. A few more minutes to feel her out and see if she'd take a chance at making things work with them. "So, when would we start? You know, doing all the PR stuff that makes me rich and famous?"

"Oh…" She spread her hands wide then clasped them together.

"I'll put a proposal together and pitch it to my bosses. If they go for it, then I'll call you and arrange a meeting. Does that work?"

He nodded. "Yeah. Sure." He wanted to pound his head into the tile floor. How could they be talking business when all he wanted to do was wrap her in his arms and hold her forever? Maybe she really didn't have any feelings for him. "Was there anything you need to tell me? Or want to tell me? Anything, you know, on your mind?"

She glanced at the ceiling as she shook her head. "Don't think so." She blinked fast and for the first time, Danny got the feeling she was holding something back.

What she'd said on the trip versus the way she'd made love to him didn't jive. How could she not want the intimacy they shared? "Okay." He backed up toward the door, giving her the space she'd assured him she wanted. Ten times worse than watching her walk away from him at the courthouse, feeling as if losing her was losing a limb... Or his heart. He turned to the door then flipped back around. "Dammit, Vic. We've got something here. Something special."

The raw emotion in her eyes made his chest tighten. They sparkled with moisture and all but begged him to stay.

VIC WAS LOSING THE battle to hold her ground. How could she, when Danny finally said the one thing she'd both dreaded and wished for.

Talking with Zoe had opened her eyes. She'd absolutely come to terms with her feelings for Danny. She also remembered why she didn't want to fall in love again. Those two things had warred in her head and in her heart for hours.

Danny took a step toward her. "Don't throw it away, Vic. Give it a chance." He took another step and focused on her so hard that she thought he might see into her head. "This is about trust isn't it?"

She pressed her lips together, wanting to deny the question when she couldn't without lying to him. "I don't know if I know how..." She didn't know what to say, how to make him see that maybe she'd never trust him the way she wanted to or should.

"How what? How to trust me? That's it, isn't it. Because of the guys that hurt you before?" He shook his head, his eyes imploring her.

Seeing that pain absolutely crushed her.

"Remember what you told me in the forest? You said, 'I'm not her.'" He was talking about Nikki. "We'll, I'm not them. I swear to you I'm not them." He took another step toward her.

Leaving him at the courthouse had nearly devastated her. Just these few hours alone without him had pounded home exactly how much he meant to her. Then he'd knocked on her door, and it was if he'd somehow felt her sadness and come to chase it away.

Like a dope, she'd fallen in love with him. Maybe that's why she'd insisted on keeping her distance from him last year. No maybes about it. She'd known from day one, minute one, second one. The instant she'd laid eyes on him, she'd known. He was a man who could hurt her and she didn't do that anymore.

Danny glanced up at the ceiling, ran another hand over his head. A gesture she'd become familiar with when he was agitated.

A hot tear slipped free at the same time he met her gaze and she blinked hard to keep more from falling.

His eyes narrowed, zeroing in on her. "All right. I'm going lay it all out. I didn't come here about the PR stuff. I came here because—" He clenched his jaw, his mouth a grim line as he nodded twice. "Because I want you in my life." His voice cracked on the words and Vic's façade cracked with it.

She couldn't blink the tears away fast enough. Her heart tripped along faster.

Danny took three strides until he stood right in front of her, everything she'd ever wanted in a man and more. A man who showed her over and over exactly what mattered most in life. In his eyes, she saw the love she felt for him mirrored back at her. He watched her for the longest time and she blinked back more stupid tears, waiting to make sure she'd heard him right. "I want you..." he repeated slowly, watching her every nuance, "...in my life." Gently he scooped a fat drop of moisture from the corner of her eye as her heart soared. "I'm not going to hurt you, Vic. I swear I'm not. I just want to make you happy."

"You do?" Even she heard the longing in her voice.

Then he smiled. The crazy, gorgeous, playboy smile she knew

from a year ago. "Yeah. I do." The grin faded as he brushed away more tears. "I want permanence and strings and lots of attachment." He brushed his lips across hers. "I want spin the bottle, truth or dare, sleeping bag sex and hot springs kisses." He kissed her again and she tasted the salt of her tears. "I want to go to sleep with you in my arms at night, and wake up with my hands on you in the morning."

"Danny—"

"Shh," he said softly, "I'm not done." He kissed her again, teasing her with his tongue on her upper lip. "I love you, Vic. I don't want to be without you."

Vic might've floated off the floor if Danny hadn't been holding her close. She opened her mouth to his inquisitive tongue and let him kiss her. He was gentle and tender and felt like home. She put all the words she'd hadn't yet told him into their kiss. He owned her heart and soul and she gave them freely.

Danny finally pulled away, breathing hard, his eyes sparkling with love and confidence. "Here's the deal, Vic. Straight up honestly. We're going to play a little game called Yes or No. I'm going to say something and you're going to answer with a yes or a no. Got it."

"I—"

"Yes or no. Those are your options."

She still had things to say, but she gave him a little leeway. "Ok—yes."

He took a breath and let it out. "When we're together, we set the sheets on fire."

She bit back a smile, but suspected he saw her lips twitch. Last night, they'd definitely set the sheets on fire in their hotel room. Her hip had precluded them from having actual intercourse, but they'd managed to work around it with the most amazing oral sex Vic had ever had. "Yes."

Nodding, he narrowed his eyes. "I'm *not* the only one who has feelings when it comes to the two of us."

"Danny—"

He stopped her with a finger against her lips. "Yes or no."

If he'd let her talk, she'd be happy to tell him how she felt. "Yes."

"I'm not the only one who wants to strip and dive under the sheets for a few rounds of Find My Hot Spot."

She rolled her eyes, because leave it to Danny to be so…so…damn adorable. "Yes."

His smile faded and eyes grew serious. "I want you in my life. Period. Just you and only you. I don't know what would've happened if you'd called me last summer. I don't know if I would've fallen in love with you like I did this past week. Yes, I said it again," he said because her eyes had grown saucer wide at the L-word. She never dreamed he'd be saying all this to her. "I don't know if it was time or circumstances or that I got to see just how amazing you are in every way. But I'm glad I found you. Glad that I know myself well enough to know what I'd lose if I lost you. I love you, Vic."

Never had anyone said something so heartfelt to her. Never had she fallen so hard so fast. Her heart opened up so wide and filled with so much love, she didn't see how it had any room in her chest. All for this man. She opened her mouth, not sure where to start.

"Yes or no," he whispered. "Are you on board with that?"

He wanted honesty. He wanted cards on the table. "Yes. Absolutely yes." The relief, the euphoria washing through her made her tremble. She kissed him, soft and sweet, her heart knotting in her throat and tears stinging her eyes. "I wanted you from the very beginning. And this past week, I fell in love with you. I couldn't say anything, because I promised you I wouldn't. I didn't want to scare you or make you think about…" About that woman who wrecked him so badly. More damn tears slid down her cheeks. "And once I realized I loved you, I had to face getting hurt again. I wanted—"

"Shh." He kissed her softly, stroked tears off her cheeks. All she needed was the love in his eyes and his sweet touch. He'd become the one man she could count on no matter what came their way and together they could handle anything. His mesmerizing smile chased away her tears. "It's all good, babe. It's all good."

His mouth brushed across hers in a gentle caress and Vic let go of all her worries.

CHAPTER 28

ERIC STARED AT HIS phone as he took the path to Zoe's condo, processing the news from his boss that he'd been expecting. Shoving the phone and thoughts of work out of his head, he rapped on Zoe's condo door then rubbed his palm across the smooth skin of his cheek. He'd made Danny wait while he shaved. Despite his brother swearing that chicks loved stubble, Eric hated the itch. Did Zoe like the stubble? Maybe he shouldn't have shaved. What if she wanted more alone time before he made an appearance? Just because he realized he had serious feelings for her didn't mean she felt the same way.

Zoe opened the door, her eyes widening when she saw him. His pulse picked up when he caught her familiar vanilla scent. She'd changed into a purple tank and matching loose fitting sweats that flowed with her curves. He wanted to yank her close and hold her tight.

"Hi," she said. "This is a surprise. Oh my God, you shaved. I almost didn't recognize you. Come in. You okay?"

"Yeah. I'm good. Just needed to talk for a minute." He glanced around, making sure they were alone. Two sets of French doors brought in tons of light and opened to an outside patio. Immaculate hard wood floors flowed from the spacious great room to the large kitchen. He'd been here the night they'd packed for his boss's house, but it had been late and at his urging they'd turned on as little light as necessary and Danny had been texting him nonstop. Now, he didn't detect anyone else. No siblings or parents or best friends to get in the way. All he had to do was find a starting point. "Nice place."

"Thanks." She sucked in her bottom lip and Eric itched to do the same thing. She headed toward the kitchen and he followed. "Want to buy it?" she mumbled. Then louder, "Can I get you something to drink?"

He definitely wasn't supposed to hear that first part. "Are you selling?"

She spun around, blue eyes wide.

He tapped his ear with his good right hand. "Excellent ears. Why are you moving?"

Her eyes watered, she swallowed hard and blinked a few times. Her clear distress had him instantly concerned. She lifted her phone from the countertop and waved it, before setting it back on the granite separating the kitchen from the great room. "My boss left half a dozen messages over the last week. I tried to call him from the hotel last night when you were in the shower, but I got his voicemail. I guess he got tired of waiting. He fired me while we were in court."

All her concerns had been warranted and he hadn't ever said a word about it. He felt like shit. "What the hell? How could they do that? They know everything we've been through. It's headline news." Eric strode nearer, watching her struggle to hold it together. He pulled her in as close as he could with his damn sling and her splint. "Those idiots. They don't know what they lost."

She hugged him fast and pulled away. "I think they do." Zoe swiped at her eyes. "You should probably know too." She paced into her living room then faced him. "Here's the deal. I'm not the successful realtor that everyone thinks I am. I sold one house. One. My old college roommate's dad was moving and he knew I wanted to be a realtor. He'd already planned to sell his house to a friend—they both have more money than God—and he basically handed me the sale. I used it to leverage a spot at a very reputable agency. After that, I made a plan with every new listing, I did the marketing. I did everything I was supposed to do, but no one stuck with me. The couple of houses that did go into escrow fell through." She shook her head, her gaze far away. "I had no idea what I was getting into. I had no idea how competitive, how cutthroat the whole industry is." She looked at him and shrugged, clearly defeated. "You see? I'm not who you thought I was. I'm not the successful agent busting everyone's balls." She sat on the edge of her sofa, head in her hands. Her despair crushed him.

Eric sat next to her. "Looks like you and I have even more in common. I got a call from my boss too. Just now on the way over here. We're both looking for new jobs." She gave him a sidelong—*what the hell*—glance and he lifted an eyebrow. "We can stand in the unemployment line together."

"Oh, Eric. I'm sorry. Because of your boss's house?" At his nod, she shook her head. "Uh, that sucks."

"A hell of a way to celebrate a week of running for your life, that's for sure. I apologized. Told him I never thought we'd be followed. I never would've gone there if I thought his place was going to be trashed. Blake emailed me the list of everything he replaced and an itemized bill. There wasn't anything broken that couldn't be fixed and he took care of the major stuff like windows and drywall. I offered to pay for anything the insurance wouldn't pick up, but apparently that wasn't enough to cover my transgression."

A few silent minutes passed and Zoe sighed. "This is so wrong. I have no idea what I'm going to do. I thought I was supposed to sell real estate. It's what I always wanted to do. I have to figure out something completely different."

Eric rubbed his palm up her back. Wanted her to feel his support. "You don't have to figure it out alone." He waited until she met his gaze. "Look, Zoe, what happened this past week—"

"I know." She put her palm out to stop him. "It was stress. Adrenaline. Thinking we might die. I know how you feel about me. It's all right." She sucked in her lip again, a telltale sign of her insecurity. How had he never noticed that before last week? Because they'd never spent any significant amount of time together. Because he was too stupid to see a good thing when it was right in front of him.

"How do I feel about you, Zoe?" He pushed a chunk of her curly hair behind her ear, waiting for her to meet his gaze.

She shook her head. "Look, I know we got closer, Eric. You saved my life so many times, I lost count, but ultimately, I'm still the pain in the ass I was before last week happened. I'm always going to be bossy and controlling and—"

"Zoe."

She looked at him with the saddest eyes and he wanted to hug her tight until he got the smile back. Instead, he came up with the next best thing. "You've met my mom, right?"

She glanced up, brows pinching together. "Of course, I have."

"You probably don't know that she's one of my heroes. She's one of the toughest people I've ever met. And the things she's done for us, for my dad…" He shook his head, swallowed back emotion. "During the kidnapping, one of the psychos fixated on her." Remembering that time still had the power to make him sick. "The things he said he was going to do to her, right in front of us, if she put up a fight…" He nodded, clenched his jaw to fight back tears. "So she didn't. Didn't fight him. To save us. I'll never forget it. She walked right out the door with him into another room." Exhaling hard, he shook off the memory that still gave him nightmares. "My sis ended up saving her, how about that?" He grinned, always wished he'd been there to see it, even though hearing the commotion had scared the piss out of him.

"Anyway…" he got back on track, "I think maybe I was afraid I wouldn't meet someone who cared about me the way my parents care about each other. So maybe I didn't try hard enough—or look hard enough at what was right in front of me." Eric cleared the knot in his throat. "You probably know my mom's really strong and that my dad is crazy about her." She nodded, tears in her eyes as she watched him. "They're a really great team. I always hoped I'd find someone as strong as my mom." She nodded again and looked away, and Eric realized she wasn't really listening to him. He lifted her chin until she met his gaze. "I did when I met you."

"What?" she whispered, the word small and surprised.

"You think your strength is a detriment." He shook his head. "It's not." How did he make her understand? "You and I made a great team out there." He stroked his finger along her bottom lip, surprised by how such a simple touch could reach inside him so deeply. "I just wanted to get to know you better. I think I did that this past week."

"Haven't you heard anything I've said? I'm not what you think I am."

"Bullshit. You think because this agency let you go that

suddenly you're not worthy? Not smart? Losing this job doesn't change who you are inside, Zoe. It just changes how you'll make a paycheck." Eric stood and paced toward the French doors, afraid if he stayed too close, he wouldn't get all the words out because his mouth would be sealed to hers. "When we were separated at the courthouse today…" he turned so he could gauge her reaction, "…when I didn't know if or when I was going to see you again, it was like someone turned off the light and I all I had was this giant dark void." Her pretty eyes widened and she stood. She really had no clue how much she meant to him, how much he admired her strength and her backbone. "Going back to my apartment, going anywhere, without you…doesn't feel right." He shook his head. "What I'm saying is…I have feelings for you, Zoe Turner. Very strong feelings."

Zoe clamped a hand over her mouth as tears brimmed her eyes.

A few measured steps later, he hooked his finger into the thin strap of her tank and tugged her closer.

Zoe swiped at her eyes and flashed him a shaky smile. "That was kind of sexy," she whispered.

He battled a grin, because it was just like her to make him laugh when he shouldn't. Plus it still hurt when he smiled because of his swollen lip. He leaned close, his mouth barely brushing hers.

"So, like on a scale of one to ten," she breathed, warm air washing over his cheek, "where might those feelings be?"

She wanted cards on the table. Fine. "Mm…" He glided his lips across hers, teasing, tasting. "Somewhere between fifteen and eighteen."

Her eyes snapped open. "That's not really on the scale yo—"

He kissed her. "Shh." And kissed her again. Her eyes fluttered closed and she pressed against him. Soft lips opened under his and he slid his tongue into her mouth because she was so damn sweet. Chocolate sweet. She moaned and her palm moved up his chest and around his neck, bringing him closer to all those lush curves that had been teasing him this whole week. Eric put his arm around her, angled her closer to his right side even though it sent a sharp bolt of pain across his shoulder. Her kiss was worth it.

Slow. Deep. Satisfying. The kind of kiss that preceded the same kind of sex.

"A few nights ago, when we kissed like this," he whispered at her mouth, "I said you'd be in serious trouble if I had a condom." He palmed one luscious ass cheek and brought her tightly against him, showing her exactly what waited for her if they kept this up.

"I think I might really like your serious trouble." She teased him with her tongue.

That was all the answer he needed. Without removing his mouth from hers, he walked them toward the stairs, shuffling along in their awkward—her splint/his sling—gait. Slowly, step by step, they moved toward her bedroom. He knew where it was from the night she packed, but he hadn't been in it. He paused at the four-poster bed with white canopy. It suited her perfectly. The fantasy room for the modern day woman. Strong enough to make the little girl fantasy a reality. The perfect spot to get naked and roll around in the sheets for hours at a time. At least one day when they could roll around and not scream in pain. Still, it worked for now too. He pulled back the matching white comforter. With a blush on her cheeks and her eyes soft with emotion, she helped.

Eric ran his fingers through the softness of her curls. "I've been wanting to do this all day," he murmured. Just like he wanted to touch every inch of skin, hear every sigh and see all her passion when he made love to her.

Zoe stood on tiptoe and brought his mouth to hers, slowly, taking her time and sending his pulse hammering faster. She tasted like chocolate and he angled her lips for more. Her sigh hit him chest deep.

Without pulling away, Eric grabbed the strip of condoms he'd stashed in his back pocket and tossed them on the bed.

Her gaze flicked from the condoms to his eyes. "I see being trapped in the wild has honed your preparedness skills." She systematically unbuttoned his shirt. She'd forgotten about her job situation and he loved the determination in her blue eyes, the clear intention that she wanted this as badly as he did. When her lips connected with his chest, his heart thrummed faster. Her hands reached the button on his jeans. "Ouch." She eased her bad wrist closer to her body. "Gonna take both of us to get this."

"See, there's that teamwork I was talking about." Their lips fused as his jeans and her sweatpants hit the floor. He pulled back long enough to ease the sling over his head. She took his shirt off next, careful of his shoulder. Showering him with reverence, she erased any speck of doubt he might've had about this moment and what she wanted. Easing the straps of her top over her shoulders one by one, he took the same care when it came to her wrist.

Unlike her sister's tall willowy frame, Zoe had curves for days. Full breasts that tapered to a small waist and flared again with sweet hips.

Goosebumps rose as his fingers grazed her bare shoulders. He bent, brushed his lips along her neck, loving the way she tipped her head, offering more. Running his palm down her side and ignoring the throbbing in his shoulder, he traced the outside shell of her ear with his tongue. "Damn, you feel good," he murmured. He followed her curves one-handed, down to the elastic band of her pink bikini underwear. She helped strip them off and he grazed his fingers along the ultra-soft skin of her thighs then back up again. Her eyes tracked him from head to toe with a long stop in the area below his stomach. He hoped to hell his rampant erection didn't scare her.

Her cheeks flushed and she snaked her arm around his neck and brought his lips to hers, brushing softly before opening for his tongue. The tight points of her breasts teased his chest and revved his blood. Eric needed to show her how much he cared and tried to take his time. He palmed her ass, moved his thigh between her legs and loved the moan vibrating in her throat. After a minute of long, lush melding of mouths and tongues, the heat turned up.

Zoe's kisses took on new urgency. The doctor's rule about avoiding strenuous activity was about to be obliterated and Eric didn't give two fucks. She pushed him back until his ass hit the sheets. It took a few extra seconds of awkward positioning to get situated and his shoulder burned like a hot iron brand. No matter how badly he wanted to pull her beneath him and drive into her, that wasn't happening today.

Clearly, she realized it because after they got his boxer briefs off, she straddled him. "I like this teamwork thing," she huffed at his mouth before sitting up. His dick jutted thick and hard in front of her and she pressed him against the wet heat of her entrance and the small dark racing strip of tight curls, gripping him firmly and throwing spots in front of his eyes at the sweet torture.

At this rate he wouldn't last a minute. He adjusted on the pillow and grimaced.

Zoe froze. "I hate this. You're in too much pain."

"I'll survive. Trust me, we're not stopping."

"What can I do then? To help?"

Thank God she asked. "There is something you can do. Something I really *need* you to do."

"Anything. What?"

He eased his good hand up along her thigh until his thumb rested right on her clit. She all but froze for a second time. "I need this…" He circled the hard nub and she gasped. "…on my mouth. Now." He circled again and she dropped her head back. The move jutted her breasts forward. God, he wanted to touch them too. "Zoe, now. Straddle my face."

"Oh my God. No way! I'll kill you. I can't do that and not put any weight on your shoulder, much less balance with this splint!"

"I have extreme faith in you. Do it."

She huffed out an exasperated breath. "Now who's being bossy." Her straight delivery had him laughing even as she moved up his body. Then she was there. His. He licked either side of her clit at the same time he palmed her breast. She pushed against his mouth in the sexiest fucking move that destroyed his patience.

"Hang onto the headboard," he told her.

He just needed to consume her. Slowly, he parted her tender flesh with his tongue and tasted her for the first time. Spicy, warm, wet and so ready for him. He licked at the swollen nub begging for attention and Zoe gasped, grabbed his hair and held on tight. Her reaction spurred him on and Eric dove into her pleasure with new determination.

Zoe's muscles tensed and if the *oh Gods* coming out of her mouth were any indication then he was close to his goal. He tortured her with long licks, quick licks, open mouth kisses and hard sucks. When he finally pressed on her clit with his tongue as he pushed two fingers inside of her, Zoe broke apart in his arms, her internal muscles clenching his fingers like a vice.

Eric drank her in, slowed his tongue until he rested his head against her thigh, listening to her ragged breathing. He didn't think he'd ever been this hard in his life. His dick begged for release.

"Oh my God…" Her fingers stroked through his hair. "Okay, that deserves serious retribution." She moved down, careful of his shoulder as she got into place on top of him. Her mouth connected with his and the smoking hot kiss revved him hotter. Then she watched him, her eyes shining bright, her skin flushed. She smoothed her fingers over his cheek. "Have I told you how much I love this?"

"What? Sex?"

She laughed. "No. I mean, yes, I love sex. This sex. Eric sex. But I was talking about the clean, smooth version of your face." Ha! He couldn't wait to tell Danny he was oh so wrong! She bent low, her breath warm on his lips before she kissed him lightly. She eased back, slowing them down again, creating an intimacy they hadn't shared before. An intimacy he'd never shared with another woman.

Her smile faded as they looked into each other's eyes. "You smell really good," she whispered. The pulse in her neck beat a frantic pace and matched the extra beats of his heart.

"So do you," he rumbled. He loved the scent of her on his face. He stroked his good hand down her spine, over her ass and back again.

"Better than the campsite stink I acquired the last week." She lifted a sculpted brow.

"Even at your worst, you didn't come close to my stink."

She nodded stoically. "True."

He never thought he'd banter with Zoe this way, never thought he'd find so much frickin' joy in it.

"Why are you grinning like that?" she asked, those pretty eyes narrowing.

"Because I've got you right where I want you." Eric leaned up slowly, watching her eyes until they closed a fraction of a second before their lips touched. He forced himself to go slow. To savor every kiss, every sigh, every little sound in her throat that told him how much she loved everything he was doing. He still tasted chocolate and smelled vanilla soap.

Her sneaky little hand eased down his side and tucked under his ass and Eric pushed against her, rubbing his erection exactly where she'd feel it most.

"Zoe..." He whispered her name between long, deep kisses. Kisses that totally wrecked him. She was a combination of bold and shy. Fierce and soft. Daring and tentative. He never knew which part of her he was going to get, but discovering her for the first time was like opening a surprise package when it wasn't a holiday.

She wrapped her hand around his erection and Eric clenched his jaw. "I've waited long enough," she whispered in his ear. "Let's do this thing." She leaned over and returned with the strip of condoms he'd brought. She didn't bother with the perforation, she just ripped the first one with her teeth and pulled out the condom. That was more like the woman he knew. Eric's chuckle turned into an inhale as Zoe rolled the condom on. When he looked up, he caught her gaze, a cross between playful and...horny. She waggled her eyebrows in a quick gesture and Eric laughed. He couldn't remember the last time he'd laughed right before making love.

And yeah, that's what he was doing with Zoe. This wasn't a quick fuck or something he took lightly.

"Why are you so serious all of a sudden?" Her quiet words derailed him. Earlier, she hadn't been paying attention and now she read him like a damn book with large print.

"Because. This is important to me. I want to get it right." He realized he wanted that more than anything. "I want to roll you over and drive inside you, Zoe. So deep inside that you don't know anything but the pleasure I'm giving you."

Leaning down, she kissed his lips softly. "That is so hot. So sexy. And so not happening until your collarbone heals. So, while we wait for that to happen, let me take care of things."

"I like how you think," he murmured against her lips.

"I bet that's not the only thing you'll like." She adjusted over him and placed his erection right at her entrance. His brain fogged over as she pushed down and forced the tip inside.

"Damn, you're tight," he muttered. And it was blowing his mind on so many levels.

"We won't let that stop us." She brought her mouth closer to his and stroked her tongue inside. "Okay now," she said, coming up for air. "Let's keep it movin'."

"Back to the bossy thing, I see." But as he said the words she pushed down more causing a sharp gasp from both of them. "You okay?" He waited, watched her.

She nodded, exhaled. "I'm good. Really good. Really incredibly good. Don't mind me... I'm just going to keep going."

Eric sputtered a laugh, a dangerous thing in the position he was in. "Don't make me laugh. I might come."

That made Zoe laugh. "Well, isn't that the point?"

"No. Not yet." He lost the smile. "Not for a long while yet." He pushed up and gritted his teeth at the hot, tight fit. Being inside her was like a homecoming. It was where everything fell into place, his heart and his soul.

Zoe's eyes widened. She gasped. "You are well-equipped for this activity. God did pretty good by you."

Eric nearly laughed again and he couldn't afford to lose control. "Zoe. I'm serious. Shut up."

Her smile slayed him. "By all means. Let me just get to wor— Ah, yes," she hissed when she pushed down. One or two more good tries and he'd be in deep. Just where he wanted to be. This time, he kissed her. Took her mouth in a possessive kiss meant to own, destroy and conquer. Zoe took and gave back more. Stroking into his hair, she held on tight, balanced on her splint and gripping his good shoulder. Every time she pushed down she dug her nails into his skin, marking him, driving him closer to release.

Breathing hard, Zoe stilled with him as deep inside as he could get. Eric soaked in the heat of her, the tight clasp of her body as she squeezed him with internal muscles.

"Oh my God," she panted, her warm breath stroking across his neck. "You feel really good."

"And we haven't even started," he huffed back. He pushed up again, nearly took her off her knees.

Zoe inhaled. "Oh my God. You might kill me, and it would be like the best way *ever* to die."

Eric stroked his thumb across her cheek and pushed a damp lock of hair out of her face. "Where the hell were you hiding this sense of humor for the past year?"

"I don't know. It just comes out when I feel comfortable with someone."

"Meaning you never felt comfortable around me?"

"Meaning I liked you from the day I met you. You held the door open for me. Twice. Look, I know I'm not the easiest person to get along with. Casey kids with me all the time that I'm a bitch until you get to know me. Then I'm just a bitch you know."

Eric grinned. "You're not a bitch. Bossy maybe. Okay, definitely bossy, but—"

"Hey. Quit while you're ahead." She kissed him again and brought him back to all the sensations that he'd been trying to distract himself from.

ZOE DIDN'T WANT TO love this too much, but it was incredibly hard to avoid the way Eric made her feel. Like she was more than just a fling or one-time screw. That worked for her since she'd never made love to a man without being in love with him. Except for now. Except she was lying to herself because she did love him. Sure, she'd done her best to avoid him and maybe acted...okay...not especially great in the beginning, but it didn't seem right to make a move on her sister's future brother-in-law. So she'd kept her distance as much as possible.

Look where that got her.

Not that she was complaining. No how. No way. Zoe wanted this moment. More than anything. Eric proved over and over that he was dependable, capable, and the kind of man a girl only dreamed about. He was so sweet and oh-so-battered and all she wanted to do was make him feel good.

Every time she picked up the rhythm, moved a little faster and stroked a little harder, Eric gripped her hips and slowed her down. He seemed to have a plan for this evening that involved slow, drawn out pleasure, and she wanted him to come *now*. Okay, it wasn't any big news that they thought in opposite directions. She desperately wanted to give him the same pleasure he gave her. She wanted to show him with her body exactly how she felt about him.

And seriously, after the week he had, no one deserved release more.

Sometimes a girl had to take control.

Zoe took Eric's good hand and held it above his head, taking the opportunity to gently kiss the massive bruise on his collarbone, then trail her lips near his ear. "Okay, I'm bossy. It's a personal flaw." She squelched his laugh with an electric kiss on his lips. It only took him a second to overpower her, and that strong hand cupped her head, held her steady. She loved the way his fingers buried in her hair before traveling the length of her back to grab her ass and adjust her over him as he pushed up.

"Mmm," she moaned into his mouth as he filled her. He hit a bundle of nerves inside that threatened to end this party really quickly and she was determined to get him off before she came again.

Zoe sat up and the move drove him deeper. Her vision glazed over as she looked down at the gorgeous man beneath her. She trailed a finger in the valley between his washboard abs, loving the soft skin over hard packed muscle. His hair stuck up in spiky strands and the bruises on his face and shoulder reminded her of just what they'd gone through the past few days. Her heart opened up as she stared into those forever-blue eyes.

His hand took its own journey as he stroked up her thigh, her waist, and ended on her breast where his thumb circled her tight nipple. Tingles raced from her breast to the spot where they connected. His touch set fire licking through her veins.

Zoe lifted and pushed back down, started a ride she hoped would make him as crazy as he was making her. Just watching the intensity on his face was almost enough to send her over the edge. His gaze clashed with hers and his hands moved to her hips, guiding her, showing her how he liked it without saying a word.

Holy crap that was sexy. So was the way he clenched his jaw, fighting his orgasm, no doubt waiting for her to come again. What a guy.

"You know," she said, "It's okay to make this first time quick and dirty. We can go slower the next round."

His eyes lit with fresh fire and narrowed a fraction more. "Who are you and what have you done with Zoe? Did you just say 'quick and dirty'? Because I can make that happen."

Before Zoe had a chance to process his words, Eric gripped her hips and drove up inside her, filling her, stretching her and making her gasp with a pleasure so intense her lungs seized. With his jaw clenched tight, he continued the barrage, taking control again despite being on the bottom. Zoe loved it. Every beautiful, sexy second of it. She loved how reverently he touched her, how much passion he put into every kiss.

Eric kept a steady pace, driving her closer to another release as he pushed inside her over and over again. No slowing down at this rate, Zoe balanced right on the edge, holding the line, waiting for Eric before she fell. Until he adjusted his hold on her, dragged his thumb from her hip to her clit and slicked over it, back and forth.

Zoe went off like a bottle rocket. It happened that fast. One second she was out of breath from Eric's exquisite length filling her and the next she was in the stratosphere with lights flashing and stars erupting behind her lids. Her muscles tensed and euphoria spread through her veins. She was barely aware of the guttural moan coming from her mouth as she panted Eric's name.

His roar happened a second later and she felt the undeniable throbbing inside her as he hit his own climax. Time seemed to stop as they flew, as each sweet wave of bliss washed over them.

Sweat slicked their skin as they gasped for air and Zoe collapsed on top of him, keeping her weight to his good side. Long seconds ticked by and his arm stayed tightly around her, sending a very clear message. *You're not going anywhere.* Turning his head, Eric closed his mouth over hers in a gentle kiss, a long, sweet melding of lips and tongues that sealed the act with delicious perfection.

"I think I love you," she whispered, when he came up for air. The room got really quiet. Oh shit. What the hell had she just done? His *strong feelings* didn't necessarily mean *love*. Before she could backpedal or come up with an insane excuse as to why she'd blurt out those crazy words, Eric put his mouth to her lips.

"No. Shh. Don't panic." The fact that he seemed to know her so well scared her and made her happy at the same time. "I see it in your eyes," he said, only confirming her thoughts.

The slow smile spreading across his face matched the tenderness she saw in his eyes.

"I'm pretty sure I fell in love with you during our second kiss. The one where I said, I want you to owe me. You not only evened it up, but now I owe you." His eyes sparkled a devilish glint. "Fair warning…I plan on taking a long time to even us up. A very long time."

Zoe loved the sound of that.

CHAPTER 29

Three weeks later

ZOE STOOD IN THE middle of her empty condo, sadness filling her almost completely. In the scheme of life, she shouldn't be upset, but losing this place just freaking hurt. This gorgeous condo meant success. It signified that she was someone to take seriously. Now it signified her status as a failure.

A strong arm wrapped around her shoulders, and Eric pulled her against his chest. Closing her eyes, she soaked in his comfort. "I'm sorry," he whispered. "I know this place was important to you."

She clutched his arm, kept him tight and held back stupid tears. He was only proving her point. He mattered. Not some damn two-bedroom, two-bath condo. He didn't try to make light of the situation or skip around it. He faced things. One of the qualities she loved most about him.

"Look on the bright side, Zoe. Maybe you didn't have it long, but you made a good return on your investment." True. She'd come out ahead, by selling the place for way more than she paid for it.

"Location, location, location," she mumbled, not yet in the swing of things. Her whole life had flipped upside down in a matter of weeks. Everything from the top to the bottom had switched up, and she was too overwhelmed to handle so much upheaval all at once.

"Change isn't necessarily a bad thing." He squeezed her for emphasis. "And you still have a lot of your furniture. It's just a little spread out." She chuckled at his attempt at humor. Some of her stuff had gone to Vic's place, since her old roomie had taken most of the furniture, and some had gone to Eric's apartment to replace old furniture. Either apartment felt like home—literally—these days. "My mom is a big fan of the saying, 'Everything happens for a reason,'" Eric finished.

Danny stomped out of the room she'd used as an office, his arms loaded with a big box. "This is it," he said. "Last one. I'll load it up and meet you guys at the apartment." He lifted an eyebrow as he strode by. "Hey, no messing around either. We've got a schedule." And boom, he left dust in his wake.

"Is he going to be like that as a boss?" Zoe asked, watching him go. The four of them had done a lot of talking the last few weeks. Mostly involving Danny's—and now Eric's—business. They'd recruited Zoe to help with everything from general office work to marketing, and it seemed better than sulking, so she'd signed on.

Eric chuckled as Zoe turned in his arms. "Someone's a little excited to see Vic. And speaking of roommates, how do you think that's going to go?"

The roommate situation. Now that was exciting. "It'll be fine. Vic is unpredictable, fun and honest to a fault. Anyone who knows her, knows those things about her. It's part of her overall charm."

Eric leaned down, teased her lips with his. "I happen to like *your* charm." This was the *messing around* that Danny had warned them about.

Zoe nuzzled his nose, perfectly happy to disobey Danny's directive. "Aw, see...and Casey's always said I'm an acquired taste."

His chest vibrated in a growl. "I happen to love the way you taste too." And with that, he kissed her.

VIC HAD CONSOLIDATED HER makeup and finished wiping down the now empty drawer, excited to make space for her new roomie. The front door squeaked open, and she came out of the bathroom, dodging boxes and wiping her hands on a rag. Danny, Zoe and Eric had been hauling boxes and furniture for over an hour.

"I'm back," Danny said, as he kicked the door closed behind him. "Last one." Breezing past her, he dumped his load in the second bedroom. Without missing a beat, he returned, wrapped her in his arms and set his mouth on hers. He tasted like peppermint and Danny.

"Mmm," Vic purred when he pulled away. "My other roommates never kissed me like that."

"They better not have," Danny groused, walking her back toward their bedroom, where Vic had been busy making room for his things.

"Aw, you're jealous. How sweet." Vic kissed him again, loving the way his hands brushed along her sides and teased her breasts. "Where'd the other two go? Did they go back to their place without saying goodbye? That's lame."

"Uh…" Danny froze while kissing her neck. "That would be my fault. I kind of told them to take a hike. No pun intended. After watching you all day and not having time to touch you, I'm seriously at a breaking point." He rubbed against her to show exactly what was about to break.

"Ah-ha. So, I have you to blame. Usually when my new roommates cross me, I give them the silent treatment."

Danny chuckled, fully in the process of unhooking the back snaps of her bra. "You can try, but I'll be having you screaming in no time."

Vic yelped when he nipped her ear, but her insides melted like butter over fire. The tiny part of her working mind squawked a warning. "Danny," she said, holding his hands still before he eased off her clothes. "You really don't think this is happening too fast? Us moving in together."

He froze then met her gaze, his eyes full of love and confidence. Nodding, he took out the band holding her hair back. "I'll admit it's happening fast. But it's not a mistake, if that's what you mean." He brushed his lips across her softly, lovingly. "You know my folks met when they were in high school. My dad knew from the second he laid eyes on my mom that she was the one for him, just like I know you're the one for me. I want to come home to you, go to bed with you, wake up with you. Moving in together might be fast, but it's definitely right."

His lips cruised over hers again and any remaining doubts Vic might've had disappeared into nothing.

"What about Zoe and Eric?"

"What about 'em? Eric is totally whipped. If he wasn't ready to live with Zoe he wouldn't be. Now, time for talking is over. It's time for fu—"

"Oh, one last thing! I forgot to tell you, the office called earlier. We've got a meeting scheduled for this Friday. You'll finally get to hear everything we have planned for the company."

"Mm…great." He tossed her onto the bed and followed her down, totally consumed with peeling off her leggings.

"Did you hear me?" She laughed at his single-mindedness as his weight pressed her down into the mattress.

His lips played beneath her ear, his tongue tasted.

"Danny, I need a shower. I'm disgusting. We can't do this now."

"Delicious. Salty. Sexy. Love it. Not stopping." He peeled off his clothes with the speed of a gigolo. Her gigolo. Then it was skin on skin just the way she liked it.

She sighed into his mouth as their lips collided. "I did miss you," she whispered between kisses. "How am I going to survive when you're on a camping excursion? When you're gone for long weekends?"

He pulled back, his eyes solemn and so full of love that Vic held her breath. "Here's what's going to happen. You're going to come with me and we'll tell the office that you can't properly do the public relations job if you don't experience the excursions. Then once you guys make the business as big as you seem to think it can be, then I won't have to go as often. Besides, camping is only a fraction of the list. Most everything is local." He brought his lips to hers and Vic's heart expanded. She loved him so much. Loved the way he showed his love for her too. The past three weeks had been magical. If she'd had any doubts about the old Danny— Danny the Player—making a return appearance, they'd been squashed within days. His full attention, his absolute devotion, made falling in love with him that much easier.

"Danny," she whispered between kisses, "we have so many boxes to unpack." In answer, he pushed inside her, and Vic gasped at the fullness and complete perfection. "On the other hand… boxes can wait."

"Mm-hmm." His low growl sent tingles down her spine.

She ran her fingers through the short crop of his hair. "I could get used to this."

His intense gaze zeroed in on her. "Plan on it. Every day. Multiple times." He stroked into her with a slow and steady glide that sent delicious sensation curling in her stomach and had her moving up to meet him. "For the rest of our lives," he whispered. "This is just the beginning."

EPILOGUE

Seven months later

"YOU COULD'VE LEFT ME some hot water, bro. Does Vic put up with that shit?" Eric groused, whipping a fresh T-shirt over his head and finger combing his wet hair as he came out of his bedroom.

Danny grinned from the dining room table—mission central—since Eric and Zoe's place was the bigger apartment, his shaggy hair damp from his shower. "Uh...don't have that problem at my place. We conserve water." He waggled his eyebrows for emphasis.

They'd just finished a day at the beach teaching a bunch of Boy Scouts the fine art of surfing. Not a bad way to make a living. Granted, his parents had needed time to digest the news, but with business booming, they couldn't really complain. It helped that Eric used his legal knowledge to review and draw up contracts with equipment companies, as well as waivers and release forms. At least his education was being put to use.

Danny had been right. In the past year, they'd grown the business more than enough to support the two of them and technically it supported three. Zoe had done so well with the marketing that she'd moved into business expansion, which freed the guys up to spend more time actually working. If you called surfing, biking, hiking and kayaking—among other things— working. Some days Eric felt guilty taking money from people just to play. But, if someone had to do it, may as well be Danny and him.

"Any word from them?" Eric asked, patting the little pouch in his pocket.

"Not yet. Vic said she'd call if she was running late and I haven't heard from her so…"

Eric checked his phone on the counter. "Same with Zoe."

"You're nervous." Danny grinned.

"No, I'm not." But he was.

"Yes, you are. I just don't know if it's because of their meetings or your proposal."

"And you're not nervous about their meetings?" Eric fired back. Because Danny should be.

Danny considered the question. "You know, not really. Life is good already. If the meetings didn't go well, then fuck it, life is still good. If they were successful, it just means…more. I don't *have* to have more."

Eric loved the serenity his little brother had found. Vic had given him a solid foundation and he'd flourished in it. Danny had a good point. Life was pretty damn good. Hopefully tonight—after his proposal it would get even better.

Checking his watch, Eric started his prep for the night. He'd picked up a dozen red roses on the way home and spread petals over their bed along with a trail to the bathroom where he arranged a dozen candles with a bottle of wine on ice.

Danny leaned on the doorframe of the bedroom. "What if she comes in here before you're ready?"

"She won't." Eric came out of the bathroom and placed the remaining roses in a slim vase. "We'll make sure of it." The key turned in the front door lock and Eric nudged Danny into the hallway, closing the door behind him. "Shh. Go." He shoved him toward the den.

Zoe pushed through the front door with Vic right behind her. "Hi!" She glowed with news as did her best friend. "We timed it just right," Zoe said. Eric loved every version of Zoe, but the red powersuit and sky-high heels definitely got his blood pumping.

Danny snatched Vic in his arms at the same time Zoe reached Eric and wrapped her arms around him. The next few seconds stayed pretty quiet as Eric got a taste of Zoe's warm mouth.

She pressed up against his growing erection and cranked his pulse rate higher.

Eric pulled away before he got too far ahead of himself and ruined Zoe's surprise. "Okay, what's the news? Something good?"

At his question, Vic moved away from Danny's lip-lock. "Oh, you don't know the half of it," she gushed, stripping off her black blazer of her pantsuit, kicking off her stilettos and dragging Danny over to the table. "Sit down. Both of you."

"Uh oh. It's sit down news," Danny teased, the old glint back in his eyes.

Zoe and Vic looked at each other. "Who's first?" Vic asked.

"You," Zoe said. "With this morning's news. Then I'll tell them mine."

Eric glanced at Danny's amused expression, sensing the potential for an avalanche of information.

"Okay," Vic began, clapping her hands together like a toddler at a birthday party. "This morning I secured three sponsors."

Danny sat forward, his eyes cranked wide. "Sponsors? For real? Sponsors?"

"Yes." Vic glowed with triumph. "I didn't want to mention it in case one or all of them didn't come through. Pacific Surf is on board for a dozen surfboards and equal number of kayaks. The Excursion Store is in for all camping gear necessary for up to two dozen and..." She paused, looking between them, "Chevy is in for two commercial vans that hold fifteen."

"What?" Danny stood. Held onto the table as if he needed it for balance. "You got all that today?"

Vic nodded, her smile luminous. "This morning. I timed it so that all parties involved knew they were investing in the next big thing. Once I had one, I had them all." She gestured to Zoe. "Your turn."

"I met with Francisco Vega, CEO of Western Star Technology." Zoe had been cold calling local businesses for months already, her tenacity, a thing of beauty. "They are a rapidly growing start-up with six hundred employees and counting. Mr. Vega loves the idea of team building excursions and is giving his employees incentives to pick from your list of activities. The longer the activity with team members, the bigger their yearly bonus. And he plans to foot the bill for excursions. Seeing as how his profits topped sixty-five million last year, I believe he can afford it."

Danny sat down with a hard thump, his eyes glazed over, probably thinking of the logistics for spacing out six hundred new clients.

Zoe's brilliant smile came Eric's way before she gestured to Vic who continued.

"Because Zoe managed to call me with this news before my afternoon meeting, I was able to add it to the agenda. When I mentioned to my boss how Zoe had this new influx of clients to the business, it sparked an idea because her husband—who happens to be a producer—is looking for a new take on an outdoor reality show. Kind of like how *Extreme Makeover* was a feel-good for the family. This could be along the same lines."

"How?" Danny asked bluntly.

Vic sat next to him. "Babe, every day you work, you come home with a story about someone accomplishing something they've never done or a story about people helping strangers pull through. Every day it's something different and it's always inspirational."

Eric thought back on the past few months and had to agree. Maybe it was one of the reasons he loved this job so much. Not necessarily because of the freedom of the outdoors, but the fact that he and Danny were seeing it all brand new through their clients' eyes.

"After Vic's meeting," Zoe said, picking up the conversation again, "she called and told me her news and I called *back* Mr. Vega and asked if he'd be interested in a reality show type setting for his workers, just to feel him out. Now obviously we couldn't put all of them on the air and—more importantly—not all of them would want to be anyway, but it's a way to bring more exposure to his company and get that team building experience all in one shot. Two for the price of one. He told me he'd think about it. Even if he says no, Danny has plenty of clients who'd love to participate in something like this."

"Holy shit," Danny whispered. Poor guy…almost looked a little sick to his stomach. "But this is a total crapshoot, right?" he asked.

"Yes, and no," Vic replied. "Show biz is always a crapshoot, but the fact that we have sponsors and clientele, and my boss happens to sleep with the producer looking for material...let's just say there's a reason we talk about luck and timing when something goes right." Her phone rang and she dug in her purse to find it. "It's my boss. Hang on." She punched the screen. "Hello?" Listening, she nodded and her eyes widened. "No way. You're kidding me. When?" Her smile blossomed more. "Small world at that. Yeah, he's right here. I'll tell him. Thanks." She ended the call and dropped her phone on the table.

"What now?" Eric asked.

"Danny, do you remember a kayaking trip a couple of months ago. One of the guys had a close encounter of the dolphin kind. Then he realized the dolphin was—"

"Tangled in some netting. Sure, I remember. A few of us managed to cut the little guy free and he was so happy he gave us a show."

"The man who helped you, Craig Moscot, he's my boss's husband, the producer we're talking about. You've already jumped through your first hoop and didn't even realize it."

"Holy shit," Danny mumbled again.

"Not a bad day's work." Zoe looked at her watch. "I say we celebrate with a drink and dinner. Who's with me?"

Danny checked his watch. "Oh, shit!" He grabbed Vic's hand. "Come with me." Then hustled her outside.

"What's with him?" Zoe asked, trailing behind them.

Eric followed her to the open door. "Dunno." He patted the velvet pouch in his pocket, biding his time.

"What's that?" Looking up, Zoe covered her eyes against the glare of the setting sun.

Eric stepped farther outside. "No effin' way," he murmured. "I'm gonna kill him." Overhead, a skywriting plane already had the letters M-A-R-R- in clear white lines and was working on the Y.

Zoe slapped a hand over her mouth. "Is he proposing to her?"

Yes, Eric was going to kill his little brother. Didn't matter that they were best friends. He was simply going to wring his neck.

Finished with the Y, the plane worked on an M.

Danny stood by—Mr. Casual—as the minutes ticked by and

the letters slowly spelled out *MARRY ME VIC*. To which Victoria Lopez screamed her excitement and jumped into Danny's arms making it hard for him to pull the ring out of his pocket. Little fucker.

"C'mere," Eric said, taking Zoe by the hand and closing and locking the door behind him.

She laughed. "Uh...a little overkill, don't you think? You're locking out the newly engaged—" She stopped when Eric pulled out the pouch and got on one knee. That hand went back over her mouth.

Eric tipped his head toward his brother. "That little dipshit knew I was doing this today so he had to go and...forget it." He tipped the bag and out came the two-carat diamond she'd been secretly coveting for the past six months. Vic had been instrumental in sharing that little secret of hers.

Looking into her wide eyes, he began. "Zoe, I love you with everything I am. I waited because I wanted to make sure you were comfortable with the idea of forever, but I've known for a long time now that you're the one I want to spend the rest of my life with. I want to be the one you turn to on good days and bad. I want to always be the great team we've become." He thought about his parents. "I want to embarrass our kids when we kiss in front of them and when I grab your ass when you walk by." She laughed at that and he went for the finale. "I want to be your forever, and I want you to be mine. Will you marry me?" He held out the ring.

"Oh my God, Eric. It's beautiful."

He waited as she stared at it, his heart in his throat and not exactly sure what she thought. "And...is that a..."

Her eyes flashed to his. "Yes! Oh my God! Yes! Yes! Yes!" She dropped to her knees in front of him. Her sweet kiss turning passionate in a heartbeat as she wrapped her arms around his neck and sucked the living hell out of his lungs.

"It's not skywriting," he finally mumbled when they broke apart.

She stroked her hands through his hair, her smile soft and sexy. "I don't need skywriting. I just need you."

A slam at the door interrupted their kiss, and they got to their feet as Danny unlocked the door and Vic and he rushed in with the good news. "We're engaged!" Vic squealed, showing off a pretty sparkler comparable to the one Zoe wore.

"So are we." Zoe held out her hand too and both of them screamed and hugged.

The four of them ended up going out for those celebratory drinks and dinner, and Eric's surprise waited for when they got home.

Zoe stopped short in the doorway when she saw the rose petals leading to the opened bed and trailing into the bathroom—all set with candles waiting to be lit. "This is way better than skywriting," she said, wrapping her arms around Eric's neck. "Because it took time and effort and you put a lot of thought into it." She kissed him sweetly. "I'm in such a good mood, I might even let you be on top."

Eric laughed. He'd done a lot of that in the past seven months. Zoe brought him so much happiness it didn't seem fair to the rest of the world. Sometimes during any given day, he caught himself grinning for no other reason than remembering one of her deadpan one-liners or funny faces. He stroked his hands down her back until he cupped her ass and brought her into contact with the hard-on he'd been sporting since the drive home. "But you're so good on top. Why ruin a good thing?"

"I created a monster that first time, didn't I?" Her palm moved over the real monster and Eric thrust against her hand, his blood pumping hotter and faster.

He kissed her slowly, taking his time, working her up. "If it'll really make you feel better, I'll be in charge tonight." With that, he picked her up and threw her over his shoulder in a fireman's hold.

"Eric!" Zoe shrieked as he moved into their bedroom. "What are you doing?"

"I call it, getting this engagement off to a fine start. And before you say anything else, you need to know right now, there will be *no* engagement party."

"You can say that again," she mumbled, her voice distant. But it was her hands, working his jeans over his hips as he walked that had him laughing. "Would you pick up the pace? The blood is rushing to my head."

"That's not the only place it's rushing," he said, tossing her on their bed a second later. Eric pounced after that and he didn't remember how or when their clothes came off, he only knew that he'd found his forever in Zoe.

The End

Enjoy this sneak peek from the crossover book in the Adrenaline Highs series

IMMINENT DANGER

by Dee J. Adams

For Abbey Washington, dancing is more than a dream, it's a way to forget her past. But being at the wrong place at the wrong time makes her the sole witness to a stabbing and brings back horrible memories. Since the killers saw her just as clearly as she saw them, Abbey is now a loose end that needs to be tied up.

Blake St. John is working toward his PI license and hopes to find the man who hurt his brother in a kidnapping. He quit chasing his quiet co-worker, Abbey, months ago. But now that she needs protection, he takes on the role of bodyguard and all the feelings he tried to bury for her come back with a vengeance.

Abbey's past makes it hard to trust and an attempt on her life forces her to realize that time is running out as the killers get closer. Now, she must risk it all or face a life without the one man who showed her how to love.

CHAPTER ONE

"COMING THROUGH," ABBEY CALLED. The farther she jogged down the large cavernous Sports Center hallway, the more it emptied out as people rushed toward the stage for the sold out concert. She'd never felt more like a salmon traveling upstream. Everyone wanted to see Seger Hughes when he made his entrance. Including her. Unfortunately, she doubted she'd get back in time.

Her boss, Julie Fraser, had accidentally left the courtside Lakers tickets she'd promised to Seger in an envelope in the car, so being the all-around gofer/get-it-done-girl, Abbey had to retrieve the tickets. Abbey never put anything off for fear it might come back to bite her in the ass later. She had *do it now, do it right* mentality and didn't expect that to change.

She really had no right to be pissy about this unexpected run, since she hadn't paid for the concert tickets anyway. A ton of perks came with the job of being an assistant to an Oscar and Emmy winning actress, but with those perks came the reality that as long as she accepted them, she was on the job, which meant unexpected things cropped up...like making runs to the car for a forgetful actress.

The credentials around Abbey's neck gave her all-access to the venue, so getting in and out wasn't the problem. Doing it as fast as humanly possible so she could see Seger open the show was the problem. She didn't want to miss her favorite song, *Always Believe.*

Of course, getting back faster also put her in Blake St. John's vicinity for that much longer, but she was willing to put up with him for the sake of seeing Seger live. She rolled her eyes at the thought as she jogged down the now almost empty hallway. A few late concert-goers—all VIPs—straggled in.

She had to be honest with herself about Blake. Putting up with him wasn't the problem. It was putting up with her pounding heart and sweaty palms every time she was around him that bothered her. Blake had admitted to falling *head over ass in love* with her the minute he met her. She seriously doubted *that.*

Now that Julie had married Blake's boss, Troy, it seemed as if they were forever in each other's company.

Perfect.

Not so much.

Abbey picked up her pace as the end of the corridor grew closer. All she had to do was get out the door, get to the car, grab the envelope and run like hell back to see the concert opening.

At the door, she threw her momentum against the heavy metal and shoved it open to the dusky evening. She nearly barreled over the guard watching the area from the outside.

"Oh my, God! I'm so sorry," she said to the tall, dark-skinned man with a tight Afro haircut, bushy beard and *event staff* stenciled on his T-shirt. She hoped her apology would take the stink eye out of his angry face. His quick once-over sent chills down her back and his lecherous smile gave her the impetus to keep moving. "Really! I'm sorry," she said jogging backward toward the car. "I'm in a hurry!"

He didn't wave or say a word, just watched her go, and Abbey turned and ran full out for the car, her VIP badge bouncing against her chest, her lungs heaving as the hot air of a Southern California summer night made her sticky.

The car wasn't parked that far away because Julie was a VIP after all, and that did afford her a good amount of luxuries in her life. But the cars that had parked on either side of Troy's black BMW—a mint green Jaguar on one side and a white convertible Mercedes on the other—had boxed in his car, so getting in the door without scratching anybody's paint job became an exercise in sucking in air and sliding sideways inside the passenger door.

Abbey took two seconds to get her breath as she leaned her head against the seat rest. God, she needed a vacation. Or a dance job. Either one would make her deliriously happy.

With her two seconds gone, Abbey looked around the seat for the envelope containing the Lakers tickets. Not in the glove compartment, not on the floor, not under the seat. She checked the center console. Bingo. Hallelujah.

She sucked in another breath to exit the car then started running back to the concert. She slowed as she neared the same door she'd come out of a few minutes ago. No security guard in sight. God, what if the door was locked? What if she had to run all the way around to a different entrance to get back inside?

So much for seeing Seger's opening song.

Glancing around for the guard, Abbey grabbed the handle. Before she had a chance to pull, it blew wide open and a man tore out moving at hyper-speed. Her heart nearly exploded as they collided. Impact knocked them both down and he cursed as he sprawled on top of her. The panic in his dark eyes registered as fast as the bloody cut on his cheek. Had that happened just now?

"Are you o—"

"Move," he finally shouted as he scrambled to his feet. That seemed excessively rude since he'd been the one to knock her down. The guy wasn't much bigger than her, mostly bald with an average face. The next second, he was up and running, and just as Abbey got to her feet, the closed door crashed open again. At least this time she had enough distance behind the door to keep from getting bowled over by the two guys who came running out.

Her pulse raced as she watched the two men tackle the man who'd knocked her down. Abbey took a step toward them, her hand against her pounding heart.

One guy threw a hard punch and the man underneath screamed. The fear and agony in the sound made her cringe.

"Run! Get help! Hurry!" he screamed.

What? Wasn't he the bad guy if he was being chased? Especially since one of the men on top of him was the same guard wearing the event-staff T-shirt?

Both men looked back and seemed to see her for the first time. The new guy had a big Fu-Manchu mustache, sunglasses, baseball cap and a giant knife glinting red and wet in the parking lot light. Seeing that—plus the deadly look on both their faces—dried up every bit of spit in Abbey's mouth.

Run! Get help! Hurry! The words flashed in her brain as the danger hit her head on.

"Get her!" the man with the knife yelled.

The black man pulled a gun from a shoulder holster as he rose to his feet.

Fear strangled her heart. *No fucking way!*

She ran to the door and yanked on the handle. Her shoulder nearly came out of its socket when the door didn't budge. Locked! *What the fuck?* Abbey glanced back as she took off running along the side of the building, with the black man on her tail and the other guy leaning over the injured man, still lying on the pavement.

Holy shit!

Abbey flew over the cement, her pulse beating hard and loud between her ears as she raced along the curve of the wall to the front of the building. The cars on her left would provide a better hiding place, but she needed people. She needed to get lost in a crowd.

But what if this guy didn't care about a crowd? What if she was leading a maniac into a crowded concert because of what she'd just witnessed? What had she witnessed? A stabbing! *Ohgodohgod!* The man had screamed because he'd been knifed, not punched. The blood on the knife had been his blood!

Sweat popped out of every pore and the overhead parking lights blurred as she continued to haul ass as fast as possible.

She dared a glance behind her. The man was catching up and Abbey was breathing too hard to find her voice. A pop-pop sounded behind her and she waited for the bullets to hit. They didn't. She would've screamed for all she was worth if she had a second to take in extra air. She checked behind her one last time as she came to the edge of the building and cut right.

A brick wall stopped her. Strong arms came around her and this time, the scream dying to get out, let loose.

"Abbey! Abbey! Jesus, it's me. What's wrong?"

Wild eyed, Abbey focused enough to make out Blake, all six foot three inches of lean muscle and dark auburn hair. His stunning blue eyes were filled with concern. She wanted to leap into his arms for protection, wanted to take a second and enjoy the relief of having help, but the more seconds that ticked by, the closer the man came. Just because she didn't see him, didn't mean he wasn't there.

"Run!" she screamed, yanking him back toward the stadium doors. "Hurry! Run!" No other words formed on her parched tongue. Pulling air into her fried lungs hurt. "Gun! He has a gun! Inside!" There, that seemed to help because Blake was pushing her ahead of him as they sprinted into the building, flashing their badges.

"Get inside! Everyone!" Abbey yelled to the event staff and public still walking to their seats. "He has a gun! There's a man with a gun!" Her shout got everyone moving in all directions. Event staff closed the doors as security drew weapons and urged people away from the glass doors.

With armed security closing in, Abbey finally slowed as she backed up toward one of the alleyways leading into the concert. Peeking around Blake's shoulder, she kept her eyes on the door the whole time, waiting for the man chasing her to come into view.

As the seconds ticked by into minutes, as the security slowly closed in on the doors, clearly intending to venture outside, Blake disengaged Abbey's tight grip on his hand and pulled her against him.

"It's okay. You're okay. I think we're safe."

Safe. The word, the relief, triggered a release. She refused to cry and her breathing got ragged as she fought back tears and buried her face in his soft black T-shirt. There was no denying the absolute certainty that she'd barely avoided a brutal death. She just needed a minute to regroup.

"It's okay," he murmured into her hair. "I've got you. I've got you." His arms wrapped around her tight and Abbey squeezed him close, held on like her life depended on it. As the possibilities seeped in, she couldn't manage to breathe.

Blake pulled away and she needed his strength too much for that. She wanted the comfort he was so good at providing. "Abbey, look at me," he ordered.

But she didn't want to face him. She especially didn't want him to see her so weak. It seemed that's how he always saw her. When she was at her most defenseless. She hated it.

"Abbey!" He barked her name again and this time Abbey met his gaze. True concern clouded his gorgeous blue eyes as he held her face in his big hands. "Breathe," he told her. "Breathe with me. C'mon. In and out. You know the drill."

The first time they'd met, she'd had a panic attack in a broken elevator and he'd talked her through it. Her sister and parents had always been the only people capable of calming her down from an attack before then. But Blake had a way about him. A confidence. He was a couple of years younger than her, but seemed to have an old soul that talked to her.

Abbey just refused to listen.

"Abbey!" Blake said sharply. "Look at me. Concentrate."

She blinked, focused and followed his lead, taking long breaths and releasing them slowly until she had a rhythm, until the air flowed into her lungs the way it was supposed to.

"There you go. That's my girl." Blake wrapped his arms around her again and Abbey let him. She not only let him, she burrowed deep into his chest and breathed in his woodsy fresh scent. He always smelled so good and avoiding him had become harder and harder over the months since her their bosses had married.

She didn't get nearly enough time in Blake's arms before fresh chaos erupted in the form of police invading the lobby. Though it seemed the danger had passed, now they had the aftermath.

Blake let her go and pulled out his cell phone from his back pocket.

Abbey crossed her arms and forced herself to stop shaking. "Who are you texting?"

"Troy."

She bobbed her head. Good. Troy would know what to do. He was one of the best private investigators in the city and he knew dozens of officers in multiple stations. Abbey moved toward the police who swarmed the area. Two uniformed officers came her way. "Tell him to hurry," she said over her shoulder.

"I did." Blake caught up to her, put his arm around her shoulders and Abbey didn't try to pull away.

Imminent Danger is now available in ebook and paperback.

Also by Dee J. Adams

High Stakes Series

AGAINST THE WALL

OVER THE TOP

OUT OF THE BLUE

UNDER THE RADER

The Adrenaline Highs Series

IMMINENT DANGER

A LITTLE DANGER

ALWAYS DANGEROUS

ABOUT THE AUTHOR

After graduating high school in Texas, Dee J. moved to Los Angeles to pursue acting. For twenty years, she acted in television and worked behind the scenes as an acting/dialogue coach for sitcoms. Writing happened accidentally after a vivid dream and the urging of her husband to "Just write it down." Three weeks, fourteen hours a day, and four hundred and fifty (long hand) pages later, she had her first novel. Dee J. loves writing books filled with action, mystery and love. (Not necessarily in that order.) Her experience in show business led to her narrating many of the books in the Adrenaline Highs series for Audible.com. She is the wife of a wonderful man and mother to a fabulous daughter. She's a dog lover all the way, with a fondness towards Boxers and Pit Bulls. She is a member of several organizations, including Romance Writers of America and SAG-AFTRA.

For more information on Dee J.'s books please visit:
www.deejadams.com

Dee J. can be found on
Facebook: http://www.facebook.com/DeeJAdamsAuthor

Twitter: https://twitter.com/DeeJAdams

Goodreads:
http://www.goodreads.com/author/show/5107047.Dee_J_Adams

Amazon: http://amzn.to/MuznPw

www.ingramcontent.com/pod-product-compliance
Lightning Source LLC
Chambersburg PA
CBHW030031180626
46810CB00001B/310